# Thief

## of

# Curses

Book 1

Jessie D. Eaker

*To my parents who provided bunches of encouragement, love and gave me the coolest name on earth.*

# Contents

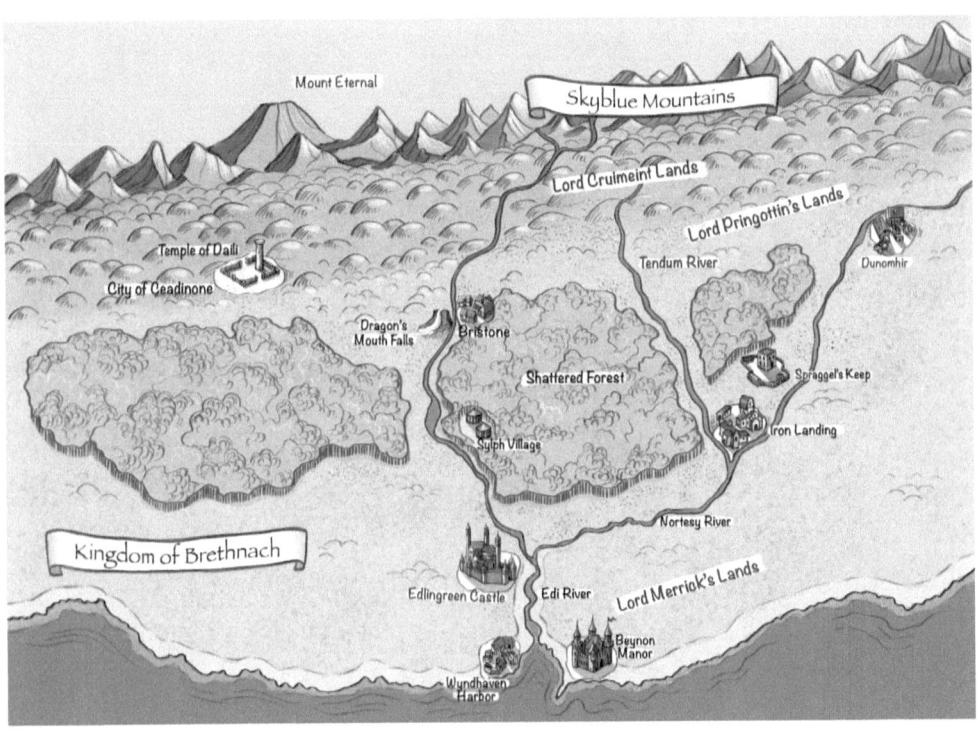

# CHAPTER ONE

# Loose Gold

I brushed the soft end of the quill against my lips while contemplating my journal. I had spent the better part of the afternoon gazing up at the cobwebs clinging to the rafters just over my head, trying to think of something witty to say. But to no avail. Inspiration had to be a woman because—just like her human sisters—she was snubbing me.

Breathing in the familiar scents of old paper and ink inside an even older and musty keep, I sighed. This was serious business. A world-famous knight-scholar-explorer should at least have a record of his exploits. You can't trust the minstrels to get it right. They always embellish too much. And Creator forbid the historians! They would bore you to tears. So I had no choice but to take this one on myself. I had saved my meager earnings—and they were truly meager—and bought my first blank scroll. It *had* to be a scroll, of course. They just looked so *official*. I had carefully laid the parchment out on the workroom's only table, easily the most refined piece of furniture inside of Revenhille Keep, where it sat ready to receive my first words.

But how to start?

I glanced at an abandoned scrap of paper lying on the floor and frowned. I had attempted to sketch my profile, thinking an illustration might be the way to start. However, the ink lines did absolutely nothing to capture my true likeness: brown eyes, a masculine chin, and chestnut brown hair—reluctantly kept short because my master threatened to kick me out if I didn't. My not quite twenty-year-old face was rather square, and while not one to turn heads, it was at least a solid representation of maleness. My mother had described me as pleasantly plain in my letter of introduction to my master. Whatever that meant.

I took a deep breath and focused on the parchment in front of me. Well, I guess there was no better place to start than the beginning. Keep it simple. Something the reader could easily latch on to. I dipped the quill into my bottle of ink, and being careful my hand didn't shake, I boldly wrote the first words in my journal: *Thus begins the recorded deeds of Coren Hart.*

I smiled in satisfaction at my creation. It was direct, to the point, and hinted at the adventures to come. I liked it.

But then I glanced at my family name. *Hart.* I wasn't especially fond of it. I had often wondered why I couldn't have been born to something more dramatic, like Everhart, or Bravehart, or even Bloodhart. But just *Hart* was so plain. The teasing I'd endured when I was younger certainly didn't help. The boys called me Hart the... well, you get the idea.

I nodded. It might be a plain name, but one day, everyone would know it. Sometimes you just had to work with what you were given.

Making sure the ink was dry, I rolled up the scroll and pulled out a special red ribbon to tie it up with (red was just so official). Now I, Coren Hart, was ready to record the knight-scholar-explorer adventures as they happened to me—or *when* they happened to me.

I was sure they would start soon. At least, I was pretty sure. I was only a scribe apprentice now. But that was just the beginning. One had to take the long view. I glanced at the wide leather band laced around my left wrist and thought of what lay hidden beneath. I frowned. Finding a way to alleviate my *problem* depended on it. I tried not to think about it too much, but my life had definitely taken a turn for the worse since it had appeared. It tended to make my luck run toward the bad kind.

The *very* bad kind.

My free hand crept to the lump under my shirt, and I drew reassurance from its gentle warmth. I was grateful to my master for giving me the amulet. Before receiving it, my life had been pretty much intolerable. But now the amulet counteracted the worst of my terrible curse.

*Most of the time.*

A thunderous pounding rattled the old keep's door. My heart leaped into my throat, and my almost tied ribbon went floating Creator knew where. The journal scroll flew from my fingers and sailed across the work table. It bounced once and fell to the floor on the opposite side, no doubt unwinding itself across the room. My scrolls tended to do that. It was an unfortunate side effect of my problem.

The pounding came again more demanding than before. "In the name of Lord Wort, open this door!" The voice was deep, gruff, and accustomed to command. "The master requires a reading!"

In my panic to get the door, I jumped up and promptly stumbled over my stool. I crashed against the worktable, not only knocking off the pile of scrolls on the other end, but turning over my inkwell and pen too. The feathered quill floated lazily away in the sudden updraft. I cursed and chased the inkwell unsuccessfully as it rolled across the table, leaving a trail of black ink, as it too escaped to the edge and fell to the rough wooden floor on the other side. My heart skipped a beat. For some reason, it looked like a trail of splattered blood, and I shuddered at the thought. Creator! An omen. I made a warding sign.

I grabbed a conveniently located rag (spills were a common occurrence for me) and tried to blot the wayward blood. *Ink! I meant ink!* Master would scold me severely if I got anything on those ancient scrolls. I shuddered to think what my punishment would be; last time it was holding a metal rod on the top of the tower during a thunderstorm!

Another loud banging came from the door. "Open up, I say! *Immediately!*"

I turned toward my elderly master, hoping for some assistance. Unfortunately, Master Spraggel was sprawled in his favorite chair, sound asleep—and snoring. Loudly. His feet were propped up on a stool, in front of a gently glowing hearth. A thin line of drool darkened the man's white beard. His gray robe was wrinkled and splotched with oil and ink stains. *How could he sleep through all that banging!* I firmly believed that my master was as old as creation itself, if not even older. In fact, I could easily envision Spraggel at the beginning of time telling the Creator he was doing it all wrong!

Seeing as how no help was coming from my master, I threw down my rag and ran for the door. But in my haste, I forgot about the stool and tripped over it again, falling flat on my face just in front of the door. This turned out to be a good thing. Because before I could rise, the door, constructed of heavy oak boards and iron bands fastened with steel spikes, suddenly split diagonally from top to bottom. With a loud clap, a line of daylight suddenly appeared in the door, and in its newly halved state, toppled into the room, one piece at a time, barely missing my nose. I sneezed as a cloud of dust kicked into my face.

I crawled away from the opening, gaping in amazement. *What had happened?*

A large man stood silhouetted in the doorway. My eyes went up and up. He was several hands taller than myself, Spraggel, or anyone else I'd seen for that matter. The dark-haired man was broad-shouldered and had arms the size of small trees. A pearl white snarl gleamed from inside his carefully trimmed black beard. The man wore a well-made white shirt, dark pants, and brown leather boots. He was awesome—in an evil lord sort of way.

But what really made an impression on me was his sword. It was beautiful—fully as long as the man's well-muscled arm—and seeming to gleam unnaturally, like it was radiating with a light all its own.

The large man had to duck under the door frame in order to enter. Three scroungy but well-muscled men entered behind him, their expressions grim.

"Where is the reader?" the man demanded. He spoke with an accent I couldn't place—definitely not from one of the surrounding lands. "Tell him Wort is here for a reading, and he had better hurry unless he wants this deteriorating hovel leveled!" He lowered a deadly gaze toward me, and I could swear his eyes seemed to be on fire.

I nodded in near panic. I quickly got to my feet and, stepping in a pool of spilled ink while I was at it, ran to my sleeping master.

"Spraggel," I shook him. "Master Spraggel, wake up. We have a customer wanting a reading."

The elder slowly raised his head and smacked his lips. "Now where was I, oh yes, Kornealius still owes me for that last script..."

"No master," I interrupted and pointed to the big man. "*New* customers."

Spraggel blinked and stared at me in puzzlement before looking to where Wort stood. "Oh! We have customers. Why didn't you tell me? Now we mustn't be rude to them. Offer them a seat and bring some..."

Wort roared and swung his sword at the scroll table, cleanly slicing through the top and one of its legs. The damaged table collapsed, raising yet another cloud of dust.

I couldn't believe what I had just seen. Surely that was no ordinary sword. It went through the table like it was made of air.

"You waste my time, old man," yelled Wort. "I want a reading. Can you do it?"

"Why of course I can, but there was no cause to split my table in two. I'll have to charge you for that. I don't tolerate such behavior—"

Wort pulled the sword's scabbard from his belt and held it out to Spraggel. "READ IT!"

Spraggel gave him an exasperated frown. "There's no need to be rude. If you aren't a little more polite, I'll have to ask you to leave."

I shook my head nervously and whispered. "Master, I don't think that's a good idea. He looks dangerous."

Spraggel cocked his jaw and squinted at Wort. "I think we could take him."

Putting on my most polite smile, I turned to our guest and took the offered scabbard in my upturned palms and presented it to Spraggel.

Spraggel shot Wort one last look of warning before examining the piece. His expression quickly changed to one of surprise. He took it gently and ran a light finger over the raised runes. Spraggel studied them intently. "Why, I haven't seen such as these in a long time. These runes are ancient Tomarrian, which means this is truly ancient. That language died off at least five hundred years ago." He held it up to the light. "Beautiful workmanship. No doubt the Tomarrian's indeed made this." He looked up at me. "Coren, bring me my volume on ancient weapons, the *Armeda ne Emour*. Second shelf, fifth to the right. Moonhagen is the author."

I jumped to comply. It never ceased to amaze me how Spraggel could remember the exact placement of every book and scroll in his workroom, when most times he could barely remember what he had for breakfast.

The volume was indeed exactly where he said. I had not seen master refer to it before, but judging from the shelf it was on, I knew it was a very valuable book. I carefully took it down; the old leather was dry and dusty. Since our only table had just been destroyed, I gently opened it for Spraggel and held it out balanced on my open hands. The parchment bound in the book smelled not merely old, but absolutely ancient.

Spraggel flipped through the pages and began to hum obnoxiously. I turned and grinned apologetically at Wort. "He does that when he's reading. He can't help it really."

In reply, Wort just glared at me.

Two of the men behind him slowly spread out, covering both sides of the room yet within easy reach of the windows, effectively blocking all the exits. This was not looking good.

Spraggel stopped at the page he wanted and nodded. His finger traced down the page. "Yes, just what I thought. This is the scabbard for *Havoc's Sword*. A powerful weapon. Apparently, it was forged to combat the Dark Avenyts, but it's unclear if it was successful." He looked back to the scabbard. "Let's see. Roughly translated the runes say, 'Woe to the one who welds Havoc's Sword for it is cursed to cause only destruction." Spraggel flipped the scabbard over. "And on this side, 'This sword must never touch *Ruin's Shield* for the Earth's end will soon follow."

Wort nodded. "As I was told, there is a shield to go with my sword."

Spraggel looked back to his book and ran a finger down the page. "It says here that the sword was hidden away with only the king's lineage knowing where?" He glanced up at Wort. "No offense, but you don't look to be from that family."

Wort smirked, the tension in the room rising. "It was a gift from someone needing a favor."

The old man glared at Wort suspiciously. "It must have been quite a favor."

Wort only gave a wide, toothy smile in reply. It sent a shiver down my spine as I grew increasingly uncomfortable.

Spraggel looked back to his book. "It's not clear if the shield was paired with the sword or was to be used separately. It says here that the sword and shield were considered too powerful, and both were hidden after the war. They were only to be used again should the Dark Avenyts return."

Wort leaned forward and took the scabbard from Spraggel. "Where is this Ruin's Shield now?"

Spraggel shook his head and closed the book. He took it from me and clutched it to his chest, while I shook out the cramps in my arms. That book was heavy!

"It doesn't say," Spraggel continued. "But there is a footnote saying the information came from the *Scroll of Nobem*." Spraggel stroked his long gray beard. "Last I heard, the warrior-priests of Daili had the scroll in their temple. They have a habit of adopting such objects."

Wort nodded. "Good. You have done well." With a smile, he put Havoc's Sword back into its scabbard. He pointed to the volume that Spraggel held. "That book you hold. It is a book of weapons, is it not? Does it tell of others? Of all kinds of weapons?"

Spraggel shook his head. "Not all of them. Just the ones known to the Ulegious Empire and even then only the most famous ones." He leaned forward. "Do you know the author didn't include the Sheldities weapons because he thought them barbarians?"

Wort stroked his beard thoughtfully. "Are there other books like it?"

Spraggel frowned and clutched the volume to his chest. "There was only one copy made of the *Armeda ne Emour*. There isn't another like it."

Wort grinned. "Sounds interesting." He reached forward and plucked the book from Spraggel's hands. Without looking, he handed it to the one man standing just behind him. The man had a poorly healed scar pulling one corner of his mouth slightly higher than the other, giving him a permanent sneer.

He took the book and tucked it protectively under his left arm. He smiled and laid his right hand on the hilt of his sword. I think he was actually hoping I would try to take it from him.

I stepped up to Wort. "Hey, give that back. It's an important book with information that cannot be replaced. Besides, I didn't think you could read."

Wort shrugged. "You're right. I can't read. But I'm sure those priests you mentioned would love to have it. Perhaps even trade the location of the shield for it."

"But wait!" Spraggel stepped forward. "I hope you're not planning on seeking Ruin's Shield. You already have the sword, and they should not be near each other. The warning was very clear—the Earth itself would be destroyed."

Wort ignored this and turned to his men. "Phelan, you're with me. Dai. Rid. Kill them. There must be no witnesses. And be quick about it. I leave immediately for this temple."

*Kill us!* I glanced at each of the windows and door, but there was nowhere to run. They had us cut off. I frantically looked around for a weapon. My sword was under my bed in the loft above, so that wouldn't do me any good. Then I spied the table leg that had been lopped off, right beside the wayward ink bottle. That chunk of wood was big and thick, it definitely had club potential.

Wort strode out of the room with Sneer Man following behind and Spraggel's book under his arm. Neither of them so much as glanced our way.

The remaining two men surged to take their place. Each was well-muscled and broad of chest. The man furthest from me had a scar across one eye and wielded a wicked-looking mace. The other wore a leather helmet with a single horn protruding from it and held a very dangerous looking sword.

I felt a flash of warmth underneath my shirt as my amulet suddenly heated. It meant my bad luck had tried to do something horrible, but the amulet had countered it. I briefly considered jerking off the charm and letting my luck have its way, but just as quickly decided against it—*much too dangerous*. My curse would make things even more unpredictable.

I dropped to one knee close to the table leg and clasped my hands before me. "Please, I beg of you. We're but simple scribes. Please don't kill us!"

Helmet-man smirked and raised his sword. "Sorry, bloke. It's just business. Noth'n person'l."

I quickly reached for the fallen table leg, but instead my hand closed on the wayward ink bottle. *Oh no.*

As the sword started its descent toward my head, I instinctively threw the ink bottle at his face and leaped to the side. The bottle hit him squarely in the nose and splashed ink into his eyes. The sword, now without power, landed where I had just been, barely missing me.

"Agh! That stings!" helmet-man yelled and wiped his eyes, trying to get the ink out. He only succeeded in smearing it across his face. It would have been comical, had he not had such a deadly expression. "When I catch you, I'm going to cut out your liver and eat it!"

I yelled over my shoulder, "Master! Run!"

Behind me, Spraggel huffed. "Nonsense. Why would I run when I have them right where I want them? I guess I'll have to teach these youngsters a thing or two." He began to rummage through his pockets. "Now where did I put my sword?"

I finally reached the table leg and swung it up just in time to block helmet-man's chopping stroke. The impact stung my hands, with the sharp blade biting deep into the wood. We each tried to pull our weapons back but found the sword stuck. He gave a hard jerk, and I simply released the leg. He stumbled backward at the sudden weight and tripped over my fallen stool to land squarely on his backside. I guess I wasn't the only clumsy guy in the place.

"Master!" I looked back over my shoulder. "If you're not going to run, how about a little help here!"

But Spraggel continued busily digging in his robe pockets and tossing the contents on the floor: a small scroll, a chunk of bread, a vial of some blue liquid. *Where was he getting that stuff?* I'd seen strange things come out of his pockets before and surmised he had some kind of enchanted robe.

After pulling out a sock, he reached deep into the pocket—up to his elbow. His eyes went wide. "Aha! This will do nicely."

The remaining henchman with the scarred eye, managed to work his way around the various broken bits in the room and now was in striking range of Spraggel. He reared back his mace to clobber my pre-occupied master. I leaped in his direction, but knew I would arrive too late.

Spraggel pulled out his hand—and it was filled with a fistful of gold coins. Not copper, not silver, but *royal gold* coins. The kind where each coin was easily worth a smallholding. And there had to be a dozen of them. *Where was master getting those from?* I'd never seen him with that much money before.

Spraggel frowned and shook his head. "No, that wasn't it. I wanted my sword." *And he tossed them on the floor!* Royal gold coins! Just tossed them on the floor! My brain couldn't wrap around it. He was throwing away a fortune!

The round coins rolled in all directions. Both henchmen froze, their eyes bulging with greed. Fearing they might not get their share, they both quickly dropped to their knees and began searching for the coins. Lots of fighting and name-calling broke out between them. I managed to snag one on my way over to Spraggel.

I grabbed him and pushed him toward the ladder to the loft. The door was still blocked by the warriors on their knees.

"Up, master."

Spraggel nodded toward the men. "But what about them? I need to beat them soundly to get my book back and prevent Wort from getting the shield. I've got to have my sword."

I shoved him up the ladder. "Mine's under my bed. You can use that one."

Spraggel made it up two rungs then turned to me. "That old thing is more rust than good metal. I need something with a little edge to it."

"And I'd prefer the edge not be coming at me. Now, *UP!*"

Master finally took me seriously and started climbing. Behind me, the men continued arguing. Seems that one of them felt a little cheated. This was a good thing because it gave me time to start up after Spraggel stepped off.

"Look!" one-eye yelled. "They're get'n away. Wort'll kill us if we don't finish." They then agreed to have their discussion a little later.

*Well damn.* I raced the rest of the way up the ladder, making it to the top just as helmet-man started up. I rushed to my bed, grabbed my trusty sword, and ran back to the ladder. I grinned down at him. "You know you won't make it. All I've got to do is push the ladder. Nothing personal, you know!" I swung my sword at the cord holding the ladder in place—and it bounced off. It didn't even dent it. I tried sawing, but that didn't work either. In frustration, I reared back and brought the sword down with all my strength and—

Broke my damn blade!

It snapped at the hilt, sailing across the room to stick point first into the wooden floor a fingerbreadth from one-eye's boot. He glared up at me and made his way to the ladder.

Spraggel muttered behind me. "I told you it was too rusty."

Disgusted, I threw the remaining piece at the man below me, but it just bounced harmlessly off his helmet. He turned his ink-stained eyes up at me and growled.

Looking around, I grabbed the chamber pot (unfortunately empty) and threw it down on top of our attacker. He deflected it to one side, continuing on up.

*Damn!*

"Coren!" called Spraggel. "This way. Quick!"

I turned to see Spraggel looking at me from outside the loft's small window. He waved at me and smiled. "Hurry!"

I ran to the window and stuck my head out. The timber rafters stuck through the sides of the building, giving just enough room to stand on, and if you took big steps, you could make your way along the side. I quickly climbed out and carefully stepped on the rafters behind Spraggel, trying not to look down. Even though we were only on the building's second floor, we were still a good way up. This old keep was built into the side of a steep hill. Below us was nothing but some *very* sharp looking rocks. If we jumped, we would definitely break something, most likely our necks.

We made our way along the rafters toward the back of the building. Unfortunately, Spraggel stopped at the corner. "Well, Coren," he said, rubbing his chin. "I think we've come to the end of our path. There are no rafters on the back."

I looked behind me and saw helmet-man poke his head out; his ink-covered face had a definite snarl. Scar-eye's head quickly followed, also looking none too happy.

"Master Spraggel," I said. "Looks like this is it. I appreciate all you've done for me."

Spraggel chuckled. "My lad, you're forgetting your *condition*. It's not going to let you die just yet. It might be unpleasant, and probably will hurt a lot, but you won't die from it."

"But master, I don't see how..."

Suddenly, a thunderous shout came from the front of the building. "*Who in the Creator's hell stole my gold!*" That had to be Wort. "I had thirteen gold royals in my purse. Now they're gone! I want to know who stole them. And when I find you, I'll tear your heart out with my bare hands! But if you give them back right now, I'll go easy on you. And I do mean *now!*"

Helmet-man froze with one foot on the rafters and one inside the window. He looked terrified. His partner covered his mouth in fear.

I turned to Spraggel. "You didn't take those coins from Wort's purse, did you?"

Spraggel shrugged. "Not on purpose. It's supposed to link up with my storage chest, but sometimes it has a mind of its own. It's not my fault the pocket chose Wort's purse instead." He leaned away from the wall and waved to the now pale helmet-man. "Good sir. I think we have you at a disadvantage. Unless you leave us, I'm going to have my apprentice yell at the top of his lungs that you've got your lord's gold, which I actually believe you do. However, if you withdraw and tell Wort we're dead, then we'll keep our silence."

Helmet-man nearly spat. "An' wha' say I jus' kill you both now?"

Spraggel nodded toward me, and I raised a hand to my mouth.

Helmet-man waved us off. "No, no, stop... you win." His eyes narrowed. "But you bett'r nev'r cross paths wit' us again."

He then promptly withdrew.

I slumped against the wall. That had been close.

We waited until we heard the men outside depart and then waited a little longer to make sure they were gone.

Spraggel leaned toward me and whispered. "Wort was right about one thing. I'm sure the warrior-priests of Daili will gladly exchange the shield's location for my book." He looked off into the distance. "You realize that we can't let them get Ruin's Shield."

"But, Master," I protested. "How are we supposed to stop them? They outnumber us six to one! And that sword. You saw what it did to our door and the table."

Spraggel grew solemn. "You're right. Havoc's Sword is a myst weapon. One that can cut through things as easily as a knife slices through the air. And unfortunately, so is Ruin's Shield, with myst that will repel anything put against it. Both are very powerful weapons. Too powerful, in fact. That's why they were hidden."

I paused a moment as the information sank in. *Myst.* The ethereal substance behind what some would call magic or sorcery. The myst I knew provided light in the deep of night or let people travel great distances in the blink of an eye.

My hand unconsciously rose to the lump under my shirt. Myst also powered amulets to keep one safe.

I shook my head. "But why hide them? Seems they would be wonderful weapons to have."

Spraggel nodded. "One would think. But myst weapons don't always work like you think they should. If the sword were to strike the shield, you could get an unpleasant reaction. Something called a myst deadlock. Each of the mystic items will draw in power to best the other. And they won't stop until they can't draw in anymore."

My eyebrows rose. "And since myst is needed by all living things..."

He nodded. "We all die."

We were silent for a moment. "That would be bad," I said.

Spraggel snorted. "Slightly." He leaned over and touched me on the arm. "I think it's time to go in. But be on guard. It could be a trap."

I carefully stepped across the rafters and poked my head in the window. Empty. I waved to Spraggel, and we both climbed inside.

I carefully descended the ladder, and after making one final check for intruders, stood for a moment to survey the mess. Shortly Spraggel joined me and returned to his chair by the fire. All I could do was sigh as I began to pick up the pieces of the work table and door. Replacing everything was going to be expensive.

Spraggel stroked his long beard, returning to our earlier conversation. "Wort must not get that shield. He must be stopped at any cost. And let's not forget he also stole my book. That alone could be big trouble if it got into the wrong hands."

Determining it couldn't be fixed, I dropped the table and stepped back, catching the ink bottle under my foot and nearly falling. I picked it up and threw it out the window as far as I could.

Spraggel stroked his beard. "I would normally go see Lord Pringottin and see if he would send some men after the thieves. But he's away and not expected back for several months. He's left Javillia, his master at arms in charge, but that old soldier won't send anyone anywhere without Pringottin's permission." Spraggel sighed dramatically and buried his face in his hands. "What *are* we going to do?"

I stroked the leather band around my left wrist, thinking of what lay hidden just beneath it. I couldn't hide my growing grin. *This could be the start of my adventures. And the beginning of my cure!* "Why don't we go after him ourselves?"

Spraggel looked up at me in surprise. He got up from his chair and walked over to me. "But we're only scribes. We don't have the funds or the arms to launch such a quest."

I dug into my pouch and pulled out the remaining gold royal. "What if we use this? It could surely pay for us to get there."

He stroked his beard. "But what about help? We'll need a few good fighters and weapons."

I nodded excitedly. "We could find some good men to go with us. We could use this to pay them."

Spraggel smiled and patted me on the shoulder. "Excellent idea, my young apprentice. Truly brilliant and so charitable of you to offer up that gold piece. I'm so *glad* you thought of it."

I suddenly realized that I had just been suckered. Spraggel was going all along. He just wanted me to offer up the gold.

But I couldn't help but grin. Maybe this would be the start of my adventures. Maybe even a solution to my problem.

One my father had passed to me eight years before.

A curse of very bad luck.

# CHAPTER TWO

# The Lady Had a Hawk

The town of Iron Landing was bustling with mid-morning activity as Spraggel and I entered through the main gate. The wide street just inside was lined with merchant stalls, some matter-of-factly drab, while others were draped in painfully bright fabrics flapping in the breeze. Some men and women moved purposely along the thoroughfare, while others stopped mid-stride to chat with their acquaintances, forcing the flow of people to move around them. Over the background noise of the crowd, sellers hawked their wares while goats, pigs, and oxen complained in their pens. Dust rose from the dirt streets mixing with the smells of people, animals, food, and manure. The noise and smells were overwhelming.

I loved it.

It was a perfect, early spring day to enjoy it. While the air was still cool, it was warm enough that my jacket was all I needed.

Where I grew up, there wasn't a town this large nearby, so I was always fascinated whenever we came. Spraggel and I didn't come that often since Iron Landing was a four-hour walk from Revenhill Keep. But I loved the activity of the town. Its trade in ore from the nearby mountains ensured a constant stream of goods and people. In fact, Revenhill Keep had originally been built to protect the mining road into Iron Landing. But that route had fallen out of use when the traders shifted to a road further west.

Spraggel, on the other hand, hated the town, or towns in general for that matter. He said towns had too many people, and almost all of them were greedy, lying bastards.

When I first heard him say that, I couldn't restrain from commenting. "Don't you think that's a little harsh?"

He considered this for several heartbeats before answering, "I thought I was being rather generous myself."

So while my master may not have been particularly happy we were in town, I was ecstatic. And my first order of business was a new sword.

"Yoo-hoo!" a female voice called.

I slowed and looked around. I didn't see anyone. Spraggel continued on ahead.

"Up here!"

I looked up. I was standing in front of a two-story building displaying a sign high above the door with a faded blue ox in profile and the name Ox Head tavern on it. Above it, leaning from a narrow window above the sign and smiling down at me, was a beautiful woman with long dark hair. She was wearing a very low-cut blouse which exposed most of her large and pearly white breasts—and she was leaning out quite far while waving a lace handkerchief. I stared dumbfounded as she blew me a kiss.

"Hey there. Why don't you come up and see me? I could use some company from a handsome young man like you."

I couldn't help but blush. Spraggel grabbed my arm and pulled me away. "Sorry Merellia," he called, directing us back into the flow of traffic. "But this fellow has a social disease. You wouldn't want him."

"Disease!" she pulled back. "Pray tell, what's he got!"

"He's moneyless."

She stared for a moment and then laughed, flicking her handkerchief daintily. "You're right. He wouldn't pass muster." She leaned forward. "But what about you, Spraggel? Do you have some time to spare?"

I looked at Spraggel in shock. I couldn't decide if it was because he knew her name or that she knew his. "You know her?"

Spraggel nodded. "Indeed I do. She plays a mean Devil and Taylors." He called up to her. "Sorry, love. But I've got some business I have to attend to. Maybe when I return, I'll let you beat me."

She chuckled. "Promises, promises."

Spraggel gave a slight bow. "Until then, my lady."

She waved as we walked off. A few moments later, I could hear her accosting some other male walking down the street.

Spraggel leaned in close. "You have to watch out for these town folk. They'll take everything you have, down to the last bit."

"I can't believe she knew you."

"Well, young man. I may be old, but I'm not dead. And don't be deceived by her looks. She really is very good at just about any game of chance, especially where it entails separating a young man from his money. She definitely knows how to use her assets as a distraction."

"And you're not distracted?"

He smiled. "That, my boy, is my secret." Spraggel drew me down the street. "Now our first order of business..."

"Is getting me a decent sword."

Spraggel looked skeptical. "I actually think we need to find some brave and strong warriors. Then we'll know what we'll need in the way of supplies." He stroked his beard in thought. "But we do need to leave quickly so we can catch up with Wort." His head came up. "Why don't you go look for some horses. I'll ask around about our help."

I was uncomfortable letting Spraggel pick the help. No telling what he would come back with.

"Let me come with you, master. I can help you talk to them."

He shook his head. "No, Coren. I need to do this myself. And don't worry. I won't pick someone weak."

I didn't share his confidence but couldn't argue too hard. I grabbed Spraggel's sleeve. "Remember, master. They have to be strong and brave and have their own horse. And they need to be loyal too! We don't want them running off when we need them."

Spraggel shrugged me off. "Yes, yes. I know exactly what we need!" He hurried off calling over his shoulder. "Meet me at the Inland Sea at noon."

As I watched him walk away, I couldn't help but have a bad feeling.

A little over an hour later, I stepped away from the stables less than impressed. The horses all seemed overused with a few even in poor health. I sighed. They would not do at all. I had spent my early years working in the stables before my father died. So while I may not have known much about swords and fighting, I did know a thing or two about horses. My only hope was another stable on the other side of town. Maybe they would have better.

I entered the main street again, finding it more crowded than before, with quite a collection of people of all shapes, sizes, and classes. I checked the sun. I still had perhaps an hour before I would need to head over to meet Spraggel at the Inland Sea. It was the only tavern in town Spraggel would go to. (The rest were out to cheat you, or so he claimed.)

I stepped around a cart blocking my path and came face to face with the strangest sight I had ever seen. A woman—with her long blonde hair pulled back in a tight braid and dressed in a white shirt, leather vest, and brown leather pants—was walking toward me.

Now, a woman in pants instead of a dress by itself was unusual, but not *that* unusual. Rather, it wasn't the woman that had caught my eye. Instead, it was what rode on her shoulder—the largest hawk I had ever seen. The bird was huge, at least an arm's length from head to tail, and beautifully majestic, with dark brown wings, a reddish breast, and a fringe of white along its tail. It rode on the woman's shoulder as if it were royalty, gazing intently ahead, yet giving the impression it saw everything around it.

The woman, seeming unaware of the stares her companion invoked, moved through the crowd with a bold grace. She looked to be a little taller than me and not too much older. A deadly looking sword hung on her hip, and she carried a pack on her back. I had to admit; she was pleasing to look at. But when she glanced my way and her blue eyes locked on mine for only an instant—I revised my estimation. She was indeed beautiful—as beautiful as a she-wolf staring at her prey. I quickly looked away.

As we approached each other, the bird swiveled its head to watch me. I didn't sense any evil intent from it, just a curious intelligence.

As we passed, I turned to follow them with my gaze, only to find the hawk's dark eyes tracing my path. I was definitely impressed.

And then I felt it. Just a slight tug at my waist, and I instantly knew what had happened.

"Hey!" I yelled. And launched after the boy running away from me and now carrying my purse—it was all the coin we would need for the horses. "Stop, thief!"

He dodged away, heading straight down the street.

But before I had taken two steps, I felt a rush of wind go past, and the faint caress of a feather on my cheek, as the large bird sped by me. It easily caught up with the boy and sunk its claws into the thief's coat. It gave a loud screech, and the boy fell to the ground in fear.

"Get it off me!" yelled the boy.

I drew up before the bird, which had spread its wings, forcing the onlookers back. The bird's owner brushed past me and held out her arm. "Come, Zofie. You shouldn't attack people."

The bird gave out a squawk and bent down to nose the stolen purse. The boy eagerly released it from his grasp.

Then the hawk looked right at me. I could swear it was trying to tell me to get the purse.

"I believe that's mine," I said.

The woman gave me a skeptical look and turned to the bird. "How do I know it's really yours?"

"The boy just stole it."

The hawk nosed the stolen purse yet again, then raised its head giving a bobbing motion.

The woman nodded knowingly. "Now I understand." She reached down and picked up the purse, pausing to whisper something to the hawk I couldn't make out. In reply, the bird looked away from her, and in a single flap of its wings, leaped into the air. The boy didn't hesitate to spring to his feet and flee into a nearby alley.

The woman handed the purse to me. "You should take better care of your money. You're lucky Zofie saw him running. She can't help but chase running things. It's just her nature."

I was disappointed. So the bird had only acted on instinct. For a moment there, I thought it had been trying to help me. I saw the hawk alight atop a nearby building, watching us.

"Thank you for your help in getting my purse back."

The woman shook her head. "Don't thank me. Thank Zofie. Personally, I wouldn't have helped. Anyone who can't protect their own stuff *should* have it taken from them." She held out her hand palm up. "And now it's time for my reward."

"Reward? You just said it was the hawk that saved me."

"True. But I have to feed her, and it's not cheap."

I sighed. "What if I bought you a cup of ale instead?"

She shifted impatiently and put a hand on her sword. "That would be nice, but I'd rather have the money."

Well, I guess even heroes can be thieves. Spraggel's words on the greed of the townspeople echoed in my mind. Maybe he was right.

Reluctantly, I opened my purse and pulled out two copper coins. I laid them on her palm.

"You're kidding. That's all? I just saved your butt."

"You saved my purse."

"Butt, purse, in your case, they're all the same."

I sighed and put another coin on her palm.

"You're getting warmer..."

The hawk gave a loud squawk from atop its perch, interrupting her. The woman suddenly closed her hand. "I guess that's good enough. Zofie is impatient to be going again." She gave a brief nod. "It was good doing business with you. My name is Risten. Risten Brightmare, should our paths cross again." And she turned away.

I called after her. "No offense, but I hope we don't!"

She held up a single hand and waved in dismissal.

*Damn women.* They always got the best of me.

I glanced at the leather band around my left wrist. My curse loved to use them to taunt me. I would be sorely glad if it just disappeared.

My eyes went large. *My amulet!* In panic, I felt inside my shirt. I breathed a heavy sigh of relief upon touching the charm that lay against my chest. I made sure it was secure inside my shirt before turning back to my original direction. I had been afraid that maybe the pickpocket had gotten that too. It was the only thing that kept my curse under control. That would be even worse than losing my money. Not for me so much, but for those around me.

For I had a very special kind of bad luck curse. One that could kill.

I should know. That's how I lost my father.

The other stable had a much better selection with several horses suitable for the trip. But naturally, they were more expensive, and with the saddles and tack, were going to take all our transportation budget. I had been hoping for some left over to buy a sword, but with the added horse expenses and what that blonde woman took, I only had a silver coin and a few coppers left. Not nearly enough for a sword.

I made my way to the Inland Sea to meet up with Spraggel. I was running a little late, but I doubted Spraggel would be upset with me.

The Inland Sea was a small tavern and owned by a man named Mikney de'Glougeman—one of the few people in town Spraggel thought was decent enough to socialize with. I was sure being able to finagle a free drink or two had nothing to do with shaping my master's opinion. But for me, Mikney usually charged double. The man didn't like me for two reasons. On my first visit, my bad luck had caused a cask of his best ale to fall and break open. It had unfortunately broken on his foot too. He'd hobbled around for a couple weeks while it healed. That was before Spraggel had gotten me my special amulet to control my curse. Can't say I blame him for holding a grudge. The second reason he didn't like me was because of his daughter Maggie. I think he was afraid I'd try to take advantage of her or something. Not that it was a possibility. For one, while she was cute, she was too young for my tastes—not more than fourteen at most. And the other reason, *I just wasn't going to pass on my curse.* It was going to stop with me: no wife, no children—the single life for me. That was unless I managed to break it, which from what I knew, would be a monumental task and could take years. So if I couldn't stop my curse by finding a cure, I would at least ensure I was the last of my line to suffer.

Breakfast had been a long time ago, so I was looking forward to something quick to eat. We still had to arrange repairs for the tower door and buy some supplies, so we wouldn't be able to leave until the morrow.

I stepped into the dimly lit room, the only illumination coming from the open door and a window above. The interior had bits and pieces of ships tacked up on the walls. Originally, they were only from Mikney's own wrecked vessel, but over the years, his customers had brought him other pieces of unfortunate ships. He always managed to find a spot for them on his walls and was always eager to recite their story.

I paused in the doorway, savoring the smells of food and ale, until I finally spotted Spraggel sitting at a table speaking with the owner's daughter, Maggie. Spraggel had a soft spot for her—she always laughed at his jokes, even when they weren't funny.

Someone else was sitting with Spraggel, but I couldn't make out who. They had their back to me, and Maggie partially blocked the view. But I could see a sword hanging at their hip, so it was no doubt our hired help. The sword was a good sign. At least they had their own weapon.

I approached the table. Maggie looked over at me and broke into a broad grin. "Coren! How are ya! Spraggel was just tell'n us you're going off to save the world."

Leave it to Spraggel to exaggerate just a bit.

I gave a slight bow. "Doing good, Maggie. And you're looking very fine yourself."

She blushed clearly pleased. "Oh, go on."

I glanced to the side and saw Mikney glaring at me. Daggers were in his eyes. I just hoped none were in his hands.

"Uh... I'm fairly starving. How about some of that ham you're famous for."

She bounced on her toes. "Sure thing." And hurried off to get the meal. I turned my attention to the person sitting with Spraggel, and my mouth fell open.

"You!"

Risten raised her glass. "Hello again. How's that purse doing?" She winked at me.

Spraggel leaned back in his chair. "Good, you two already know each other."

"Sort of. Her hawk caught a pickpocket that tried to steal my purse."

Spraggel chuckled. "Fortunate for you, she was around."

"True, but she charged me three copper coins for the privilege."

Spraggel furrowed his brow. "Only three? That *was* a good deal."

I gave up and pulled out a chair and sat at the table in the only open spot between the two of them. Just then, Maggie reappeared and sat a plate before me with a huge chunk of bread and a generous slice of ham. It was larger than the normal portion.

"Thanks, Maggie. This looks good."

Risten leaned toward me and whispered. "See that man over there? I think he's getting ready to rob the place."

Both Maggie and I looked in the indicated direction, but all I saw were two men arguing over who was supposed to buy the next round.

"I don't see anyone..." I glanced at my plate. Wait, something was missing. I looked to Risten, and she was smiling around my slice of ham. "Hey!"

She shrugged as she chewed. "I just gave you a valuable lesson concerning your food. Like your purse, never leave it unguarded." She winked at me again and proceeded to take another big bite.

Maggie frowned at Risten and touched me on the shoulder. "I'll get you another piece."

Glancing over at Mikney and his deepening scowl, I shook my head. "Don't. You'll get in trouble with your father. I've still got the bread."

I did a quick look to make sure I actually did have the bread.

Spraggel leaned forward. "I'm glad you both get along so well. This journey could take a few months."

I paused with the bread halfway to my mouth. "You mean you hired *her*?"

Spraggel nodded. "She comes with good recommendations. She used to be in King Xernow's guard in Brethnach."

My eyebrows shot up. "The king's guard? But wasn't Xernow assassinated?"

Risten's eyes narrowed and leaned in my direction. "I protected my king to the best of my ability. His death was due to treachery from his own family." She leaned back in her chair. "And I left because I didn't particularly like the new king. He's nothing like his father." Risten put her feet on the edge of the table and took a big bite of my ham. Her blue eyes bored into mine, daring me to pursue the topic further.

I had heard something about the King's assassination. Apparently, one of his heirs, a daughter I believe, decided not to wait for the king to pass on and killed him. But a younger son found out and killed the murderer. It was apparently quite the spectacle since both daughter and son were powerful myst users.

I considered Risten. King's guard or no, I couldn't help but stack her up against Wort. After all, she was a woman, and Wort had that myst sword. I was afraid Spraggel's judgment might have been a little clouded—he had a soft spot for women.

"Master, are you sure she's a good choice? Wasn't there someone stronger? And shouldn't there be more than one?"

"Well, I did see some that might have been stronger, but when they heard I was going up against Wort, they all declined. Apparently, he has a bit of a reputation."

Risten watched the conversation with interest.

"But she's a woman... How can she possibly go up against Wort? That man... he split our door and table in half!"

Spraggel cocked his head to one side. "Could any of us go up against Wort? Not hardly. The objective is to get to the shield before he does—and get back my book. Going up against him is definitely *not* in the plan. Risten is our muscle in case something other than Wort gets in our way."

"But how do you know she's not just boasting?"

Spraggel leaned forward, a sparkle in his eye. "Why don't you go up against her? Have a little mock fight." He looked at Risten. "You wouldn't mind, would you?"

Risten grinned. "Not at all. Do I get to kill him?"

Spraggel leaned forward and patted her hand. "Sorry, but I need my apprentice in one piece. Think you could do that?"

She frowned. "It would be more fun to kill him."

I looked back to my bread. "I would, but I don't have a sword." I *had* practiced quite a bit, and she *was* just a woman. I could probably beat her on strength alone.

Risten rocked forward in her chair and leaned across the table. "We don't actually have to use swords—we could just fight with sticks. First one to land a hit wins."

She leaned in very close. "I'll even sweeten the deal. How about I bet you my sword against all the ale I can drink tonight?"

"I don't know..."

She sat back in her chair. "Unless you don't have balls enough to fight a little old, *helpless* woman."

My face turned red. That got me. "I'll do it." And held out my hand. We shook on it. It was then that I had my first doubt about the bet— her grip nearly crushed my hand!

Spraggel called across to the room. "Mikney! Can you accommodate us?"

Mikney went to the wall and pulled down two long sticks. They looked like sawed-off boat oars. He handed one to each of us. "I keep these around for just such an occasion," he said. "Some drunks always want to prove themselves. The sticks make sure no one is killed. Just do it out back so nothing gets broken." He turned and grinned at me. "I'm going to enjoy watching you in action... Action being getting your butt kicked." He snickered and walked off.

Risten and I took our sticks, walked through the kitchen, and out into a small courtyard. I noticed that Risten's hawk, Zofie, was perched on the roof overlooking the yard. She watched as Risten and I squared off, giving off a loud squawk of what sounded like displeasure as we took our positions. Spraggel, Maggie, Mikney and a few others lined up along the tavern wall to watch. Spraggel leaned on the side of the building sipping his ale, while Maggie stood beside him wringing her hands. Mikney was taking bets.

Risten shook out her arms and positioned herself across from me.

I smiled and nodded toward her. "Ready when you are... *love.*"

Risten's expression grew suddenly angry. She quickly raised her mock sword and charged, swinging her stick downward. I easily stepped back and caught it with my own, but then she stepped on my foot, pinning it firmly in place. *What the...?* I staggered, nearly losing my balance. She leaned in and grinned. "You're a virgin, aren't you?"

"What! That's..." I struggled to pull my foot lose. *That was none of her business.*

Her smile hardened. "Because you have no idea how dangerous a woman can be."

Then she brought her knee up into my groin. I doubled over in instant agony, falling to my knees.

Risten tapped me on the back with her stick sealing her victory. "And don't call me *love,*" she said as she turned away. "Only one person ever called me love... and he's dead."

Applause broke out around me. Risten did a very regal bow to her audience.

Spraggel raised his mug and called to me. "Coren! I forgot to mention that she knows how to fight dirty."

I put my forehead on the ground and groaned. *Now he tells me.*

Risten enjoyed her victory by having quite a few rounds that evening, which left my sword fund pretty well gone. Not to mention, my crotch hurt every time she walked by.

As the evening wound to a close, we all agreed to meet at the oak tree just outside town at sunup. Risten left for her room at another establishment, while Spraggel and I went upstairs to ours. Mikney maintained a few rooms for letting out and grudgingly let us have one that was unoccupied.

Since there was only one bed, Spraggel slept on the straw mattress while I bedded down with some blankets on the floor. Bless Maggie's heart, she made sure I had a couple extra ones. And naturally on the way up, Mikney pulled me aside and whispered that if I went near his daughter, he would do a lot more damage to my privates than Risten had. In fact, the damage would be permanent.

I laid down on my blankets and tried to sleep. But I was too wound up from the day's events and the thrill of what was coming in the morning. Sleep wouldn't come. After laying there listening to Spraggel snore, I finally decided maybe some fresh air would help.

I made my way out back and into the dark courtyard. Tonight was the night of the new moon, so the courtyard was completely black. Reaching inside my shirt, I took out my amulet and pulled off the small cloth bag over it. It easily filled the courtyard with its light, nearly blinding me. The amulet glowed all the time, but I kept it in a small black bag which hid the illumination. That's how I knew it was working to keep my curse under control.

It contained a handy little spell. Master Spraggel had explained the principles behind it when he gave it to me. Spells use *myst* which all living creatures have, but most people can't see or feel. However, there were a few individuals that could not only see it but use it to do or make things. The spells themselves were nothing more than a series of commands on what to do with the myst: take myst in, process it, stuff happens. Since my curse was a very complex spell, it took longer to process the myst. However, the amulet was a vastly simpler spell. It was able to suck up the myst around me *before* the curse got to it. So while the curse was trying to cause me all kinds of misfortune, it had an empty quiver, so to speak. No arrows to fire. But the amulet spell had to do something with the myst it consumed, so it turned it into light. A *lot* of light.

With the courtyard now being well lit, it was easy to pick out the privy. I wondered if I should put my light away since I could have easily located it by smell. I went in and closed the door behind me. The amulet lit the small interior very well—probably better than during the day. I was seeing things I really didn't want to see.

I finished my business and heard someone outside.

"Are you the one called Coren?" A female voice asked through the door. The accent was unfamiliar and the voice one I didn't know. But it was a solid voice, its quality almost musical.

"Yes, I'm just coming out." But when I pushed on the door, I found she was blocking it.

"Please don't open the door yet. I have something I need to tell you. It's about Risten."

"If you're going to tell me not to call her *love*, I've already found that out."

The woman on the other side chuckled. "Sorry about that. Risten is my cousin, and while she means well, she can be a little forceful at times."

"That's an understatement. Now, pray tell what is important enough to keep me trapped inside this odorous chamber?"

She chuckled again. She had a very charming laugh. I couldn't help but wonder what the woman looked like. You can never tell from voices, but she sounded close to my own age.

"To make up for the problems my cousin has caused, I left you a present on your blankets. I intended for you to wake up to the surprise, but it was hard to miss the light coming off your charm."

A gift? I was surprised. Well at least one person in the family had manners. But I sensed that wasn't all. "And? There's more to it, isn't there?"

"Yes... Yes, there is. I... I need you to watch out for Risten. She is bold and excellent with a sword. Few can match her. But she's bull-headed and thinks just a bit too highly of her own skills."

"She did a pretty good job of proving she doesn't need my help. So why me?"

The lady paused. "Let's just say, I'm a good judge of character. Risten has had a very rough year. We both have actually. She's withdrawn from most people, and she desperately needs someone to watch her back."

I tried to see through the gaps in the boards, but I couldn't make out anything. "I will do as you ask," I said. "I would have watched her bitchiness's back without you even asking."

"I give you my thanks. And I will be going now."

"Before you go, why the secrecy?"

I sensed sadness from the other side. "I am not nearly as fair as my cousin. I'm afraid you would not find me pleasant to look at."

And suddenly, I noticed the pressure on the door release and the presence on the other side left. "Wait! What is your name?"

I quickly stepped outside to find no one around. *Where could she have gone so fast?*

After looking around a bit to no avail, I went back to my room. Spraggel was snoring louder than when I left him.

I pulled back my blanket, and my mouth fell open. That lady had been serious.

A beautiful sword and scabbard lay in my blankets.

# CHAPTER THREE

# Swordplay

I lounged beneath the branches of an ancient oak, just outside the city and beside the road leading north. It sat atop a small hill with a clear view of the road below. Tiny buds dotted its branches and prepared to leap forth with the advancing spring. Our three horses—two to ride and one to carry our supplies—grazed nearby content to nibble at what little grass was coming up. All were saddled and packed for the trip. My master and I had arisen well before dawn and collected our mounts. Spraggel even complimented me on my selection. I had spent the money well and gotten good deals for them, again I was thankful for my years as a stable boy before my mother apprenticed me to Master Spraggel.

I yawned loudly and tried to stay awake. I hadn't been able to sleep until well past midnight. I pulled my sword out to look at it again. It was beautiful—perfectly balanced and highly polished. The hilt had a fairly wide guard with a dragon's head engraved into it. There was also an inscription on the blade with perfectly formed letters in a language I did not recognize.

Spraggel had been just as surprised as I when I showed it to him. He said the sword was finely crafted and thought it was fairly old. The scabbard, on the other hand, had a slightly different style. Spraggel seemed to think it was of a more recent make—perhaps a replacement for an original that had been damaged or lost. Upon finishing his examination, he had patted me on the back and gave me a word of advice, "A sharp mind is far more deadly than a sharp blade." He smiled. "However, the blade can definitely help someone see your point."

I put the sword away and leaned back against the tree. I wish I knew the name of the lady that had given it to me. Unfortunately, my master had slept through the gifting, so he had not seen her. Whoever she was, she deserved to be thanked. And thanked again. But I couldn't help but wonder why I would merit such a fine present.

"Risten's late!" pronounced Spraggel. I lazily cracked one eye and glanced his way. He was pacing around the tree with arms folded. He'd already said that at least ten times.

"Maybe she's not going to show. Drank our ale and ran." Although based on the sword I'd been given, I doubted that was the case.

I glanced down the road and spotted a lone rider in the distance headed our way. The figure looked female. I guess she'd finally decided to show up.

I stood and brushed off my pants. "I think that's her coming."

While she traveled up the road, I got the horses ready and checked the gear. I was just pushing Spraggel up into his saddle when she rode up. She looked a little rough around the edges. "I'm sorry for being late."

I couldn't resist. "What's the matter? Did you have a little too much to drink last night?"

She frowned. "No... well, maybe a little, but that's not why I'm late. I seem to have lost an important piece..." Her eyes locked on my new sword. "*You little thief!* You took it!" She threw her leg over her horse and jumped to the ground, striding toward me.

I looked up at her in surprise. "You mean the sword? I did not steal it. Your cousin gave it to me last night."

Risten looked furious. She rested her left hand on her own sword and held out her right. "She should not have done that. Give it back."

Suddenly, the hawk sailed under the tree, and with a thump, landed on my shoulder, nearly knocking me over. Her claws sunk deep into my coat: I could feel their sharpness against my skin. It gave me quite the scare. The bird spread her wings and gave a loud squawk, lowering her head toward Risten as if preparing to fight.

Risten froze in place, her hand gripping her sword. The two stared at each other. Zofie gave another loud squawk as if daring her to move and shifted nervously from foot to foot.

Risten glared at her a moment longer and finally took her hand off her sword. "Crazy bird," she wheeled and strode away.

The hawk relaxed her wings but kept a wary eye on Risten as the woman gathered her horse's reins and climbed back into the saddle. Without looking at us, she directed her mount toward the road.

I carefully peered up at Zofie, not quite sure what to do. "Ah... Risten. Could you get your bird?"

Risten gave me a dismissing wave and continued to ride slowly away.

I shrugged my shoulder repeatedly trying to get Zofie to move, but she stubbornly stayed in place. I sighed. I guess she was going to ride with me the whole way.

I pointed toward Risten. "Zofie, don't you think you would be much happier riding with Risten?" The bird looked at me, a sadness in her dark eyes, and gave a soft chirp. She launched herself after Risten to land on her shoulder. Risten didn't shoo her off but didn't acknowledge her either. Zofie rubbed her head against Risten's. "Stop it, will you!" Risten shouted. "But I meant what I said, you are stupid!"

It occurred to me that Zofie must be a very special hawk. I knew that hawks could be intelligent, but this one must have been the pick of her litter, or clutch, or whatever hawks are called.

I mounted my own horse, and Spraggel and I followed along behind her.

"Hey! Wait up," I called. Zofie swiveled her head to look at me, but Risten refused to speak.

I sighed. This was going to be one very long journey.

We made good time on our first day. The road was well used and followed the Nortesy River upstream. We encountered a few travelers coming in our direction, but none had seen any sign of Wort. Either he had taken a different path, or he was far outdistancing us.

Risten hardly said a word the entire day. She and her bird rode in silence. Zofie would occasionally launch herself into the sky and be gone for perhaps half an hour before returning to her perch. Spraggel, on the other hand, was his usual chatterbox self, explaining to me about how the trail we were on had been marched by countless armies, from numerous kings, during this and that war. As soon as he started, my eyelids began to droop.

But I did manage to learn a few things. The road took us through an empty field. Spraggel explained that a little over a hundred years back, a Lord Bryst had fielded a large army and camped in the meadow we were riding through. However, the lord never advanced beyond that point. Apparently, he had an attack of severe hemorrhoids and couldn't get back on his horse. He was too stubborn to ride in a cart, so the army sat until nearly winter. Finally, unable to stand it any longer, the physician of the count he was fighting snuck out and treated Lord Bryst. The cure was so successful that Lord Bryst packed up his army and went home.

I considered Spraggel's story. "Master, so the moral to the story is that a single act of kindness can stop a war?"

Spraggel nodded. "Yes, but not without cost. Despite having prevented a war, that nameless physician was declared a traitor and summarily exiled."

I looked at him in surprise. "Exiled? That seems rather harsh."

"Indeed. We humans are strange that way. We don't like to help the ones we're against, even if it will benefit ourselves." Then he brightened. "However, that physician did go on to make quite the fortune selling hemorrhoid remedies."

We made it to a small village without difficulty and took lodging at an even smaller inn. I was all in favor of taking advantage of the inns while we could. Spraggel had said we were headed into a less settled area, so encountering a place to stay would become less frequent.

After bedding down the horses in the stable and seeing that Spraggel got his ale, I went outside to a grassy clearing beside the stables and pulled out my new sword. I hadn't had a chance to practice with it yet, and I'd been dying to try it all day. I had only an hour of daylight left, and I wanted to make the best use of it.

I went through a couple of stances and was surprised at how good the sword felt. Although it was a little shorter than my last one, it was perfectly balanced. Even in my novice hand, I realized it was a masterpiece of craftsmanship. I had read one of Spraggel's books on the subject, so I at least knew a little. I tried to copy the movements I had memorized from the book, but I was dissatisfied. The sword felt great, and I thought I was going through the motions correctly, but my movements were rough and felt off balance. In past practices, I had blamed it on the condition of my old sword, but with the new one, it was obvious the problem was me. I was missing something. But what?

I caught movement out of the corner of my eye and looked up to see Zofie circling above me. The hawk sailed into a nearby tree and alighted on a limb with a good view of the clearing. To my surprise, she settled down, watching me intently as if waiting for me to continue. I shook my head. No doubt my movements were somehow attractive to her: sort of like a kitten and a ball of string. I shrugged. Well at least someone would be entertained.

I practiced a few more basic moves until the evening sky began to darken. It was then I felt another presence. I froze mid-stance. Under the tree where Zofie perched, a figure was leaning against the tree trunk: Risten. Creator, that woman was quiet. I waved to her, but she remained motionless. I could just make out her frown.

*Well, be that way.*

I could feel her eyes on me as I went through my stance one last time. Even I could tell it wasn't very good, and I sorely wished I could figure out what I was doing wrong.

"Waste of a good sword," Risten muttered. She stepped forward and held out her arm. "Zofie, come!" Anger was evident in her voice.

The bird hesitated, looking from her master and back to me while dancing from foot to foot. She seemed unsure what to do.

"Stupid bird," Risten muttered and impatiently snapped out her arm again. "Come! Or I'll leave you to the fool." This time the bird immediately dropped onto the offered perch. Risten turned, carrying her hawk, and walked toward the inn.

I watched her leave and gritted my teeth. Just because she didn't want me to have the sword was no reason to make fun of me. I pulled out my oil rag and began to wipe down the weapon. "I'm no fool!" I called after her. "I'll make you eat those words."

She neither paused nor looked back.

After calming myself while rubbing down my blade, I went inside and joined Spraggel for supper. Risten chose to eat by herself at a table in the corner while feeding Zofie bits of meat from her plate. I was still pissed at Risten and didn't want to even look at her, but my eyes had a different idea, and more than once, I found myself watching them.

Risten and Zofie obviously shared a special bond, which was evident from the way Risten smiled when she spoke to the bird or gave her a choice morsel. They seemed happy together. And yet, they had an air of tension about them. I couldn't place why I thought that. It might have been from the way Risten's head jerked toward the door every time someone came in, or how she touched her sword when someone's voice got a little too loud. Whatever it was, something bad must have happened to them recently. I gave a silent prayer to the Creator that whatever it was didn't come looking for us.

When it was time to retire for the night, we all huddled into a single attic room reserved for guests like us that wanted out of the weather but didn't want to pay too much for the privilege. Spraggel took the only bed, while Zofie roosted in the room's open rafters. Risten, on the other hand, gave us a wary look and took her blanket to sit with her back against the far wall. I didn't think she was going to get much rest that way but was too tired to give it much thought. I threw my blanket on the floor and was out before I closed my eyes.

It seemed like I had been asleep only a few minutes, when my eyes flew open, my heart pounding. I had a fleeting memory of a searing heat at my chest and a voice echoing in my head: a deep, dark voice that was vaguely familiar and made me shiver.

I calmed myself and felt for my amulet. Its gentle warmth was still there, meaning my curse was safely in check. But the voice—it generally meant the curse was trying to awaken. Which was not good.

Rubbing my face, I knew there would be no more sleep for me. I sat up and noticed the room's only window had its shutters open. Standing in it was the silhouette of a large bird. Light from the approaching dawn reflected off her eyes, so I could tell that Zofie was watching me. But after a moment, she turned to continue looking out the window. I couldn't help but wonder what she was thinking. She really was a very beautiful hawk, almost regal. Maybe I'd ask Risten where she got her— *if* she decided to answer me.

"Thanks for cheering me on today," I found myself whispering.

*Creator! Now I'm talking to the bird!*

Zofie's head swiveled back in my direction. She cocked it to one side, considering me, before giving a single chirp and turning back to the window. Whatever night element had her attention, it was definitely more interesting than I was.

Letting Zofie have her time of peace, I laid back down and fished out my amulet. I ran my finger over its intricate design which I could feel even through its cloth bag. I clutched it tightly. It was such a thin protection from my curse. My life had greatly improved since Spraggel had given it to me, and I could never repay his kindness (although my master was making me try). Such amulets were fairly common, but usually reserved for the nobility or rich merchants. He never told me where he got it or how much it cost him, but I suspected it was expensive when compared to how much I'd seen us earn as of late. Spraggel had his faults, but overall, he was a better master than I deserved. He had even mentioned that I should consider taking over for him when he passed on. I didn't know if I could. The curse would be with me until my death—unless I found some way to break it. But for that, I needed the nearly impossible.

I glanced over at the snoring Spraggel. This trip was rough on him. He was probably too old to be going on such an adventure. My eyes roved to the blanket-covered lump against the wall. And what about Risten. She wasn't exactly fitting in. While she felt trustworthy, would she stick with us when things got tougher? We were going up against Wort no less. Did we really stand a chance of getting to the shield before him? We didn't even know where it was.

My eyes drifted back to the window, and I could see the barest hint of blue in the sky. Zofie was watching me again. I took comfort in that for some reason. "Are you looking out for us too? We can definitely use the help."

Zofie gave a short chirp and looked back out the window. Then, spreading her wings, she launched herself into the coming dawn.

The next few days all went pretty much the same. We would ride all day with Risten barely saying a word, and once we found an inn, I would practice until dark with Zofie watching. Then when night was falling, Risten would come looking for her hawk and walk away without even acknowledging me.

And with each passing day, we both got a little angrier.

On the fourth day, the sky turned cloudy mid-afternoon, ushering in an early nightfall. I expected we might see rain before dawn. We stopped at the only tavern in the village of Broadbrook. It was a little larger than most we had stayed at, and I hoped I actually got a bed this time instead of a blanket on the floor. While Risten saw to our horses, Spraggel and I went inside to make arrangements with the inn master. I didn't dare let Spraggel go in by himself because, while he was a learned scholar, his haggling skills were... not very smart.

We found the main room crowded with several men gathered around the tables. In the center, seven of the men wore the red livery of Lord Cruimeint—clearly, they were some of his personal guard. They were also well into their drink and laughing rowdily over some story one of them was telling. I frowned. Lord Cruimeint ruled the northern lands of the kingdom. He was a stern man, and those in his employ tended to reflect those same attitudes, usually with clubs and knives. So I refrained from looking in their direction and tried my best not to attract the group's attention. Thankfully, Spraggel was too tired to offer much conversation with the inn master, and quickly agreed to my suggestion that, due to the hour, we retire soon to our room. I turned from the inn master and walked headfirst into what I thought was a solid wall of red. Stepping back, I realized it was someone's coat, and as my eyes traveled up—and then up some more, I saw it was one of Lord Cruimeint's men. He smiled down at me, his face red from too much drink. He stank from ale and too much time on the road.

"Sorry," I said, taking a step back and wincing at the squeak in my voice. "I didn't realize you were there."

His smile got even bigger, and behind him, the room suddenly grew silent. "That's a very nice sword you have there. It looks like one I've seen before. I'd like to look at it."

I was no dummy. If I showed him my sword, I would likely never get it back. But on the other hand, if I refused, he could take that as an insult, which could lead to a duel, and so he would get it anyway—only I'd be dead.

"This old thing." I patted the hilt. "It's not worth your time. It's been giving me trouble, and I think the blade is about to snap off..."

I made shooing motions at Spraggel, hoping he would head on to our room. But unfortunately, my master decided to be... well... Spraggel. He just stood there watching.

The soldier held out his hand. "I'm not asking again." The menace in his voice was clear. "Let me see your sword."

I swallowed, trying to figure some way out. But with the door several steps behind me, and Spraggel glued to the spot, my options were definitely limited.

And then two unexpected things happened. The amulet at my chest suddenly went white-hot. I had just enough time for the pain to register before it stopped. I immediately knew what it was: my curse had tried to activate, but thankfully the charm had caught it.

But I didn't have time to ponder it because out of nowhere, something large thumped onto my shoulder and dug its claws into my coat. *Zofie!* The bird squawked in warning, lowering her head and spreading her wings.

The soldier's eyes grew wide, and he reached for his own sword. "What in the Creator's hell?"

And from behind me, I heard Risten's voice. "Are you trying to pick a fight with one of my party?"

The big man's angry expression quickly softened as he leered at her. He evidently liked what he saw. My sword forgotten, he brushed me to the side. "Well, aren't you the pretty one? I'm going to need to get to know you better... much better."

He reached for her, but Risten deftly stepped aside, leaving the man to grasp empty air. He tried again, and again, but couldn't seem to touch her. His companions laughed from their table. One called out, "A little too quick for you there, Ide."

The big man's face reddened. He focused on Risten again and moved forward with more caution this time. "If you know what's good for you, *my love*, you'll come to me."

I groaned. This was going to be bad.

Risten's boots rang loudly on the rough wooden floor as she stepped quickly up to the soldier, and while being a head shorter, she looked right up into his face. "What did you just call me?"

He grinned, entrapping her in his huge arms. "I called you, my love."

Risten stood rigid. "That's what I thought." She then grabbed the front of his shirt and firmly planted her knee in the man's groin. There was a moment of complete silence in the room as the deed sunk home. Then the large man bent over, and like a giant oak tree, toppled to the ground.

I gritted my teeth in sympathy, almost feeling the pain myself. He was going to have trouble riding tomorrow.

The room quickly filled with the sound of chairs scraping the floor as the other soldiers in the room rose, hand on their own blades. Those not with the soldiers quickly made for the exit.

Risten's sword appeared in her hand, and she held it ready. I looked to her—severely outnumbered by six armed men—and then at the door, where I found the same men blocking the room's only exit. So I made the only logical decision possible. While Zofie squawked a challenge from my shoulder, I drew my sword, stood at her back...

And tried my best to look deadly.

Risten glanced at me over her shoulder, her eyes flicking quickly to my face and then to the raised sword. As she turned back toward the men, I could swear she *grinned*.

She raised her voice. "I really don't want to fight you. I've fought alongside Lord Cruimeint's men up at Potters Hill a few years back. We worked together to clear out a group of bandits. Lord Cruimeint's men are mostly a fine bunch, and I have no wish to make them my enemy."

A man older than the rest peered forward, looking closely at Risten. "I fought on Potter's Hill, and only the king's guard stood with us to clear that thieves' den. But I don't recall seeing you there. And I would surely remember a lady of your... stature." He grinned.

Risten snorted. "That was several years ago and before I received my full... ah... stature. I was a late bloomer. You likely saw me with Arnest Valervick: best swordsman this side of the Skyblue Mountains. He led the charge, and I was always right behind him."

The old man's eyes grew wide as recognition sunk in. "It *was* you! Valervick's apprentice!" He rubbed his chin. "If it hadn't been for Valervick, our losses would have been very high. With his help, we didn't lose a single soldier." He turned to his companions. "I think it best we lower our weapons, if nothing else out of respect for old Valervick." He sheathed his sword.

Grumbling, the men around him lowered their weapons.

Risten smiled and likewise sheathed her own. She turned to say something to me when I saw a huge shadow rise up behind her. Two sizeable hands grabbed her from behind and lifted her off her feet. "I told you, you were mine," said the large man. He must have recovered from Risten's blow.

The older soldier called out. "No, Ide. Don't...!"

But Risten didn't hesitate. She locked her arms around the ones holding her, and in an unbelievable move, she swung her legs over her head and wrapped them around her attacker's neck. She squeezed tightly and twisted. Over balanced, the man toppled to the floor with Risten landing on top. The man struggled to get away but could do nothing as his face turned blue.

"Please, my lady," the older man pleaded. "Don't kill him. He's a pain, but I do need him. I'll see that he is punished properly."

Risten glared up at the older man, and for a moment I didn't think she was going to let go. But after three heartbeats, she sighed and released the man. While she rose, the man's companions quickly went to him and helped him sit up. The old man lectured him in a quiet voice, telling him he was lucky to be alive. And all the men gave her a concerned look.

Seeing no further fighting was coming, Zofie drew in her wings and hopped over to Risten's shoulder. The bird began to leisurely groom her feathers.

Risten leaned close to me. "I just saved your butt again." She put a hand on my shoulder. "I think you owe me."

"Owe you?"

She turned to the soldiers. "This has given me a powerful thirst," she announced. "How about you, men? What say we put this misunderstanding behind us with a couple rounds of good ale."

The older man stood and smiled. "An excellent idea."

Risten patted me hard on the back. "And my companion here will be happy to pay." She lowered her voice so only I could hear. "I did say you owed me. Consider yourself lucky it's only a few rounds. By rights, I should just take your head off for nearly losing the sword."

I stared at her in shock. "You wouldn't."

She lowered her gaze, and I suddenly had no doubt she would.

I quickly turned to the room. "Drinks for everyone! Ale on me!"

A victorious cheer arose in the room. Spraggel made sure he was the first one served. Risten patted me on the back before going to get her own mug of ale.

I muttered to myself. "I think I liked it better when she wasn't talking to me. At least it was less expensive."

The next day our travels returned to the quiet we were accustomed to. And that evening, after finding lodging at a wayside inn, I found time to practice in a nearby field with Zofie watching.

I was glad that I hadn't had to fight the previous night. My stances were still off. Badly off. I seemed to be getting worse. At one point, I ended up tripping myself and falling onto my backside. I got up, brushing off my pants.

"Your stance is wrong."

I started at the voice behind me and turned to find Risten leaning against a nearby tree. Zofie sat on the limb above her.

She continued. "If you're going to carry a finely made weapon, you damn well better be able to defend it."

"Come to make fun of the apprentice scribe? I know I'm doing it wrong, but I don't know how to make it right!" I turned back to my practice. "So just leave me alone so I can figure this out."

Risten stared at me a moment and then shoved off the tree, heading in my direction. "You're an idiot."

I spun to face her. "And you're a real bitch."

Risten smirked. "At least we understand each other." She walked up beside me. "Take the start position of your first stance."

I stared at her, unmoving, and she waved at me to hurry up. *What did I have to lose?* I moved to the first stance.

She leaned down and patted my right leg. "Move this one back slightly and spread your weight a little more. And Creator! Bend your knees!" I did, and it felt strange, but it didn't feel wrong.

She pulled out her own sword and assumed the same stance. "Here, do as I do. I'll go through it with you slowly. Don't worry about getting it exactly right, that will come later. Be sure to watch the placement of your feet."

She then moved through the form I had just been attempting, and I copied her. As our swords moved in tandem, I could see instantly she was very accomplished at this: she had an unwavering grip and fluid movements. *Graceful* was the word I'd use. By the time we finished, I had a new respect for her abilities. I had been very fortunate, when I first challenged her, to have received only a kick in the crotch—because she could have just as easily taken off my head.

She didn't pause. "Let's do it again, but a little faster. And watch your footwork."

We repeated those same movements again and again until the first stars began lighting the sky. Slightly winded, I wiped my forehead on my shirt sleeve. "You're good." I couldn't help but compliment her.

She frowned. "And you're terrible. I've never seen such a sloppy stance. My grandmother could do better than you." She got a faraway look in her eye. "At least that's what my old master said after taking me through that stance. It was the first one I learned."

"You mean Master Valervick? He must be really tough."

Risten put her sword in her scabbard and turned away. "He was. But he's dead now."

*Oh hell. What do you say to that?* "I'm... I'm sorry, I didn't know."

"But now you do. So use his sword well. Don't shame my master."

*Her Master's sword! Oh, my Creator!*

My mouth came open, but no words would come out. She slowly walked away.

Finding my voice, I called after her. "You can have it back. I didn't know it was your master's. Your cousin..."

I saw Risten hold up a hand and shake her head in the dim light. She turned toward me. I could make out a shimmer around her eyes. "No, this is for the best. It was her right, and my master would have wanted it this way. I was just having a little problem..." I heard a faint sniffle and then she continued. "Letting go."

Zofie swooped down to land on her shoulder, and together they went inside the inn.

I was dumbfounded. After hearing that story, there was only one thing I could possibly do, which was to swear on the sword and my honor, that I would make her master proud so that he could forever rest in peace.

# CHAPTER FOUR

# The Curse Reveals Itself

I wiped the sweat from my brow and looked up at the late morning sun. Nary a cloud marred the deep blue sky. It seemed the day would be rather hot—very unusual for this early in spring. The horses weren't happy about it either and plodded along the dusty road a little slower than usual. As the day had warmed, I had taken off my coat and vest and packed them away in my saddlebag. I had also pulled my amulet out so that it was outside my shirt. Even in its protective cloth bag, the charm was always warm, and I just didn't want the extra heat.

It was the twelfth day of our journey, having crossed a rickety bridge over the Tendrum River the day before and turned toward the northwest. With the crossing, I knew the easy part of our journey was behind us. I had studied the maps alongside Spraggel, so I knew the land would become more rugged with less farmland, fewer villages, and more patches of deep forest.

However, despite the increased hardship, the mood in our little party had definitely improved over the last few days. Spraggel rode beside me, happily explaining the history of the land. My master was certainly a fountain of knowledge, and I really did try to listen to him. I only wished he wouldn't try to share all his knowledge with me at once.

I glanced over my shoulder to the ever-watchful Risten riding behind us. She caught me looking back and frowned. I couldn't help but smile. She also had become more talkative—if you can call going from one to five word answers talkative. But for her, it was progress. And when she didn't want to talk, I respected her silence. She obviously had a lot to think about.

As for myself, I was in good spirits too. My blade work had finally begun to improve. In the early mornings before we left and the evenings when we stopped, Risten would take time to work with me on my stances. While she was still an insulting bitch, she was definitely competent and someone I was quickly learning to respect. So with a smile on my face, I closed my eyes and basked in the sun's radiance.

My pleasant thoughts were abruptly interrupted as the warmth of the sun was cut off by a canopy of branches over the road. I had to blink at the unexpected transition to deep shade as our path led us into a thick clump of evergreens. The horse's hooves echoed off the trees, and I couldn't help but have a sudden uneasy feeling. Even Spraggel was affected and paused in his lecture. Unbidden my hand crept to my sword.

We rounded a bend in the road, and up ahead I could see where the darkened woods ended and open sunlight began. However, a silhouette was standing in the middle of the road. As we approached, the shadow transformed into an unkempt, long-haired, mid-aged man. He had a wicked-looking spear and wore the tattered coat and pants of a once purple and gold uniform—the king's colors. We drew to a halt and two other men, one wearing an eye patch and the other moving with a slight limp, emerged from the brush and took positions behind us. They too wore the same tattered uniforms. I couldn't help but notice they bore the grim confidence of hardened men used to fighting—and killing. It was obvious they were deserters, which could only mean one thing.

"Hello, travelers," called the mid-aged man in front of us. "I'm sorry, but I'm not allowed to let you pass unless you pay a toll."

Spraggel called back. "My fellow, this is the king's road. There are no tolls." He eyed the man's spear. "But for argument sake, how much of a toll would that be?"

The man grinned evilly. "Everything you've got." He leveled his spear at us. "Now how about you get down from your horses so we can take inventory. If you don't give us too much bother, we might even let you live."

Risten leaned forward in her saddle. "How generous of you, but I think you've got this wrong. You and your mates are the ones in danger of losing your lives."

The man gave a deep laugh. "A woman, a boy, and an old man against us three? You think too highly of yourself."

Risten smiled and shook her head. "You missed one. We also have a stupid bird. *Zofie!*"

From high above, the hawk gave a shriek. The mid-aged man looked up just in time to get a face full of feathers, talons, and beak.

Risten leaped from her horse and pulled her sword in one smooth motion. She raced to the rear and engaged both the men holding spears. She easily slipped past limping man's weapon and drove her sword's pommel hard into his solar plexus. He gasped for breath once and went down. His eye-patched companion stabbed forward, but Risten wheeled and blocked his thrust, knocking it aside. Eye-patch retreated a step, refusing to fall for Risten's feint.

Risten called over her shoulder. "Coren, protect Zofie!"

I leaped off my horse and pulled my own sword. The mid-aged man in front of us was using his spear as a club, trying to keep the hawk away from his face. I leveled my sword at him. "Drop your spear now or the hawk will eat your eyes."

With blood dripping down his face from the many claw marks, he whipped his spear up to point at me—the point was steel, and it looked very sharp. He tried to knock away my sword, but I had practiced that move and countered, forcing his spear down and away.

Just then, Spraggel rode forward holding out his own sword out to distract the man. Trying to defend against the rider, the man swung up while taking a step forward, making a gallant attempt to slice me with his sharp point, and re-aim it at Spraggel. He almost succeeded. I jerked back as the spearhead raked across my shirt—and unfortunately, caught the piece of leather holding my amulet.

It sliced the leather neatly in two.

I watched in horror as the amulet came loose and fell to the ground. As my protection against the curse came away, I heard a faint, yet deep, evil chuckle. The same dark laugh that haunted my dreams.

My blood ran cold.

"Spraggel! Get back!" I yelled.

Simultaneously, the horse stumbled and the girth holding the elder's saddle broke, throwing him to the ground. He quickly rolled to keep the recovering horse from stomping on him.

The man turned his spear to me. Zofie squawked and flew toward his face, but the man got his spear up in time and knocked her away. Hard. She squawked in pain and fluttered to a large shrub nearby, falling within its branches.

Behind me, the man with the limp that Risten had knocked to the ground, rose and charged her with his spear. She managed to knock it aside, but not before it clipped the rear of my own horse. It immediately reared and in panic started bucking furiously. One of the stray kicks caught the man solidly in the chest and sent him sailing through the air to land flat on his back. He did not move.

Eye-patch lunged forward to take advantage of the distraction, but Risten stepped inside his guard and hit him in the chin with the pommel of her sword in a quick uppercut. But the move had more strength than she intended. We all could hear the crunch of bone as something broke in the man's jaw, and the bone sank into his head. He collapsed, dead before hitting the ground.

The mid-aged man in front of me, the only one of the three left standing, bared his teeth. The spear held tightly in his hands.

I immediately loosened the grip on my sword, letting it slip from my fingers and fall to the ground. "Don't!" I yelled. "You won't live through it."

He pulled back his spear to thrust at me...

And then everything seemed to slow down.

*The spear came toward me... His foot came down on a stone he hadn't expected, and he stumbled... His foot rolled, and his ankle turned... It gave an audible snap as the bone broke... The momentum of his thrust carried him forward... His spearhead lowered and caught in the ground... The man continued forward bending and breaking the spear shaft in half but leaving a sharp point at the break... Unable to stop, he fell on his spear, impaling himself through his heart.*

He died instantly.

And with it came that faint, malicious laughter.

*Dammit! How I hated that curse. Three more have joined the list of those it has killed.*

I dropped to my knees and scoured the ground. It didn't take but a few moments to find the amulet still in its black bag, and what was left of the leather strip. I quickly retied them back together and slipped it over my head, tucking the amulet safely in my shirt.

I breathed a sigh of relief and looked up to see Spraggel getting to his feet. He couldn't straighten up—he definitely hurt something in the fall. He hobbled after his horse, which had wandered away in the excitement.

Risten was in the bushes looking for Zofie, and I hurried to help. I heard a faint chirp and saw the hawk sprawled on the ground, her right wing was bent at an odd angle and her eyes glazed in pain.

"Found her!" I called. I knelt beside her, not knowing what to do. My heart sank. *It was all my fault.*

Risten ran over and roughly shouldered me aside. She gently scooped her up, cradling the bird in her arms. Zofie squawked in pain when Risten gently probed the injury.

Carefully holding the large bird to her chest, Risten stepped back out to the road and wheeled on me. Her face was a mask of anger and fear.

"What in the Creator's hell just happened? I've seen things turn sour on a battlefield, but nothing like this. Three men died all because of accidents. Not that I mind their passing, but it felt *wrong!* The blow I gave that man should not have killed him! I've used that same move in a hundred fights and practiced it a thousand times more, but it's never caved in a man's jaw." She pointed to the man that had fallen on his spear. "And that one... how could it happen like that? A spear just doesn't snap like that."

I looked down, sighed deeply, and then confronted her angry eyes. "It's me. I killed them. Or rather my curse did."

"*Your curse?*" She looked from Spraggel back to me. "I find that hard to believe. It was like something was guiding them to their deaths."

Spraggel hobbled over, a hand on his back and a pained expression on his face. "Unfortunately, it's true. He has a hell of a curse."

Risten shook her head, her face turning red. "And just *when* were you going to tell me about this little curse?"

"Risten, I..."

She stabbed her finger at me. "After we were all *dead!*" She turned away. "Some student you turned out to be. I thought you were some-one that I could count on. I *trusted* you!"

Now I was getting mad. "Trusted me! Don't get so high and mighty.

I'm not the only one with secrets. What about you? When were you going to tell us your little secret?"

Risten became suddenly calm. "I don't know what you're talking about," she said coldly.

I moved toward her. "Like hell! I'm not as stupid as you think I am."

Spraggel held up his hands and tried to intervene. "Now children..."

I ignored him. "You're good Risten. *Very* good. My guess is that you're a master. A real-life *sword-master*! One of the best of the best when it comes to swordplay."

"And what if I am?"

"Then why would a sword-master come with a boy and old man, chasing after someone with a Creator blasted enchanted sword?"

Risten cocked her jaw and narrowed her eyes.

Spraggel put a hand on my arm. "Calm down, Coren."

But I couldn't calm down. I looked into Risten's face, and in a gesture that had become all too practiced for me, rested my hand on the sword at my hip. Risten's gaze flicked to the blade. At first, I thought she was thinking I might draw. But then it hit me. My eyes went wide in realization. The sword, Risten's master's death, even coming with us despite the general warning not to.

"It's because it's personal, isn't it?" I said softly.

Risten frowned.

"Wort killed your master. And you're going to get revenge."

Risten and I stared at each other. Nothing moved around us. The pounding of my heart loud in my ears.

Spraggel grasped my arm with both hands. "Coren, you've gone too far..."

"Deny it!" I shouted. "You want revenge. You want it so badly you intend to go head first against him. Isn't that right? You had no intention of following Spraggel's plan. When were you going to tell us that? Your death wish is going to get us killed faster than my curse!"

She drew up nose to nose with me, and I had a close view of her flaring nostrils and wide white eyes. She was beyond angry. "You are a Creator damned *idiot* if you think that's all there is to it!"

Spraggel tried to separate us. "Now you two, don't fight. Normally, Coren's curse is kept under complete control by his amulet. That thief just accidentally cut it off him."

Risten's eyes grew wide. "Accidentally cut it off. More likely that *thing* directed the spear so it would *be* cut off." She shook her head and stepped away. "I feel like I've been betrayed. I'm not sure I can go further with you two. I can handle thieves and brigands like those all day. I don't even need to kill them. But I need someone to watch my back. Not someone to break my neck if I happen to fall at the wrong time. I saw what happened, and it shouldn't have happened that way. What I saw today was high myst powers at work—unpredictable and very dangerous."

She bowed her head over her bird and gently rubbed the hawk's head. Her expression softened. "And Zofie's broken her wing," she said sadly. "You even hurt the stupid bird!" She stepped away. "I've got to see if I can do something to help her."

"Risten..." I started, but she turned away from me, heading toward her horse.

I took a step after her and suddenly found her sword pointed at my throat.

"You stay away from us. You're too dangerous," she said, turning away and sheathing her sword.

"Zofie and I are leaving."

Risten shook me just as the nearly full moon was rising above the trees. I stared at it groggily, wondering why I was looking at it—until Risten shook me again.

"Your turn to watch," she said.

At first, I was trying to figure out why she was waking me—it had to be near midnight. As my sleep-filled brain gradually came alive, I remembered: there could still be some surviving thieves, so we had agreed to take turns watching. I had been asleep for nearly three hours, but it sure didn't feel like it.

Risten had calmed down enough to realize she couldn't leave us immediately and so was delaying until morning. Other than that, she had not shared her plans, but I could guess they involved returning to the last village we passed through and seeing if she could travel with another party. I blinked. What were we going to do?

I sat up, rubbing my face, and began extracting myself from my blankets. Satisfied that I wasn't going to lay back down, Risten crawled into her own pallet and was asleep in only a few heartbeats. She had good reason to be exhausted. In addition to taking first watch, she had fought off those men, then worked with me to bury them, not to mention the shock of Zofie getting hurt. That would exhaust anyone. She had coiled up an extra blanket next to her to make a nest for Zofie, but Risten's sleeping form cast a shadow over it. I couldn't see how the bird was doing. I didn't hear anything, so I assumed she was sleeping too.

Not for the first time, I wished we were in an inn: a big deep feather bed, a goblet of wine. I slapped the back of my neck. And no bugs.

Spraggel was curled up on his side of the fire, snoring loudly, as usual. His back had eased up with rest, so I thought by tomorrow he would be well enough to ride, provided we take it easy.

We were all on edge from the attack earlier that day. The mood was definitely chill as we went about our tasks. I tried to apologize for my harsh words, but Risten wouldn't talk to me.

Can't say I blame her. I guess I should have told her about the curse from the start. But I tended to keep that information to myself because of the reactions exactly like the one I got from Risten. I sighed and stirred the fire. *What were we going to do without Risten?* We couldn't go ahead without her. We'd never stand a chance against whatever the road might throw at us. And worse, I doubted she would travel with us if we also turned back. I sighed. Even if we could talk her into going with us, could we trust her? She was out for blood, and our whole plan was to get there ahead of Wort, so we didn't have to engage him.

I pulled myself up and went for the water bag. Not surprisingly, I found it empty. Spraggel must have drunk it all and not wanted to hobble to refill it (and likely forgot to tell me when something else attracted his attention.) I stood and stretched. There was a spring just a short walk away. I would refill it and quickly return.

After checking on the horses, which seemed slightly miffed that I didn't have any food with me, I moved to the edge of camp, pulling out my amulet and carefully slipping off the bag around it. The light spread brightly in front of me. Too bright, in fact. On the side of the hill, you would be able to see me all the way back to Iron Landing. So to dim the light, I grasped it in my left hand and allowed a faint glow to seep through my fingers. Even with the reduced light, I had no trouble finding the faint path and making my way down the hill. It wasn't that long until I heard the sound of running water just ahead of me. I froze mid-step. And I could hear something else. I believed it was humming.

Female humming. And I knew the tune. It was a ballad about a prince searching for his true love.

Who could be out in the wilderness on this deserted stretch of road? Surely not more of the bandits. My first thought was to go back to get Risten. But if it was someone directing other bandits to us, I didn't want to lead them back to our camp.

I tightened my grip on the amulet and covered it with my jacket, plunging myself into deeper darkness. Then quietly, I pulled my sword. After waiting a few moments for my eyes to adjust to the moonlight, I slowly crept forward. I wasn't as good at the stepping noiselessly as Risten was, but I thankfully had the gentle babbling of the stream to help hide what I did make.

As I approached the spring, I could make out a figure beside the water—a distinctly female form. And she was still humming. It was a beautiful melody. I couldn't help but wonder what she should sound like when she sang. She definitely had a good voice. I heard a gentle splash and realized she was sitting on the edge, dangling her feet in the water.

If I remembered correctly, just up ahead was a small pool. Some long-ago traveler had built a dam across a natural depression in the stream's path. In warm times, I'm sure it brought welcome relief from the heat. But during this early-spring time of year, the water was outright cold. The pool was naturally screened by some thick bushes and a few trees which were just coming into their foliage and did little to block my view. Even without my light, the nearly full moon illuminated the area, and I couldn't see any deep shadows around which might hide another person. But then again, you couldn't be too sure.

She must have felt my presence. Because through the bushes, I saw the shadow of her head come up. "Is someone there?" she asked. I heard a loud splash. Was she going into the water?

And the voice was familiar. I had heard this accent before. It had a solid, almost musical quality.

I quickly pulled out my amulet, flooding the area with blinding white light. I blinked in the sudden brightness and saw in its glare—

A discarded blanket lying on the ground.

I heard splashing in the water and scanned across it. Midway, I saw a woman's head poking out of the water and moving away from me. Her long dark red hair was loose and spilled gently in her wake.

"Stay away from me!" she yelled, but pausing in her flight when she realized the water was getting shallower nearer the other side and would not conceal her if she moved further. I could see her looking for an exit, but the bushes were too far away.

I quickly scanned the area, relieved to see that no one was around. She appeared to be alone.

She kept facing away with her head just barely above the water. "Do you normally sneak up on an unsuspecting lady when she's bathing! I hope you weren't thinking of taking advantage of me. And since I'm naked, I don't have much in the way to steal!"

*What!* "No, I mean... I wasn't... *Naked!*" I was completely flustered. "I... I heard someone... and I thought it might be bandits."

"Well, since you got such a good look, do I look like a bandit to you!"

"I didn't... I mean, no..." I slumped. This wasn't working. "I think I had better just leave."

"Wait..." she called, I could hear her teeth chattering. "Are you from that camp up the hill?"

I paused. "Yes."

"And you won't harm me...?"

"I give you my word. I will not harm you."

"Then I'd like to talk to you for a bit. But would you put out that blasted light and turn around. This water is damn freezing cold."

I did as she asked and put my amulet back into its bag. The area instantly plunged into darkness, and while putting away my sword, I moved a few steps back toward camp to give her some space.

I heard her stepping out of the water behind me.

"Where did you come from?" I asked. "We didn't see any other travelers on the road. Did those bandits take you captive?"

She chuckled, but I could hear the shiver in her voice and the rustle of cloth. "No, I'm traveling with a small party. We... we saw what you did to those men and were a little frightened. So we hid."

"And so you think we're the bandits."

"You very well could be. You've got that swordswoman. She seems very strong."

I heard her step around a bush and on bare feet come closer.

"Risten's not that bad. A bit of a bitch at times, but she's got a good heart."

The lady stopped behind me. "Hmmm." I couldn't help but feel I was being scrutinized. "You know you're cursed, don't you? You've got a real nasty one."

The statement took me completely off guard. "You can see my curse?"

"Indeed. It's by far the most complex myst-spell I've ever seen."

If she could see my spell, then this lady was indeed one of a rare breed of myst users that can not only see myst workings, but could create *new* spells. Most could only manipulate existing spells working within the bounds of what had been crafted. These people were far beyond that.

"Then that means you're a..."

"Yes, I'm a myst-seer."

I tried not to let it, but my hope rose. "Could you remove my curse?"

"I don't know, but I can look. Close your eyes and turn around."

I hesitated. "You *are* covered, aren't you?"

She laughed, clearly amused. It was almost musical. "Do you think I would come after you stark naked? Not likely. Besides, *the night will be my cloak.*"

She was quoting from a famous sonnet. I finished the verse. "*And the stars will be my guide.*"

She laughed again. "That's good. I see you've read *The Great Travels* by The Poet."

I turned to face her and could make out the shadow of what looked like a blanket draped over her head and shoulders. "I've read about half of *The Great Travels*, but I haven't finished it yet." I didn't tell her that Spraggel had to practically tie me up to get me to read it. "It takes a little bit to... ah... get through."

I heard her step closer. I could feel her warmth.

"Hmmm," she said. "That is definitely a very complex spell. And look at the myst running through it! All these different components. And... that's weird, the anchor is in your left wrist... very unusual placement.

They usually put them on the chest so they can't be... ah... amputated." She sighed. "There's no easy way that I can see to stop it. Whoever did this was a true master. How did you get it?"

"I inherited it from my father, who got it from my grandfather. Before that, I'm not sure."

"Hmmm..." She paused, studying me. "It's also got some kind of protection piece. It... I don't believe it. Truly amazing. It will let all kinds of bad things happen, but it won't let you get killed."

"That's the weird part of this curse. It causes bad luck to everyone, including me, but at the same time, won't let me die. It always causes bad things to happen to prevent it. In fact, that's what you may have seen when those men attacked us. My protection amulet got pulled off, and when one of them tried to kill me, the curse got to him first."

I felt her take another step closer and touch the amulet hidden in my shirt. "But I can see this little charm is doing a good job of keeping the curse at bay. It's much simpler than your curse, but a nice piece of work too."

She sighed and gently patted my chest. "I'm sorry. But there's nothing I can do. This is far beyond my ability. Stopping a running curse is difficult at best, but this one is something else. Maybe if I had been allowed to continue my studies, I could have learned more about these."

I nodded, my hope diminishing. I knew it would be this way. Another myst-seer had looked at it and told me basically the same thing. Still, I always had hope. "That's all right," I said. "Thanks for looking."

"And you looked too!" She laughed. Thank the Creator, she couldn't see my blush.

She was still resting her hand on my chest. And it felt nice. "So are you an apprentice too?" I asked.

"I am... or rather, I was. My master and I parted ways almost a year ago. My fault really. I don't know when I'll get to study again."

"Surely, there's another master that could teach you."

I felt her hand tense on my chest. "A master isn't the problem. You see, I'm also..." she paused and took a sharp gasp. "Dammit." Her voice acquired a new urgency. "It's time. I've got to go back. I've been gone too long." She removed her hand, and I saw her shadow moving away.

"Will I see you in the morning?" There was something about this young woman. Something different...

"No, I'm sorry, Coren. We leave in a couple hours, and you won't see me go." I heard the bushes rustling, and her shadow disappeared.

"Can you at least tell me your name?"

But she didn't answer. In a few moments, the rustle of her movements was gone, and I realized I was all alone: the only sound came from the babbling of the spring.

I sighed and stepped back up the trail to get the water bag and finish my original task. I wish I could have gotten her name. Maybe I would run into her in the morning.

And then it hit me.

She called me by name.

*But I never told it to her.*

# CHAPTER FIVE

# A
# Second Curse

S itting on a large rock next to camp, I watched as Risten arose at first light. She was surprised to find me still on watch. I think she was hoping to sneak away before I awoke. Spraggel was supposed to have taken over for me a couple hours before dawn. Since I knew I couldn't sleep, I decided to give the time to someone who could use it.

But the mystery of last night's young woman bothered me. Something just didn't add up. And I had been stewing over it since she left. How did she know my name? She could have heard one of the others use it. But then why hadn't we seen her or her party? And her accent? It was unusual. Cultured. I know I had heard it before.

Risten quickly went about breaking camp. She pulled a bit of dried bread from her pack and chewed on it as she worked. She would occasionally glance in my direction, but otherwise seemed to be taking great pains to ignore me.

I awoke Spraggel and started making our own preparations to leave. I finally couldn't stand it anymore. I just stepped between her and her horse until she had to look at me.

She gave me an exasperated look. "What?"

"Did you notice another group of travelers yesterday? When I went to get water last night, I met a young woman. She said she had seen us, but it seems odd we haven't noticed anyone before."

Risten stepped around me impatiently. "Where did you see her?"

"By the pool down the hill."

Risten busied herself with checking the stuff in her bags. "I haven't seen another group. Are you sure it wasn't a water nymph? What did she look like?"

"I know it wasn't a water nymph. They're rare, but I've seen one of those before." And I had. There was one in a pond not too far from Spraggel's tower and close to where I gathered wood. The nymph kept luring me into the pond, even though it only came up to my waist. I kept coming home with wet pants until I learned to avoid her. And I hate being wet. I think the nymph just wanted to annoy me.

"No," I continued. "This girl had red hair, but I didn't get to see her face. It was dark, and she asked me to cover the light."

Risten shrugged. "Oh well, it was probably just a dream. I know how you young men are. I bet she was naked."

I blushed. "It was no dream. I definitely saw her."

The conversation ground to a halt as Risten continued to make ready to leave. If I was going to do something, it had to be now. I took a deep breath.

"Risten," I said. "I'm sorry about yesterday. I was really out of line. And we should have told you sooner. Please don't leave us."

She looked at me from the corner of her eyes. "I'm sorry. I just can't travel with you. You have no ill intent, I realize that, but you're too dangerous. I've seen what damage a spell can do."

She turned and patted me on the shoulder. "I'm not angry with you anymore. And you can keep the sword. Keep practicing, and one day, you might be able to keep from falling on your butt."

I nodded, disappointed, and looked at my feet. "So what are you going to do?"

She sighed and gently pushed me to one side so she could finish saddling her horse. "I'm going ahead. *Without* you two. I can make better time anyway. If I don't catch up with Wort on this trail soon, it means he's found another road to this Temple of Daili. I'll catch up to him there."

"And if you catch him?"

"I'll take him down," she said coldly. She turned to face me. "You were right. I do want revenge. Not only did he kill my master, but he also murdered a lot of other people that were very important to me. And after he's dead, I'll take Havoc's Sword back to Edlingreen Castle where it belongs."

Spraggel hobbled over, still stiff from the morning, and joined the conversation. "You realize that women aren't allowed in the Temple of Daili. They worship war and firmly believe that women are little better than slaves."

Risten shrugged. "Doesn't matter. If he's there when I arrive, he'll have to come out sometime."

I nodded and noticed something missing. I didn't see the hawk.

"Where's Zofie? Is she all right?"

Risten paused for just a moment and then resumed tying on her blanket. "She passed on last night. The broken wing was too much for her."

Now I felt even worse. My curse had caused her to lose her feathered friend. They were together all the time. "I'm sorry. I know you loved her."

"Yeah. She was a stupid bird."

I wasn't quite sure what to say after that, so I watched in silence. Spraggel did too.

Having made the final adjustments, she took the horse's reins and swung up into the saddle. The horse danced under her, eager to be away. "Don't try to follow me." She looked me in the eye. "I'll kill you if you do."

And I thought she would too.

She turned toward the path, but her horse nickered nervously and danced to one side. *What the...?*

Up ahead on the road and walking slowly, deliberately, in our direction was a large wolf. You could see the ripple of its powerful muscles, and its huge paws blew puffs of dust with every step. The wolf was a beautiful creature with an unusual reddish fur. Yes, beautiful, but it looked deadly.

And it was coming right for us.

Spraggel hid behind me while I pulled my sword. I took up a defensive position, putting myself between Spraggel and the animal.

But surprisingly, the animal stopped on seeing me pull my sword. Still only a short distance away, it sat down on its haunches, watching us intently. Risten's horse was clearly uncomfortable and danced under her.

"Don't, Coren!" Risten hissed. "Let's not kill it. The animal probably just wants to sniff us. I don't think it's going to hurt us."

I couldn't believe what I was hearing. "It's a wolf, Risten. Wolves eat people."

The animal reared back its head and gave a loud howl. The wolf paused and then did it again. I swear I could feel my insides vibrating.

Risten fought to keep her horse under control. Our other horses tried to jerk loose from their tether.

The wolf stood and sauntered toward us, moving slowly and deliberately. I raised my sword and prepared for it to lunge. But then it repeated its prior action and sat down again.

"Oh, I get it." Risten swung her leg over her horse and hopped down, shoving the reins at Spraggel. She strode purposely toward the wolf.

"Risten! I'm not sure that's a good idea."

"It's all right. I know this wolf. She's an old pet of mine."

"*Pet?*" Spraggel and I said together.

She stepped to the wolf and patted its head, looking over her shoulder and giving us a 'see there' look.

I scratched my head. "You just lost your bird, and now you have a wolf?"

Spraggel stroked his beard in thought. "And this wolf just happened to find you?"

"And just how many pets do you have following you?" I asked.

"Bunches. I was quite the wild child when I was little. They seem to like following me." She laughed nervously.

I scratched my head. This was just too bizarre. And why did I get the impression Risten was lying, and not very well either. First her bird dies, now a wolf appears, and I met a naked lady last night.

Spraggel stepped around me and bent down to examine the wolf more closely. "Your wolf is in exceedingly good shape to have been following unnoticed through the forest." He bent closer. "And a female I might add."

My master slowly stood, his knees creaking as he rose. He seemed amused about something. "And just what is the wolf's name, may I ask?"

"It's ah... Dog. I wasn't very original back then."

"A wolf named Dog?" I asked in disbelief. I glanced over at Spraggel, who smiled knowingly at me. I had seen that look before. He gave it to me when he knew I had all the pieces to a problem, but just had to put them together. *What had he figured out?*

Then it hit me. It all made sense. The bird, it's intelligence, the mysterious girl, and now a wolf that knew to stop when I drew my weapon.

I put my sword away and folded my arms across my chest. "I don't think Dog is her name. I think her name is actually *Zofie.*"

Spraggel mumbled under his breath, "Took you long enough."

Risten shook her head and laughed again. "No, it's actually Dog. I raised her from a pup."

I pointed to the wolf. "Zofie, are you going to let her keep calling you a dog?"

The wolf stood and trotted to me, slowing to a stop right in front of me. I squatted down and looked into her eyes; I could see the intelligence behind them. This was no simple wolf, just as the hawk had been no simple bird. The wolf looked over her shoulder at Risten and whined.

Risten put her hands on her hips. "Are you sure you want to do this? It isn't what we talked about last night."

The wolf gave a short bark.

Risten blew out a big breath and walked over to join us. "You're right. That's Zofie. She is actually my cousin and was a completely, normal human until last year when a curse was put on her."

My eyebrows went up in surprise. "She's cursed too?" That wasn't what I was expecting. A myst spell maybe, but not an active curse.

Spraggel stroked his beard and nodded. "I thought that might be the case."

Risten frowned. "Yeah, it makes her take on the form of an animal. On the night of the full moon, it changes her into a different one, a new animal every cycle. Last moon, she was a hawk, and the one before that..." she shivered. "A snake. That one wasn't fun at all."

Zofie gave a short bark in agreement.

I nodded. It made sense. A myst spell could transform something, but it was only a one-time thing. Only a curse could continually cause someone to shift form, or include active protections against being removed. Which also explained why they had been hiding it. From my own personal experience, people treated you differently when they knew you were cursed. Especially something they could see. I was suddenly conscious of the leather band on my left wrist, and I resisted the urge to touch it. The evidence of my curse was under that band.

Yet there was one piece I still didn't understand. "But last night wasn't a full moon. That's not for a few days yet."

Risten dug her boot toe into the earth trying to free a rock. "Breaking her wing yesterday triggered it. When Zofie is injured, the curse makes her transform that very night. It heals whatever is wrong in the process. The curse was intended to torment her and not allow her to die too soon."

I nodded thoughtfully. "But she's a myst-seer. Can't she just undo her own curse?"

Risten shook her head sadly. "She can't. I don't know much about myst and spells and seers, but from what she's told me, the curse uses up all her myst. She can't get to any of her own to recast it. Not to mention, it has protections built into it. So she's stuck until we can find someone strong enough to break it."

Spraggel leaned in. "Did you try getting a counterspell, like the one Coren has?"

Risten kicked a loose rock into the grass. "We did. But this curse has some kind of powerful protection built into it. It burns out any that try to counter it."

Spraggel looked up in surprise. "Which explains why you wanted to separate from us. Zofie's curse could burn out Coren's protection amulet, and with his curse loose, doom us all."

Risten pursed her lips and nodded. "You're right. I was afraid to have *two* curses among us. From what Zofie's told me, curses are very complex myst spells. There's no telling how they would interact with each other." She sighed. "So there you have it, our true condition. But it doesn't change anything. We're still separating from you two. The risk of the two curses is just too great."

"I'm not so sure." I reached out to stroke Zofie's fur but stopped myself. One normally didn't rub a girl's head, so Zofie might not appreciate it even if she was a wolf.

I cleared my throat. "Last night, Zofie touched my amulet and nothing happened. It was through my shirt, but that shouldn't have mattered."

Risten turned to Zofie. "Is that true? Did you touch it? That was a huge risk."

Zofie nodded her large head and gave a big wolf grin.

Spraggel stroked his beard. "It doesn't surprise me that it didn't react. The amulet is custom-tailored to Coren, so there was probably nothing for Zofie's curse to latch on to."

Zofie padded over to Risten and put a paw on her thigh. Risten folded her arms across her chest. "I take it that means you think we should continue together?"

Zofie gave a short bark.

Risten looked up at us. "Just so you know, one animal sound means 'yes' and two mean 'no'. We worked out that system a while back." Risten scratched her head. "I don't know Zofie. Look what a spell did to you. I don't know if I can protect you."

Zofie extended her head and took Risten's hand gently in her mouth, pulling her toward me until we were standing in front of one another. I thought I knew what Zofie wanted. I held out my hand, offering to shake. "Risten, please reconsider and come with us. Before we started, Zofie asked me to watch your back, and I would be honored if you would let me."

The sword-master looked at my hand and then back to me. Hesitantly, she reached out and took it. We shook, wolf spit and all.

I squatted down in front of Zofie, holding out my hand to her. "And what about you? I swear to watch your back, too."

She lifted her paw and placed it in mine.

And with that, we were a team again: a cursed apprentice, a senile old man, a crazy sword lady, and a cursed shapeshifter.

Wort didn't stand a chance.

After Spraggel and I finished breaking camp, our small group continued our quest to get to Ruin's Shield before Wort. And some of the things I had seen Risten and Zofie do previously began to make sense. Zofie would leave us frequently to scout ahead. While Risten would use her 'yes' or 'no' answers to understand what lay ahead. I realized she had been doing this all along even when she was a hawk, but I hadn't known what to look for.

They really made a good team. Honestly, I was a little envious. I had never had a close friend—relative or otherwise. Spraggel was as close as it got. But while he was indeed was a good friend, with our considerable age difference, I would never be his peer. My lack of friends was just another effect of my curse.

Along mid-afternoon, Spraggel and I were in the middle of a discussion of whether the ale from the northern lands was better than the brews from the south (which had been a topic of heated conversation since our last wayside) when we were interrupted by three sharp barks. I looked up. *Three?* What did that mean? Zofie was nowhere to be seen, so I turned to Risten who was riding behind us. To my surprise, she urged her horse into a fast trot and wedged herself between Spraggel and I. This caused our mounts to have to sidestep to make room for her. *What in the Creator's hell had gotten into her?* I fought to get my horse back under control.

"Sorry," she said over her shoulder, angling into the brush beside the road and nudging her horse forward. "Whatever you do, don't admit I'm with you. I'll explain later." And she quickly rode deep into the woods and out of sight.

I looked to Spraggel. He looked back at me with the same expression of utter confusion I'm sure I had on mine.

Only a heartbeat later, we heard it. Horse hooves. *Many* horse hooves. And they were coming from behind us, approaching rapidly. In reflex, I reached for my sword—only to grasp empty air. *What!* I looked to my saddle where I kept it while riding, but it was gone. I looked behind me thinking I must have dropped it when Risten rode by, but there was no sign of it.

I looked up in horror. "My sword is gone."

Spraggel looked grim and shook his head. "It's probably for the best."

"But what if it's Wort?"

Spraggel's eyebrows went up. "Oh, I don't think this is Wort's party. No, it's something completely different."

Spraggel then turned his horse toward the edge of the road, and I followed suit, moving completely off to the side. All the while, the sound of the horses grew louder. It didn't take but a few moments more to see the riders as they rounded the final bend.

My eyes widened. I counted twenty riders, going in pairs, on large war horses. They wore the king's livery of purple jackets and golden pants, and each had a sword and shield on their saddles. As was customary, Spraggel and I dismounted and awaited their approach. I hoped they just passed us by, but that was not to be.

When they drew close, their leader, a captain from the looks of his uniform, held up a hand and the men slowed to a stop before us. All the horses in the party danced in place eager to be on their way. And I felt uncomfortable in their gaze—several held crossbows at the ready.

"You two there," the captain asked gruffly. "What is your business on the king's road?" He was a middle-aged man with a neatly trimmed beard, mostly gray, and a scar on his right cheek.

I opened my mouth to answer, but Spraggel beat me to it. "Good day to you, captain. My apprentice and I are on our way to Daili. We hope to do business there. We had heard that the high priest was looking for someone to transcribe some books that were damaged when the library's roof leaked."

"You're a scribe?"

"Yes, captain. One of the best around. We can do legal documents and..."

The officer cut him off with a wave of his hand. "I have no need for a scribe." He turned toward his men. "Search them."

Three of the soldiers dismounted and approached. Spraggel and I stood motionless as they patted our clothing and then went through our belongings. I tried not to show my irritation since protest would likely just make it worse.

"It's not here, captain," announced one of the men.

Their leader looked up the road and sighed. "Remount."

The soldiers snapped to obey, and the captain turned to us with a frown on his face. "We are looking for a young woman that stole an heirloom of the royal family. And the king wants it back. We had received a report that she may have been headed in this direction. She's of normal height and has light red hair, freckled skin, and keeps her hair cut unusually short. She is also likely traveling alone." He leaned toward us. "You haven't seen anyone like that in your travels, have you?"

I tried not to show my surprise. They had to be looking for Risten. She had been traveling alone, or it would have appeared that way if you didn't know that Zofie was her cousin in animal form. And she did seem intent on avoiding the king's soldiers.

Spraggel didn't hesitate in his reply. "I'm sorry captain, but we've not seen anyone like that. But we can definitely keep an eye out." Spraggel leaned forward. "By chance, is there a reward?"

*Reward?* My master didn't usually go for such things. Besides, the king didn't reward anything, or at least the new one didn't. He just commanded. Then it hit me. Spraggel was digging for information.

The captain's eyes narrowed at my master. "None, other than being allowed to keep your head. Serving his majesty Branwynn Xernow should be enough of a reward by itself."

Spraggel nodded emphatically, seeming to take the captain's warning to heart. "Indeed. We will report seeing such a woman immediately."

The captain nodded once and held up a hand to motion his men forward, but paused. "Oh, and one thing more. If you do happen to see her, do not try to capture her yourself. She has murdered over a dozen people." He gave a grim smile. "Executed might be a better word."

Spraggel's eyes went wide. "You mean when the old King was murdered?"

The captain nodded. "She was one of the traitors. And a thief to boot! Got away with an old sword, one of the king's family heirlooms. She's not someone to take lightly."

He didn't wait for us to say anything further, but motioned his men forward and they thundered on up the road.

Spraggel and I turned to each other, no doubt with the same thought, but I voiced it first. "Could Risten...?"

Spraggel shook his head. "The description doesn't match exactly. A myst user can alter someone's appearance, but it's forbidden. But, then again, I'm sure someone would do it for the right price."

"She herself said she was in the king's guard."

Spraggel took his horse's reins and pulled himself up into the saddle. "I admit it doesn't sound good. But Risten did say she would explain. Let's at least give her that courtesy."

I nodded in agreement. But there was something else bothering me. "What was this execution the captain mentioned?" I knew the last king was assassinated by his daughter, and the only reason she was caught was because she hadn't expected to be challenged by her younger brother.

Spraggel snorted. "See what you miss by going out to practice your sword instead of drinking and trading stories?" He sighed. "Maybe one day you'll learn that it's not all about the ale."

I rolled my eyes. As if I believed that.

Spraggel got a faraway look in his eyes. "No one knows for sure because most of those involved are dead, and those that survived aren't saying much. But rumor has it that Princess Olwenna, and her followers, killed all of those loyal to her father to ensure there was no opposition. Apparently, it involved swords and a lot of nobility in a locked room." He shuddered. "It was pretty brutal."

I followed my master's example and mounted myself. I thought back to the incident with the drunk that wanted my sword. Being a sword-master, Risten could have easily killed all six of Lord Cruimeint's men. But she didn't. And when we encountered those bandits on the road, she had been trying to disarm rather than kill. I shook my head. "Risten is a bitch sometimes, but I just can't see her as a murderer. I think Risten will kill if she has to, but it's not something she seeks out."

Spraggel nodded. "And on that, my young apprentice, we agree."

I saw movement out of the corner of my eye, and Zofie bounded out from the brush and onto the road. She gazed up at me, panting and almost smiling. She seemed very pleased about something. And then a moment later, Risten led her horse out, carefully picking her way toward us. And in her hand, she held my sword.

"Hey!" I shouted. "You took my sword."

She shrugged and handed it back to me. "Sorry. I knew it was the king's soldiers from Zofie's barks, and I didn't have time to argue. They're basically good people, but they will sometimes collect tolls on items they take a liking too. I just didn't want to take a chance of losing my master's sword."

Spraggel cleared his throat. "The king's soldiers were looking for a woman. And she sounded a lot like you."

Risten smiled. "Let me guess, they were looking for a woman of medium height with very short, red hair." She held up her blonde braid. "Does this look red?"

Spraggel looked down at his saddle. "A myst user can change appearances. And you were in the king's guard." Our horses danced nervously beneath us.

Risten looked indignant. "I'll have you know I got this blonde hair from my mother. So don't talk to me about a myst spell." She turned to Zofie. "Isn't that right?"

Zofie barked once.

Spraggel leaned forward in his saddle. "Risten, child. Let's get to the point. Did you steal the king's sword? And more importantly, did you kill those loyal to the old king?"

Her expression turned dark. She stepped over to me and jerked my sword free of its scabbard. Then taking a step back, she reversed it. I gasped as she grabbed the naked blade with her left hand, raised it pointed upwards tightening her grip. I could see a tiny trickle of blood flow between her fingers and down the sword. "I, Risten Brightmare, swear upon my master's blade that I did not steal the king's sword, and I did not kill the king's people."

Zofie went to her and put a paw on Risten's leg, before turning to us and giving one loud bark in agreement.

Spraggel and I looked at each other. Zofie whined beside us. Risten was using a powerful oath—one that required another to receive it. Should we refuse, it was customary to take the sword used in the oath and snap the blade in two.

Spraggel gave a slight nod in my direction. I sighed. So it was to be me. I nodded back and got down from my horse. Then, standing before Risten, I extended my own left hand and grasped the naked blade next to hers. I felt the sharp blade cut my own skin.

I looked into her face and found in her eyes a strange mix of anger and relief. "I, Coren Hart, accept your oath and do likewise swear to use this sword to take your life should we find your oath to be false."

She released her grip leaving the sword with me, which I immediately wiped off and put away. Spraggel dismounted and pulled out some binding cloth and ointment. Over her protests, he began to wrap Risten's hand. My master spoke as he worked. "You shouldn't have done that Risten. We believed in you. We just wanted to hear you say it."

She shrugged. "I had to do it. It was the only way to belay your concerns. I'm innocent of any crimes against the old king. I would have never done anything against him." And then she added softly. "I loved that man. We all did." Zofie whined and suddenly turned to walk ahead of us up the road. Risten followed the wolf with her eyes and shook her head sadly.

Spraggel finished with Risten's hand, and he turned to me. He began to bind my hand. "Your hands look more like a swordsman's now than a scribe. I wonder if you'll be able to even hold a quill when we get back."

She turned toward me. "But he's a long way from being a true swordsman yet. Which is another reason I took your blade. I didn't want you doing something stupid like pulling your sword, which will get you killed quicker than your next heartbeat." She swung up onto her own horse. "Which reminds me. We need to discuss sword etiquette."

"Etiquette?" I grimaced.

Risten nodded. "Indeed. It's how someone with a sword should behave, especially around someone else who has a sword. Not being polite can end up with somebody dying." She looked over at me and grinned evilly. "And at your current level, I would guarantee it would be you."

# CHAPTER SIX

# Abduction

A few days later, Risten announced that Zofie had picked up the scent of a party only a day or two ahead of us. And it wasn't the king's soldiers. She could tell by their scents—one of the advantages of being a wolf—that there were seven in the group. And she was pretty sure they were Wort and his men. This was good news since we were finally catching up to them. However, it did pose a new problem: how were we going to get around them?

Risten, Spraggel, and I discussed it around the campfire later that night. There had been no waysides on the road for the past few days, so it was another evening spent outdoors on the damp, hard ground. Zofie, like the last few evenings, had left us to hunt. Or I assumed it was to hunt. At least, I never saw Risten feeding her, and she had to get her food from somewhere. She would typically show up a couple hours after we made camp to lay down beside Risten. Which was fine by me.

Zofie was an excellent deterrent for most night creatures that might show an interest in us.

Spraggel sat on a stump close to the fire. "We're going to have to go around them at some point," he announced. "Despite Risten being a sword-master, we won't be able to pass them without a fight. One which we would likely lose."

I sat cross-legged across the fire from Spraggel. "If we try to blaze a trail through the forest around him, we'll go slower and never get ahead of them."

Risten rested on her blanket a little ways away from us with her hands behind her head and her saddle serving as a pillow. She had one knee raised, and the other leg draped over it swinging freely. "Wort doesn't worry me," she offered. "Seven men are nothing."

Spraggel and I exchanged a glance. Risten continued to bring up going after Wort, and we didn't want to encourage this. So we ignored her comment.

Spraggel reached into his robe pocket and, after a moment of searching, extracted a rolled-up map. While he laid it out, I went to look over his shoulder. "I say we cut through the Shattered Forest." His finger traced a path along the paper. "According to this, it gets a bit hilly, but would shave quite a bit off the trip. The forest is just west of here. Once we enter the forest, we simply continue due west until we run into the Edi River."

Risten's leg stopped swinging. "Isn't the Shattered Forest forbidden? That's Sylph territory. From what I've heard, you can't let their tall, slender look fool you. They're tough. They say they're mean, ugly, and very tall."

"How tall?" I asked.

"About twenty hands."

My eyebrows went up. I didn't want to think about someone that could look me in the eye while on my horse.

Spraggel frowned. "Don't frighten the boy. It's forbidden because it was reserved for the Sylph for their part in defeating the Dark Aven-yts." He cleared his throat. "While it is true they can be dangerous, they generally keep to themselves."

Risten snorted, but Spraggel ignored her. "If we just skirt the edge of their territory," Spraggel continued. "We shouldn't run into them. Any objections to trying this? I'm open to other ideas."

Risten and I looked at each other and shrugged.

A thought came to me. "And what if we do run into them? What will they do to us?"

Risten gave an amused smirk. "No one has lived to tell."

That kind of put a damper on further conversation.

I looked up at the sky, seeing the full moon coming over the trees. It made me think of Zofie. It was past time for her to come back to camp.

"Risten." I glanced in her direction. "Tonight's the full moon. Will Zofie change again? She only transformed three nights ago."

Risten shrugged. "Probably." Her leg was swinging furiously. I got the impression I'd asked a sensitive question. I'd learned that Risten was like that. She didn't try to avoid difficult questions; she just re-fused to answer them. Probably because she was so bad at lying.

"Should someone be with her?"

There was that pause again. Risten shifted her position and re-crossed her legs. "She doesn't want me," she said softly. "The process is... difficult. She claims she just wants to be left alone." Risten leaned her head back and looked up at the moon. "You see, the transformation is two-part: she first transitions back to a human, and then into the next animal. She said there was a good reason for doing the spell that way, but she lapsed into myst-seer talk and lost me. But what I do know is that it's painful for her. Extremely painful. Worse than having a baby while getting all your teeth yanked out." She turned her eyes back to-ward me. "That's why she was at the pool that night. The cold water numbed the pain a little. When she turns back into a human, she comes to find me, and then we have a short talk before she goes through her next transformation."

The exchange made my heart hurt. I understood exactly what she was going through. Before Spraggel gave me my amulet, I was burned, stabbed, pushed down, trampled—all of it just shy of killing me. And most of the time, I went through it alone. *Abandoned.* I felt like I didn't have a single person that cared whether I lived or died. I felt extremely lucky that my curse was sort of controllable now.

And a little guilty.

I stood up. "She should not be by herself."

Risten looked up at me, angry. "She said she wanted to be left alone. She doesn't need some apprentice scribe chasing after her."

I looked up at the moon. "You're right. I am just an apprentice scribe. But I'm something you're not. Cursed. And I know that despite what she said, I'm pretty sure what she really wants is someone to just hold her hand."

Risten jerked upright. "You don't understand. I've *tried!* But nothing I do seems to make it better. All I do is make her hurt worse." She looked down. "And Zofie is a proud person. I think she's just ashamed of it. She told me to stay away."

"I believe you. I've even said those things myself." I grabbed the water bag and a blanket. "But what you heard was the real purpose of the curse talking... to make her feel ashamed and isolate her. To make her feel alone." I continued out of the firelight.

Risten called after me. "You'll be sorry. I've tried to help her, and she nearly bit my head off, literally!"

I heard Spraggel talking to her behind me. "Let him go, Risten. Better than any of us, he knows very well what she is feeling."

I pushed the bushes aside and stomped out into the darkness. I thought about pulling out my amulet but decided against it. While it would make it easier for me to find her, it would also make it easier to avoid me.

The full moon was high in the sky, which helped, but there were wisps of clouds gliding across it, which dulled the light. Plus the forest and bushes made lots of shadows too. So, how was I going to find her? I began looking for something with a lot of cover. She would likely feel vulnerable during her transformation, and even though she might want to be alone, she would be afraid to venture too far away.

Just then, I heard a groan. I looked to my right. It came from over behind a clump of trees in deep shadow. I carefully made my way toward it. Behind a large bush which shaded most of the moonlight, I found a dark shadow breathing heavily and whimpering. I carefully knelt beside her and gently took what I thought was her front paw. I didn't do anything else—just lightly held her paw. I saw two glimmers of eyes look up at me and then shut.

Gradually, a pale blue glow spread over her, turning the air around her translucent and obscuring her form. Yet within, I could see her shape begin to squirm and writhe, while her whimpers increased to an agonizing whine. Her paw turned blazing hot, as if it contained an entire bed of burning coals, and even in my light touch, felt almost too scorching to hold. An odor drifted from her that was part dog, part human, and part something unpleasant I couldn't identify.

I closed my own eyes and gritted my teeth, cursing whoever did this to her. It was horrible. No person should be subjected to such torment. Zofie could never have done something to deserve something so terrible.

Yet she had withstood it. Had done so for many months through many other transformations. While I was appalled at her suffering, I couldn't help but admire her raw courage for surviving it.

Her panting and whimpering became louder. And with an almost scream—I felt her transformation start: the nails on her paw thinning and flattening, fingers growing and extending. Gradually, the whimpering died and the blue glow faded—until it was again pitch black, and I was holding a very female hand.

I waited in silence until her ragged breathing had slowed. "Hey," I said softly. "I have some water if you're ready for it."

I heard her lick her dry lips. "That would be very nice," she said breathlessly. "That was a bad one. Must have been because I just transformed a few nights ago."

I held out the bag and shook it so she could find it in the dark. "I hope I didn't offend by finding you. Risten said I shouldn't, but I felt I had to. I know how lonely a curse can make you feel."

I couldn't see her in the dark, but I heard her shifting around. She groaned. She felt for my hand and finding it, gently squeezed. "Thanks. You knew just exactly what to do. When I go through this, I just want someone to be with me, but I never could get Risten to understand. She'd try to rub or pat me... or Creator forbid, hug me." She shuddered. "That just made it hurt worse. My nerves get all messed up when I transform and it just... burns." I heard her take a swallow. "And she would cry the whole time too."

"Risten cry? I can't imagine that for some reason."

"Oh, she'll cry all right. She really did have a mutt named Dog when we were younger. She bawled like a baby when it got hurt."

I held out the blanket. "I brought this for you. I thought you might get chilled."

She chuckled. "You are so thoughtful. I could get used to this." She took the blanket, and I heard her wrapping up in it. "I burn up during the transformation, but afterward, I cool off fast."

"Do you want to go back to your cousin now?"

She sighed. "I guess I should, but give me a moment to rest. Transforming takes a lot out of a girl."

"Should I bring her here instead?"

"You mean you'd leave a poor defenseless lady, naked and alone in the forest?" she teased.

"I... didn't mean. I... I wouldn't..."

She touched my arm. "I was just teasing you. I have so little time, I have to make the best of it."

I reached up and took her hand into mine. It felt... good. "So how long do we have, you know, before the next part."

"I guess Risten told you." She sighed deeply. "About an hour, sometimes a little more. There isn't any logic behind it that I can see."

"You mean you can't read your own curse?"

"Of course not." I could almost hear her smiling. "It would be like trying to look at my own backside without a mirror. You can catch a glimpse, but you just can't see it all that well." She leaned closer. "Enough of that. No more about curses. I'm sick of curses. Let's talk about something else. Something normal people talk about."

"Like what?"

She thought for a moment. "How about... do you have someone you like?"

I blinked in shock. That was definitely a change in topic. I scratched my head nervously. "You mean, do I have a girl?"

"Yes, you ninny. Do you have a girl?"

"No, I've just not been around that many."

"What about the girl back in Iron Landing? The one in the tavern. She was cute."

"Maggie? No, she's nice and everything, but she's way too young for me. Besides, her father and I don't get along."

"Then what about Risten? I think she's pretty, and you two seem to have hit it off."

I chuckled. "Only when our swords are drawn." We were silent for a moment listening to the night sounds. "By the way," I continued. "Thank you for the sword. I've never thanked you for it properly." I paused, searching for words. "But I don't understand why you gave it to me. I'm just a scribe, and you saw from my first go with Risten that I didn't have any training."

I saw Zofie's head come up. She seemed to be looking up at the stars. "To be perfectly honest, I don't know either. A long time ago, I was told I would know who should have it. And when I saw you on the street in Iron Landing, I just... knew. I knew it deep in my heart and in every fiber of my being that you were worthy to have it."

"I certainly don't feel worthy, but thank you." My leg was falling asleep, so I shifted around. There was another question I wanted to ask, but I couldn't figure out a polite way to put it.

"Let me guess." I could hear her smiling. "You'd like to know why the sword was mine to give and not Risten's, right?"

I laughed. "You got me. She definitely had a different opinion."

"You see, many years ago, Master Valervick performed a great service for our family, and in reward, my father gave that sword to him. Unfortunately, when the master died he had no heirs, so ownership of the sword returned to my family. Being the eldest, it came to me, and I decided to give it to you."

"Well, thank you again. I will do my best to make you proud in the master's memory."

"I have no doubt," Zofie said with confidence. Then she shivered. "I'm unusually cold tonight. Can I come closer."

I scooted toward her and sat beside her. She leaned against me. "Is that better?"

"Much."

I felt her put her head on my shoulder. She seemed so small now.

She sighed again. "I feel different with you. You're very relaxing. Not bad looking either." She giggled. "Quite handsome actually, in a scribish, boyish, kind of way."

I couldn't help but chuckle. "Thanks, I think." I looked toward her shadow. "It's not fair really. You've seen me, but I've never seen the real you in the light. I bet you're quite pretty."

And leave it to me to not just break the mood but to shatter it.

Her voice turned suddenly serious. "Nor will you ever."

"What?" That wasn't what I was expecting.

She leaned away, breaking the contact between us. I could see her shadow stand. "Could you get Risten for me. I need to talk with her... Ugh!"

"What is it?" I asked in sudden panic, rising to stand beside her.

"It's started. It shouldn't be this quick." She stumbled away from me, and I heard her retching. I moved toward her shadow and waited until she finished. She staggered and grabbed my arm. "This one is going to be worse than the last. I can feel it." I felt her waver. "I think I had better sit down."

"Right." I put my arm around her, and I gently helped her back to her original spot. "Do you want me to get Risten?"

"No. She can't help me. And there's no time... Ugh! Damn, it hurts." She grabbed my hand tightly. "Listen," she said in a rush. "When I complete the animal transformation, I will likely faint. It's too much of a shock... Ugh!"

"Is there anything I can do?"

She suddenly grabbed me by the shirt and pulled me to within a hand's-breadth of her face. "Swear you won't look at me. Not until it's done."

"Zofie..."

She pulled me tighter. "*Swear... ugh!*" Her voice softened to a whisper. "*Please?*"

I sighed. "I swear, on my honor, I won't look."

She released me and fell back. "Thank you." she breathed so softly, I almost couldn't make out the words. And then she writhed in agony.

I gently took her hand, and keeping my word, closed my eyes. I gritted my teeth at the sounds she made as she went through the agony of her next transformation. I could certainly understand why Risten might shed a tear, because I shed a couple myself.

After suffering for what seemed like an eternity, she finally gave a stifled scream, and then began to change. My eyes flew open to see her once again glowing with a translucent blue light. But this time, the hand I held grew gradually smaller, slowly changing, and her whimpers and gasps became shriller and shorter. The lump of shadow beside me also grew smaller and lost its human-like shape. I hunched closer and closer, trying to hang on to her shrinking limb, until I thought my back would give out.

Finally, the shudders and squeals stopped, and the blue glow faded. Placing my hand out, I gently touched some soft fur and felt her breathing rapidly. As she had predicted, she had indeed lost consciousness. Plus she was definitely smaller now—much smaller. Her new form could easily rest in both my hands. Carefully, I scooped her up and held her close. While I wasn't exactly sure what she had transformed into, I had my suspicion.

I picked my way back to camp (I only tripped twice) and stepped toward the still bright campfire. Risten must have kept it going so we could easily find our way back. She looked up anxiously when I entered the firelight. "Did you find her? Is she all right?"

I nodded and held out my arms. There lying in my hands, resting peacefully, was a beautiful, red-coated squirrel.

Risten screwed up her lips and blew out a frustrated breath. "Well, somebody's going to be pissed when she wakes up. She hates rodents."

The next day, the weather which had been warm and sunny, suddenly turned cooler and it started raining. This was not a welcome change—I hated being wet. The horses didn't seem too thrilled about it either. All they wanted to do was huddle under the tree where they had been tethered and not move. Mine snapped at me when I went to saddle him.

And poor Zofie. When she'd awoken to find herself a squirrel, she had—I don't know what else to call it—a squirrel fit. She chattered at me, and then Risten and Spraggel, squealed, rolled on her back, climbed up a tree to jump down in front of me, and then do it all again. I was exhausted just watching her. I think she was having just a little trouble adapting.

Once we got started, we turned north off the trail as Spraggel suggested, and after a fireless camp, made the Shattered Forest the following day. There was definitely not a line on the ground saying this is the forest, but you could tell because the forest went rather abruptly from small maples and pines to large ancient oaks and elms. And I do mean large. You couldn't put your arms around them. The leafy canopy overhead was thick and blocked most of the light, even though the early-spring leaves weren't fully grown. It gave the forest a gloomy cast. In full summer, the forest floor must be dark all day long.

The nasty weather stayed with us. The trees would catch the steady drizzle and convert it to huge drops, which would plop down on your head unexpectedly. Mine would usually roll off my head and down my back. Did I mention I hate being wet?

By silent agreement, we did not talk much, and when we did, it was in whispers. Speech seemed to carry unnaturally far; our voices echoed off the trees, making us jumpy and anxious. You could hear the sound of the horses' hooves and then again their echo a heartbeat later. If a wind blew through, the sound of the rain falling off the trees was nearly deafening. It was definitely spooky. I found myself looking over my shoulder frequently.

In her new animal form, Zofie stayed close to us. I think she was afraid of the larger animals. I had heard an owl at one point. There were likely lots of animals that would love a nice tasty squirrel.

And unlike her other transformations, she liked to ride on the front of either my horse or Risten's—sometimes on the saddle and sometimes on its head. She would chatter at us constantly. In my miserable wet state, I finally asked her if she could quiet down. When I said that, Risten threw a rock at me.

The path we were following was little more than a deer track. About mid-day, we came to a particularly thick section of forest. Long twisted limbs entwined over our heads, and the path became hard to distinguish. It seemed to grow deadly quiet. The only sound was the dripping of the rain and the sound of our horse's hooves crunching the long-dead leaves. I didn't like it. Behind me, I heard Risten draw her sword. I shot her a glance, but she just shrugged. Apparently, she didn't like it either. I drew my own sword. Zofie must have felt it too. She suddenly ran up my arm and jumped inside my coat, where she turned and poked her head out the top. *Ugh.* She was wet.

Spraggel sensed it too and reined in to a gradual stop. Risten and I pulled up beside him, and we huddled close.

"Something doesn't seem right," he whispered. "I feel like we're being watched."

Risten nodded. "You noticed it too. But I've been searching the trees, and I don't see anything. It could be our imagination."

Spraggel stroked his beard. "Well, we can't go back, so I guess we have to take our chances. Just be on the alert and stay close." He urged his horse forward, and I followed right behind him. Risten brought up the rear. I turned in my saddle to look at her and noticed she was not only holding her sword—but was also holding a knife in her teeth. Seeing me looking, she grinned evilly around it.

There was a bend in the trail ahead that cried out for ambush. It was unusually grown up—and dark. Spraggel rode cautiously through it but saw nothing. I followed, and behind me, I heard Risten settling into her saddle. Zofie ducked her head inside my shirt. Looking from side to side, I rode through the dark patch and came out where the forest lightened slightly. I breathed a sigh of relief. That must have been my imagination. I drew up beside Spraggel and waited for Risten to join us.

"I don't like this forest," I said. "I hope we can be done with it before dark. I definitely don't want to camp in here. "

Spraggel shifted in his saddle. "I don't like these woods either. I'm nearly sure that someone is watching us."

I nodded agreement and turned toward the sound of Risten's approaching horse to ask her opinion. But the horse didn't stop, riding right on by us.

And Risten wasn't on it.

# CHAPTER SEVEN

# Prisoners

Spraggel and I quickly turned our horses and went back down the trail—we went carefully, looking for any sign of Risten. Zofie left the safety of my shirt and climbed to the top of my horse's head, looking quickly left and right. We rode until I was sure we were at a place where I had seen Risten last. I slowed to a stop and glanced at Spraggel. He shook his head.

Turning yet again, we retraced the path one more time, looking for any sign of her. The forest was unusually quiet with only the sound of our horse's hooves on the soft, wet leaves, the jingle of their tack, and the gentle sound of rain hitting the trees. Slowly I led the way along the trail, with no sign of her. It was like she had just vanished.

Suddenly, Zofie started chattering and leaped down from the horse. She started digging in the leaves. Reining in, I threw a leg over my horse and hit the ground before he had stopped moving. I knelt beside Zofie and immediately saw something shiny through the forest debris. Brushing them aside, I saw it was Risten's sword hidden under a layer of leaves. And whoever had put it there knew what they were doing. The ground looked undisturbed. Without Zofie, I'd never have found it.

I quickly stood, looking around. "Risten!" I called. I received no reply. Even the normal bird sounds were missing. Spraggel dismounted and led his horse over. He stood close by while I knelt again beside the sword. I picked it up and examined it carefully. There was no blood on it, so she must have been completely overpowered to be taken sword in hand and without a single blow. Zofie and I combed the ground looking for some clue as to what might have happened. But there were no footprints, nothing disturbed in the brush. Close to where I had found her sword, I spotted a clump of hair lying beside the path. And it was black, unlike Risten's blonde. It looked to be about a fistful, like someone would pull out of an attacker. I grinned sadly. At least Risten had gotten in one good lick.

I held it up for Spraggel and he nodded. "Sylph."

I stood, dropping the hair, my fear confirmed. "So the Sylph abducted her right about here. But I'm not seeing any tracks other than our own." I glanced around. "What I don't understand is why they took just Risten. Why not ambush us all?"

Spraggel leaned in. "Let's look at this logically. The horses are untouched, our belonging were ignored, Risten's sword was left behind. There can be only one conclusion why they didn't take us too."

I stood and wiped my hands on my pants. "And what might that be?"

Spraggel raised a single finger to the air as if making an earth-shattering proclamation. "We're of the wrong sex."

I nearly choked. "You mean they took her because she's a woman?"

Spraggel shrugged. "It's the only explanation. But now that we know who and why, the next question is, how?"

I looked to Zofie, who was holding her little paws in front of her looking very forlorn. "Zofie, how's your smelling? Could you sniff her out?"

She gave me an ugly look and put her paws on her waist, chattering wildly and pointing at her nose and giving short barks. I think she was trying to tell me she wasn't a dog.

Since turning into a squirrel, I noticed Zofie wasn't as easy going as she once had been. In fact, everything about her was done fast, her running, her eating, her sleeping. It was like the world ran too slow for her. I was beginning to think that the form of the animal she had taken affected her personality.

"All right, I get it. Then do you have any idea which way they went?"

She gave a single chirp and pointed up. *The trees!* I looked up and scanned the canopy of tree limbs. They very easily could have come at her from above—no doubt dropping on her when she wasn't expecting it. And likely that's how they moved her out, hoisting her up into the thick foliage. I sighed in frustration. We'd never find her.

Spraggel motioned me closer, and I leaned toward him. He spoke in a whisper. "And if we couldn't hear them take Risten, then I would wager my last piece of gold that we're being watched even now. No doubt to make sure we don't try to follow them."

"Are you suggesting we climb the trees? I don't think my horse will like that."

Spraggel looked insulted. "My boy. Why do all that work of running them down, when we can make them come to us? All we need is some bait."

I shook my head in confusion. "What?"

He suddenly jerked Risten's sword from my hands and shoved me hard. I fell rather ungracefully on my backside and looked up at him in disbelief. He raised the sword high.

"And just like in The Poet's *Betrayal of a Robin*," he announced rather loudly. "You have failed in your task. It's all your fault! If you had been watching, this would not have happened! There's no way we can best Wort now! You must pay for your incompetence!" He swung the sword at me, and I scrambled to get away. It landed rather half-heartedly where I had been.

"Do not think to run because I will have your life!"

I managed to get to my feet and raised my hands in front of me, carefully backing away. What in the Creator's name had gotten into him? And then something clicked in my brain. The *Betrayal of a Robin* was a long and boring epic about a knight who was betrayed by his king, but the knight ended up turning the tables on the king. And Spraggel's *'I will have your life'* was a line from the epic where the knight pretended to be dead. I gasped. *That old rascal.* He was telling me what to do without telling our watcher!

I deliberately stumbled and fell backward, landing on my rump again. I held an arm in front of my eyes and tried to look terrified. "No, master! Please forgive me," I shouted. "I was doing my best!" It sounded a little stilted to me. Acting was not one of my strengths.

Spraggel drew back his sword.

"Please Master! *Don't!*"

Spraggel placed his foot on my chest and pushed me backward. Then he jabbed the sword down, the blade passing between my body and arm to lodge in the ground.

I eyed the sword. He'd come a little closer than I was comfortable with.

Squeezing the sword between my arm and chest, I screamed in mock pain. "Eeee! You have killed me!" I fell back with my eyes shut.

With his foot still on my chest, Spraggel grunted and yanked the sword out of the ground. "That will teach you to betray me. May your soul rot in damnation." He wiped his blade on my coat and walked away. I barely heard him whisper. "Zofie, stay with him."

I felt Zofie climb on my chest, and I heard her whine in mourning. She was playing it up too. Everyone was an actor.

I heard Spraggel mount up and take all the horses and go back the way we had originally come. Then all was silent except for Zofie's whining. Even the rain stopped. (But the ground was still wet and was soaking through my coat.)

And so I waited, eyes closed, listening for some small sound of approach. A fly buzzed around my head and landed on my nose. With no opposition, it called its buddies, and they held a festival on my forehead. I silently cursed them in three different languages. Zofie finally noticed and waved them away with her tail.

After what seemed like hours, I heard the faint sound of someone dropping to the ground close by. Very light footsteps approached. If the rain had continued, I probably wouldn't have heard them at all. I waited patiently as the steps halted a short distance away. I tried not to breathe. Something nudged my foot, but I stayed still. The person nudged my foot again a little more forcefully. There was a pause, and then they slowly approached again. Zofie chattered in warning.

The person said something in a language I didn't recognize, but it sounded like ancient Andronise. I think the person was trying to call Zofie. I could just imagine the watcher trying to save the poor squirrel from heartbreak. Or more likely, save the poor squirrel for dinner.

I slit my eyes and could see a bare foot come down beside me, painted forest green and emerging from a leaf green trouser leg. Zofie gave a short bark and I immediately leaped up, grabbing the person's leg and throwing my weight against it. The person attached to it instinctively turned but quickly lost their balance, falling onto their side. While I fought with their kicking feet, Zofie went for their face. The person yelled and tried to get Zofie off. This was enough of a distraction for me to wrestle them onto their stomach and pin their arms behind them. Even after I sat on their back, the person struggled until they exhausted themselves. Panting hard, the person lay still, turning their head to one side. Zofie leaped up on my shoulder and chattered in victory.

Inspecting my captive, I at first thought they didn't have a face, but upon looking closer, I saw their head was actually covered by some kind of thin cloth mask. No doubt, it helped hide their eyes. Wondering what a Sylph looked like, I pulled it off and discovered our captive was one very pissed female. The Sylph had greenish skin, close-cut dark hair, and a slightly longer face than a human. She appeared to be older than me, definitely a mature woman, but I didn't think her quite to middle age. And I could tell through her baggy clothes that she had a slender build and was quite well muscled. If I hadn't pinned her quickly, she likely would have captured me. She struggled again, giving one last frantic effort to free herself, but finally gave a frustrated cry when she couldn't win free. She lay still, breathing hard.

"What have you done with my friend?" I demanded. "Where have you taken her?"

The Sylph didn't answer.

Thinking she might not know Ellish, I tried the two other languages I knew, Andronise and Urticia, but she again wouldn't answer.

Her only reply was short, and she spat after it. The words were different from the Andronise I knew, but sounded similar. I was pretty sure she was making some kind of commentary about my ancestry.

*Now what?* Did I dare call to Spraggel? She could have a partner. I hope my master didn't go too far.

"Spraggel!" I called softly. And upon receiving no reply, tried again louder.

I looked back at Zofie. "I don't suppose you could go look for him, could you?"

She pointed to herself and gave a couple of short barks. Then put her paws on her waist while giving me a very disgusted look.

I sighed. "Please! I'm a little busy at the moment."

Fortunately, I heard the jingle of horse gear and the clomp of hooves coming up the trail. Spraggel rounded the bend and gave me a proud smile. "Excellent work. What's he..." He looked closer. "Uh... *she* got to say."

I shook my head. "I'm not sure she understands me. She's speaking in what sounds like a dialect of Andronise."

"Andronise? That's odd." He slowly got down from his horse. "The last report I read had them speaking Urticia because of their neighbors to the north."

Spraggel pulled a rope from his pack, and he tied her hands and feet while I held her. When we were done, we sat her up against a tree, where she glared at us.

Spraggel tried to speak to her in a language I didn't recognize. She just stared at him. He tried another, and then a third. On the third, the girl answered back. She spoke rapidly and spit in my direction at the end. It still sounded like Andronise to me.

"What did she say?" I asked.

Spraggel shrugged. "It was a little fast for me, but it was something about where we're going to spend the afterlife."

Spraggel spoke to her again, and she looked away.

"Hmmm." Spraggel crossed his arms and stroked his beard. "I'm not sure if she understands anything I'm asking her." He thought for a moment. "Well, unfortunately, we can't have her going back and telling the rest of her tribe that we're coming to rescue Risten. I guess we'll have to kill her."

I saw the woman's eyes suddenly flick in Spraggel's direction and then back to the ground. My master saw it too. I began to suspect the woman understood us a little better than she was letting on.

I kicked at some loose leaves. "Yes, it's sad, but I agree. We'll have to kill her. Do you think stabbing is the best? Strangling might be better since it wouldn't leave a mess, but she might suffer more."

She suddenly started struggling at her bindings. I smiled. The woman was only faking. She knew perfectly well what we were saying.

Zofie must not have seen the signs. She leaped onto the woman's lap, and defiantly facing us, held her paws wide as if to block us.

Spraggel slowly knelt down in front of the woman and the agitated squirrel. "Don't worry. We're not going to hurt her. We were merely trying to find out if she understood us. And she does." He looked to the woman. "Don't you? Now would you please tell me where your people have taken our friend?"

She raised her head. "You are trespassers in our forest," she said in strongly accented, but perfectly understandable King's Ellish. "That is why we took the girl. She is passage price! You're blessed we didn't take two people because we were unable to get the passage price from the men ahead of you."

Spraggel leaned forward. "Did you say men were ahead of us? Were there seven of them, and did one of them have a sword that would cut through anything?"

She looked at him suspiciously. "There were indeed seven men. And the big one destroyed many trees just by swinging his sword. They came through yesterday on a trail to the south."

My master nodded thoughtfully. "His name is Wort, and he stole something important from us," Spraggel said. "And on top of that, he's trying to find a shield to go with that sword. One that can't be penetrated. We're trying to get to the shield ahead of him so we can stop him. Thinking this would help beat him, we took a short-cut through your forest. But it looks like he's taken the same path."

The woman's eyebrows went up in surprise. "You refer to Ruin's Shield, do you not?"

Spraggel's eyes widened in surprise. "You know of it?"

"Indeed. It is spoken of in our legends. A very powerful shield. Too powerful. Some say it is cursed. Together with the sword... very bad."

"We're trying to stop him," Spraggel stood, stretching out his back. "We must keep him from getting the shield."

But she didn't answer. Instead, her gaze turned to Zofie. "What kind of squirrel is she? She seems to almost talk."

"That's Zofie," I said. "She's actually a girl about my age. But she's had a terrible curse put on her and was changed into an animal. It's her cousin that you took."

Still standing on the woman's lap, Zofie dropped to her haunches and grasped her paws in front of her like she was begging.

The woman frowned and considered the squirrel. "How do I know you aren't lying?" She tilted her head and gazing up at Spraggel. "What guarantee do I have?"

He shrugged. "You don't. We only caught you to make you speak with us. But I swear on my honor that we mean you no harm and that we must stop Wort from reaching the shield."

"And what will you do if I tell you where your friend is."

Spraggel shrugged again. "The answer would have been the same either way. I'm going to set you free."

The woman cocked her head in surprise.

Spraggel continued. "And after that, we're going after our young friend. It would just be easier if you helped us. But you can't stop us either." He reached down, untied her feet, and then released her hands. She watched quietly and unmoving until he was finished.

Spraggel leaned in and offered her his hand. She looked at it a moment before taking it and letting him pull her up. The two stood close, considering the other. At a couple of hands taller than my master, he had to look up to see her face. She stepped in closer to Spraggel and smiled. "You are clever and brave. You told the boy exactly how to catch me. I like that." She ran a finger across his chest. "What your name be?"

My master swallowed. "Spraggel van Deviante."

She suddenly grinned and quickly wrapped her arms around him, pulling him into an embrace and squeezing him tightly to her. I grimaced when I heard his back pop. "No man has bested me in all my years. My name is Yvonnani, daughter of Yuridi. So I think I will enslave you with my beauty and take you as my husband."

Spraggel's muffled voice came from her chest. "But you're just a young thing. What could you want with an old man like me?"

The Sylph chuckled. "Thank you for the compliment, but I am not young. Not hardly. We Sylph age more slowly than you humans. I would wager we are close to the same age. And you are very handsome, with a very fine beard." She felt along his back. "And more muscles than you would think hiding under your robe. You would make a fine husband. I would be the envy of all the other women." She gave him one last squeeze and pushed him an arm's length away. "But that will have to wait. I will take you to where your friend is being held. But I cannot help you release her. That, you will have to do yourself."

"Thank you," I said.

The woman shook her head. "Do not thank me. I said I would take you to your friend, but there is a condition, if you can bear it."

"And that is?" Spraggel asked.

The woman grinned. "You have to go as my prisoners."

At Yvonnani's direction, we dismounted a good half league from our destination and led our horses the rest of the way. And it was a good thing we had the Sylph woman with us. Not only would we have become completely lost, but she called out to several hidden sentries as we approached. They each came out of their hiding places to salute her and report on their progress. I had no idea they were even there.

I studied them as they spoke. Like Yvonnani, they were tall and extremely thin with that same green skin color. I had given Yvonnani a real laugh when I asked her why they painted their bodies. Turns out it's their natural shade.

I also noticed one other characteristic: the females were much taller than the males. Yvonnani had at least a couple hands on them. I thought that perhaps she was just a big girl, but we encountered another female, and she too was of similar height.

We finally topped a slight rise, and there below us was their village. It was built on a wide stretch of cleared land bordered by an even wider river—its other shore just barely visible in the distance. These were surely the backwaters of the Edi River. Bare ground was visible from the base of the hill where we stood, stretching from the water's edge to the south, to a series of huts to the north. I could also see what looked like a long narrow pier leading out into the river. Several small boats were tied to it, and I thought I could make out some fishing nets drying. The sun had dropped considerably in the sky, and we had to shield our eyes to see through the glare. Sunset was rapidly approaching.

There was quite a commotion going on below us—some kind of festivity seemed to be in progress. A group of Sylphs were gathered on a high spot close to the riverbank cheering and yelling. On another smaller mound, even closer to the water, three Sylphs wearing long black robes and high, pointed head-dresses were beating large drums in a slow, steady rhythm. But it was what was at the river's edge that drew our eyes: a woman dressed in a flowing white gown and tied to a tall post. Her hands were bound at the wrists and drawn up over her head.

The woman was Risten.

And she was laughing her head off.

Spraggel turned to Yvonnani. "Is this the ritual you were telling us about?"

Yvonnani nodded. "Indeed. She is tribute and will be sacrificed to the River God. He will come soon."

Zofie sat on my shoulder and whined.

"That's barbaric," I breathed.

Yvonnanni's face grew stoic. "It is not what we desire either. But we have to feed the River God, or he will attack our boats and snap our nets. Then with no fish, we will starve." She nodded in Risten's direction. "We have even given her medicine to make this as easy as we can for her."

I could understand the problem with the River God, but not the solution. There had to be another way.

Spraggel slapped me on the back. "No time to waste. Get down there and release her."

"Shouldn't you create a diversion? I mean we *are* interrupting their ritual." I eyed Yvonnani. "Wouldn't they be angry at that?"

Yvonnani stared out over the water. "The village might be angry if you were to actually get away. But they will not try to stop you now." She paused. "The River God is near."

I narrowed my eyes. "How close."

"*Very* close." She pointed to the water, and in the middle of the river, I saw something big break the surface. It dove back down, but the wake was clearly visible.

*Creator!* I had better hurry. The hill below me was steep and had too many loose stones for a horse. I was going to have to run. This was going to be close.

"Zofie, you stay here." And I started down the hill.

"Good luck!" called Spraggel behind me.

I didn't respond and focused my energy on getting down without breaking my neck, hopping quickly from one clear spot to another. Presently, I felt something land on my shoulder.

"Zofie. I told you to stay back."

The squirrel gave two short barks. *No.* She wasn't going to leave her cousin.

"Then watch out. I don't want to accidentally hurt you."

Once I reached more level ground, I ran flat out. The wake behind Risten was getting closer. And it was huge.

The Sylph gathered on the nearby hill saw me running. Much to my surprise, they started cheering. They pointed and talked excitedly. All except an elderly woman with an elaborate headdress of spring flowers and vines who sat in their midst and watched expressionlessly. She had the air of a leader.

The Sylph men in black robes, priests for lack of a better word, continued to beat the drum, but gradually accelerated the pace of their rhythm. While not showing any emotion, they too eyed me with interest.

Risten, on the other hand, was laughing her fool head off. They had taken her armor and replaced it with a thin white garment that was almost transparent. The gentle breeze coming from behind me made it flutter and mold to her lithe and well-muscled body. I knew from traveling with her that despite her fighting skills and general crude manner, she was a modest person. Somebody was definitely going to be very angry when the drug wore off. Especially when she realized I was the one that rescued her.

I pulled up panting, almost colliding with the stake. She looked over her shoulder at me.

"Hi, Coren," she laughed, hanging limply from the rope. "I wondered when you were going to get around to saving me." She laughed hysterically.

I moved around in front of her, splashing into the water lapping at her toes. I examined her bonds. Her wrists were tied securely above her head and attached to a lead rope from the top.

"Risten, you don't know what you're saying. They've given you some kind of drug."

With my back to the river, and standing in the shallow water at the edge, I tried to reach them. Zofie immediately leaped off my shoulder and began gnawing at the ones holding Risten's feet.

She laughed again. "I know. I don't like it, but it's so funny." Her cheeks were flushed.

"Just be still. I'm trying to get these off." I pulled out my knife and started sawing, but the stupid cord wouldn't cut. My angle was bad, and the blade was just not that sharp. I wished I hadn't left my sword on my horse. Zofie was having better luck and managed to free her feet. I reached down and pulled the cords away before returning to work on freeing Risten's hands. The squirrel leaped from the ground to me and then to Risten's shoulder, chattering in her face.

"Oh, hey cousin. You came too." She laughed. "This is so backward. I should be saving you, Zofie. Not that I did that well against your brother Wynn. That bastard. But don't you worry. We'll figure out how to remove the curse and get our sword back from Wort."

Sword *back?* From Wort? Could she be saying that Havoc's Sword was actually theirs? Wort had said it was a gift. When this settled down, I was definitely going to have to have a talk with those two. "Risten, hang on," I said. "I think I've almost got it."

"Thank you for saving me," she said very seriously before breaking out laughing. "I've taught such a strong student, soooo strong... and soooo handsome."

With one final cut, the cords sliced in two. She slipped free from the pole and collapsed into my arms, causing me to drop my knife in the process. Zofie leaped aside just in time to keep from being crushed. I staggered under her unexpected weight. With our faces a hand's-breadth apart, Risten gave me a stupid grin and landed a wet kiss on my lips. "I'll have to thank you properly when we get back." She gently patted me on the cheek. "You're so sweet..."

Then she looked at something over my shoulder, and the smile faded. "But what should we do about that." She pointed behind me.

I turned toward the river in time to see a giant snake-like head rise out of the water. It gave a deafening roar and slowly approached, rising until its shadow fell over us.

The crowd of Sylph on the hill went crazy, screaming and yelling in delight.

Risten laughed. "I think it's hungry."

# CHAPTER EIGHT

# River Gods

My feet were frozen to the ground as the River God approached. And I had to agree with Risten, it did look hungry.

The monster was huge and seemed to grin with a mouth full of gleaming white, dagger-sharp teeth. Two large eyes sat atop its head with long sharp bristles across its face. The beast had no legs that I could see, but its body was covered in thick green scales, and a jagged ridge of horns ran down its back. I couldn't help but wonder just how far into the water its body went.

The monster reared back its huge head and let out a roar so massive I could feel the organs inside my body shake. It rose out of the water to a height equal to the hills surrounding us. The light from the setting sun was directly behind it, making the beast seem to glow with a heavenly light. The sight triggered some ancient fear deep within me, and

I could understand perfectly why the villagers might think the monster, a god.

The Sylphs watching from their hill cheered the River God's arrival. Some were chanting in a steady drone to match the beat of the drums. It also explained why none of them tried to stop me. They were hoping I'd get eaten too!

The River God tensed and Zofie squeaked in alarm—I knew what was going to happen. I backed away from the water as fast as I could, still holding a very limp Risten around the waist.

The monster lunged, moving faster than I thought possible for something so big. A loose river stone found its way under my foot and I stumbled, falling backward and taking Risten with me. The monster's teeth snapped closed exactly where our heads had been only a few heartbeats before. It blew a hot breath in disappointment, and I nearly gagged at the stench. It pulled back, raising its head, and roared to the sky.

Risten sprawled most unladylike on top of me and pressed distractingly close. She stroked my face. "Coren, I like you too, but this is not the time. Zofie's here and she might get jealous."

My eyes grew wide at an unexpected searing hot pain. And it was coming from my chest. *Hot! Hot! Very Hot!*

I rolled Risten off to sprawl beside me and reached inside my shirt to pull out the amulet. It burned my fingers, and the cloth sack containing it was smoldering. It had never done this before.

No doubt the curse was trying to protect me, but the charm was fighting to keep it under control. And it was succeeding so far at least. I briefly considered taking the charm off. The curse would definitely keep me from getting killed, but there was no telling what the cost would be. The curse would be just as happy to have my arms and legs bitten off, or even worse, cause Risten or Zofie to be killed. It would do whatever it took to keep me alive.

I let the amulet drop outside my shirt, the smell of burning cloth making it hard to breathe. The monster hesitated and seemed to be searching for us. Maybe I could draw it away from Risten. I stood and swung my hands over my head and shouted, stepping parallel to the shore and trying my best to attract the River God's attention. But the monster ignored me. Risten sat up, and the sleeves of her gown caught the wind. The monster's large head swung in her direction and pulled more of its bulk further up the shore, mowing over the pole Risten had been tied to and snapping it off.

The gown! The monster was focusing on the white cloth of her gown. All I had to do was take the gown off Risten... I looked at her and realized that was not going to happen. Not even the Creator himself could protect me from Risten's wrath if I left her naked.

But... there was an alternative. I ran to her and shoved her back down so the dress wouldn't flutter so much. Then I grabbed the material of her gown about her knees, and using my teeth, ripped a sizable chunk from it that left most of her legs bare.

"Hey," she called, trying to slap me away. "You're messing up my pretty dress."

Grabbing up the cloth, I frantically waved it over my head and backed away. I turned just as the monster was rearing back to strike, but it paused, seemingly confused over where to attack.

"All right, you overgrown grass snake! Come and get me!"

I continued my frantic waving. It finally decided it liked me best and moved to follow me. That had been the plan, but seeing it turn its huge bulk and sharp teeth in my direction, made me wonder about the wisdom of that decision.

I ran toward the hill with the Sylph villagers on it, and sure enough, the monster followed behind me. I grinned. Served them right. A commotion broke out, and their cheers quickly turned to panic. They scattered, diving off the hill and running for the forest. All except the elder with the elaborate headdress. She sat there calmly on the hill in her reed chair as if daring the monster to approach.

Dammit. I couldn't let the monster kill her. I reversed direction and went back the way I had come. As I passed close to the beast, it took the opportunity to lunge at me. I dived for the ground, losing some skin from my hands as I slid to a stop. I heard the monster's giant jaws snap shut over me. It raised up to again scream in anger, its movements were becoming more agitated.

I rolled onto my back and reached to pull the amulet away from my chest. *Hot! Really hot!* It had burned the sack enclosing it completely away and charred a hole into my shirt. It was glowing so bright I couldn't look directly at it. I had to get away from the monster, or something really bad might happen.

I jumped up and resumed running back toward Risten. She was sitting up and looking at her hand, clearly puzzled. Zofie was sitting on her shoulder. "Move Risten! Move away from the water!"

She turned her puzzled gaze in my direction. Zofie was chattering up a storm. Slowly, Risten got to her hands and knees and began to unhurriedly crawl away.

I looked for anything I could use as a weapon. Even if I had my sword, it wouldn't do anything more than make it angry. There was no way it would penetrate those thick scales. Then I spied the pole Risten had been tied to. It lay just at the water's edge where the monster had snapped it off.

I was desperate. I ran to the pole, and on the more pointed end where it had broken, I tied the white cloth allowing it to flutter like a flag. Groaning with the exertion, lifted it to stand up vertically, propping its butt end on the ground. It was a long shot, but maybe the monster would try to eat it and get indigestion or something.

The pole was on the heavy side and hard to hold as I angled it toward the monster. My arms trembled with the effort of holding it steady. And I gritted my teeth against the pain as the amulet tried to burn a hole through my chest. It felt like a hot coal.

The monster crept closer, its grinning mouth opening, exposing its needle-like teeth. I would only get one chance at this.

*Please, Creator, make this work...*

And then I heard a tiny tinkling crack like a fine glass breaking—

*Creator, no!* A deep, dark laugh echoed inside my head and sent a chill down my spine. Glancing down at my chest, my horror grew.

*Oh no.*

The amulet had cracked. My curse was free.

As it had before, time seemed to slow as devastation took place around me. *Over on the hill, the drum heads the Sylph had been beating suddenly broke... One of the drumsticks snapped in half, the loose piece knocking out a female bystander... A sharp wind came out of nowhere, sending leaves and twigs flying... A tall tree in the center of the clearing gave a loud crack and fell over, pulled up by its large roots... The falling tree flattened one of the village huts... Out on the water, a huge swell appeared and crashed on all the boats tied to the pier... They sank immediately.*

My horror grew. The curse had never been this bad before. I glanced over my shoulder and saw Risten had just decided to try and stand, her now shortened gown flapping in the suddenly stiff breeze. Zofie stood on the ground beside her, urging her on.

At just that moment, the monster lunged toward me... hard and fast. But just as it started, it caught a glimpse of the now standing Risten and her white gown flapping in the wind. The monster, suddenly attracted to her larger white gown, tried to alter the direction of its strike, but its huge body was still uncoiling, pushing it forward. It continued to lift its head as it focused on the white gown. Which was just enough for its chin to catch my pole, and with momentum behind its body, the monster impaled itself through the head. I leaped out of the way when it reared back, shaking its head, only to crash back down, driving the pole deeper. Upon impact, the pole splintered, sending a painful shower of sharp debris at me, cutting my face, arm, and sticking in my clothes.

The monster fell over onto its side, gave one last breath, and was still.

The Sylph on the hill went immediately quiet. The world seemed to stop in shocked silence with the only sound coming from the water lapping gently on the shore. Then the Sylph burst into angry shouts, and I knew our troubles weren't over yet.

Risten plopped back down on her butt and stared at the monster. She too had received cuts from the debris, but none looked too serious, and she obviously wasn't feeling any pain.

I looked around in sudden panic. *Zofie!* I scanned the area. I didn't see her. She had been standing next to Risten. I stepped carefully to where she had been. Risten's eyes went wide, and I saw what she was looking at.

Zofie lay unconscious, a piece of splintered pole sticking from her shoulder. And it was covered in blood. I gently scooped her up and held her in the crook of my arm. She was breathing at least, but the wound looked terrible. I would need to get her bleeding stopped quickly and bind it.

I shook my head, the guilt rising within me. This would force Zofie yet again into a painful transformation. Just how much pain could one person stand? Maybe Risten had been right when she first tried to leave with her. Maybe I *was* too dangerous. Behind me, the last of the sun slipped behind the horizon as if it were afraid of me too.

A ring of Sylph formed around us, each holding a very sharp steel-tipped spear. And they looked angry.

While I had kept Risten from being eaten...

The curse was definitely free.

I sat on a mat inside a Sylph hut, my legs spread before me and my back against a support in the wall. I rubbed my eyes. I was exhausted.

It was completely dark inside except for the faint glow coming from around the door, allowing me to see the shadows of my boots. The hut had a dirt floor and no furnishings except the single woven mat I sat on. I sighed and tried not to feel my cuts and bruises—not to mention a few pulled muscles. I was afraid to shut my eyes lest sleep creep up on me. Zofie might need me.

Her squirrel form lay in my lap unmoving. I gently stroked what little fur wasn't covered in bandage. She hadn't regained conscious-ness since being injured. Yvonnani had helped me dress her wound, but after that, the elder had ordered me placed in the hut with two guards outside. The only break had been when Yvonnani brought me a plate of what looked like fried bits of fish and some clumps of fried bread. It was tasty; a welcome change from my usual fare. I just prayed they weren't cut from the River God.

Darkness had long since fallen and outside the entire village had gathered around a large fire in its center. I had caught a glimpse of the activity when Yvonnani had brought my meal. My back was to the wall closest to the activity hoping to hear better, but it didn't help. They were speaking that dialect of Andronise that I had trouble with. I could make out about every third word.

From what Yvonnani had told me, and what I could pick out of their discussions, there was general disagreement within the village on what to do about the death of their River God. Most of them weren't pleased. Other than depriving them of a primary source of entertain-ment, they feared the other River Gods would come to avenge their friend. Someone had suggested that I be sacrificed to appease them.

Another seemingly smaller group, argued that I had done them a favor in killing the monster. Sacrifices were no longer required, and it saved many lives. This group was led by Yvonnani. I couldn't help but wonder if Spraggel was with her.

The Sylph hadn't seemed too concerned about Risten or Spraggel, and so, weren't imprisoned like me. Risten had passed out from the drug she had been given and was sleeping it off back in a different hut—which was why Zofie was in my care.

I ran a gentle finger down Zofie's head. I hoped she would be all right. She had told me the transformation would heal everything. Still, there had to be a point where her curse couldn't repair her.

My ears perked upon hearing a new speaker. This one was concerned about what to do with the body. They were saying it would start to rot before too long, but they were afraid to cut it up—again because of potential revenge from the other gods.

I felt Zofie stir and shift position, but she did not awake. There was something else I was concerned about. My curse. I felt for the amulet still around my neck and ran my thumb over it. For the hundredth time that evening, I felt the crack running diagonally through the crystal. The curse had broken it, had overloaded it to win free, to keep me alive, and to torture me some more. I looked down at Zofie. It wasn't fair. It wouldn't be long until she transformed, and I dreaded Zofie's pain. She had seemed to hurt so bad last time.

I wondered how she had gotten her curse. It was a nasty one. Not only did it mark her and make her an easy target for some hunter to take down, but it also tortured her at least once a moon, and sometimes more. Whoever had given it to her must have been very angry. Or just liked to be cruel.

Zofie gave a squeaky moan and shifted positions. Her body was heating up. No doubt, the change was coming. I gently picked her up, and by touch, placed her on a woven straw mat next to me. All I could see was a lump of shadow. From the last time I know she didn't want to be touched while transforming, so I knelt over her and held her tiny paw as delicately as I could. Her moans increased and she grew hotter.

"I'm sorry," I whispered. "I caused this transformation. I wish there was something I could do to make it easier."

Then, as I knelt over her, I felt something very strange: an icy-burn in my left wrist—right where my curse anchor was. This was quickly followed by the oddest sensation, like something connecting within me, as if one part moved into another. *What the...?* The odd feeling was immediately replaced by a searing pain on the skin of my chest. *Creator, it hurt.* I jerked open my shirt and saw a small circle glowing blue on the left side of my chest, just above my heart. I had seen pictures and knew instantly what it was: a curse anchor.

And it hadn't been there before.

The glow went out, and just as quickly as it happened, the feeling was gone. I closed my eyes in disbelief. What horror had my curse done now?

Zofie moaned and I looked back to her. A dim blue glow began to spread over her as her transformation started, obscuring her tiny form. She didn't whine or moan like before, most likely because she was unconscious, but her tiny body became burning hot. I then felt her paw start to grow, getting larger and larger, as did the rest of her body, stretching and elongating... until a translucent human length blob lay before me. Just as the blue glow began to fade, I reached over and covered her with the blanket I'd requested from Yvonnani. I had known Zofie would need one.

The movement startled her. "Who's there? Where am I?" Zofie's shadow sat up in alarm, and I heard the movement of the blanket as she pulled it closer around her.

"It's Coren," I said softly. "And keep your voice down. The guards outside don't know you're in here." I reached for the water bag and held it out so she could feel it. "Water?"

"Thank you," she whispered as she took it. "The last I remember you were fighting that monster and then... nothing." She took a long drink. "I was hurt, wasn't I?"

"When the pole shattered, you were hit by the flying wood. Took a pretty bad cut."

"And the monster's gone?"

"Dead."

She stoppered the bag. There was a long pause. "You saved Risten." I felt her lean toward me and feel for my face. "That was very brave," she said. She stroked my cheek. Her touch was very soft.

And then she slapped me.

"Hey, what was that for?"

"For being an idiot!" she whispered as loudly as she dared. She pulled back in anger. "You could have gotten killed."

I sat back slightly aggravated. "And Risten could have been eaten. Is that what you wanted?"

"No, but it was still dangerous. Why didn't you just pick her up and run?"

I snorted in disbelief. "I know I'm a man and all, but she's not a petite thing. She's heavy! We never would have made it."

"You should know, you had your hands all over her."

"What! You're not making any sense. She wasn't wearing much of anything! I had to touch her to untie her."

"I don't have to make sense!" Her voice broke. "They're my feelings, and I'll deal with them as I see fit!" And I heard her tears come. "I could have..." She sobbed. "...lost everyone."

We sat in silence for a few moments as I waited for her tears to pass. I felt sorry for her. She'd been through a lot. Were I in her place, I might do more than just cry.

"I'm sorry." I scratched my nose, not knowing exactly what to say. "It's my fault you had to transform again. My curse caused you to get hurt."

I heard her sniffling. "I'm not fond of transforming, but at least I get to be human for a bit. It's very frustrating not being able to talk."

I couldn't help but smile even though I knew she couldn't see it. "But I must say, you were a very cute squirrel."

She chuckled. "I bet you say that to all the girls."

"Only the cute ones. Which I'm sure you are." I leaned back against the wall. "Maybe I'll see your real face one day."

There was an unexpected pause before she answered. "Maybe."

But her tone made clear she didn't believe it. I heard the rough blanket moving, and while I could only see shadows in the dark hut, I could make out her settling it over her head.

She changed the subject. "So what's going on now? And where is Risten?"

"I'm being held by the Sylph until they figure out what to do with me. They've been talking all evening. One side wants to kill me, and the other side wants to make me a hero. You just happened to be in my care when they took me in." I leaned forward and sat cross-legged. "As for Risten, she's in one of the other huts sleeping off the drug they gave her. Yvonnani said she'll be all right in the morning. Might have a headache though." I looked toward the door. "And Spraggel is probably with Yvonnani trying to talk them out of killing me. Which I sincerely hope they don't try, because my curse is now unfettered. No telling what it would do."

I heard her gasp. "Oh, your amulet... I don't see the charm anymore. Your curse must have overwhelmed it."

I sighed deeply. "And now I'm a danger to everyone around me. My friends. Even you. I never know what it's going to do next. Sometimes it's quiet for a while and then... boom, it strikes."

She scooted forward. "Do you mind if I look at it again?"

I shrugged. "Be my guest."

"I'm going to touch your chest." And I felt her light fingertips walk gently over my shirt to touch the amulet.

"It's definitely dead now," she said. "There are pieces of the charm left, but nothing that would work. If it wasn't for my own curse, I could repair it for you." Her fingers moved to touch over my heart. "Wow, I know I said this before, but your own curse is a very complex one." She was silent a moment as she studied it.

"Can I ask why you're looking at my chest? The curse anchor is on my left wrist."

Zofie chuckled as her fingers continued to follow the unseen lines. "I can see why you might think it odd. What I'm doing is tracing the lines of myst in the curse which are only visible to a seer. Typically the curse anchor is placed on the chest, which is close to the highest concentration of myst in the body. Mine's that way." She paused in her tracing. "But your curse if different. It is easily the largest and most complex curse I have ever seen. In fact, it extends well beyond your body. The curse anchor was likely placed on your wrist because that provided the best anchor point for such a large curse."

"Oh," I said, very impressed. She certainly knew a lot about myst workings.

"And another strange thing about your curse," she continued. "I don't see any way to end it. Typically it's put right out front. Some kind of event or ritual that will bring the curse to an end. Unfortunately, it's usually something very difficult, if not impossible, but it should be there."

I was afraid that might be the case.

She sighed sadly. "They do it on purpose, you know, to drive home how hopeless it is." She paused. "It's cruel."

"What about yours? Does it have a way to end it?"

She didn't answer immediately. Outside, the crowd booed loudly at someone's comment.

"It does," she finally said. "It's when I die. Like I said, it's a reminder from its maker that I can end it myself at any time."

I wasn't sure what to say. She sounded so—defeated.

I took her hand. "Don't give up. There's got to be a solution. I'm going to find a way to get rid of mine. I'm not going to pass this along any further." I nodded. "Might as well get rid of yours too."

She snorted. "For mine at least, I'm not sure that's possible."

"Not possible?" I asked. "Then I'm your man. I'm an expert on the impossible. My curse does impossible things every day. So I know the impossible really is possible. And if my curse can do the impossible, then why can't I?" I grinned. "So I figure if I can do mine, yours will be easy."

She squeezed my hand and chuckled. "I'm not sure I completely agree, but if you could... that would be wonderful."

We sat for a moment, neither one of us knowing what to say next. She finally took her hand back and once more started to trace the lines of my curse. "You said this was passed down from your father, who I assume got it from his father. Is there anything in your family history about it?"

I shrugged. "Not that I know of. We always seemed pretty normal. We used to run a stable and raise horses. The finest in the land. In fact, my father met my mother when she accompanied her family to buy a draft horse. As mother tells it, he was so taken with her beauty that he offered to give her the horse for free—if she would marry him. But mother said no. She told him that while the horse was pretty, he, on the other hand, was not!"

Zofie laughed. It was a most enchanting sound. "So where are your parents now?"

I squirmed, suddenly uncomfortable. "My father died when I was young," I tried to keep my voice neutral—I chose not to tell her that I'd been responsible for his death. It wasn't by my hand but, with this curse, it didn't have to be.

"Mother remarried, but I haven't seen her in a couple years. Her new husband doesn't like me. You know, the curse thing."

"Oh." Her fingers continued to lightly brush my chest but stopped abruptly. "This is interesting. Your curse has some very unusual parts to it. I'm not sure exactly what it does, but it seems to be leading some-where outside of you. That is really, really strange."

"Strange?"

"Yes, curses, or any myst working for that matter, don't usually reach outside..." She broke off and shifted closer. I felt her press where I had felt that mysterious pain earlier "Creator! I don't believe it. Your curse has somehow reached out to touch mine. I've never heard of a curse doing this."

"Right before you started to change, I felt something in my chest."

"That must be when it happened." I saw her shadow look into my face. "Our curses are somehow connected now."

My ears picked up at a change in the sounds outside. Had the villagers finally reached a decision?

I leaned in close. "It sounds like they will be coming for me soon. I don't want to involve you in my trouble. I'll go out, so they don't come in and find you."

"But..."

"Shhh... It'll be fine. But I need to get away from here, so I don't accidentally hurt you. I think Risten is two huts over, try to sneak in over there."

Without waiting for an answer, I stood and strode to the door, pushing it open. The guards didn't stop me, and I soon saw why. Yvonnani was approaching the hut and, behind her, every eye in the village was watching. None of them looked happy.

"The village has reached a decision," she said. "Come with me." Yvonnani turned and started back the way she had come.

My heart sank. This wasn't going to end well. I glanced over my shoulder, glad to see the guards following behind me. Hopefully, that would buy Zofie some time to slip out. No telling what the Sylph would do if they were to find that an extra person had slipped inside with their prisoner.

I was escorted to where everyone was gathered by the village's central fire. Whispered conversations stopped as I approached, and silence spread through the crowd. Spraggel waved to me from the front. I was surprised he didn't have a pen and paper trying to record what he was seeing. It was no doubt a rare event to observe the workings of the mysterious Sylph.

I was led to stand before the elderly woman I had seen on the hill. She still wore the elaborate headdress and was seated on the same chair woven from reeds. She looked tired, and from her drooping eyes, I thought it was well past her bedtime. But when I stepped before her, she came instantly alert and frowned, clearly irritated with me. It was as if she wondered why I hadn't allowed myself to be eaten like a good outsider.

Yvonnani took her place beside the old woman, and I immediately noticed the resemblance. They had to be related. Mother and daughter, perhaps?

Yvonnani spoke. "This is our village elder Yuridi, daughter of Yvinnque."

I gave her a slight bow. "My name is Coren Hart."

The elder raised her hand and pointed to me. Surprisingly, she spoke perfect Ellish. "Human named Coren Hart... Through the years, many have tried to save the sacrifice only to end up being the sacrifice themselves. You're the first to not only save your friend and yourself, but to kill our River God. This is not something we can take lightly, but we have no precedent to fall back on. We have not been able to reach consensus on what to do with you." She lowered her hand and leaned back in her seat. "From time immemorial the River Gods..."

But I lost track of her words as a strange feeling came over me. I heard the sounds, but I could pull no meaning out of them. An odd sensation grew in my chest. It felt like someone was pulling a string through my heart. And it burned. Intensely. I put my hand to my chest and staggered against one of the guards. A strong hand clamped on my arm to steady me.

And then, just as suddenly, it was gone. *What the Creator was that?*

The village elder ignored my stagger, no doubt taking it for fear.

"Therefore," she continued. "We will let the River Gods decide. You will be tied to the stake at the water's edge. If a god comes for you, then you will take the girl's place and be the sacrifice. If they do not come, you will go free."

I grimaced. My curse was going to love this. And sure enough, a cool breeze blew through the camp, making me shiver. One of the vines in the elder's headdress broke in two, and a large piece fell off and into her lap. The wood in the campfire suddenly collapsed, lifting a cloud of sparks into the air, and someone yelled as they had to beat the flames out of their clothes.

A loud, inhuman roar echoed eerily across the river. Murmurs erupted across the gathered villagers but were quickly silenced when another roar sounded—this one closer. The villagers instinctively huddled nearer the fire. Then came a soft booming sound, immediately followed by others in the unmistakable sound of footsteps—something on four legs was approaching. Something with *very big* legs. The roar came again, sounding even closer.

Just then, the clouds parted, and moonlight gradually lit the area, revealing a very large shape approaching. The villagers broke and ran away from the river toward the forest. Yvonnani put a hand on her mother's shoulder, but the two stood firm as they watched the approaching bulk. I wanted to run, but for some reason, I was anchored in place—my feet wouldn't move.

There was another loud roar, and the shadowed creature suddenly stepped into the firelight. I couldn't believe my eyes. It was a giant turtle with thick leathery skin of a dark, dark green, four huge legs thicker than the biggest oak tree, and a shell that could have easily fit a dozen huts inside it. Its sizeable head was raised as high as a second-story roof, and its two large eyes stared straight at me. It opened its mouth and gave another bone-chilling roar.

Unbidden, I stepped toward the monster. In panic, I tried to stop myself, but my body wouldn't respond. It had to be the curse. *What was it doing?* The turtle and I stopped in front of each other. I heard the villagers behind me talking excitedly.

Slowly the turtle lowered its head until it was at the same level as me. It opened its mouth wide, and I could see its large pink tongue inside. I couldn't help but think that maybe my curse had run into something it couldn't protect me against. That this was it. I was going to die. Not by anything noble like a lion or a dragon. No, I was going to get eaten by a turtle.

The turtle's giant mouth moved closer. The tongue flicked out and...

Licked me. A juicy one from bottom to top.

*What was going on!*

The head pulled back, and I couldn't believe it when its large eye winked at me. I stared in wonder as it suddenly hit me what this monster actually was.

*It was Zofie!*

# CHAPTER NINE

# Secret Plans

Zofie slowly lowered her massive body until her shell rested on the ground, and then she brought her head down to my level. She looked at me expectantly, as if she were waiting on something. I could swear she seemed extremely pleased with herself.

I had no idea what she wanted me to do. I found my legs back under my control, and I stepped up to her head, which was nearly as tall as me. I whispered close to where I thought her ear was. "What do you want me to do?"

She rolled her head in small jerks as if she wanted me to come closer. But I was already next to her so that meant she... I hoped I was right. I found some footholds on her leg and shell and managed to climb on to her neck and then carefully stepped to the top of her head. I sat and crossed my legs.

I involuntarily gave a yelp as her head immediately rose into the air until I was as high as the top of the tower back home. (I knew from that business with the lightning.) Her head rocked as she stood, and I was suddenly afraid I was going to fall off.

I stole a glance at Spraggel, who had not moved the whole time. I could make out that he was smiling. He'd evidently figured it out too.

The villagers started to creep out of the woods and stare in awe as they excitedly whispered among themselves. But the elder didn't look too pleased. I felt she was just a hand's-breadth from ordering spears thrown at us.

But once again, Zofie stole the show. I felt her head rock and then... She spoke.

"Villagers!" she announced, in a deep booming voice, and pausing to allow the sound to echo off the trees and hills. I could clearly tell it was Zofie because she retained her unusual accent, although her voice was pitched quite a bit deeper. It was strange that she could form words with the mouth of a turtle. There was no doubt some kind of myst-spell involved, and I suspected I knew why. My own curse had done some customizing.

She continued. "I mourn the loss of the one you call River God. He was truly a great creature. However, I also celebrate his passing because it is time to move toward a new relationship with the river. One without the isolation of the past." Again she paused. She gently turned her head to face another part of her audience. She was good at this. "This man has proven his worthiness to take on a great quest. A quest to save the very world we live in. Did you know that he seeks to stop the one that stole Havoc's Sword and now seeks to stop that same ruthless man from claiming Ruin's Shield? You of all people know that this cannot happen."

She paused again, and a murmur spread among the people.

My eyebrows rose in surprise. They knew about the two weapons? I was going to have to ask Spraggel about it. Maybe these people had been involved in the war many years ago with the Dark Avenyts, too.

Zofie continued. "I have decided to help this man in his quest. I will see that he gets ahead of the villain and stops him before he can succeed. But..." She bowed her head. "As large as I am, I cannot do this by myself. I am only one. To succeed, I need your help. I need the help of each and every one of you." She looked up and scanned the crowd. "We must work together. Will you help us? Will you help us save not just this village, not just this forest, but save the entire *world?*"

She paused. Not a sound could be heard. I thought she had pushed it a little too far. Why would they get involved? Then suddenly from the back, there came a single clap, then another as a rhythm was established. A slow beat of hands coming together. Others joined, and then more, until the whole village was clapping in that steady beat, feet joined in the rhythm, gradually increasing in tempo and growing louder. It grew faster and faster until they burst into shouts saying something that roughly translated as 'we are with you.'

The elder started to stand, and Yvonnani grabbed an arm to help lift her up. The village immediately fell silent again. The elder raised both arms in the air and spoke. "The River Gods have spoken sooner than we were expecting. We beg your forgiveness at not understanding." She turned to her people. "We will help them in their quest to stop the evil one from obtaining Ruin's Shield!"

And the village went crazy shouting their agreement.

Zofie gave me a moment of fright as she slightly bowed her head. "I thank you for your help. All of you." She turned toward the elder. "I will return at morn. Please make whatever preparations you need so that we may start our quest quickly."

The elder nodded. "We shall."

Slowly Zofie turned her bulk around and headed back into the river.

I leaned forward, spread my arms, and did my best to hug her giant head. "Zofie! That was amazing! Not only did you keep me from becoming fish food, you even got them to help us! You definitely have a way with words. Where did you learn to do that?"

She didn't say anything, but instead continued on out into the river.

I sat up in alarm. "Ah... Zofie, you know I'm still up here, right? I'm not really fond of water. Especially deep water." The Edi was the largest river on this side of the continent and was especially deep and wide at this point. I swallowed and tried not to look down. I was deathly afraid of deep water. It was deep, black waters that had claimed my father and nearly killed me.

"Zofie, can we go back now? I'm not really comfortable out here."

But she continued with the river getting deeper and the shore moving further away from us. And it was dark out, with only a three quarter's moon low on the horizon. I looked behind me, and the light from the village seemed very far.

"There, that should be far enough," she finally said and stood still in the middle of the river. "Now we can talk for a bit. My voice carries so far, I needed some distance to have privacy."

I lay down on her head and tried to look into her face, but it was just too big. "Zofie, this is probably a bad time to mention it, but I don't do well in water. You know how I don't like to be wet... well, I had a bad experience one time. So, can we go back to shore?" I was babbling.

"Coren, please bear with it for just a little bit longer. I will return you. I just need you to do something for me first."

I winced, having a good idea of what was coming. "Anything within my power."

"Good." She sighed. "Coren, you're a good traveling companion, and I like being around you, but... can you please tell me why I've turned into a big talking turtle? In all the time I've been cursed, I've only transformed into normal creatures. Animals that actually existed. But there is no turtle in the world this size, and definitely none that talk."

"Well," I winced. "I don't really know, but... I think it was my curse. I felt it do something when you were transforming." I put a hand on her head. "I'm sorry. I had no idea it would do this."

She blew out another heavy sigh and shook her head slightly. "Curses will sometimes compete for myst and not work properly. But not like this. It's like your curse adjusted the settings on mine, which shouldn't be possible. And while I appreciate the ability to speak, it's a little unnerving."

I got to my knees and tried not to look off the sides. It made my fear a little more manageable. "But look at the bright side, you've got the entire village helping us now. And it's all because of you pretending to be a River God. If you hadn't transformed into a turtle, that wouldn't have been possible."

"I guess you're right."

"That speech was something else too. Very quick thinking on your part. I wouldn't have thought to ask them to help us. You seemed to know exactly what to say. You're a natural leader."

Zofie chuckled. "I bet you tell that to all the turtles."

I sat back down, smiling. "Of course not, only to River Gods."

Zofie shook her head gently, rocking me back and forth. "One more comment like that, good sir, and you go in the river." We were quiet for a moment, the only sound coming from the gentle lapping of the water around Zofie's shell.

"So what do we do now?" she finally asked.

I laid down on my stomach and rested my cheek against her head. It felt kind of nice. "The only thing we *can* do; continue our quest to find the shield before Wort does."

"I guess you're right." I tensed as she started moving again and turned back toward shore. "But Coren?" she asked.

"Yes."

"You have to keep your curse from interfering with mine any more. It scares me."

I sighed.

*Not as badly as it scares me.*

I lay back and shut my eyes, the hot mid-afternoon sun lighting the inside of my eyelids and baking my face and arms. Sweat soaked my shirt. *Creator, it was hot.* Not as bad as the previous day, but bad enough.

I sat on top of Zofie's head as she waded up the river. Only her head and about half of her shell were above the water. And behind her came a long barge, which she pulled using thick ropes tied around her shell. It had to be tiring work for her. Yet she was determined, and we made a slightly better speed than if we were pulled by horses or tried to pole our way upstream. This was our third day since leaving the Sylph village, and our guide insisted we were close to reaching the end of our River trip.

Spraggel had suggested I continue to sit on Zofie's head to prove to the Sylph that I was still in the god's favor. She said she didn't mind, but I felt awkward up there. One false tip of her head and I'd be in the water. And that thought alone was enough to terrify me.

Not to mention, I couldn't swim.

The Sylph had generously volunteered to take us upstream on a large flatboat, just big enough for our four horses, supplies, and a few of their tribe. But their generosity did have its limits. The edge of their territory was as far as they would escort us. Their lands ended at the Dragon's Mouth—a very tall waterfall that stopped water traffic from going any further upstream. Of course, the trip wasn't solely for us. The ever-practical Sylph had managed to fit some furs, baskets, and sweet tree sap on the barge, which they planned to trade with the small human village atop the falls. At least that way, they would not return empty-handed.

By going up the river using Zofie power, we were quickly making up time we had lost due to our encounter with the Sylph. Despite the river running a good bit east of our intended path, our faster speed would hopefully put us close behind Wort.

I cracked an eye and glared up at the sun. I stretched and decided to roast my back for a while. I carefully rolled over onto my stomach, being mindful of the edge. I didn't want to accidentally roll off.

"Hey, be still up there. You're giving me a headache." Zofie said as quietly as she could, which actually wasn't all that quiet. Her voice carried pretty far. I'm sure everyone in the boat could hear her. We tried not to display too much familiarity, afraid the Sylph might figure out that Zofie really wasn't a River God. So I did most of the talking and she gave, hopefully, vague answers.

"Sorry." I exhaled heavily. "It's just so hot up here."

"How are we doing?"

What she actually meant was: 'How is Risten doing?' I sat up and looked back at the barge. Risten was still sitting on one side of the boat with her back to the rail. She was sharpening her sword and oiling it. No doubt putting on a display so the Sylph would not mess with her. She glanced my way and caught me looking at her. She just glared at me, giving her blade a nice hard stroke with her whetstone. I turned back toward the front. "About the same."

On the first day of our trip, she had mainly knelt by the rail, hanging on for dear life. The drug the Sylph had given her had left Risten with a major hangover. Yvonnani tried to help by offering her medicine, but the sword-master flatly refused. She was pretty much done with the Sylph, having been captured, drugged, and left for fish food.

Spraggel, on the other hand, had been in deep conversation with Yvonnani since before we had left the village. She had volunteered to come with us, but I think it was only so she could continue to talk to Spraggel. They had definitely taken a liking to each other.

I laid back down on my stomach and put my hands under my cheek. "Do you think Risten's still pissed at me? She's just sitting there sharpening her sword."

"Definitely."

I looked back over my shoulder again, and she was sighting along the blade of her sword in my direction. "I guess I shouldn't have told her about our curses interacting?"

Zofie chuckled, her head bobbing up and down. "Yes, not very wise."

I settled back down again. "I thought she would understand. But now she's determined to separate us. I honestly believe she'd kill me if she didn't think my curse would stop her."

Zofie chuckled again.

A couple of days into our journey, I had decided I needed to bring Risten up to date on what had transpired while she was passed out. But I wasn't sure how to slip away from the Sylph without offending them or making them suspect us. I mentioned this to Zofie, and she came up with the solution. That evening around the campfire, she rose to her full River God height and actually commanded us to leave while she talked to the Sylph alone. They were extremely pleased.

After taking a short walk away, I informed Risten and Spraggel of what had happened during Zofie's last transformation. When Risten learned my curse had somehow connected with Zofie's, she became concerned and very angry. She demanded that I leave Zofie alone—like I had a choice in the matter—and threatened to depart with her right then if I didn't. It took quite a bit of talking to calm her down and get her to see the problems that would cause. She finally agreed to stay with us until reaching the falls, but after that, she and Zofie were leaving us. I couldn't help but wonder if my curse would even allow us to be separated.

And that was the thing that worried me. Since influencing Zofie to turn into a turtle, my curse had been unusually quiet. In the past, it had demonstrated periods of calm, but it usually came back within a day or two, causing absolute calamity. But this time, it had been almost four days and not a peep. No broken ropes, no wetting of supplies, no hidden rocks in the river.

*What was going on?*

There was one more thing going on with my curse. I pulled up my shirt and looked down at my bare chest. I kept hoping it had disappeared. Over my heart, where I had felt the pain of Zofie's transformation, I had a new curse mark. One that hadn't been there before. It was about as big as a gold royal and perfectly round with complex symbols around the edge. Inside the circle were the shapes of four animals and the phases of the moon. I noticed it the morning after Zofie had turned into a turtle and showed it to her the first private moment we had. She was as surprised as I was and said it looked like her own curse mark... and it was in the same place on her chest too.

*What exactly had my curse done?*

I looked at the leather wrist guard covering my own curse mark. I briefly considered taking it off to see if my mark had changed. But just the thought of seeing it again reminded me of my dead father's face. I was filled with such loathing that it made my stomach queasy. No, I just couldn't look at it again. At least, not yet. The curse had saved me at his expense, something I truly did not deserve.

I heard shouting behind me and guiltily dropped my shirt back into place. I turned to find our guide waving his arms and pointing to shore. Apparently, we had reached the point we needed to disembark. I relayed the message to Zofie, and she turned toward shore, carefully selecting a place that she could ground the barge safely.

I waited for Zofie to put me down, but she continued to hold her head up high. I thought she had maybe forgotten me. "Uh... you can put me down now. You've got to be tired of me stomping around up here."

She instead stepped out of the rope attached to the barge. "I must speak with you alone," she announced more for the others than for me. "I have guidance I must give you." She turned back toward the river.

From behind me, I heard Risten call out to us. "Coren, you bring her back, now!" Standing up, I saw her running after us, clearly not pleased.

I held out my hands in a shrug. "She's got the reins, not me."

Zofie stepped back into the water, headed for the other side.

Risten ran to the edge. "Stop right this instant!"

Zofie continued into the deeper water. "I will return shortly. I must speak with him... alone."

I sat back down on her head, eyeing the water as it crept up her shell. I was sort of getting used to it.

"What's going on?" I asked.

"Be patient. I just wanted a few moments to explain something." She sounded sad. I grew concerned.

She moved on in silence, passing the middle of the river and then continuing on toward the other side. The river was wide here, and the current not too strong but steady, so it was taking a bit to get there. On the other riverbank, it was heavily forested, so there was no way she could pull herself out of the water. But she angled a little further upstream and found a small tributary, which managed to have just enough space to walk up it.

"How did you know this was here?" I asked.

She chuckled. "It's part of being a turtle. I could feel the difference in water temperature, so I knew it had to be coming from another source."

"So how do you know how to do that? You're still a human under all that shell."

She lowered her head, and I jumped off onto the bank of a crystal-clear stream. It was just the right height that she could look at me without having to lay her head down. "When I transform..." She tilted her head to one side. "I seem to know exactly how to use my new shape. It's not surprising, really. That would have been a normal part of the spell used to create the curse."

"What do you mean, a normal part? Don't you just shape it like you want it then stick it to the person."

She nodded. "That *is* what we do, but not exactly. Why go to all that trouble to recreate a spell that been perfected by someone else? Instead, you just incorporate that other 'proven' spell into whatever you're doing. It's a lot easier and less prone to mistakes."

"You mean there are a standard set of spells that everyone uses? Like common groupings of letters to make words?"

She laughed. "That's a good analogy. It's works very similar." She suddenly glanced away, and while her turtle expressions were difficult to read, I felt her demeanor grow dark. "But that's not what I brought you here to discuss."

I got the distinct impression I wasn't going to like this.

She took a deep breath. "Last night, Risten told me she had a conversation with one of the Sylph about the trail ahead. They have scouts all up and down the river, so they have a good idea of what's going on. He let it slip that a party of seven men were spotted leaving their forest a couple days ago. And one of the men had a special sword."

"Wort," I breathed.

She nodded. "The men were headed for Bristone, which is a small village near the top of the Dragon's Mouth. Risten is planning to leave us behind tomorrow and try to catch him there."

"But he has that sword."

She gave an almost human sigh. "She doesn't think it will matter since she believes her skills are so much better than his."

I rubbed my chin in thought. "While she is a sword-master, there are seven men and one unstoppable sword."

She nodded. "That's what I told her. She doesn't actually know that her skills *are* better, she just thinks they are..." She paused and took a deep breath. "I probably shouldn't say this because Risten is sensitive about it, but she's great with the forms and practiced with her master quite hard, plus she accompanied him on many battles, but she hasn't actually been in that many real fights. The one with the thieves was probably her first real swordfight on her own."

"But she killed one of them."

Zofie shook her head. "Remember what happened? Risten didn't use her blade. She slammed the hilt into his jaw. She was trying to knock him out. She may be a sword-master, but she's never bloodied her blade before. I'm afraid she'll confront Wort and not be able to follow through."

I held up my hand. "I'm not sure I agree on that. She regularly kicks my butt, and her skills are top-notch. I don't see why she wouldn't be able to go through with it?"

Zofie sighed. "I've known Risten all my life. We grew up together. She's not the dark-hearted person you think she is."

I shook my head. Were Zofie and I talking about the same person? The Risten I knew definitely had a dark streak.

Zofie continued. "Regardless, I believe there is a good chance she might lose to Wort in an actual fight. And I can't lose her. I've lost so much already. I can't let her be killed." She looked down and stirred the water with her front foot. "So I have to go with her to try and keep her alive."

A strange sadness came over me. *Separate?* I knew we would have to part at some point, but I was hoping it wouldn't be so soon.

"However..." Her mouth pulled back in a turtle approximation of a smile. "There is an alternative. If you're up to it. You and I could go and *steal* his sword instead of fighting him."

"What? Steal his sword? Wouldn't we have to—I don't know—get close to him to do that! I imagine he doesn't let that sword out of his sight."

"The village is famous for what is called its Dragon Pools."

"Dragon pools? I think I've heard of those."

She nodded. "They're pools cut from the rock by the action of the water. The water flows into them before going over the falls. The pool is only a hand's-breadth from the edge. All you have to do is lean over and watch the water plunge straight down for several hundred feet."

"I knew they were tall, but... wow."

She grinned. "But that's not the best part. There is a custom that bathing in the pools at midnight by the light of the moon grants one eternal bravery. So you *know* Wort is going to do that. If we can catch him there, we can simply take the sword while he's bathing. If we arrive too late, we'll just have to take it while he's sleeping. Either way, it has to be tonight."

I pointed to her shell. "Isn't there a slight problem with stealth here? You do stand out a little."

"We'll have to leave at dark and, when we get there, force a transformation..."

"Wait," I interrupted, holding up a hand. "*Force* a transformation? The only way I know to force you to transform outside of a full moon is to hurt you."

She cocked her head to one side. "It's not like you're going to kill me. A carefully placed jab of your sword should be fine."

"But..."

"You shouldn't worry about hurting me. A sword strike is nothing compared to the pain of transformation."

I opened my mouth to argue, but after watching her transform, I really couldn't think of anything to say.

Zofie continued. "My transformations follow a sort of pattern, so I'll be a bird next time."

"Pattern?"

"My... I mean the person who cursed me, incorporated a pattern to the transformations. They start with a small mammal, and then go to a reptile, next a bird, and finally a large mammal before returning to a small mammal. I've now gone through a couple cycles, and it's always been the same. I'm fairly confident my next one will be a bird. If I'm big enough, I can fly in and snatch the sword by myself. And if I'm too little, then I can be your lookout." She extended her head toward me. "I know we can do this."

I stroked my chin in thought. I was sort of disappointed. I had expected her plan to be very farfetched, but it sounded almost *doable*.

"What about the others," I asked. "It's still a couple hours to dark, and when we pull out, they'll miss us immediately, well... at least they will you."

"I'll make up some kind of excuse. I *am* a River God, so I'm expected to be mysterious. They won't be able to follow me once I get in the river. I can see fairly well at night in this form. If we leave at dark, it should only take us a couple hours to reach the falls and then only a couple more to climb them. I can travel pretty fast if I'm not pulling a barge."

I turned and walked away a few steps before turning back toward her. "You realize, I'm not a good choice for this. My curse..."

"Has been unusually quiet."

I paused with my mouth open. "You noticed too? Which means it won't last. It could come out at the worst moment."

Zofie shook her head. "I'm not so sure. Something happened when our curses connected. Yours has started to regulate mine, but I think mine is somehow inhibiting your bad luck. It must be working like your charm did, consuming all your curse's myst to regulate mine."

I shook my head. "But you don't know that. And there will be no room for error in this attempt. My curse could easily kill you. And then, well, you'd be dead." Creator, that sounded stupid.

She extended her neck to its limits until we were only a hand's-breadth apart. "Please! I know we can do this, and it will keep Risten from getting herself killed."

I sighed deeply. I looked to the ground and then back to her. "All right, I'll do it. I always was a sucker for a pretty turtle."

"You will! Thank you!" She stuck out her large tongue and licked me from bottom to top in one long, very wet stroke. I tried to think of it as just being thoroughly kissed, but it didn't help.

I still felt wet.

By the time we got back, the Sylph had fixed a meal of fried fish and vegetables. They planned to leave us the next morning and wanted to give us a good meal before they said their good-byes. Zofie went off into the river to forage a distance away but was clearly visible from the camp. I took the opportunity to inventory my belongings, looking for something she could wear temporarily while in her human form. I was sitting cross-legged on the ground, tying the few things I'd selected into a bundle when Risten approached me.

"Coren, I need to speak with you." She squatted down beside me. Her tone was flat.

I tried to nonchalantly stuff the bundle back into my bag so she wouldn't become suspicious. If she found out, she might literally kill me—or at least try. "What... what do you want?"

She looked around to make sure we weren't being watched. "Why did Zofie take you away earlier? She won't talk to me."

I looked back to my bags and breathed a sigh of relief. Zofie and I had made up this story on the way back. "She just wanted to tell me good-bye, since you both will be separating from us soon. With her voice carrying so far, it's been difficult for us to have a private conversation." I looked into Risten's face. "I'm going to miss her, but I understand you're only protecting her. My curse is a liability after all. But we did make a promise to see one another again after our quest is done."

Risten seemed to relax and sighed sadly. "I'm sorry I'm pulling Zofie away, but it's for the best. Although, to be truthful, your curse is only part of the reason." She looked over her shoulder to make sure Zofie was still a ways off. "Zofie has lived a very sheltered life until recently. She doesn't have much experience with the way the world works and how cruel it can be—she's not had to deal with people very much, little alone young men. Until just a few months ago, she was still playing with her dolls and storybooks."

I somehow couldn't imagine the Zofie I knew playing with her dolls now. The books part though, I might go along with. She could match me one-for-one on a wide variety of topics. She'd even read all The Poet's works!

She looked over her shoulder again, checking on Zofie's location. "I'm afraid she's grown a little too attached to you. I don't know quite how to put it, so I'll say it bluntly. She's well above your station, and her future has already been determined. It would be better for all if you encouraged her to move along and never saw her again."

I blinked at Risten, not sure what to say. She was basically implying that I wasn't good enough for Zofie. And it made me angry. True, I was not of noble birth—*and* I was only a cursed apprentice scribe—but I was not trash. My irritation bubbling inside, I opened my mouth to reply. But I stopped mid-breath, thinking of the evening. If I wasn't careful, I could spoil our plans. Instead, I gritted my teeth and swallowed my anger. It would be better if I just played along.

I looked down and nodded. "I understand." But anger still burned in my chest. And it was growing.

*Why?* I asked myself. *Why does this upset me?* I had long ago decided that I would not have a female companion. Zofie was just one more female passing through my life. Why was it making me so angry?

Risten patted my shoulder. "I knew you'd do the right thing. One day, you'll understand."

Unexpectedly, I heard a loud rumble of thunder. We both looked up to see a storm cloud rapidly filling the sky. It was late afternoon, but in a matter of minutes, the sky quickly darkened until it looked like dusk. A bolt of lightning struck a nearby tree, setting it ablaze, and a wicked wind began to whip the trees. In the distance, I saw Zofie's head come up to peer in our direction. She turned toward us, coming double-time. The cook fire the Sylph had been using flared higher than their heads as the kettle of oil suddenly tipped. The lines holding the nearest tent snapped, and it fluttered in the breeze. I took all this in, my horror growing. The curse! I thought it was being suppressed. Risten looked at me with growing concern, when her hair suddenly stood on end. I felt a tingling of sparks in the air and was reminded of that time on the keep's roof during the thunderstorm. I knew exactly what was going to happen.

I leaped toward Risten and tackled her to the ground. A bolt of lightning hit the dirt where she had been standing, blowing a deep hole in the ground. I knew we both felt the shock of its hit.

Just then Zofie stepped out of the water near us, and suddenly the air stilled, the fire died down, and the sky began to clear. And that tightness in my chest eased. I looked at Zofie in shock. If I had any doubts before, I certainly didn't now. She really was suppressing my curse. If we were separated too far, it would activate. I had to go with Zofie.

Risten cleared her throat. I looked down and realized I was lying on top of her, our faces less than a hand's-breadth apart. "I guess I should thank you for pushing me out of the way, but if you're expecting another kiss, you're sadly out of luck."

I grinned nervously, thinking back to the drugged kiss she gave me when I rescued her before. "So, you remembered that?"

Her eyes narrowed, and she smiled wickedly. "A woman never forgets her first kiss."

*Oh Creator, was I in trouble.*

# CHAPTER TEN

# Dragon's Mouth

A s dusk was falling, Zofie made an excuse that she was still hungry and went to forage for a little longer. After she was gone, I checked discreetly to make sure Risten wasn't around. Fortunately, she had gone hunting with a couple of the Sylph and hadn't come back yet.

Being careful I didn't attract attention, I picked up my bundle and made off up the path leading upriver. I hadn't gone more than a hundred steps before I came face to face with Spraggel. *Oh no, what am I going to tell him?*

He pushed off from the large oak he was leaning against and held out a small leather pouch. "Here, you'll need this. I didn't see you pack any food, and you'll likely get hungry."

I scratched my head. "How did you know?" I had been very careful not to be seen.

"You've had a guilty look about you since you came back from across the river. I've lived with you long enough to know when something's up."

"But..."

"Shush!" He waved his hand in dismissal. "Don't say anything else. I don't know all the details, and I don't *need* to know them. I just have to trust that you know what you're doing. Just swear you and the girl will return in one piece."

"I can't swear, but I'll do my best."

Spraggel nodded gently. "I'll accept that. Now go. I'll try to keep the others occupied."

I nodded once and took off up the trail. Just up ahead, Zofie was waiting for me. We had agreed that her booming voice would carry, so we didn't speak as I approached. Without a word, I climbed aboard, and we turned up the river. I couldn't help but feel strange as we left everyone else in our party behind. We were truly on our own.

Darkness quickly fell as Zofie slogged up the river, and soon the only light we had came from the stars and the gibbous moon. For me, it was a little unnerving since I could only make out shadows in the river around me. Zofie, on the other hand, had no trouble seeing— night vision being yet another enhancement from her latest transformation. Not for the first time, I wondered why my curse was interacting with hers this way. It was definitely strange. But I really wasn't that surprised. My curse was astonishingly good at finding new ways to torment me.

Zofie set a fast pace. Unlike when she was pulling the barge, she stayed close to shore. This allowed her to stay in the water, but not fight against the current as much.

The quiet swish of her feet was unnerving, though. It kept reminding me of the water all around us. I scooted over to the edge of her head and looked down at the solid darkness below me, broken only by an occasional patch of white foam stirred up by Zofie's steps. Looking into the black current, I couldn't help but think back to when my father had drowned. He had died saving me.

I still remembered the day, watching with a child's fascination, the rain-swollen river near my home. Its current swift and a dark muddy brown, carrying trees, bushes, and even a small house by. I had only been twelve. But I strayed too close and slipped in the wet mud of the river bank. The angry river didn't hesitate to suck me in and carry me away while stuffing foul water into my mouth and dragging me beneath its torrential current. I slammed into a flooded tree and clawed its bark for purchase as the eager current sucked at me. My father had seemed to magically appear at my side, but we were both lost in the current. I heard my father gasp out something, and then I felt a searing pain in my left wrist.

The next thing I knew, I was lying on wet ground, coughing up water, while a strange man knelt over me. He was saying something to me, but I couldn't make out the words. I turned my head to the side and saw my father lying next to me. Only, he was white and still—and he wasn't breathing.

I jerked myself back to the present and gave a shuddering sigh at the memory. I touched the reassuring solidness of Zofie's head, but I knew the dark water recognized me. Calling me to rejoin her beautiful black currents. I could feel the terror from it in my bones.

I shivered and moved to the center of Zofie's head. It took several minutes before my panic passed.

"Are you all right?" Zofie risked a whisper, still incredibly loud by human standards. "I feel you shaking."

I unwrapped my arms from around myself and took a deep, and only slightly shaky, breath. "I'm fine." I patted her head. "At least I'm not wet."

She quietly chuckled.

We traveled in silence after that. Both of us were trying not to attract too much attention. The forests around us were dark and spooky. No telling what things might be lurking just inside them. I heard a wolf howl in the distance. It was quickly followed by an answering cry that didn't come from any creature I knew.

After traveling for a couple hours, I was fighting going to sleep from the rocking and the darkness. Suddenly Zofie spoke and gave me quite a fright. "Coren, can you feel it?"

"Huh?" I snapped, suddenly awake. "What!"

"Can you feel it?" she repeated.

She slowed to a stop. "Listen. You might hear it."

I held my breath. Over my own pounding heart, I could hear the gentle gurgle of the water swirling around us. From the direction of the shore, I could hear an owl hoot and the wind gently brush the trees. I strained for something else. And there in the distance, I could barely make it out: a dull roar. The Dragon's Mouth.

Zofie lurched forward, nearly knocking me off. "We're almost there!" Excitement was in her voice.

The roar gradually grew louder until we rounded a bend in the river and heard it full force. I could see lumps of white foam ahead and lights from the inn up above.

And those lights were really high. *Much* higher than I was expecting.

"Uhhh...? Zofie, just how tall are these falls?" I tried to measure the distance, but it was nearly impossible in the dark. "Climbing that would be really difficult in the day, little alone at night."

Her head swiveled left and right. "There has to be a trail up to the top. I heard the Sylph mentioned they occasionally trade with them. But I don't see anything."

"Let's try the other side."

We were on the western shoulder of the river, so Zofie moved toward the eastern side and was soon climbing up the other bank. It was fairly steep but not impassible given her large body. "There!" She pointed with her head. "I see a trail."

We moved closer and discovered a lightly used but heavily rutted road paralleling the river. It was a tight squeeze, but Zofie could make her way along it. As we traveled, I heard the falls gradually get closer and closer, and when I thought we should have arrived, I discovered we still had a long way to go. *Just how big were these falls?* The path had developed an upward incline, and when I caught sight of the river below, we had already risen twenty or thirty feet above its surface. The air became heavy with mist, and my clothes were quickly damp and cold.

It was only a few hundred feet further before we came to a wide clearing in front of a sheer rock wall. Zofie let me down so I could investigate.

I reached inside my shirt and pulled out my amulet. In hopes of fixing it, I had asked a Sylph myst-caster to look at it before we left. He confirmed the protection charm portion was lost, but he had been able to get it so that it would produce a feeble glow—nothing close to the sun-like illumination it used to emit. But in this dim light, it was better than nothing.

So with the amulet providing a dim glow, I explored and found a series of steps cut from the living rock cliff. Moss grew on them in places, but generally, they seemed clear. Someone must be maintaining them. From what I could tell, it looked like they led to the top. But this was as far as Zofie could go in her turtle form.

"All right." She lowered herself to the ground and stuck out her neck. "Take your sword and wound me. The neck would probably be best."

I froze. I'd have to intentionally cut her, and I wasn't sure I could. At the time we discussed it, it had seemed easy. *Sure, I can stab my traveling partner and friend. Shouldn't be a problem. Just draw a little blood.* But now... What if I messed it up? What if my curse made it worse?

*What if I accidentally killed her?*

"Are you sure you want to do this?" I asked hesitantly. "It's going to be very painful."

"I can handle it." She said confidently. "I don't fear pain any longer. I hardly notice it." But even I could hear the lie. She noticed it all right. She went through agony every time she transformed.

I licked my lips. "And you're sure it has to be the neck."

"If it's a small wound, it won't trigger a transformation. It has to be a broken bone or a body wound."

I held my amulet high and tried to find a good place on her neck. Her skin was cool and moist to the touch—and I could feel the beat of her large heart. I really didn't want to do this. I found the spot that Zofie indicated and pressed my sword point-first against her neck. But I hesitated, unable to push it home. It just felt so wrong.

She turned her head around, startling me as we came face to face. I didn't think her neck would bend like that. "I need you to do this," she said, impatience entering her voice. "You have to injure me, or I won't transform. That's the only way I'm getting up there. And I *have* to get up there if we're going to try and steal the sword. It's the only way. If we wait, Risten will try to take on Wort and get herself killed. Compared to what I go through when I transform, it will be nothing."

"I..." I licked my dry lips. "I don't want to hurt you."

"Coren. It's all right." She said pleadingly. "Please!"

I closed my eyes and took a deep breath. I really, *really* didn't want to do this. I wished with all my heart that there was another way. As I repositioned the sword, I muttered to myself, "I wish my damn curse would do something useful for once." I gritted my teeth and leaned on the sword.

Suddenly, I heard a deep chuckle. I instinctively froze. At first, I thought it was Zofie, but I quickly realized it was of a deeper, darker tone. I groaned.

*It sounded like when my curse was going to do something particularly nasty.*

And suddenly, over top my heart, I felt a tingling burn on my chest, and a blue glow began to spread over Zofie.

I reflexively jerked back, and the sword fell to the ground. My curse was acting on its own. I couldn't decide whether to be thankful or not.

Zofie gasped. "It's starting. How...?" She broke off as she started panting. A feeble moan escaped her as the transformation took her.

The burning in my chest turned into a bonfire, and I felt as if someone was pulling molten lava out of my chest. My legs gave way, and I fell to my knees, grabbing onto Zofie's leg for support. It hurt so bad.

"Put the light away." She hissed. "Now! *Please! You can't see me change!*"

I quickly stuffed the amulet back into my shirt, and its glow was immediately gone. The moon chose that moment to go behind a cloud and plunge us into complete darkness.

"Thank... you...." she gasped.

I felt her leg begin to change and lose shape, growing smaller... rounder... more delicate. Gradually the blue glow faded, and the pain stopped. I found myself holding Zofie's left arm, but it was so dark, I couldn't even make out her outline.

"Are you all right?" I asked. She didn't answer immediately, and in a flash of panic, I reached inside my shirt.

But she suddenly leaned close, and I felt a gentle touch on my arm. "I'm fine. And please don't pull the charm out. The glow... it might draw unwanted attention." She sighed. "I'm just a little tired, but I always feel drained after a transformation." She sighed. "And this time it seemed to affect you too."

"Yeah, our curses must really be connected." I hesitated. "You know your transformation started on its own, right? I'm sorry I wasn't able to keep it under control."

She snorted. "I'm not complaining. It saved me from being stabbed." She laid a hand on my arm. "So at least for this time, I'm grateful."

I gazed at her shadow and tried to make out her features, but with no luck. Maybe one day, I'd get to see what she looked like.

I grew conscious of her light touch on my arm. It was warm against the cold mist, and I suddenly remembered that she wasn't wearing any clothes. It's a wonder my embarrassment didn't light up the darkness.

"I... I... have something for you." I stammered. I turned and by touch found the bundle I had brought with me. I pressed it into her hands. "Here are my extra shirt and pants. I rigged a rope for a crude belt, plus there's socks for your feet. I don't have extra boots."

She gave my arm a squeeze and laughed. "You are so thoughtful." She stood, and I could hear the soft sliding of cloth. "I've been naked as an animal for so long, I didn't even think about clothes."

She stepped to the side and began to pull on the shirt. The moon partially peeked out from the clouds behind her as she dressed. While I couldn't see anything but a silhouette, it was a very shapely shadow. I swallowed, suddenly embarrassed, and looked away. I was sure the image would forever be burned in my mind.

After she had pulled on the clothes and cinched the rope belt, not to mention rolling up the pants, we started climbing the stone stairs. Oh, what a climb. They went up and up, crisscrossing back and forth up the side of the mountain. I was glad it was dark so we couldn't see how far up we were. We took breaks as we climbed to rest our burning legs. We were both gasping from exertion, and our progress seemed achingly slow.

After what seemed an eternity, but was actually only a little more than an hour, we finally made it to the top. We stepped off the stairs onto a short piece of level ground bounded by a high stone wall. It looked to be some sort of holding area. I could barely make out a single gate sitting in the middle of the opposite wall. From the arrangement, there was no doubt it was used to extract a toll for those using the stairs. Which explained why the stairs were so well maintained—they were a source of income. But the other side of the gate was dark, and I didn't sense anyone close by.

I scratched my head. "Damn. How are we going to get in?"

I saw Zofie's shadow step up to the gate. "It's sealed with a myst lock. If my curse didn't drain away most of my myst, I could..." She turned toward me. "Let's try something. Give me your hand."

I held it out and she grasped it firmly. Her hand was warm; her grip strong. I kind of liked it.

After a brief pause, she said, "Yes, I think I can. Our curses are connecting at a basic level." She paused before asking hesitantly. "Would you mind if I borrowed some of your myst? I promise to be very careful and only draw a little."

I chuckled. "Of course. I trust you not to kill me."

I thought Zofie might make some kind of funny retort at my comment, since myst depletion was a rare occurrence. But her grasp on my hand suddenly stiffened. It was several heartbeats before she loosened her grip and softly replied, very, very seriously. "I will be exceedingly careful."

*Oh no, I must have hit a nerve.*

She laid a hand on the door. I felt a tingle pass between us, followed by the dull flash of an intricate pattern against the door. When she took her hand away, the gate creaked ajar.

"Wow, you're good," I said. I didn't know much about myst users, but I did know that *undoing* a spell took a lot more skill than doing one.

"I'm a little out of practice since I haven't been able to use myst for several months. I was just able to draw a little myst from you to complete the counter-spell." She pulled the door open and peered inside. I moved to enter, but she grabbed my arm. "Wait. There is an alarm charm." She raised a hand toward it and again, I felt a tingle in my arm and then saw a brief flash of blue. "Now, we can go. It's been disarmed."

She moved inside and I followed, taking a few tries to get the gate to completely close. I wanted to leave it so that anyone looking at it casually, wouldn't notice anything wrong.

Finally I got it to close, but when I looked up, I couldn't make out Zofie's shadow.

"Zofie?" I called quietly. I heard rustling cloth, and then a hooded shadow loomed near me. I quickly reached for my sword...

"Coren, it's me," Zofie whispered. She laid a hand on my arm. "I found this hooded coat on a hook just inside. I was getting a little chilly, so I took it."

I breathed a sigh of relief. "Tell me when you do something like that. You nearly scared my insides out." I took in her new shadow. "How did you see it in this darkness?"

The shadow shrugged. "It has a charm on it to keep the wearer dry. Being a myst-seer, it was rather easy to make out."

We turned to survey what lay before us. Up ahead, we could see flickering light coming from what appeared to be the windows of an inn high up on a hill. Those must have been the lights I saw from the base of the falls. Closer to the river was a smaller structure that also had a warm glow coming from the windows. But this one seemed to have a tall chimney which I could make out from the way it blocked the stars. I could also smell smoke coming from it.

Zofie stopped in front of me. I saw a shadow of an arm point in the direction of the river. "The sword is that way. From what I can tell, it looks to be at the edge of the falls themselves. Wort must be in one of the Dragon Pools." I studied the path we would have to take. There were dark shadows along the way, no doubt clumps of bushes and small trees. But our route would take us closer to the building with the tall chimney.

I cocked my head in puzzlement. "How do you know it's there? The sword, I mean."

"The same way I saw the charm on this coat. Those things just stand out to me."

"But aren't charms fairly common?" I scratched my head. "It could just be a really strong one."

"No." She paused for a moment, considering. "Trust me. I know what this one looks like."

Risten had mentioned something about the sword too. "When have you seen it before?"

She didn't answer my question—an uncomfortable silence lingered between us for several heartbeats. "I'll tell you later," she finally said.

Then she moved, heading toward the river, flitting from bush to bush. I followed but was having trouble keeping up with her with any stealth. I tried to get her to slow down. There was no telling if Wort had posted a watch, or worse yet, we startled some servant.

As we passed close to the smaller structure, we paused at the sound of rough male laughter and sloshing water coming from its windows. The smell of fragrant oils and soap drifted toward us. No doubt this served as the inn's bathhouse.

"Bring us som' mor' ale!" came a male voice from within.

I heard water spilling.

"And bring m'som' too!"

Then I heard a feminine screech, followed by the crash of several objects hitting the floor. This, in turn, was followed by a loud, meaty slap.

"I told you I'm not that kind of lady!" yelled a female voice. "You can get your own damn ale."

The door to the bathhouse flew open, and with skirts flying, one very angry serving woman stalked up toward the inn.

"Ah, don't go away. T'was just gettin' to the good part." And both men laughed.

I grimaced, recognizing their voices. They were Wort's men: Dai and Rid. The ones that had nearly killed Spraggel and me.

I leaned close to Zofie. "They're Wort's. He has to be close."

I saw a shadow nod. "That's two of them. Now, where are the others?"

The answer came almost as if on cue from beyond the inn. I saw a torchlight approaching and pointed it out to Zofie. As we watched, a group of four armed men strode purposefully toward the bathhouse. They were carrying someone between them. As they moved into the light of the door the servant had left open, I got a clear look at a limp figure with blonde hair, brown leather pants, and leather vest.

I heard a gasp from Zofie. "Oh Mother of the Creator," she whispered, making the same identification as I did.

It was Risten.

# CHAPTER ELEVEN

# Lies

I couldn't believe Risten was here. She must have snuck away too, which explained how Zofie and I slipped out of camp so easily. "We've got to get closer." I started to move, but Zofie grabbed my arm.

"I can't," she whispered. "My transformation is way overdue. I could accidentally betray our position."

"But if we get too far apart, my curse will become active."

I saw her head turn toward the bathhouse. "I..." I could hear the agony in her voice. "I can't. I mean, I won't be of any help. You're so much stronger. And..."

I felt a sudden pain in my chest: not nearly as sharp as before, but a clear indication something was going on.

"It's starting." She almost sounded relieved. "I've got to hide." She squeezed my arm gently. "Can you please save her? You're the only one that can. If I manage to put some distance between us, your curse will surely assist."

I was glad she had faith in me—and my curse. But six men *was* a little much. I sighed and looked toward the bathhouse. "I'll try."

"Thank you." She gave me a quick kiss on the cheek and took off deep into the night.

I felt the touch still warm on my cheek as I watched her shadow merge into the darkness. *Focus! Don't get all mushy now.*

I crept toward the bathhouse, avoiding the few pools of light, and carefully worked my way to an open window. The scents of bathing herbs and heated water wafted from the open windows. The openings were about shoulder height and unobstructed by glass or bars. A single wooden shutter hung from hinges at the top with a long stick propping it open. I squatted below the window listening intently.

"So you don't know what to do with her either?" came a voice I didn't recognize from inside. "Is Lord Wort still down in that cursed Dragon Pool? How does he stand it? That water's frigid!"

"Bah... the innkeeper gave'm a charm to keep'm warm in there. Feels like a heated bath to'm." That was Dai.

"But he's sitting right at the edge of the damn falls. One slip and he's headed for the rocks." I didn't recognize this voice either.

"He's been out there o'er an hour, bless ou' master's sweet soul." It was either Dai or Rid, I wasn't sure which. He laughed and took a noisy slurp of something.

I slowly stood and risked a quick peek in the window. There were two large wooden tubs with an undressed Dai and Rid reclining in each. Four armed men stood just apart from them. Two of the armed men held an unconscious Risten by her arms. I slunk back down.

"Should we take her to him? Or wait till he comes up."

I heard water splashing. "If t'was me, I'd wait. Wort can be a fit if he's disturbed doin' his thinkin'."

"And what do we do with her? One thing's for sure, she knows her way around a sword. We only got her because she wasn't expecting Blake's sleep charm."

"Bah... Blake doesn't hav' a sleep charm."

"Oh yes, he does. It's on the end of that long stick he swings."

They all chuckled.

"Let's just slit her throat and be done with it."

"That's got my vote. Clean'n up the blood would definitely piss off the servants!"

Water splashed. "Nah, we bet'r not. Wort might want t'finish what he started."

*Finish what he started? Have they fought before?* I shook my head. I couldn't worry about that now. I had to get Risten out of there. But how?

I needed a distraction. I briefly thought about Zofie, but she was in the middle of her transformation. I still had that pulling-a-string-through-my-heart feeling, but it wasn't nearly as strong as before. Was her transformation going slower than normal? I wondered what in the world our collective curses were up to.

I risked another peek and saw Dai with his back to me, getting out of the wooden tub. And I had to say, that was one ugly butt. He stepped in my direction toward the clothes hanging on a line nearby.

I steeled myself. This was the opportunity I needed.

"Psst!" I said. They all looked in my direction. And I dropped back down.

"Now what the twelve hells was that?" I heard the soft slap of wet feet coming my way. I saw him look out the windows across the yard.

"Psst!" I called again. "Down here."

He looked down at me clearly puzzled.

"Come closer. I have something."

The man leaned over further, water dripping on me. "What y'want?"

"This."

I pulled out the stick supporting the heavy shutter, and it clunked him soundly on the head. He took on a glazed look. For good measure, I reached up, pulled it back, and hit him again. He hung half-way out, unmoving under the shutter.

"Hey!" a shout came from inside the building. One of the armed men looked out the next window. After making sure he saw me, I ran toward the inn. "Stop, or I'll cut your arms off and use them for candle holders." I heard a crash as somebody slipped in the water.

I ran up the path, my poor legs nearly cramping from having just climbed the stairs by the falls. Looking back, I only got two to follow me. I had been hoping for three. Passing behind a large bush, I threw myself underneath and clamped a hand over my mouth to hide my heavy breathing.

Suddenly, a slight breeze rustled the brush over me and plucked at my hair. I heard the pursuing footfalls slow and then split with one going to each side of the large bush. On either side of me, I saw shadowed legs pause beside my hiding place.

*Did they know where I was?* I was almost sure they did. But then a cloud passed over the moon, plunging us into absolute darkness. Suddenly I heard running, quickly followed by the sound of metal on metal and the grunts of men fighting. They rather loudly crashed to the ground as they fought, punching on another, each trying to get a grip. I eased out from the bush and took off back toward the bathhouse, the lanterns from the remaining open windows showing me the way.

Behind me, I heard one of the fighting men say, "Hey, stop. It's me. We're fighting each other."

"What? But I was sure it was him."

"You broke my Creator damn nose, you fool!"

"And you ripped out a chunk of my beard."

"With your ugly face, it's an improvement."

I heard more meaty smacks as they restarted their fight. I would have laughed if I'd had any breath left.

I made my way up to the bathhouse and noticed they had pulled poor old Dai in from the window. *But how to get to Risten?* I spied a dirty work apron hanging on a peg close to the door. Quickly unbuckling my sword, I dropped it on the ground in the shadows just outside the door then quickly rolled up my sleeves. Grabbing the apron, I slipped it on, messed up my hair, and plastered a slack expression on my face. Slouching, I ran the last few steps to stand in the open door.

I could see Rid, a towel around his waist, kneeling beside a total unconscious Dai sprawled out on the floor. The two men holding Risten had dropped her and were trying to peer out the windows.

"Sars," I called out breathlessly from the doorway, trying to deliberately garble my words. I bowed to them and rambled on. I kept my face down, and my head hunched into my shoulders. "M'just a simple servant from t'house. I came straight to ya. Two of yar men and... and... they're hurt, sars. Blood and everything." I wrung my hands in pretend fear. "I didn't know wha' to do."

"I don't remember seeing you," accused Rid. He stood up, holding his towel.

My heart skipped a beat. I hoped they didn't see the sweat on my forehead. "M'sorry, sar." I looked at my feet, my hands still writhing. "Master says I'm dumber'n ox, sars. I watch the fires at night. Master says 'tis all I'm good for, sars."

Dismissing me with his eyes, one of the men turned toward the other two. "Dammit. I told you they'd be others following the girl."

Rid stepped closer, motioning to the armed men. "Go see what happened to those two idiots. The woman's tied up. She's not going anywhere." As he was stepping over her, one the men grinned evilly and kicked her. I could have sworn I saw her wince ever so slightly. Perhaps Risten wasn't as unconscious as they believed.

"Boy!" ordered Rid, looking at me. I jumped as if startled. "Bring me my clothes."

I really didn't want to get too close to Rid. He might recognize me. "But the fires, sar." I pleaded. "They'll go out."

"I don't give a damn about the fires. Get me my clothes."

I saw them hanging on a line in the back of the bathhouse. I dare not protest too much. "Yes, sar."

I went and pulled them down, trying to think of some way to untie her. I took him the clothes and held them out to him, my head bowed. Rid looked up at me and then did a double take. He roughly grabbed my chin and pulled it up. "I know you... You're no servant. You were with that scribe back in Iron Landing."

The sweat on my forehead turned cold, and I heard that deep, dark laugh again.

Suddenly, all three wooden tubs burst, sending water cascading all across the floor in a miniature flood. The shutters on all the windows suddenly slammed shut—and Rid's towel fell off. The man made no attempt to cover himself, but instead lunged toward me and pinned me against the back wall by the throat. I fought and pulled at his hands, which were as strong as iron bands.

He grinned wickedly. "I'm gonna enjoy this."

I felt my vision begin to dim. I guess I had finally found something my curse couldn't save me from.

Suddenly I heard a meaty smack, and Rid released me, collapsing in a heap on the floor. I staggered and gasped for air. Risten stood behind him, brandishing a wooden board and smiling wickedly.

"How?" I croaked.

She shrugged. "Your curse snapped the ropes at the same time the barrels burst. Very efficient. It not only freed me but gave me a weapon."

"Did those men hurt you?"

"Only my head. I don't know what they hit me with, but I've got a headache from the Creator's hell and a lump the size of Mount Eternal." She poked the unconscious man with her toe. "Where's Zofie? I know she's got to be with you. You're not smart enough to get here by yourself, and Zofie's afraid to do anything alone."

"She went to hide while she transforms."

Her lips rose into a crooked smile. "I bet she went toward the river, didn't she?"

My mouth fell open. *I'm stupid. She's gone after the sword!*

Risten sighed. "Let's go. Some protector you are."

"But she hasn't completed her transformation. At least I haven't felt more than a steady pull."

We both tore out the door heading for the river. I grabbed my sword as we went out the door.

"I've seen her delay her transformation," Risten whispered as we ran. "I'm not sure how she does it, but it's something to do with being a myst-seer. It costs her, and I've only seen her do it one time. But that one time she held it off for a full hour before it finally overwhelmed her. She said the extra pain wasn't worth it, although the transformation itself went extremely fast."

I nodded. That must be why I had that low-level pain in my chest. She was fighting her curse.

Running toward the falls, I could see a raised walk, almost a small pier, go out over the water near the river bank and then turn a corner in the direction of the falls, running parallel to the bank. It was lit by dim lanterns from poles along its length. At its end, a much longer pole hung over the water, illuminating the pool area just shy of where the water went over the edge. The river current appeared to be gentle in this section of the falls with the current getting stronger and deeper further toward the middle. But it was clear from the way the splashing water suddenly disappeared over a very sharply defined edge, that there was nothing beyond but air. And here, close to that edge, the roar of the water was loud. You could almost feel its power in your very bones. That was a lot of water, falling a long, long way down.

And just shy of the edge, I could make out the Dragon Pools: holes in the rock the swirling water had cut out over time. The pool itself was big enough to hold three or four people. There was no lantern directly over it, but there was enough light coming from the lanterns on the walk-way that we could make out a lone occupant—Wort. The water came up to his shoulders as he sat with his back to us and seemed to be staring out over the top of the falls.

We squatted behind a lone bush—our last piece of cover before hitting the raised walkway. Risten studied the area around Wort. "I don't see any guards so he must really be alone." She looked over her shoulder at me and held out a hand. "Give me your sword."

"What! You can't be serious?" I gazed back at her levelly. "You're going to get yourself killed."

"If I do, he's coming with me." She held out a hand again. "Now let me have it."

"No." I glared back. "Zofie and I came up here to prevent you from trying to fight him. You may be better than he is, but he's got that sword."

She suddenly grabbed me by the shirt and jerked me to within a finger's breadth of her face. "Listen, shit for brains, that man killed my master. He was like a *father* to me. And I mean to have my revenge. So I will have that sword, or I will pull off your arms to get it."

I smirked. "And just how are you going to take it? The moment you touch me, my curse will come up with something nasty before you've even gotten close."

"Coren...!"

And suddenly everything clicked in place. It was all so clear.

"You planned this, didn't you?" I pointed an accusing finger at her. "You knew you'd never get a weapon close to Wort. So, you told Zofie we were splitting up and that you were coming up here for Wort. *You knew* she would try to get up here before you and bring me with her. And with me, would come my sword. *Your Master's old sword.*"

"And what of it?" She gave me a cruel smile. "It's only fitting that the bastard die by my hand using my old master's sword."

"And what of Zofie? You dragged her into your death wish."

"She'll be fine. She won't approach him when she's about to transform. Especially without her powers."

I slowly brought up my hand and wrapped my fingers around the hand she was using to hold my shirt. "I will not let you throw your life away. Zofie needs you. Now let go of me before my curse does something I can't reverse."

She glared at me—our faces nearly touching. "You're right. I can't attack you." One side of her mouth went up in an amused smile. "So I'll have to do it another way." She jerked me forward and into a kiss. I tried to push away from her, but she held me firm for several heartbeats. When she finally released me, I sprawled backward and landed on my butt. She raised the sword in triumph, having pulled it out while I was *distracted*.

"You give that..." but I broke off. I heard a voice nearby. My eyes went wide in disbelief. Risten heard it too and froze in place.

"Oh, mother of the Creator," Risten whispered. "She wouldn't."

"Wort! I have finally found you," I heard Zofie shout over the roar of the falls. "I call upon your honor as a warrior to return what was stolen. The sword was given to my family hundreds of years ago in order to be kept safe. I don't know what Wynn told you, but it's extremely dangerous and will bring you great harm. I beg you to turn it over to us."

Risten and I both looked around the edges of the bush to find a lone figure stepping out onto the walkway. She was still wearing the robe she had found earlier with the hood pulled up and covering her from head to ankle. I only knew for sure it was her from my mismatched socks on her feet.

I looked over my shoulder at Risten. "What were you saying about Zofie not approaching Wort?"

Risten shook her head violently. "She wasn't supposed to do that."

In his pool, Wort turned his head to look at Zofie, but otherwise sat quietly in his pool, not in the least concerned. "You're that brat's sister, are you not?" he asked.

Zofie gave a slight nod.

"Then you know it was given to me in payment for a service. A service I completed. So go away. You have no claim on the sword. Leave now, and I might forget to tell your brother I saw you."

Zofie stepped to the edge of the ramp. "It was not my brother's to give, and that service was to kill my father's friends!"

"And what of it? It's mine now, and I'm not giving it up. Now be quiet. I'm trying to decide what other kingdom to take over first. Wynn said I could have my pick."

From up the hill in the direction of the bathhouse, I could see Wort's men had gathered themselves together and were coming our way armed with torches and their swords. They didn't look happy either.

Risten and I looked at one other. She poked a single finger into my chest. "You do something about Wort's men. Buy me some time. I'll deal with that bastard."

"We need to get out of here. If you want to kill yourself, so be it, but I won't let you get Zofie killed too."

"You let me worry about that." And she took off running toward the walkway.

"Creator!" I spat. "That woman is so infuriating!" I turned in the direction of the approaching men. How was I going to hold them off with nothing but my bare hands? I was too close to Zofie to count on my curse. Then the obvious choice was to run toward them, and once away from Zofie, let my curse deal with them. I leaned in their direction, but hesitated. My curse would likely kill them or at least seriously maim them. The thought made my stomach queasy. I glanced after Risten. She had already made it to the wooden walkway and, with sword in hand, was rapidly running toward them.

Wort saw her coming and slowly stood. The water streamed off him, and with his broad chest and thick arms, he looked like a colossus emerging from the ocean. But there was no mistaking the look of murder in his eyes. Wort knew his attacker would be at a distinct disadvantage since the pool would limit mobility. All he had to do was wait for her to step within his reach. He raised the sword high, and I could see it emitted a definite warning glow—a reminder of its terrible power.

Zofie yelled at Risten to stop. But of course, the sword-master didn't. Zofie was totally defenseless, standing alone between the two warriors.

As I watched the tragedy unfold, I knew with certainty that Risten was going to die. This was no prophesy, only simple reasoning. No amount of sword-master skill was going to allow her to kill Wort with his current advantage. And after Risten, Zofie would be next. There was no way Wort would let her live.

I swore. I had to do something to change that fate. "Please Creator," I begged. "Let my curse do something good for once."

I turned and ran after Risten as rapidly as my legs could carry me. I heard the men behind me shout as they saw me, but I was committed now.

Risten raised her own sword and was clearly focused solely on her enemy. Zofie stepped in front of her, but Risten brushed right past, upsetting her cousin's balance. Zofie staggered, and a board snapped under her foot. Risten, now with her back to her cousin, didn't see Zofie tumble backward off the walkway into the water.

*Creator, no!*

The waters in that portion of the river were swift. They caught the robe she wore and pulled her further into the current. "Zofie!" I yelled.

She floundered in the now deep water, headed straight for the edge. Suddenly, the pain in my chest grew overwhelming, and I stumbled to my knees. Oh Creator, now of all times for her to transform! I clutched my chest and forced myself to crawl out onto the walkway, fighting to get to her in time...

But the dark current swept her over the edge.

And she was gone.

*I was too late!* I pounded my fist into the boards of the walkway. I sat up, still clutching my chest. The pain was intense. And then suddenly it stopped. Had her transformation completed, or had she died?

Risten hadn't even noticed Zofie falling; she was so focused on her opponent. She had leaped onto the rocks beside the pool. It was a treacherous place and looked very slippery. Wort stood with his sword raised calmly, tracking her every move. He said something I couldn't make out and grinned. Whatever it was, it infuriated Risten, and she recklessly lunged forward. Wort was quick to counter with a rapid swing which she was barely able to duck under. But Wort was ready to swing again, and from the smile on his face, I knew this was going to be the final blow.

*Coren, you have to jump!*

Zofie? Was that Zofie! *She was alive!* I didn't question her command, although I did wonder how I could hear her over the roar of the falls.

With my feet pounding off the boards, I ran to the edge of the walkway and leaped straight toward Risten. My jump was exceptionally long—no doubt aided by my curse. I plowed into Risten and grabbed her firmly.

"Nooooo!" she yelled.

Wort's sword whizzed by my head close enough to slice off a clump of hair.

Then Risten and I sailed over the edge and into the darkness.

The black air swallowed us greedily. I felt my clothes flapping in the currents as we tumbled earthward. I lost track of Risten in our fall. All I could see was the white foam of where the water met rock rising toward me fast. It was terrifying. I couldn't find the courage to breathe.

*Don't worry. I've got you.*

And suddenly I sensed a large body loom up beside me. Faster than I could comprehend, I felt something encircle my waist. And with a sudden jerk, I was no longer falling... but flying over the water and gently rising into the air.

I could make out the last of the moonlight shining off the river, and behind me, the roar of the falls began to fade away. Through the scream of the wind, I could make out the steady flapping of broad wings, and circling my chest was what felt like a huge claw. Zofie must have transformed into a *very* large bird.

*You two are as heavy as rocks!* I heard Zofie say. *I need a place to land and soon. I can't maintain this height.*

I couldn't help but notice that Zofie's voice sounded different. In fact, it was like I was hearing it in the back of my head.

"Uh... Zofie? Your voice. It's like you're not using your mouth."

*I'm not. This form can't make words, so you're hearing me in your head. Apparently, your curse decided not only was I to be the biggest bird in all of creation, but that we also need to keep in touch. Instead of speech, I can project my thoughts into your head, and I can hear what you're thinking.*

"Does that mean you can read my mind?" I shouted. The image of her dressing in the moonlight came to mind. I suddenly panicked. There were definitely some things in my head I didn't want to share.

*I don't know.* She sounded rather upset. *This is just so strange. I'm having to be careful what I think. A girl has got to have some secrets. I really don't like what your curse has done to me.*

"So what kind of a bird are you?"

There was a pause. *I... I don't know. Your curse has really distorted this form. It feels unnatural.*

"But you're all right?"

*I... Don't take this the wrong way. But I don't want to talk right now. I've got too much to think about.*

That took me by surprise. I thought she would be pleased that we had gotten Risten out alive. It almost sounded like she didn't want to be around me.

I saw the river approaching, and I realized what she had said was true. The ground was indeed approaching faster than I would have liked.

I heard the swoosh of a sword close to my head. I pulled back making Zofie rock in her flight—she squawked in protest. Risten, in her other claw, was leaning my way trying to reach me with the sword. "You son of a jackal. When I get free, I'm going to *kill* you. *I almost had him!*"

"No, you didn't. If I hadn't pushed you off, he would have sliced you in two, and you know it."

"I... You..." I could hear her tears in her voice. "You should have let me die. I was going to take him with me."

Now I was angry. "You coward! Would your master really have wanted that? I don't think so."

I heard her sob.

*Sorry to interrupt, but I'm running out of air. I've got to put you down somewhere.*

I felt the beat of Zofie's wings change, and our forward speed slowed down.

"How close are we to camp?"

*Very close. I can see their campfire from here.*

"All right. Just put me down any..." And Zofie released her grip on me, and I fell face-first into the water. *Any place but the river!*

Absolute terror gripped me as I foundered. *Water! I was in the water!* It took me a moment to realize it wasn't deep at all. In fact, it only came up to my knees. I sat for a moment in the gentle current while I regained my composure. I shook my head. I could face down Wort and his men, no problem. But get thrown into a puddle of water, and I nearly die in panic.

Completely soaked, I stood up and scanned the sky looking for Zofie, but I didn't see a sign of her. Still carrying my sword, Risten slogged out of the water a few paces away, but didn't even look my way. I let her get a safe distance before I followed. I wanted to keep my body intact.

"Zofie?" I called softly. Maybe I could get some answers from her. "Zofie, where are you?" But she didn't answer. I stood there in the darkness, dripping wet, and listening to the night. I sensed she was close by, yet she didn't answer. I only got a low-level feeling of disquiet coming from her. Not that I could blame her. My curse had struck again. My stomach clenched in worry and guilt.

"Zofie, I know you're there."

I held my breath and listened, but still no answer. I sighed. Turning toward camp, I followed in Risten's path and tried to find my way up the bank. Every squish of my waterlogged boots reminded me of just how much I hated being wet.

Our return to camp was uneventful. The Sylph set as a guard recognized us and let us pass without disturbing the others. Spraggel was already loudly snoring, so while I was eager to tell him the evening's adventures, I let him sleep. It wasn't anything that couldn't wait.

Risten ignored me and quickly rolled up in her blanket without saying a word. For myself, I was forever grateful to get out of my own damp clothes and wrap up in my dry blanket. I set everything to dry by the fire's remaining coals before laying down myself. I gazed into the crackling embers and wondered where Zofie was. I needed to apologize for what my curse had done to her. While her presence may have a damping effect on my curse, it didn't stop it from abusing her.

But there was so much about this past night that I didn't understand. Wort had recognized Zofie. Not only that, but Risten had fought him before tonight. And who was Wynn, and why was Wort working for him? I felt both Zofie and Risten were keeping something from me. Something big.

*And you don't have secrets?* The thought came unbidden. *Like how you've caused so much misfortune that no one wants to be around you. How your own mother arranged for you to leave because she feared for her own life. And how you killed your own father.* I didn't exactly volunteer much information to Zofie either.

I turned over, facing away from the dying fire, and shut my eyes. I tried to push those thoughts away. Secrets? Yes, they likely had some, but I could probably teach them a thing or two myself.

# CHAPTER TWELVE

# Unwilling Participants

The next day, we parted company from our Sylph escort. We explained that the giant turtle had gone ahead upriver, and we were following on horseback. They accepted the story and loaded up their barge for the relatively easy trip downstream. I couldn't help but notice that Yvonnani and Spraggel seemed reluctant to part. They had been spending a lot of time together on and off the barge. I had a sneaking suspicion I might see more of Yvonnani in the future. What had Spraggel told me back in Iron Landing? *I may be old, but I'm not dead.* Well, I think this definitely proved it.

After saying goodbye to our new friends, we mounted up and resumed our original course toward the Temple of Daili. From what the Sylph had told us, if we headed northwest, we would shortly leave the deep forest, and after traveling a day or two across steeply hilled meadows, we would encounter the road to the city of Ceadinone. And in the heart of Ceadinone was the Temple of Daili.

Spraggel seemed energized by our encounter with the Sylph. He apparently had been taking notes and was planning out a book on their customs and history. Of course, Yvonnani had volunteered to help him with his research. I hadn't seen him this happy in all the years we'd been together.

Risten, on the other hand, had hardly spoken a word since our last adventure. And it was pretty obvious that I was the reason. For Spraggel at least, she would give at least two-word answers, but for me, she only showed outright contempt. I couldn't understand her anger. We had saved her life, after all. To her credit, I did find my sword propped up on my belongings that first morning. I guess it was as close as I was going to get to a thank you.

As for Zofie—she didn't make an appearance. I did occasionally spot a bird soaring high above us. I suspected it was her, but I couldn't know for sure. She also wouldn't answer when I called to her. I was fairly sure she could hear me. It was most uncharacteristic for her. I tried to convince myself that it was because we were still in a partially forested area and landing spots for someone her size must be few and far between. I tried to ask Risten about it, but she wouldn't answer. Although on more than one occasion, I caught her searching the skies, so perhaps she was a little concerned too.

Zofie didn't return that first evening, nor did she appear the next day, nor the next. And my worries grew. What if she was injured? What if my curse had made her lose her mind?

What if she was just avoiding me?

I continued to ask Risten about my concern that she was injured or worse, and I guess I finally bothered her enough that she finally spoke. "Zofie's fine," she said. "She came to see me last night while you were sleeping. She'll come around when she's ready."

On that third evening of her absence, I decided I had had enough. At midnight, I went out into the forest by myself to a large clearing I had found earlier. I stood in the middle of the grass and held up my feeble amulet so she could tell it was me. Then I started calling her. My curse had been unusually quiet, so I was reasonably confident she wasn't that far away.

"Zofie! Are you there? Won't you come out and tell me what's wrong." But there was nothing. "Please!"

Suddenly, I felt a rush of wind and the snap of wings beside me. Turning toward it, I saw a huge bird settle down gently on its rather sizeable legs. Holding my amulet high, I saw what resembled an extraordinarily large horned owl with huge eyes and a beautiful set of reddish feathers tipped in white. She had to be at least twice my height, if not more. But unlike her giant turtle form, this animal didn't look natural. It had disproportionately large wings, broad muscular shoulders, and a head much smaller than what I would expect for its size.

I drew a deep breath and let it out slowly. I knew in an instant what had happened. Zofie's form had been altered to allow her to carry heavy loads. Two human-sized loads, in fact, from the top of a cliff. My curse had protected me.

At Zofie's expense.

*Now you know,* she said. *I'm a monster.* Her wings fluttered in agitation. *I'm repulsive.*

"Is that what's wrong?" I asked. "You think I won't want to see you?" I stepped closer, but she flinched back. "Your form has nothing to do with it. I miss the conversations we had back on the river. I... I like being around you. You're the nicest person I've encountered. Won't you at least talk to me again?"

She just looked at me with her large owl eyes and didn't say anything at first.

*I can't, Coren. You scare me. Or rather, your curse does.*

I shook my head. "I'm not sure I understand. It does cause things to happen, but it's usually well behaved if we're together."

She cocked her head to one side in a very bird-like gesture. *Well behaved? LOOK AT ME! I'm a bird that shouldn't exist! And there's no telling* what else it could do. She paused. *Your curse has taken over my own. Not neutralized it. Not released it. But taken it over! Before our curses connected, I would turn into a normal animal. I knew exactly when I transformed and for how long. But now, your curse turns me into giant turtles and huge birds that don't naturally exist. On top of that, it includes attributes that aren't in the layout of my curse. And this last transformation, it delayed the change until it was ready for me to transform.*

"Risten thought you had delayed it."

*It was your curse. And the transformation hurt so bad, I was almost ready to crash into the rocks just to end it.*

She paused and briefly looked up at the night sky, before slowly lowering her gaze back to me.

*Coren. I honestly like you too. You're the first friend I've had outside of Risten. But your curse... whatever it's doing, it's doing it for you, Coren. Not for me. Not for Risten. But for you! I'm worried that it will decide to turn me into some kind of freak thing and just leave me there.*

I didn't know what to say to her. It dawned on me that everything she said was true. I felt myself deflating under her owlish stare. "I don't know what to do to stop it."

*That's the sad part. I know you don't. And it's tearing me apart inside.*

We stood staring silently at each other.

She gave a very human-like sigh in my head. *Coren, I really like being around you, and I'll continue to help with tracking down the shield. But right now, I think I need to keep a little distance until we can figure this out.* She turned and leaped into the air. *I'm sorry.*

"Wait...! I've got so much to ask you."

I reached a hand out toward her ready to plead. But I knew she was right. I let it drop to my side and stumbled back to camp. I really felt alone now.

And so our dysfunctional, non-communicative group traveled: Risten barely talking to me, Zofie not talking to me at all, and Spraggel talking non-stop.

It was almost a relief that on the seventh day after leaving the river, we arrived at the city of Ceadinone. We paused to inspect it from a nearby hill.

It was a large city, the second largest in the kingdom: tall walls surrounding it and a gate on both the north and south sides. Zofie had scouted the area from the air and reported the temple was in the exact center of the city with a narrow mote around it. And it was heavily armed. It was more of a fortress than a temple.

Risten put one foot up on a stump and leaned in the city's direction. "Maybe I'll get to cross blades with one of those temple guards. I've been itching for a fight since Dragon Falls."

Spraggel looked at her in disbelief. "Risten, have you been this far north before?"

She shrugged. "No. Is there something special I need to know?"

"Only that women aren't allowed to carry any offensive weapon in the city, which includes swords. Touching any blade longer than your own hand is strictly forbidden. The penalty is death."

Risten's mouth fell open. "What! Surely you jest."

Spraggel shook his head. "I wish I was. When we go through the city gate, you'll be searched. So prepare yourself. I suggest you give all your weapons to Coren to hold until we leave."

"Like hell am I handing over my sword," she huffed. "I'll be damned if I give it up."

Spraggel shrugged. "All right. Then you'll have to wait outside until we return." He looked back at the city. From the angle Risten stood, she couldn't see Spraggel's sly smile. "It's probably for the best anyway. Wort might show up, and we wouldn't want you tangling with him."

Risten didn't hesitate to pull out her sword and scabbard and shove them at me.

At Zofie's suggestion, we decided it would be best for her to stay outside the city and be our eyes from above. If she stayed fairly close, she and I could keep in touch using our mental way of communicating.

And as for me, I would just have to be careful with my curse.

We went to the southern gate and paid our entry taxes. This consisted of a tax on our swords, a tax on our horses, a tax on our gold—and even a woman tax. Spraggel assured us that while it was unusual in the kingdom, it was normal for this city. Risten's face turned red, and she nearly shook with rage as she was lined up with the horses and assessed just as they would any of the livestock. Despite the humiliation, she managed to swallow her anger, and we made it through with no issue. Spraggel wisely decided to rush Risten to an inn and get her off the street before it became too much for her. For myself, I was troubled by the whole process. Even the idea of putting a price on a person, male or female, just seemed so wrong.

The next morning, with the sun just barely above the horizon, Spraggel burst into our room, slamming the door loudly against the wall as he pushed inside and shattering whatever hopes I'd had for a few more moments of sleep.

Both Risten and I had chosen to lay a bit longer in our respective sleeping places: Spraggel and I had the straw bed and Risten a pallet on the floor beside us.

"Coren! Get up, lad." Spraggel kicked my bed. "No time to just lay around. I know how to get us inside the temple." He was carrying a large bundle of clothing.

I was immediately awake and swung my feet to the floor, accidentally kicking the blanket-covered Risten lying beside the bed. The room was tiny, so she hadn't had a lot of choice when bedding down.

"Hey!" she yelled. "Watch where you're putting your feet!" She covered her head with the blanket.

"Spraggel, what's wrong?" I asked, stepping carefully over Risten to close the open door.

My master smiled broadly, seemingly quite proud of himself. "Last night, I figured it out." Spraggel dropped a bundle of clothing on the bed. "How to get us into the temple."

"Can't we just walk up to the door and say, hey, we're on a mission so let us in?"

"Of course not." Spraggel frowned. "Wort arrived yesterday and is already at the temple trying to see the Scroll of Nobem. He showed them my copy of the *Armeda ne Emour* and immediately got their attention. He's trying to negotiate a deal as we speak."

Risten threw off her cover and suddenly sat up. "Did you say Wort is in this city?" She used her fingers to comb back her hair; she had loosened her braid before laying down.

Spraggel nodded happily. "Indeed he is. And since he's still here, that means they haven't given him the location of Ruin's Shield yet. But the negotiations can't be far from over. Apparently, they really want the book, but don't want to let him see the Scroll of Nobem because it's sacred to them."

I scratched my head. "How did Wort get here ahead of us? I was sure we would beat him."

Spraggel started going through the clothes he'd brought and pulled out a loaf of bread hidden in the folds. "I heard his horses were in bad shape. Apparently, he drove them pretty hard." He broke the bread and handed a piece to both me and Risten.

"We must have spooked him at Dragon Falls." I took a big bite of the bread, marveling at the taste. We hadn't had good bread in almost a month. "He's been trying to outrun us."

Risten shifted to a cross-legged position on her pallet. She pinched off a bit of her bread and popped it into her mouth. "But you didn't answer Coren's original question: Why can't we just go in and explain the situation?"

Spraggel picked up one of the items of clothing and held it up to himself. It was a long robe. "Because he's already told them he's being chased by some peace-loving heathens that want to break his magical sword. That really stirred them up. Intentionally breaking a weapon is the same as killing one of their deities. And on top of that, he told them we have a woman with us who carries a sword." He looked at us levelly. "So we'll likely be arrested if they find us."

Risten looked disgusted. "This city is really messed up."

Spraggel nodded. "And so is worshiping war. But that's not all of it. They have a charm over the temple gates to detect any female trying to get in." He tossed one of the robes to me. "Try this on to see if it fits."

I held up the robe. It looked a little big. I slipped it over my head. "And what is this for?"

Spraggel grinned. "You and I are going to pass ourselves off as priests."

Risten took a big bite of her bread. "What about me. How am I getting in?"

Spraggel dug through the pile of clothes. "Well, you're a little more difficult." He tossed her some clothes. "Please don't skewer me, but this is your disguise."

Risten held up two items... and I did a double take: one was a skimpy white halter and the other a very short white skirt.

Risten frowned. "Where's the rest of it?"

Spraggel held up a single finger. "Oh, yes. I forgot this."

He tossed her a short white hooded shirt, which opened fairly far down the front, and length-wise, looked barely long enough to reach the skirt.

"You've got to be kidding." Risten held it up in disbelief. "Don't I at least get shoes," she said sarcastically.

"Sorry, you'll have to go barefoot."

"What!"

Spraggel ducked his head. "You're going as a sacrifice for Battle."

Risten looked up at Spraggel with death in her eyes. She stabbed the air with her finger. "There is no way... I'm going... as a sacrifice... especially in this city... and certainly not in this... *costume!*" She threw the clothes at him.

Spraggel caught them and tossed them back to Risten. "I'm open to other ideas. Either you go as a sacrifice, or you stay here. It's the only way you can get in. But make up your mind quick. Rumor has it, they're going to complete the bargain tonight. The high priest has been examining my book in the same room as the Scroll of Nobem. So once the deal is struck, Wort will almost immediately learn the shield's location. We *must* get my book back so their negotiations fall apart."

Risten looked at him with the expression of someone who had just eaten a rotten lemon.

I tried to help ease her distress. "Don't worry. I've seen women around Iron Landing wear as much when it's hot outside."

Risten glared at me. "You really don't get it, do you? The taxes on the women, the prohibition on swords, and finally this sacrifice costume. Women are nothing but possessions to these priests. Animal stock." She shook the clothes at me. "And do you honestly think a woman is going to be sacrificed wearing this!" She snorted. "There will be a sacrifice all right, but it won't be her life. It will be her honor. And that's only if she's lucky."

My eyes went wide. "But... but that's just wrong!"

Spraggel had a sour expression. "Indeed, rumor has it that this High Priest Benzel has drifted from the path and developed an addiction for women. That is not the way of Daili. Priests of Daili are supposed to be celibate. In fact, this discrimination against women only came about since Benzel rose to his office."

I shook my head. I couldn't believe that this so-called priest used women like that. Sure females were frustrating—Risten as a case in point—but they were still human. This definitely needed to be stopped. I wished I could direct my curse on the priests. That would be an interesting change.

I lowered my gaze. "I'm sorry, Risten. I didn't think. We'll have to find some other way to get you inside."

She held up the halter by the tips of her fingers, letting it dangle in front of her. "Well, while you might not be very smart, you at least have some integrity." She eyed the clothes. "But Spraggel's plan is sound. They wouldn't expect one of their worthless women to actually know how to use a sword. That could be a strong advantage." She looked to Spraggel and sighed deeply. "I'll do it under one condition."

Spraggel's eyebrows went up. "And what might that be?"

Risten grinned. "That if Wort comes along, you won't stop me from killing him."

I frowned. "Risten, I don't think that's a good idea..."

Risten drew her sword and pointed it at my throat. "And one more thing. Don't you dare tell Zofie. I don't want her doing something stupid to stop me." She looked back to Spraggel. "Now are you going to meet my condition, or do you two go in without a sword-master?"

Spraggel and I exchanged a glance. He gave a big sigh. "I think encountering Wort will be unlikely, but should we, I agree to your condition."

She grinned. It was the first time I'd seen her happy in days.

Spraggel rubbed his hands together. "All right, Coren. Since that's settled, let's go find a barber."

"A barber?"

Spraggel's eyes sparkled with mirth. "Why, of course. You didn't think Risten was the only one who had to make a sacrifice for her costume." He leaned close and pointed to his beard. "No facial hair."

"Wow, you're willing to give up your beard?" Spraggel was proud of this beard. Giving it up really spoke to how dedicated he was to getting to the shield before Wort.

The elder nodded and then smiled wickedly. "And of course, they shave their heads."

"What!"

Risten laughed. "So I won't be the only one going in almost naked."

Spraggel grew serious. "And that's not all. You're going to have to take off your leather wrist cover. Priests aren't allowed to wear any kind of ornament."

I put a protective hand over my left wrist and shook my head, a sudden fear in my heart. I had kept it covered ever since it showed up after my father's death. "But that covers my curse anchor. Can't I just keep that hand hidden?"

The elder shook his head. "I'm sorry, Coren, the robe sleeves only come to just below the elbow, and the priests walk with their hands clasped in front of them once inside the temple. You'll stand out immediately with your wrist guard on. But your curse, on the other hand, looks like a tattoo to the untrained eye, and tattoos are acceptable." He gave a dismissing wave and tried to make light of it. "Besides, it doesn't stop your curse anyway."

I looked down at the leather covering as if a coiled snake were hiding behind it. In a sense, there was.

"But..." I said weakly. "Everyone will see it."

Risten's hand came down on my shoulder, and I looked up at her in misery. For the first time since meeting her, she seemed... sympathetic. She smiled reassuringly. "Coren, I have something in my background that I'm not really fond of. And I've hated it for years. But my master told me once that if you have something you despise about yourself, and you treat it as a weakness, it becomes a weakness. But if you treat it as a strength..." She raised her eyebrows and inclined her head to let me finish it.

*It becomes a strength.*

She gave my shoulder a squeeze before quickly turning away in embarrassment. "I think I'll go to the baths with you," she said a little louder than she needed to. "I'll no doubt need to be suitably bathed, and Creator forbid, *perfumed!* It'll take me a week to get the stench off!"

I looked down at the wrist guard. *A strength?* Could a curse be a strength? The thought was so alien, I couldn't wrap my head around it.

*A strength?* How could something so deadly be a strength?

As they gathered up their belongings, I took a deep breath and unfastened the leather tie. But I hesitated. *I have to do this,* I told myself.

Otherwise, the plan won't work. *I have to.* Taking another big, slow breath, I steeled myself and pulled it off. Then, for the first time in years, I really looked at my curse.

It was just as I remembered. An oddly curved, almost flowing, triangle sitting angled on my wrist. Around the perimeter was what looked like tiny writing that could be runes. In any case, they were too tiny for me to make out. And inside it was a single stylized eye, but with the eye closed. I got a chill looking at it. I had been told that it was an oddly shaped curse anchor—most were round.

*Turn a weakness into a strength?*

What did I have to lose?

I quickly joined the others in gathering up our belongings, and together we headed out to complete our preparations. But there was one item left behind lying on the bed—

My wrist guard.

# CHAPTER THIRTEEN

# An
# Unexpected Book

Risten tugged at the bindings around her wrists. "My hands are going numb. I'm telling you they're too tight!"

"Shhh..." I whispered. "You'll give us away. And they're tied just fine. Any less and they'll get suspicious." I nodded and smiled to the priest walking down the road toward us.

The priest, robed as we were in a solid black wool robe, nodded in return, but his eyes were fixed on Risten's bare legs. She was wearing the halter, skirt, shirt, and after much complaining, barefoot. But Spraggel had shown us the practical side of the costume. With a little rigging, the halter provided a way to strap her sword to her back, while the shirt managed to conceal it. Plus with Risten's well-toned legs and arms as a distraction, it was the perfect hiding place.

"A heroic death to you, brother," said the priest distractedly as he passed.

Spraggel and I nodded, replying likewise. When he was out of ear-shot, Risten mumbled to herself. "I hate this. It's so humiliating!"

I tried to ignore the image of beauty walking beside me; actually a little thankful she couldn't hit me. Risten's time spent as a sword-master was evident from the well-defined muscles in her arms and legs. She walked with a grace that spoke dancer, unless you knew her true occupation. She had already caught me staring once and would have kicked me if she could.

"I mean this in a good way, but you really do look good," I offered.

She glared at me. "You are so dead."

I forced a smile. "Yeah, yeah. You can pick over the scraps Zofie leaves."

When Zofie found out what we were doing, she was less than pleased—especially when she found out about Risten's disguise. She became so agitated that I thought she was going to literally eat me.

I felt strangely naked myself, the air cool against my newly shaved head and face. Not to mention my bare wrist with my curse anchor in full display. It took all my will power to leave the mark exposed for the world to see.

We walked up a wide stone avenue going uphill toward the temple, which was visible at the end of the long straight street. The late afternoon sun shaded the stone-paved avenue itself, but illuminated the temple so that it almost glowed a brilliant white. The temple itself was a very strange structure for a temple. It seemed more like a fortress. It had high stone walls—higher than the city—and a small mote surrounding it. A single drawbridge spanned the mote. On top of its high walls, I could see men carrying pikes, pacing back and forth on watch. And inside, rising above the walls, were three tall towers flying the deep burgundy flags of Daili. Woe to the army that tried to lay siege to that structure.

I glanced over my shoulder at the sun—we only had about an hour of daylight left. We had debated at length over the timing of our plan with Spraggel wanting us to do it as late as possible to ease our escape. However, Zofie and Risten had argued for earlier since tonight was a new moon, and Zofie would likely transform a few hours after dark. We eventually compromised and decided to go in late in the day but leave by dusk.

I looked up into the narrow strip of blue sky visible between the buildings. Way up above us, I could make a tiny spec seeming to float in a broad circle. Zofie was scouting for us.

"See anything, Zofie?" I asked quietly.

*Nothing unusual. Just the normal flow of traffic. The temple is larger than a small city all by itself. But I dare not get too much closer. The guards are very sharp-eyed, and they have some pretty strong crossbows. They nearly hit me this morning.*

The plan was simple. We use Risten to get into the High Priest's chambers. Spraggel would look for the scroll, I would run interference, and Zofie would fly us out. Should be easy. I tried to ignore the million things that could possibly go wrong. Number one on my list was my curse. So far it was behaving. Most likely it had decided I didn't need any help messing things up, I would handle that nicely by myself.

I glanced up at the sky one last time, taking comfort in that tiny spec. "Just stay as close as you can, Zofie, in case we get in trouble and need to get out."

*With these eyes and ears, I know exactly where you are. So don't worry. The only thing you have to worry about are the instincts of this body—they're a little strong. I'll just have to resist the urge to eat you.*

I chuckled to myself. "Thanks. Now I know what a mouse feels like."

Despite the circumstances, it was good that Zofie was talking to me again—at least a little bit. I desperately hoped my curse didn't do anything to drive her further away. We definitely worked well together. Plus there was just something about her that—fascinated me. *All right, admit it,* I thought to myself. *You like her.* I couldn't suppress the smile on my face.

As the temple grew closer, I wondered where they got all the riches to build it. War must be very profitable.

"Master," I said, marveling at how much younger Spraggel looked without his beard. "What exactly do these men worship? I know it's Daili, but what exactly is that? You've never told us."

"So I did forget." Spraggel nodded. "They have numerous gods, but their head God is called Battle. Now Battle had a son called Daili, which they claim was the greatest hero of all time. Daili's exploits, which date back to the Dark Avenyts invasion, were all recorded in the *Legends of the Hero*. He supposedly slew many and had quite the adventures. A fascinating read actually; I highly recommend it. Of course, it's mostly fiction, since historians have proven Daili never actually existed. But this sect has made a religion out of it. That's why that fellow greeted us as he did, wishing us a hero's death. They also collect and store great and unusual weapons—the more destructive, the better. But mind you, they only study war, they don't practice it... often. Over the years, they've found it much more profitable to sell weapons and teach the arts of war. It's not unusual for kings to bring them in as advisers before attacking their neighbors. For a hefty fee, of course."

We paused in our conversation to allow another priest to pass. But I had one more question. "So if these priests have the location of Ruin's Shield, why don't they bring it here to the temple? It seems odd that they wouldn't claim it."

Spraggel nodded. "You're right. From what I've read, something is protecting the shield. And from the looks of these people, it must be powerful." He glanced at the approaching temple gates—we were almost to them. He whispered. "Now remember your parts."

I lowered my head and whispered. "Zofie? Is the high priest's room clear?"

*Yes*, she answered. *He's still in the other tower, so his chambers are empty.*

So far, so good. Now if the high priest would just stay away for a bit longer, we'd be able to get out without a fight.

Spraggel walked up to the gateman. "Brother, we are here with a sacrifice for Battle. The High Priest Benzle requested this one personally."

The bored gateman looked up from his ledger. He fixed Spraggel with a snarl and opened his mouth to speak. "I'll have to check with the master..." But then he spotted Risten, and speech seemed to leave him. His eyes traveled over her arms and legs.

Risten had her gaze turned downward, with her shoulders slumped downward in defeat. But her long hair was loose and fell out teasingly from her hood.

I gritted my teeth. The way he looked at her made me angry. Risten likely knew she was being gawked at, and yet she took it. She was definitely strong in more than just her arms and legs.

Spraggel smiled at the gateman. "High Priest Benzle seemed anxious to have this one and requested her brought with all speed. He was concerned with the situation in Gien and their attempt at peace. That's where she's from. The High Priest thought a special sacrifice might help."

The gateman nodded distractedly, never taking his eyes off Risten. "Yes, yes, that is a grave situation."

Spraggel leaned forward. "Don't you think we should be admitted right away?"

The gateman jerked as if coming out of a trance. He nodded. "Of course. His chambers are in the center tower. Just go straight, and you'll run into it. "

"Bless you, brother." And turned to leave. I followed suit. Eager to get Risten away from the man, I nudged her just a little bit too hard, and she stumbled.

After we were a short distance away, Risten stopped suddenly and jammed her elbow in my chest. She leaned close. "If you push me like that again, I'll make sure you never have any children. Understand?"

I nodded, rubbing my chest.

"I was just trying to get you away from that gateman. He was staring at you!"

She flashed me a wicked smile. "Oh, so you're jealous now. What will Zofie think?"

"I was not jealous. Zofie and I are just friends."

Risten flashed me a knowing look but said nothing more.

We slowly made our way across the court to the tallest tower, which had a short series of steps leading up to the raised base of the structure and the entryway itself. Armed priests stood outside it, but while their eyes tracked our progress, they surprisingly did not challenge us. Apparently, the guards were used to it. I couldn't help but wonder how often High Priest Benzel did this.

We entered an open foyer with stairs in the back leading up. A priest sat at a desk just inside the door. He glanced up from his book and then just as quickly returned to it. "Top of the stairs, five flights up. Tell the guards up there, and they will direct you." He pointed toward the stairs but otherwise ignored us.

We started up the stairs. I leaned over and whispered to Spraggel, "How do you know this is where the Scroll of Nobem resides?"

Spraggel smiled. "As the incarnation of Daili himself, the high priest is supposed to be the scroll's guardian. Remember, this is one of their most sacred scrolls. So his chambers are where it's kept. In fact, not only is the scroll there, but also a small armory of their most precious weapons. Sort of an honor guard for the scroll. My sources say you go through his receiving room, and then his chambers split in two: his bedroom on the left and the armory on the right. The scroll is in the armory."

When we got to the top of the stairs, we found two heavily armed guards in full armor standing just outside the room's only door. The one on the right didn't hesitate to open the door for us. "The high priest will be back shortly. So wait in here," he said. "Just be sure to stay in the study. Going anywhere else is instant death. And remember, she is a sacrifice for Battle and must be unblemished, if you know what I mean."

Spraggel and I both nodded and entered, the door creaking closed behind us and locking with a final click. I breathed a sigh of relief. I couldn't believe we had gotten inside so easily.

We were standing in a study of some kind. A large ornate desk occupied most of the room with tall tapestries hanging along the sides and bookshelves lining the back wall. To the left was an archway, and through it, although darker than where we stood, I could make out a lavish bedroom with a bed big enough to sleep a small army. No doubt where Benzel slept and *entertained*.

On the right was another archway, and I could see several rows of neatly arranged weapons lining the walls: there were all sorts of swords, spears, knives, and other weapons I couldn't even classify. That had to be the armory.

Spraggel didn't hesitate and immediately strode into the weapons room. I quickly untied Risten's hands before we followed. Inside, at the very back, there was another archway, only this one had inscriptions carved across the outside of the arch. It was in a language I didn't recognize. On the other side of the arch was a small room with a raised pedestal in the middle. A beautiful life-size statue of a robed woman stood over it, hands clasped in front of her chest and gazing down at a large crystal case. And in the case on a red pillow sat a single scroll—it had to be the Scroll of Nobem. Sunlight illuminated it from an open window above: the light streaming down, giving it an almost holy glow. I had to admit it did look magical sitting there. Spraggel went to the case, opened it, and gingerly picked up the scroll and began to carefully unravel it, treating the ancient relic with the utmost respect.

For Risten and I, all we had to do was wait and be alert. Zofie, with her heightened senses, would let us know if the priest was going to return. Risten reached into the back of her tunic and pulled out her own sword, joining me in looking around. She was immediately drawn to the walls of weapons—especially the swords. It was quite the collection with every type imaginable. She seemed in awe as she examined each piece in detail. A few she took down and gave a couple practice swings before returning it.

I went to the back wall and carefully tested the shutters of our exit window but didn't open them yet for fear of drawing attention. All seemed in order; the window had a wide sill, and a single person could slip through it without difficulty. I was almost disappointed. Things were just going too well. Had I overlooked something?

"Zofie?" I whispered. "Everything all right?"

I didn't get an answer.

"Zofie?" My panic rising, I held my breath.

*Yes,* she finally answered. *Those roof guards aren't making it easy to stay close.*

I breathed a sigh of relief. With nothing else to do, I went back into the study and looked over the desk. There was the obligatory inkwell and quills on it, but little else. It seemed to be more for show than an actual working desk. I opened a drawer on one side and paused. Inside was a cedar wood square, slightly larger and thicker than most books, and with runes engraved around the top edge. I instantly recognized what it was: a Dupal Frame. I leaned closer. This was a myst device used to copy another item. I had seen a traveling merchant demonstrate one on a trip to Iron Landing a year or so ago. I thought it was truly amazing… until Spraggel explained that it only duplicated the outside. The inside of the object was unchanged.

I closed the drawer. I couldn't imagine what the priest was using it for, but it couldn't be good.

Moving on, I searched the rest of the desk without finding anything. I sighed. I had been hoping to find some sign of where Spraggel's book the *Armeda ne Emour* might be. Unfortunately, Wort must still have it. I turned to the shelves behind the desk and saw several ancient books. I moved closer to examine them when my eyes locked on one of the newer ones. "Well, I'll be," I said to myself. It was the *Armeda ne Emour*. Master Spraggel's book. I didn't think we would find it all that easily.

I took it down and flipped through it. While it had sat on Master Spraggel's shelf for as long as I had been with him, I had never read the book myself. Perhaps it was because it was written in Urticia and that was a language I had only recently learned. The book fell open to a finely detailed illustration of a spear with a feather tied just behind the tip. *Spear of Flight*, the caption read. Apparently, if one had the spear, they could magically fly away. Just say the destination and throw it. I snorted. I doubted something like that could exist.

I moved to tell Spraggel of my find. But for some reason, my eyes seemed to turn back to the bookshelf on their own. There at the very top of the shelf and to one side, my eyes fell on a particularly old volume. It was thinner than most of the books and seemed very old— there was just something about it that drew me closer. I moved toward it; the attraction giving me no choice.

Going up on my tiptoes, I teased the book out—careful that the thick leather cover didn't come off. It didn't have any markings on its leather binding, let alone a title. Inside, the writing was faded and the pages nearly crumbling, but I could see that the author's Ellish script was neat and precise: a female hand I judged. It started off with an introduction on the first page. As I scanned over it, I saw it was a journal, and the author was asking for forgiveness for whatever she was attempting. I nodded. This would be of great interest to a historian; Spraggel would likely give his right arm to read it. It started out detailing different kinds of curses, how they were different and similar— most of it beyond my familiarity with myst-casting. I flipped the page, and a new section started. Only this one suddenly switched to a language I had never seen. And as I looked at it, I felt it was not really even a language, but some kind of code. I sighed. And likely the ability to read it had been lost through the ages. I flipped a few more pages sadly and found more of the same with a few diagrams. Strangely, the author had left the diagram captions in plain Ellish with only the text under it coded. I shook my head. While it screamed mystery, it wasn't much use without knowing the code.

I was about to put the book back and turned one last page... then just froze. My next breath stayed stuck in my chest, despite my pounding heart. There on the page, drawn in what had once been a high-quality ink...

Was my own curse-anchor.

I juggled the book around and held up my wrist to compare it to my own. It was identical. And the curse was labeled *Abhulengulus* or *Thief of Curses...*

*Coren, you've got trouble!*

Zofie startled me, and I nearly dropped the book. She must have spotted something.

*The high priest is on the move. I was busy avoiding the guards and didn't see him leave. He's almost to the chambers.*

My heart jumped into my throat. *Creator! It's too soon!*

Just then, Spraggel shouted, "I found it!"

From where I stood behind the desk, I looked through the archway to where my master was holding up the scroll. "It says here that Ruin's Shield is located on..." Spraggel paused, his smile fading to a frown. "That's odd. It's on an island? In the mountains? Averet Island? That doesn't make sense."

I tried to interrupt. "Zofie says..."

There was loud talking just outside, and the room's door burst open. Spraggel immediately shoved the scroll back into its case. Risten tried to put back the weapon she held, while I turned to face the door and put the two books behind me. I tried to look innocent.

A slightly round man entered dressed in rich robes, still technically the black of the priesthood, but not the rough spun wool we had seen so far. He was flanked by two heavily armed men and seemed to have been in deep conversation with a group I couldn't see still outside the door. I assumed the man was High Priest Benzel.

The high priest drew up short, half-way between the door and me. Unfortunately, he and his guards blocked the entranceway.

"Who are you?" demanded Benzel.

I hoped I was playing this right. I bowed slowly. "We've come to deliver this sacrifice to you." I indicated the next room. "As you can see, she's quite the beauty."

A loud crash came from the scroll room.

Both the priest and I leaned to look through the archway. Risten was standing in front of a small pile of weapons that had fallen off the wall. She was holding a ball and chain and smiling innocently, the look of a child caught stealing sweets.

"Well yes, she is quite a beauty," said the priest, a controlled anger gradually filling his voice. "But can you tell me why a woman is holding one of our sacred weapons?"

"Ah..."

A large hand pushed the two guards to one side. And in that large hand, was the *Armeda ne Emour*. Master Spraggel's book!

*How could that be? I've got the Armeda ne Emour right here.* There couldn't be two of them. *Could there?*

A deep voice spoke from just beyond the doorway. I couldn't see the man's face, but I easily recognized the speaker.

"Let me pass!" Wort eased into the room. He looked shocked. "It's that damn boy from the scribe. You're supposed to be dead!"

I began to slowly back toward the scroll room. "I think you're mistaken, good sir. I don't believe we've ever met."

Wort stepped further into the room and pointed through the archway at Spraggel. "And you're the damn scribe himself." He turned his gaze on Risten and froze. "*And you...*" He pointed to her. "You're..." He cocked his head considering her. "*No!* I don't believe it. The hair is different, blonde and much longer, but it's definitely you..." He gave a single slow nod of his head. "You're Risten Brightmare, bastard of the old king's brother and old Valervick's study." One side of his mouth curled up into a cruel smile. "And you would have died too, along with the old King, if Valervick hadn't jumped in front of you." With his free right hand, he slowly and deliberately reached for Havoc's Sword hanging at his waist. "Which means that troublesome princess has to be close by. What is she now? A rabbit maybe, or perhaps a cow." He chuckled. "Doesn't matter really. Her brother will be so glad I killed you both."

He pulled the sword slowly from its sheath, every eye in the room watching in breathless awe as it came free—it's glow of power clearly evident. He raised it high, and I felt as if I was looking at the servant of death himself.

Wort glanced over his shoulder toward Benzel. "You'll have to excuse me priest. I think I need to bloody some steel."

# The Flying Spear

I took several steps back as Wort raised his sword. Behind him, the two heavily armored guards pulled their own swords. As a group, they moved cautiously toward us, fanning out slightly to completely block the exit. I had to admit this didn't look good.

"Zofie!" I whispered to her. "We need to get out. Can you take Spraggel?"

*Get him to the window. I'll try to make a pass and pull him out. The outside guards are trying to figure out how to shoot me. And they're doing a damn fine job!*

I pulled out my copy of the *Armeda ne Emour* and held it out toward Wort. "Wait! They've been lying to you. This is the real one. They slipped you a fake. They have a Dupal Frame!"

Wort stopped beside the priest halfway into the room and lowered his sword. He looked down at the book in his hand and then back to the one I held up, carefully comparing the two. Juggling his sword and the book, he opened the volume and flipped a couple of pages. Wort's brows drew down, evidently not liking what he saw. "What is the meaning of this? This book is not the same as the one I brought." Wort tossed the book to one side where it bounced off the armor of one of the guards. "This one looks different inside."

"It's wasn't me." Benzel put a hand on his chest. "We wouldn't stoop to doing something like that. It goes against our beliefs." He pointed in our direction. "They must have done it."

"Oh really!" I shouted back. "I'll bet you had to borrow the book from Wort there for a few hours while you authenticated its accuracy."

Wort turned an angry eye in the direction of the high priest. He grabbed Benzel by this robe and lifted him bodily off the floor. The priest yelled, and the two guards jumped to pry Wort away from their leader.

While they scuffled, I used the distraction to run into the scroll room and pushed Spraggel toward the window. I shoved both the real *Armeda ne Emour* and the curse journal into his hands. "Get to the window. We'll cover you."

Spraggel hesitated just a moment, but quickly realized it was the best move. He slid both books into his robe pocket, and they just seemed to disappear inside it.

I looked on in astonishment. "Your special pocket... How did you do that? You're not wearing your regular robe."

Spraggel gave me a disgusted look. "Of course not. I've changed robes many times since I got that spell. It was too precious to be tied to a single garment—they wear out too fast. It's made so the spell appears on whatever piece of clothing I wear." He puffed out his chest. "I thought of that one."

I shook my head in disbelief and pushed him toward the room's only window. I threw open the shutters, and he climbed up onto the window sill. He leaned out the man-sized window, and a heartbeat later, a dark shadow flashed across it, and something outside snatched Spraggel. *I hope Zofie didn't break his neck doing that.*

Now all we had to do was wait for Zofie to return. She said she could handle two of us at one time, just not three.

Wort had lowered Benzel back to the floor, but they were still arguing when Risten grinned wickedly and stepped to the arch, twirling the ball and chain. Both men turned to face her when they heard the unmistakable whooshing sound. She immediately sent it flying toward Wort. He reacted faster than one would have thought possible. He swung the sword up just in time to slice the chain effortlessly in two, but the ball continued on unimpeded and connected loudly with Wort's forehead. His eyes crossed and he fell, toppling over like a giant oak. Driven by Wort's falling weight, Havoc's Sword sunk into the floorboards, stopping at its hilt.

Risten eyed the sword greedily and tensed to lunge for it. I quickly grabbed her shoulder. "Don't Risten. It's not worth it." She glared at me, angry conflict behind her eyes, but then sighed and nodded. "You know you're useless, don't you?"

I raised an eyebrow. "So I've been told."

The high priest was a crafty little bastard and leaped for the sword himself. He grabbed the hilt and yanked, but nothing happened. It remained buried in the floor unmoving. It was as I had feared. Wort must have had a myst-lock put on the sword—it wouldn't move, unless he was touching it. Risten saw it too and glanced in my direction, quickly realizing if she had gone for it, she would have been an easy target.

"Guards!" Benzil yelled, trying to get a better grip. "Kill them!"

The two guards stepped over Wort with their weapons ready, while the priest frantically tried to pull the sword out. Risten and I fell back inside the archway.

"Dammit!" Risten spat, sheathing her sword on her back. "I can't deal with two in full armor. Especially that armor—the weaknesses are difficult to hit." She grinned and grabbed a spear off the wall. "So we improvise." She threw it at them, and I did likewise. One of the guards made a lucky pass and cut the spear in two. But it did little other than slow them down.

Benzel yelled, still kneeling on the floor. "Don't hurt the weapons! They're priceless."

I chucked a spear in Benzel's direction, but it went wide and missed, clattering uselessly to the floor. It did make the high priest realize how very exposed he was. With wide eyes, he decided that the sword wasn't worth it and quickly moved to hide behind the desk.

The fact that they were antiques didn't stop Risten and me—we just threw more. The guards, however, realized charging was not an option and decided to fall back until they could figure out how to get us without hurting the antiques. Wort started groaning and put a hand to his head. One of the guards grabbed Wort and started to drag him to cover, but not before Wort grabbed the sword and pulled it out of the floor. The guard's companion joined him, and together they dragged Wort back behind the desk. Then they quickly knocked the desk onto its side and angled the top toward us for more cover.

Risten took down a bow from the wall and a quiver of arrows. I was dubious of the string since it looked worn, but she strung the bow and plucked it a couple times. She nodded in satisfaction. After selecting a shaft, she stepped to the doorway, pulled back, and let it fly just as one of the guards was looking over the desk. It thunked heavily into the wood just below his eyes. He jerked back down.

I heard Benzel yelling to someone outside the door. "Get some archers up here. *Now!*"

It didn't look like we had much time.

"Zofie?" I called, hoping she was back. But there was no answer. She must be too far away. No doubt taking Spraggel outside the city.

Risten looked over her shoulder at me. "Some help would be nice. There's another bow on the wall."

I shrugged. "I can't shoot. At least not well enough to have them worried about it. It would be better to leave the arrows for you."

Risten made a rude noise and rolled her eyes. "You are definitely useless."

I scanned the room for something to use as a weapon. Swords were out since that was for close combat, and I wasn't that good with spears or arrows. An oddly shaped piece of polished wood caught my eye. It was flat but bent in the middle at an odd angle—almost making a shape like a dog's crooked back leg. I took it down and found it very lightweight.

Just then, an archer stepped into the doorway and pointed his arrow in my direction. Without thinking, I threw the piece of wood, and it sailed in an odd looping flight curving down and then back up. The archer ducked as it sailed over his head. He stood back up, grinning and taking aim right at me. But unexpectedly, the piece of wood reappeared from the other direction, connecting soundly with the back of his head. He collapsed.

That was definitely odd—a returning piece of wood. I wondered what kind of myst-spell made it work.

Risten was continuing to keep the guards pinned down behind the table. From the gleam in her eyes, I knew she was hoping Wort would stand up.

I looked around for something else to use as a weapon. On a shelf about waist high were five fist-sized balls of black metal stacked in a pyramid shape. I picked up the top one and found it very heavy for something its size. Just then, another archer stepped into the doorway and let an arrow fly. It sailed past Risten's head barely missing her.

I looked back to the ball in my hand. Whatever it was, it had to be better than nothing. I ran to the door and lobbed it underhanded toward the archer at the entry door. But the unexpected weight of the ball made my throw fall way short. I heard it hit with a dull thud and roll toward the wall.

*Damn! Not even close.*

The ball slowly rolled to barely touch the wall close to the entrance-way, when...

It exploded violently, filling the room with smoke and sending bits of debris flying. Everyone started coughing. As the smoke cleared, I could see a new hole in both the floor and the wall—men from the hall looked into the room with amazement.

Risten picked herself up. "Mother of the Creator, what was that?"

The blast must have awakened Wort. He stood up from behind the overturned desk, soot smudged on his face and a bright red welt rising up on his forehead. He looked angry.

I took another of the black spheres and threw it at the table shielding the men. I wasn't any better aiming this ball than the last. It again went wide, hitting the floor, rolling to the edge of the new gaping hole, and then falling through. After a brief moment, this one exploded with equal force, blowing debris back up through the hole and making the floor buckle and crack.

Unexpectedly, an arrow whizzed by my ear.

I yelled at Risten. "We've got to get out of here!"

She let loose an arrow and backed away with me. She only had one left. "I'm open to suggestions!"

"Zofie!" I yelled, looking at the ceiling. "We need some help!" But still no reply.

I filled my pockets with the remainder of the spheres and looked around for another weapon. We had already used most of the ones that could be thrown. Then my eyes fell on a single remaining spear, placed next to the Scroll of Nobem and separate from the other spears. It was painted a bright red with a single feather tied just behind the spearhead. White runes were painted on the shaft. My eyes widened. I knew those runes. *Spear of feather... no, bird... no, it was flight. Spear of Flight!*

It was too much of a coincidence. I had just seen this in Spraggel's book. I couldn't shake the feeling my curse was at work again. I took the spear down and held it in my right hand.

I ran to the window and looked out. It was a long way down. The hard-packed earth and lack of vegetation gave us no chance of a soft landing. Plus the tower sides were smooth stone, so you'd need a rope to get down.

The guards pushed the desk forward, using it as a shield. Archers were lining the hole I had blown in the wall and preparing to shoot. And worst of all, Wort had stood up and was coming around the table. Risten notched her last arrow and aimed it at Wort.

"Risten, don't waste the shot."

But she wasn't listening and let it fly. It was perfect too, aiming right for Wort's heart. But Wort's sword was already raised, and he quickly flicked it out and split the arrow in two, the pieces scattering.

Risten threw down her bow and reached for her sword.

I grabbed her arm and pulled her to the window. Risten tried to jerk away. "My enemy is the other way. I can at least take Wort out before we die."

"We're not going to die." I raised the spear toward the window. "Just trust me and put your hand on the spear. *Quickly!*"

Out of the corner of my eye, I saw Benzel stand. "She mustn't touch it! Don't let that *accursed* bitch sully Daili's spear!"

And a sudden rage came over me—deep, dark, and angry. I had never felt anything so black. Sure, Risten was a pain in my backside. But she was the finest warrior I had ever met. No one had the right to talk about her like that. It would be fitting if Benzel could sample what it was like to be a woman. In fact, I wished with all my heart that *he* would try out being a woman. Then he might see things a little differently. I glared at the priest. "You're the accursed one," I whispered.

And to my horror, something answered my wish. Inside my head, I heard that deep, evil laugh again. I felt a tingle at my wrist, and glancing down, I was shocked to see that the drawn eye of my curse-anchor was now open... and looking at me. I heard a deep voice inside my head, and it definitely wasn't Zofie. It had a deep timbre, deeper than thunder in the darkest storm, and more frigid than the glaciers to the north. I shivered in cold fear.

*As you wish,* said the voice.

I felt a pain in my chest—that familiar sensation of string being pulled through my heart. It was the same pain I felt when Zofie transformed. But she shouldn't be doing that now. It wasn't time. The sun hadn't set yet.

Unexpectedly, there was a scream of pain coming from the other side of the room. Benzel shouted, "What's happening to me!"

Every eye in the room turned toward the priest as he began to glow brightly, and the man-shaped form inside began to change. His hair grew longer, and the features of his face began to soften. And suddenly it was done. Where Benzel, a balding, overweight, middle-aged man had stood, was a beautiful mature woman, her hair the same graying brown as the high priest's and wearing the now elegant, but over-sized priest's robes. I had seen her face before—I glanced over my shoulder to be sure. It was the face of the woman on the statue overlooking the scroll.

"What happened to me?" she said in a very feminine voice. She looked down at her hands and then patted her body up and down, finally coming to rest on her face. She stepped to a small mirror on the wall and drew back in shock.

She screamed. "Help me. I'm a... a... *woman!*" She spat the word.

Wort broke out laughing. "And a damn fine one too!"

Furious, she glared at Wort. "Guards! Kill him. And get those thieves too! I want them all dead!" She looked at her hands. "And get me my myst-seer. NOW! I... I can't be a woman."

Wort's laughter finally died, and he turned back to us. "Very interesting magic! A little too interesting, maybe!" He raised his sword and started toward us.

I hefted the spear as if to throw it out the window. Risten stood facing me with her back to the window. "Hurry. Risten, put your hand on the spear."

"This is crazy. We've nowhere to go."

"Do it, or I'll drag you with me."

"If you so much as touch something you shouldn't, I'll kill you before Wort does." She quickly slipped her sword into the rigging on her back, and reluctantly put her hand on the spear.

Behind me, I could hear Wort's war cry.

I faced the window and put an arm around Risten's waist and pulled her tightly against me. She stiffened, but I didn't give her time to turn around. I shouted, "Spear of Flight, take us to Spraggel." And I threw the spear.

It suddenly moved of its own accord. With a sharp jerk on my arm, Risten and I were carried out the window and away from the tower, flying level over the temple. I could feel a slight tug on the arm holding the spear, but it wasn't much—not nearly my entire weight. Nervous, Risten grabbed my shoulder. "Mother of the Creator!" she breathed.

We gathered speed as we flew. Behind me, I heard Wort yelling. "Don't think you'll get away!"

Risten looked over my shoulder and yelled. "Yeah! And your mother was a jackal!" And then she made a very obscene gesture at Wort as we flew away.

Much to my surprise, Risten laughed: a deep, hearty laugh I had never heard from her before. She leaned back slightly and patted my cheek, her eyes alight with delight. "You know, Coren." Her hand slid down to my shoulder. "You have shit for brains, but sometimes you are really something." And gave me an awkward kiss on the cheek. "I think I'm starting to understand what Zofie sees in you."

*What she sees in me?*

I concentrated on holding tight and steering the spear... if one actually guided it. We quickly cleared the temple, then just a few short minutes later, flew over the city walls. We were flying at a height even with most of the towers, which was well above anything in the area. We were moving fairly fast too—at about the speed of a fast bird. And I couldn't help but marvel at the view.

To our right, the sun was nearly down with the last of its rays lighting a few clouds on the horizon with reds and deep purples. It presented quite a beautiful sunset. And directly ahead in the distance, I could make out the last shadows of the Skyblue Mountains, a mountain chain just north of Daili. I could even make out Mount Eternal with its strangely flat top.

According to legend, the mountain used to be the tallest peak in the chain, but something happened to it over a thousand years ago during the war with the Dark Avenyts and blew the top off. It had been a huge explosion. It was unclear if that blast had been natural or man-made. Spraggel and I used to debate about it. He was pretty confident it was man-made.

Once clearing the city, we began a gradual turn toward the northeast, where we had stashed our horses and supplies. It didn't take long before I began to recognize the area and knew we were close. The spear began to tip toward the ground, and I started to be concerned about our speed. But I had no idea how to change it.

Risten noticed it too. "Hey, Coren. Does this thing have a brake or something to slow it? Aren't we going a little too fast?"

I shook my head. "There weren't any instructions on stopping. Only on getting it started."

Risten looked at me disgustedly. "So you saved us from the priests only to kill us in a fall? Creator, you're useless."

I tried to push the spear's point back up, but it wouldn't budge. Up ahead, a giant oak tree loomed, and we headed right for it. At the last possible moment, the spear tilted its point up and slowed, but not before we crashed into the tree. I lost my grip on the spear as leaves and branches slapped me and pulled at my clothes, until I came up hard against the trunk. I must have blanked out for a moment.

When I opened my eyes, I was sure I was in the spirit world, everything was a dark green and fluttered back and forth calmly, almost seductively. But gradually, it dawned on me that the spirits resembled tree leaves, oak to be exact. And I remembered where I was.

I shook my head and immediately regretted it because my head hurt, as well as some other parts of my body. I was in the top of the tree lying across several small limbs. Fortunately, they must have broken my fall. I grabbed a nearby branch and pulled myself onto a sturdy looking limb. But I didn't see Risten.

"Risten! Are you all right!"

There was a pause, but I heard her answer from somewhere above me. "I'm fine. I've got a little problem, but otherwise in one piece."

I managed to hook my leg over the limb and pull myself onto it. I began to work my way toward her voice. "Are you hurt?"

"*You* stay put." It was a definite command.

I froze. "Stay put?" I asked. *What could possibly be wrong?* I scanned the tree for her, in the dimming light, I could only make out a foot and a hand. She appeared to be crouching.

"Coren, do you still have your robe on?"

I looked down. "Yes, but it's all torn. My shirt is fine though."

"Great. Take off your shirt and lay it on the branch where you're at. Then climb down. These clothes Spraggel gave me weren't very sturdy. The limbs shredded them, so I'm rather *exposed* right now."

I immediately understood her situation, so I did what she asked, laid out the shirt and climbed down. My broken amulet glowed gently and swung freely as I climbed down. I was an easy beacon to see. So only moments later, I heard the brush shake over my head, and finally Risten drop down in front of me.

"You wear his shirt very nicely."

I nearly jumped out of my skin and wheeled to find Spraggel behind me.

She held it up and sniffed it. "I just had a bath too. Now I'll need another to get this Coren stink off me." She grinned.

Spraggel smiled and rocked on his heels. "If I'm not mistaken, you flew in using a spear—the Spear of Flight. It fell out of use because it tended to kill the people using it upon landing."

Risten laughed. "Yeah, we figured that out."

I turned back to Spraggel. "Where's Zofie?"

Spraggel frowned and shook his head. "I was actually hoping you could tell me. She had quite the time dodging all the cross-bolts and was hurrying back to get you two. But that was about a third of an hour ago. I haven't seen her since."

Risten and I looked at each other. We hadn't either.

She immediately started moving in the direction of the city. "Zofie!"

I called her too. In my mind, I was fairly sure I could feel her presence. "She's somewhere close by, but she's not answering me."

Risten sighed. "I bet I can guess why. There is no moon tonight." She started running in the direction we had just come. "Let's split up. You angle that way, and I'll go this way."

I went in the direction Risten indicated. And after a few minutes, I began to get a sense of where Zofie was hiding. I slowed my pace and began to look around.

"Zofie!"

"Stay away!" she yelled. She was close.

I heaved a sigh of relief. "Zofie, are you hurt?" I moved toward a thick bunch of bushes.

"Just stay away," I heard her say from just behind them.

I stopped.

"You're not speaking in my mind, so you must have gone back to being human. Did you get injured and transform again?"

"I'm fine. I'm sorry I couldn't make it back to you. I was trying, but I felt the transformation start, and I had to land."

"It's all right Zofie, it wasn't your fault." I took a step toward her.

"Stay away, Coren!" she yelled in panic. "Please stay away."

I froze mid-step. This was very odd.

"Risten!" I called over my shoulder. "She's over here!" The sun was down but still dimly lighting the horizon. In the east, I could see the stars starting to come out. My broken amulet was also putting out a dim glow, which combined with the fading sun, was enough to see by.

A few minutes later, I heard Risten walking through the brush. She came up beside me. I pointed in the direction of Zofie's voice. "She's over behind that bush but told me to stay away."

Risten slowly shook her head. "What your no-good curse did to Benzel likely triggered an early transformation for Zofie. I'm not a myst user, but it probably had something to do with myst levels and there not being a moon tonight."

I nodded. "I remember her saying something about the curse running out when there wasn't a moon." I pointed to where she hid. "But how is that connected to her telling me to stay away?"

She considered me for a moment and gave a heavy sigh. "I guess it's time you found out."

"Found out what? Is it related to what Wort was saying?"

Risten started toward the bush. "Zofie. It's me. I'm coming around."

"No, don't. Just go away," she begged.

"And I'm bringing Coren with me. He needs to know Zofie. It's time we told him. Everything. Wort named us, so Coren knows who we are."

I looked up at Risten and then to where Zofie hid. "You mean about Zofie being a princess and you... the old king was your uncle?"

Risten nodded. "There's much more to it than that. But I'd like you to hear it from Zofie."

"NO! I don't want him to see me." She pleaded. I could hear her tears. "He'll hate me!"

Risten glanced at me and then turned back to Zofie. "Remember what we talked about. He will find out eventually. It's best if you show him yourself."

I heard her sobbing, but no reply.

Risten took me by the arm and slowly, but determinedly, led me around the bush.

The combination of the remaining light from the horizon and the light from my amulet gave me a clear view of what was before me. There huddled beside the bush was a small human-shaped body with a head, two arms, and two legs. Her hair was just as I remembered, long, dark red, and beautiful, only now it was tangled and hung down over her body. But sadly, that was the limit of her human appearance. Her head turned up to look up at me with tears streaming from her large bird-like eyes, and a face that was wolf-like with a dark nose, plus a shortened muzzle filled with sharp teeth. Her neck and shoulders were covered in what looked like a turtle's skin and small feathers sprouted from her arms and torso. She still had hands, like a human, but her lower half had one leg shaped like a bird's and the other like a horse. It didn't take a genius to figure out she was now a mix of every animal she had ever transformed into.

I wasn't bothered by her appearance. Not in the least. On the contrary, my heart broke looking at her. I was horrified at the depth of the curse. I thought of the times she had laughed and talked with me, and I couldn't help but admire the strength it took to hold up under its weight.

She looked down at the ground. "This is my true form now," she said. "The curse... I'm not sure if it was a mistake or he intended to torture me, but I don't fully reset between transformations. You're supposed to go back to your original form, but I... I keep a bit of the last animal every time I change."

I knelt before her, and she looked into my face. Her big bird-like eyes were wet with tears.

I reached a hand toward her, and she knocked it away. "Don't touch me! I'm a monster."

"Zofie..."

She gave a cruel laugh. "And the sad part is, even if I manage to get this curse off me, I won't go back to my original self. My form has been lost. What everyone knew as me is gone! I will forever be this chimera of a monster."

I again reached out a hand and gently raised her muzzle to point toward me. Her eyes looked at me with shame.

"Go ahead say it," she whispered. "I'm disgusting."

And I couldn't help myself.

I put my arms around her and hugged her to me. She stiffened and resisted, trying feebly to push me away. But I held her tightly. She finally relaxed, sobbing into my shoulder. I stroked her hair. "So this is why you were so secretive about what you looked like. Well, I hate to disappoint you, but you're not a monster, and I still like you a lot. I liked you when you were a hawk, a wolf, a squirrel, and a turtle. I already knew you were those things, and they didn't bother me. My friend is not this body, but the you *inside* the body."

She pulled away. "Really? You're not disgusted?"

I smiled. "No." I touched her face. "The outside is just the wrapping for the beautiful soul inside."

She threw her arms around me and hugged me tightly. And I hugged her back.

Risten cleared her throat, clearly reminding us she was still there. We both looked her way.

"Zofie, tell him the rest. He's seen what you are, but you need to tell him *who* you are."

I leaned away from Zofie. "Wort said you were a princess. What kingdom do you come from?"

She sighed deeply. "My full name is Zophia Olwenna Xernow of the kingdom of Brethnach. I'm the princess of this kingdom, Coren. You probably know me as Princess Olwenna, traitor and assassin of the king."

"What?" My mind reeled taking it all in.

She shook her head. "But that's not true. I was cursed right after my father was assassinated. My brother set it all up, the king's death, the murder of his friends, and my curse."

"You mean old King Xernow?" I asked in disbelief. "You're that princess?"

She nodded and looked down.

"Then that means..."

"I'm the true heir to the throne of this kingdom." She pulled her knees up and rested her head on them. It seemed the weight of the world rested on her shoulders. "And one very cursed princess."

# CHAPTER FIFTEEN

# Abhulengulus

All four of us were exhausted. I hadn't even bothered to find a new shirt since Risten hadn't returned mine yet. I sat on a log and chewed on the last of my dried meat and bread as I watched Spraggel across the tiny fire in the middle of our camp. He sat on a large rock, trying to read *The Book of Curses* by the light of my broken amulet. The fire was barely big enough to heat some tea and carefully hidden by the clumps of bushes around us. There would no doubt be searchers from Daili, and we didn't want to give the priests any clue to where we were.

Zofie shared the log with me, still in her mostly human form, and resting her head on my shoulder. She had sat beside me to have some tea but drifted off to sleep and slumped against me. I didn't mind. Not at all. She was wearing the robe Spraggel had used as a disguise, which was way too big for her. But she seemed content to have the hood up since it hid her completely.

Risten sat to one side on her blanket, chewing her own meal. She stared into the fire, her thoughts seemingly a thousand leagues away. No doubt, she was kicking herself for missing yet another chance to get back the sword and have her revenge on Wort. She glanced my way but quickly averted her eyes. I wasn't sure what had done it but, since the priests, Risten's attitude toward me was different. She still said I had shit for brains, but she treated me almost with respect. I definitely appreciated the change.

Spraggel turned a page in the book and then sighed. He gently closed it and looked at me over the fire. "You had to pick a book written in some kind of ancient Urticia code. It was popular around that time for authors to code their work, but it fell out of practice because people kept losing the key to the codes."

"Were you able to read it?"

"Only the parts that weren't in code." He sighed. "Maybe if I study it, I can figure it out. But depending on the code they used, it may not be easy. I did find out the author's common name was Evelend, but no family name was given."

I looked at the ground between my feet. "So, we really don't know anything about Abhulengulus, this Thief of Curses."

"Well, not from the book, but I have heard of it. "

I looked up. "Why haven't you mentioned it before?"

Spraggel shrugged. "I had no idea it was that particular curse you carried. Without the book, I would never have connected your curse mark to its name."

I nodded in understanding. "So what do you know?"

Spraggel leaned forward with his elbows on his knees. "Well... the curse itself is called Abhulengulus and the person bearing it is generally referred to as the Thief of Curses. That's probably because of the way the bearer uses it." He paused for a moment, collecting his thoughts. "It's an ancient curse... and supposedly very powerful, maybe even the most powerful curse ever created. One source claimed it single-handedly brought about the end of the war with the Dark Avenyts."

Zofie moaned softly in her sleep and shifted on my shoulder before relaxing again.

I gave him a puzzled look. "How could a curse end a war?"

He shrugged. "Who knows? The histories are a little vague about those times."

"Do you think that someone just happened to use the same curse-anchor as that one. And maybe it's just a coincidence?"

Spraggel leaned forward and looked at me, dead serious. "Has your curse ever allowed anything to be a coincidence?"

I sighed. "No." I shifted my legs. My backside was falling asleep. "So what does this curse do? How can you steal curses?"

"Well, apparently, it can take the curse off of someone else and sort of take control of it."

I snorted, frustrated that I wasn't able to find out more. The answers to controlling my curse were just barely out of my grasp. "I already know that," I said in disgust.

Spraggel stood and walked around the fire. He handed me my amulet back. "Coren, you didn't understand what I just said. It takes other curses and then brings them under your control." He stopped before me and poked his finger into my shirtless chest. He was pointing to Zofie's curse anchor. "You now carry her curse. How come you're not transforming into animals?"

I looked up at him confused. He just cocked his head to one side and paused, giving me a moment to work it out for myself. And then it hit me. "I have her anchor because I'm now the owner. I get to control it while she..." I turned toward her. "Bears the cost." I turned back to Spraggel. "That's horrible. I'm the one now causing her pain." And the mechanism behind the changes to her curse became clear. As long as it stayed within the bounds of the original curse, it could do whatever it liked with her. And as I saw with Priest Benzel, it could even cast the same curse on someone else. I sat back with my shoulders slumping as this sank in. This was truly a powerful... and awful curse.

I heard a loud snore and saw Risten had laid back and was sound asleep.

Spraggel laughed, breaking the tension. "I think I'll follow Risten's example. We've got to be up before first light to stay ahead of any pursuers." He went to his own bedroll and began to lay it out. "I'll look at the book some more in the morning, but it may have to wait until we get back home. I've got the references there that may help with translating it. And if not that, I know of someone who specializes in ancient codes."

I had a thousand questions to ask, but I knew my master was right. This would have to wait just a bit longer.

Spraggel laid down and settled himself under his blanket. "You had better get some sleep too. Wake me in a couple hours, and I'll take the next watch."

I nodded, not willing to commit. Sure, I was tired, but I wasn't about to let Zofie be jerked awake by her transformation. I'd sleep after she changed, or more likely, in the saddle tomorrow.

Zofie moaned softly in her sleep and I looked her way, but she was completely covered by the robe. I wondered what she looked like while she was sleeping.

*Princess Zophia Olwenna Xernow. King Xernow's daughter.*

I couldn't get over it. The one person I had finally started to get close to, and she was royalty. I shook my head. This explained why Risten had warned me away from her. Zofie was of noble birth and, after our quest was completed, I would likely never see her again. It made my heart ache. I'd never met a girl like her, and likely never would again.

I tried to shift my position without disturbing Zofie too much. My butt was seriously starting to hurt. In my shifting, the curse-anchor on my wrist caught the light. The eye was shut, as it had been the few times I had seen it without my wrist guard. That is until earlier today when Benzel transformed into a woman. I'm sure it was my curse, but it didn't follow the earlier patterns. Why didn't it transform Wort or the guards? I had been angry at other people in the past, and they hadn't transformed. Why him? Was it because I wished it?

I gave a short chuckle and spoke aloud. "Too bad you can't tell me, Abhulengulus."

I felt my wrist tingle, and then the stylized eye opened. In shock, I leaned away from it, feeling I should run while at the same time, thinking that was stupid—I couldn't run from my own hand, and I wasn't planning on cutting it off. At least not yet.

I heard that same deep laughter I had heard in the past. Then that cold, black voice spoke to me. *I could tell you... if I wanted.*

I held my hand as far away from me as I could. "You're talking! But you're a curse!"

*And you're talking even though you're made of slowly decaying meat.*

The curse's accent had an Urticia twang to it, and the way it articulated its words was very precise. It almost sounded like a noble.

"But why haven't you spoken before?"

*I usually don't speak to someone unless they call my name.* He made a noise like he was clearing his throat. *And now young master, what would you like for your three wishes?*

I paused in utter confusion. *Did he just say wishes?* That just didn't sound right. I shook my head. "Wishes? How can you do that? You're a curse, not a fairy."

*Drat. He figured it out. The young monkey is smarter than I thought.*

I started getting irritated. "I'm not a monkey."

I heard the curse chuckle. *Have you looked in the mirror lately? Have I got news for you!*

I felt a slight tingle over my heart and remembered how Benzel had been transformed. I froze in place. Had the curse actually transformed me when I wasn't paying attention?

Abhulengulus laughed. *I got you, didn't I? Never underestimate a thousand-year-old curse.*

Zofie jerked awake. She realized she was leaning on me and immediately straightened. She looked around the camp. "I thought I felt my transformation start. But it's not time yet."

*Oops! Sorry about that. Your princess must have felt that little jolt. Don't worry, she's got a while yet... Unless I change my mind. I wonder how she would look as a monkey? No, an ape would be better.*

"You wouldn't dare!" I shouted.

Zofie looked at me. "I wouldn't dare what?"

Spraggel woke and turned in my direction. "Are you all right?"

Risten sat up. "What are you yelling about?"

*They can't hear me, young one. I'm all in your head. And I will go on and on until you're willing to jump into the river and end it all. Just like your father!*

I covered my wrist and spoke through clenched teeth. "You... shut... up!"

It gave a short burst of laughter, and suddenly the presence I had felt before was gone. I only heard the crackling of the fire and the chirp of the night creatures. All else was silent. When I took my hand away, the eye on my wrist was closed as it usually was.

Zofie was looking at me. In fact, they all were looking at me like I was crazy. Maybe I was. I cleared my throat. "Sorry. I had a curse talking in my head."

Spraggel nodded and rolled back over. "That's nice."

Risten threw a pebble at me. "It wasn't the curse that woke me up!" She huffed and laid back down.

Zofie chuckled softly. "Don't mind Risten. She gets grumpy when she doesn't get her sleep."

Another pebble came in our direction, and we both ducked.

"See what I mean?" Zofie cleared her throat. "I take it this is the first time your curse has talked to you? That book you found must have been helpful."

I picked up the pebble and threw it out into the bushes. "I only found out what it's called. But I made the mistake of calling its name just now, and it wouldn't shut up. I wanted to ask it some questions, but it just kept talking. It was rather insulting."

"Perhaps it didn't want to tell you."

"Then why talk to me to begin with? Why not keep silent like it had all these years?" I stretched my legs in front of me and leaned back. "It threatened to turn you into a monkey and I... sort of... yelled at it."

"You're sweet." She patted my arm and gave it a gentle squeeze. "But I've been a monkey before. It was the first creature I transformed into. It wasn't that bad, although Risten didn't particularly care for it." Her hand was warm on my cool skin.

She started to pull it away, but I took her hand in mine. A bold move on my part, but she didn't seem to mind. "Curses are created things," she said. "So maybe your curse is made so it can't volunteer information. So it annoyed you to avoid your questions."

I nodded in understanding. "That sounds exactly like what it was doing. If it wakes again, I'll remember not to allow it to upset me."

We sat in silence for a moment.

Zofie cleared her throat. "I'm sorry for using you as a pillow. I haven't been sleeping much lately. And I always get tired during the new moon."

"Princess, you can use... ouch!" Zofie smacked me in the arm.

"Listen Coren, let's get one thing straight," she said sternly. "Don't call me princess. I'll smack you every time you do. Right now, I'm just Zofie."

I rubbed my arm. "All right... ah... Zofie."

The hood nodded. "Thank you." We were quiet for a moment, and I returned to our earlier topic. "You said you were tired during a new moon. Why is that? What has the moon got to do with it?"

She sighed. "That's when myst is at its lowest. Everyone's myst. Most people don't realize it, but for us myst users, it limits the amount we have to manipulate. And for me, my curse just runs out of fuel, so to speak, and I revert to my true form during this time." She shuffled her feet and looked down. "I don't mean to brag, but I'm rather talented when it comes to using myst. So the curse was designed to use up all my myst when I'm at my peak. That's why I transform during the full moon to help use it up. But during my low, I revert." She turned in my direction. "I will say something sucked me dry right after I dropped Spraggel off. It was most unusual."

I cleared my throat. "That would have been me."

"And how so?" she asked, surprised.

"High Priest Benzel made a comment about Risten, and it set me off. It activated my curse somehow and turned him into a woman. I'm sorry. You could have gotten hurt, but I didn't know it would do that."

"So you actually used my curse on someone else?" I could hear the shock in her voice.

"Well, it wasn't actually me, it was Ab..." I cut myself off. I didn't want to wake the curse up again. "Let's just call him Abe."

"Him? How do you know it's not a female?"

I thought about the voice for a moment. "Definitely male. He... it... had a deep voice and an ancient-sounding accent."

She raised a finger in thought. "Let me see your chest."

I grinned. "You mean the one you drooled on."

She gave my shoulder a playful slap. "I don't drool."

I twisted so she could see. She gasped. "My curse-anchor. It's on your chest."

"My curse stole it."

She shook her head. "But I'm still... you know, and you haven't changed."

"That's because I own your curse now." I looked down. "Yet you take the consequences."

"Wait, let me look at you." She shifted on the log to face me while I also turned toward her.

A moment later, she spoke. "I'm always amazed at how complex your curse is. Truly amazing. And I can see my curse now. It appears to be... I'm not sure how to describe it. Joined or absorbed into yours."

The hood rose to look at my face. "I would need to study it, but I think it's actually incorporated my curse into itself. Like learning a new ability."

"But why would it be made to do something like that?"

"Perhaps to better torture you."

Now that's one thought I didn't like.

I looked into her darkened hood, wishing I could see her eyes. I spoke softly, afraid I might be asking the wrong thing. "How did you get your curse? If you don't want to tell me, you don't have to."

She gently pulled her hand out of mine and began to nervously play with a strand of hair that had escaped her hood. "It was my brother."

My mouth fell open. "Your own blood kin did this to you?"

She nodded. "Wynn has always had a dark streak. I just never realized how dark it was."

I waited, feeling she had something else to add, but she said nothing further.

I cleared my throat. "So if Wynn cursed you, those rumors about you killing your father can't be true."

The dark hood looked down. "I... You see... It's just difficult to explain." She brooded for a moment more, then suddenly turned in my direction more animated than I had seen her all evening. She looked at me for a moment from the safety of her hood and then slowly reached up and pulled it back, revealing her chimera face. "I can show you if you want. How I came to be cursed and how Father died. It happened the same evening." She smiled nervously. "I feel you have a right to know. As The Poet said, *I have no further secrets to reveal...*"

I interrupted and finished it for her. "*For I have shown you the deepest, darkest reaches of my soul.*" It was another from one of The Poet's sonnets—a sappy love poem about a man pining for his true love. I had memorized it at Spraggel's insistence. He said the ladies loved it. Apparently, he was right.

Zofie chuckled. "I love how you do that. No one's been able to complete my quotes for me." She searched my eyes. "So, would you like to see the memory of that evening? That is if you don't mind me using a little of your myst. You have plenty around you now, so you're in no danger. I only need a little."

I could tell this was costing her. I took her hand again and leaned forward. "I would be honored."

Zofie looked at me and took a deep breath. "It might be disorienting at first, but it will quickly pass. Just remember, you'll not only be looking through my eyes, but you'll in essence... be me."

My eyes went up in surprise. "Are you sure? That seems like a very intimate thing to do."

She shifted on the log. "I have to say, it does worry me a bit, but not for the reason you think."

Zofie shifted her grasp on my hand, and we intertwined our fingers. She leaned forward until I could feel the warmth of her closeness. With her other hand, she gently touched my cheek.

"Then what reason does it worry you?" I asked.

She looked at me steadily for a moment. "Because you might not like me after you see this."

"I don't..."

Her fingers stilled my lips and then moved back to my cheek.

I felt where she touched me grow very warm as she worked her spell.

She leaned closer and barely whispered, "I really did kill my father."

And a heartbeat later my world dissolved around me and I was there, seeing the world through Zofie's eyes.

# CHAPTER SIXTEEN

# Betrayal Of A Princess

*I*sat on the edge of the bench at the foot of my bed and gave a last few brushstrokes to my dark red hair. I had grown weary of the servant's fussing and had dismissed them, preferring to finish the task myself. I had decided that I would leave my hair down for this evening's celebration— just two simple clips to hold it away from my face. Nothing too extravagant. I generally preferred to put my hair up on summer evenings, with lots of ribbons and maybe a few flowers. But tonight I didn't want to upstage my brother—it was his birthday after all.

I was dressed in a splendid gown of rose pink with white lace across the hem and sleeves. It too was simple, covering from my neck to ankle, but elegant enough for a princess and thankfully loose, as the evening was rather warm. It was a gift from my brother, and while I had others more flattering, not wearing the gown would have hurt his feelings.

Laying my brush aside, I looked down and paused to run a finger across the new necklace I wore. It too was simple, a silver chain and a pendant with a single blood-red jewel encased inside it. It was also a gift from my brother. True, it was his birthday, but he seemed to be trying to make amends for his recent behavior. While I personally thought the necklace was the ugliest thing in the kingdom, I wore it anyway to show my acceptance of his apology.

As for my own gift, I had sent him two books. One was a recent title, popular with the young men, about the adventures of an explorer lost at sea. And the other a more serious work about the value of friendship and honor. I hoped he didn't think the latter too moralizing.

I swiveled toward the woman sitting on the bed behind me. Risten, dressed in her best uniform, perched on the side of the bed, with one leg tucked under herself, a sword in her lap, and a polishing cloth in her hand. Her boots, already shined until they were almost blinding, sat on the floor beside her. I sighed and wished, not for the first time, that Risten would let her hair grow out just a little. She kept it painfully short, yet just long enough for the bangs to hang in her face. And my cousin had such lovely hair too—a shade of red just a touch lighter than my own dark red, but without the curly waves I detested.

I sighed heavily. "Risten, aren't you going to change? We'll need to go soon."

Risten pushed the cloth down the length of her sword one last time. She held the shiny blade up to the light as she scrutinized its edge. My cousin didn't even glance my way. "I told you I'm not wearing a dress. The brat can't be expecting me to wear one anyway. I think he meant it as a joke. You know he's not very fond of me."

I turned in my seat to look at Risten directly. "He sent you a personal invitation and even included that lovely dress." I leaned forward. "You are part of the family, you know. You could go as my cousin instead of my bodyguard."

Risten looked up from her blade as she slid it into its scabbard. "He may be your brother, but I don't trust him. So I'm happy to go as your guard, as I always do."

I sighed. "You really should try to get along with him. He is the next in line should something happen to me."

Risten looked at me levelly. "Zofie, it's my duty to make sure that doesn't *happen. I swore on your mother's grave that I would take care of you." Risten winced, no doubt kicking herself for speaking of my mother.*

*I blinked at her a moment remembering the other event that had happened on this day. I dropped my hands in my lap and sat quietly, looking at the floor. "Today is the day, isn't it? The day my brother was born. And the day mother died."*

*Risten stood and came to stand beside me. She gently touched my arm. "One life came into the world and another went out. It's the way of things."*

*I quickly pulled out my kerchief and dabbed at my eyes, fearing the threatening tears would damage the servant's work on my appearance.*

*Risten nudged my shoulder. "It's hard to believe it's been fifteen years since she passed. I remember the king's tears, the servants running here and there, and the officials in a panic. But you were kneeling beside your mother's bed, sitting so quietly, clearly not understanding what was happening. But still you sat there like a soldier at her post."*

*"Well, I was only five."*

*"I was barely ten myself and crying my own tears. Lady Winstella was my favorite and treated me better than anyone in the castle." Risten smiled. "I decided I had best get you out of the way lest you be trampled, so I went and took your hand. You just looked up at me with those wide innocent eyes and asked if your mother was dead. I had no idea what I should say to a small child, so I simply said yes."*

*Risten's face almost glowed with pride. "And you stood up with me and said, you had to be strong for father. You were the lady of the house now. And I knew right then what my role in life would be. I knew it with a certainty I felt down to my toes. You were the kind of person I wanted to serve." Risten wiped her own tears with the back of her hand. "And so I took you to my room and kept you there, fending off anyone that tried to take you, until the king himself came for you."*

*I had heard this story many times, but I hadn't thought about it from an adult's perspective before. "Was father angry? He was no doubt grieving himself."*

Risten chuckled. "Well, he wasn't angry, but he wasn't exactly pleased either. The next day though, I found myself assigned to Master Valervick and began to learn the sword. I think your father decided that if I was going to protect you, I had best learn how."

I stood up and hugged her. "I do appreciate all you've done for me over the years..." I stepped back and grinned wickedly. "But that doesn't mean you can't put on a dress."

Risten slapped her palm against her forehead. "Creator! You're persistent."

"I can't help it."

Risten smiled. "Which is why you will make an excellent queen one day."

There was a knock at the door, and a servant poked her head inside. "It's time, your majesty."

I immediately smoothed down my gown while Risten slipped on her boots and checked that her sword was secure.

I turned to Risten. "How do I look?"

Risten examined me critically. "Any suitors coming tonight?"

I rolled my eyes. "Thank the Creator no."

"Then too bad for them. You look beautiful."

I chuckled, and we grinned at each other. Unexpectedly, a rumble of distant thunder came through the room's open windows on the other side of the bed. The shutters had been thrown open to allow what breeze there was into the room. I glanced out at the dark clouds gathering in the distance, quickly moving to obscure the setting sun. A white streak suddenly cut across the deepening sky, making me flinch.

"Looks like there will be a storm this evening," I said, turning away from the window. "I hope it doesn't dampen the party."

Risten snorted. "Would serve him right if it did. The Creator should rightfully dispense some justice."

I turned toward the bedroom door. "Now Risten."

Risten fell in behind me. "You heard what he did in the city? And he's only fifteen!"

*We moved down the hall, and any servants we encountered quickly backed up to the wall and bowed as we passed. I sighed. "Those are only rumors."*

*"Why are you defending him?" Risten asked, clearly irritated. "It's exactly something he would do. Prank my ass. Those poor girls were clearly traumatized by what he did. Abducting them against their will and then draining most of their myst! It doesn't matter if they were commoners or royalty, they should not have been treated that way."*

*"But the magistrate cleared him of the charges."*

*"And did you notice that same magistrate now seems to be wearing new clothes and a gold ring."*

*"It couldn't have been that bad..."*

*Risten grabbed my arm and turned me to face her. "I can't believe you don't see this for what it is? He needlessly hurt people."*

*I considered my cousin before answering. "I'm not blind. And I've already confronted Wynn about it. He swore it was a misunderstanding and that he'd never let something like that happen again." I smiled. "Now, why don't we drop this for now and let my brother have his moment."*

*Risten searched my face, clearly having more to say, but frowned and raised her chin. "As you wish."*

*I furrowed my brows in disappointment. I really didn't like to disagree with Risten, especially not tonight of all nights.*

*Risten, evidently trying to ease the tension, changed the subject. "How is Mistress Ginneley? Is she coming tonight?"*

*She was my much loved, myst-casting tutor and easily the oldest person in the castle.*

*I shook my head sadly. "No, she's still not feeling well. This makes two weeks she's taken to her bed. I visited her just this morning, and she still looked ill. I fear she may not have long to live."*

*Further conversation was cut short, as the steward met us at the ballroom entrance, and after fussing over this and that, announced Risten and I to the gathered crowd. It was a relatively small event, as these affairs went, with only* about fifty or so nobility and close friends. There could have been ten times that number, but Wynn had insisted it be a small affair. It would be more fun, he had claimed.

I smiled as I walked into the room and down the center aisle toward the raised seats at the head of the room. My father, King Tiernan Xernow, sat in the middle on his favorite chair, another indication of this evening being a small affair. Father hated his formal throne—said it hurt to sit on it too long— preferring his smaller, well-padded chair. He was dressed in a fine dark purple jacket and a white shirt underneath with pants of gold—the colors of the king- dom. Behind him on the wall was an elegant tapestry with the crest of the kingdom on it—a regal griffin done in the same shade of royal purple as my father's jacket.

Master Valervick stood just behind the king dressed in his formal black uni- form. As usual, he was scowling. The only time I had seen him smile was when he was watching Risten practice and finally master some difficult movement. Only then would Valervick's marble face crack into a gentle grin.

My brother Wynn stood as I entered. I had to admit he was a most hand- some young man. Like me, he had dark red hair, which he kept long and in a tight braid down his back. He also had the same smattering of freckles across the nose—a mutual gift from our departed mother. He was already broad of shoulder and a full head taller than I. But his best feature was his smile, which displayed his beautifully white teeth. His jacket and pants were white like his shirt, giving him the air of an angel.

As Risten and I approached, he was displaying his handsome smile but, for just a brief moment, it faltered as he noticed that Risten followed not in a dress, but her uniform and sword. But like the lightning outside, the expression only flashed for a moment, before his smile quickly returned. Only I, who knew him the best, noticed the change. It strangely troubled me that he had reacted. Per- haps he really was trying to make amends with Risten.

When I neared them, Wynn leaped from the platform to escort me to my seat at the king's right. Father smiled broadly at his son, clearly pleased. Risten took her place standing beside the platform close to me, while Wynn formally bowed to the king, then to me, and finally gave a sweeping bow to the gathered crowd which burst into applause.

Father reached over and patted my hand. But his hand was ice cold. I looked closely at him and noticed he seemed a little pale.

I leaned closer and whispered. "Father, are you feeling all right?"

He patted my hand again. "I'm fine child. Just a little tired, that's all." I noticed that my father had a new ring on his finger. I wondered if it was also a gift from Wynn.

Father stood and began the festivities with a few comments about his son. I only listened with half an ear, since I had helped him write the speech. Instead, I surveyed the crowd noting all the familiar faces of the kingdom. I was surprised that I didn't see any of Wynn's close friends. Most everyone in attendance were allies of my father. All except one. He was standing beside Wynn's chair on the opposite side of the raised platform. He too was a quite attractive man, with a carefully trimmed black beard and a strong face. I leaned toward Risten and whispered in her ear. "Who is that man next to Wynn?"

Risten shook her head and leaned close to answer. "I'm not sure," she whispered back. "I think I heard your brother call him Wolf or Watt or Wort. Something like that. But don't worry, he appears to be your brother's guest, not your father's."

I sighed in relief. "Thank goodness. I was afraid it was another suitor. I've told father I'm not anywhere near ready to marry, but he doesn't listen to me."

"Persistent, isn't he?" Risten grinned.

I returned the grin. "Where do you think I got it from?"

There was another rumble of thunder outside, only this one sounded closer.

Father finally finished his speech and sat back down, while those gathered applauded. It was now my time to speak, and I started to rise, but my brother beat me to it.

Wynn raised his cup of wine. "I would like to propose a toast to our king."

Well, Wynn always did like to improvise. I followed his lead and did the same. The crowd responded by raising their own cups in salute.

*"May our good king live forever!" Wynn announced.*

*The hall flashed white as a bolt of lightning cracked outside the high windows and reflected off the walls. It was immediately answered by a loud boom of thunder.*

*And then Wynn did the strangest thing.*

*He upended his cup and let the wine trickle to the floor.*

*The crowd gasped in horror, and I stared transfixed at the insult. "Wynn, what..."*

*Suddenly the doors of the ballroom were flung open, and six heavily armed men stepped inside.*

*Father leaped from his chair. "Wynn, what is the meaning of this!" he shouted indignantly.*

*Wynn smiled, his beautiful teeth on full display. "I think it should be obvious, Father. It's time to bring in the new and get rid of the old." He threw his cup over his shoulder. "I think it should be obvious which is which." Wynn looked to the man named Wort. "Kill them all; they're friends of my father. None of them leaves alive."*

*I didn't hesitate. Risten and I had practiced assassination scenarios many times. Springing to my feet, I reached inside myself and activated a myst-spell. Instantly a blue-tinted bubble sprung up around the king and the guests in the hall. Risten also sprang into action and launched herself at Wort. But as Wort drew his own sword, my eyes grew wide in horror. It couldn't be. That sword had been locked in our deepest tombs. I had only seen it twice, and both times only my father had accompanied me—our family's darkest secret.*

*It was Havoc's Sword. A blade with a history as dark as those it was designed to defeat. It was able to cut through anything.*

*Without thinking, I reached again inside myself and activated a thread of myst which I sent toward Risten. But Wort's sword was already swinging. It would arrive too late. My cousin was going to be cut in half...*

*But Master Valervick had also recognized the sword and moved the instant he saw it. He shoved Risten out of the way. As she fell, I saw the master twist as I had seen him do a thousand times to avoid a strike, but it wasn't enough...*

*The sword caught his right arm at the shoulder, cleanly slicing it off.*

*Valervick collapsed. Risten dropped her sword and crawled to her beloved master, tearing up her own jacket to try and stop the bleeding. "Don't die," she kept repeating as if it were a chant. "Don't die." As he lay there slowly bleeding to death, his bright eyes looked up at her, and with his left hand, he reached out and grabbed her by the shirt, pulling her against him. Then he smiled. "Best student... I ever... had." The arm fell away as he died. Risten collapsed on his chest sobbing.*

*My heart knotted as the scene played out, but I had my own problem to deal with... I saw a flash and instinctively dodged. The ball of flame crashed into the wall behind me. I reached within myself and drew up a wall of myst. The second ball crashed into it, exhausting itself on the ethereal surface. Behind it, my brother grinned. "Don't forget, I'm over here. It's my birthday, after all." Other balls of fire crashed against my barrier.*

*"Give it up, Wynn, you know I'm an expert at defensive shields."*

*He nodded. "I'm counting on it." He turned to Wort. "Touch her barrier with your blade."*

*Wort plunged his sword at the barrier. It hesitated at the wall, but with a sudden pop, the barrier was gone. I braced for the backlash of myst—but it didn't come. Instead, my father screamed within his own barrier and fell to the floor.*

*"What...?"*

*But I didn't have time to think about it as more balls of fire flew at my head. I reached deeper inside myself and tapped a more complex spell which opened a small portal. The balls entered and disappeared. A heartbeat later, I heard an explosion outside the hall where the balls had emerged. I staggered, feeling weak. Was I running out of myst already? No, I could feel that I had plenty. Then what was wrong?*

*"Impressive," said my brother. "Too bad you spent all your time on defensive spells."*

*Suddenly, I felt something long and slender encircle my throat. I reached for the counterspell and quickly shattered it. But it made me feel even weaker—*

a cold sweat broke out on my forehead. I had to be running out, but how was that possible after only a few spells?

"I think that's enough now, dear sister."

I looked over to find that Wort had broken the barrier protecting my collapsed father. And to my horror, I saw him pointing Havoc's Sword at Father's throat. I froze.

Risten, wiping the tears from her eyes, reached over and took her master's sword. With a sword in each hand, she launched herself at Wort. Her face a mask of fury.

But Wynn smiled, and an ethereal cage of emerald green enclosed her. Risten bounced off the wall in shock and then thrashed against it in her fury. But she was unable to break through.

I fell to my knees, the world seeming to swim around me. I glanced at my father—he looked bad too, lying limp, sweating profusely and breathing hard in short gasps.

Although I fought to hold it, I felt my shield protecting the guests falter—and then fail. Their screams echoed through the halls.

How was he doing this?

And then it connected. The necklace. Father's ring.

I paled. Oh please Creator, no.

I reached to jerk the necklace off, but a strand of myst encircled my wrist and immobilized it.

Wynn squatted down in front of me. "Zophia, my dear sister, what is the first thing we are taught as myst users. Isn't it that myst users have a large supply of the stuff, but most people don't? And when you run out. You die. So what would happen do you think, if you were to link up a myst user with someone who wasn't one. So that every spell they cast drew from that poor someone. Do you think they might look like father? Slowly dying."

"You bastard!" I tried to shout, but it only came out as a whisper.

"I gave you the necklace and father a new ring, both specially spelled so any myst drawn by the necklace wearer would come from the ring bearer. And every defense spell you put up, drew our father closer to death. Until now, he is almost sucked dry. Almost. But just one more good draw should do it. One more spell and father will die."

"I won't do it," I spat. "I'll let myself be killed first."

"As I thought you would. So I arranged for something special sister. Something to haunt you until the day you die." He smiled. "I laid awake many a night thinking this up. I hope you like it."

Risten was going crazy in her confined cage—throwing herself bodily against it.

I looked up at my brother. "Why? Why all this?"

Wynn considered me for a moment and then simply answered. "Because mother died." He said it like it should be perfectly obvious from just that statement.

Wynn pointed a finger at me, touching it to my chest, his expression turning serious. "Zophia Olwenna Xernow, Princess of Brethnach, I curse you. I give you the curse of Eternal Transformation!"

The jewel around my neck turned hot, burning into my flesh. Father screamed in agony.

A blue glow surrounded me, and I began to change. I screamed in my own agony as bones crunched and warped, my organs came undone and moved inside me, and my skin seemed to melt and reform.

And I felt the excruciating pain of each and every change.

When it was done, I blinked in surprise that I was still alive. I looked down to find my pink gown puddled at my feet, and my body covered with short brown hair. In a daze, I examined my hand, opening and closing the slender, hair-covered fingers until it dawned on me what I had become: a small monkey. I looked up at my brother, large as a giant looming over me, not believing what was happening.

Risten had collapsed sobbing in her cage, one hand still beating on the cage.

Wynn laughed out loud, echoing through the now deathly quiet hall. "Sister, I always said you looked like a monkey in a dress. Now you really are one."

Outside, there was another flash of lightning and an immediate pelt of thunder—then the sky opened up, and the rain fell.

# CHAPTER SEVENTEEN

# A
# Master's Gift

Zofie pulled her hand away from my cheek, and I blinked in momentary disorientation. It felt like I had been in her memory for hours, but judging from the fire, it couldn't have been more than a few moments.

Zofie's eyes were leaking tears, but she was smiling. No doubt reliving it had been difficult for her. "Are you all right?" she asked.

I nodded in shock, my eyes wide in disbelief. "That was so horrible... and what he did to you..." I took her hand and squeezed it. "I don't know how you withstood it."

She squeezed it back. "I have a couple of good friends."

I breathed a sigh and ran a hand over my newly shorn head. "So, what happened after? You obviously made it out somehow."

She slowly shook her head. "I'm not exactly sure. The shock of the transformation, the death of my father, and Wynn's betrayal were too much for me..." She bowed her head. "I fainted, I'm ashamed to say.

When I awoke, it was dawn of the next day, and we were leagues away from the castle heading upriver by boat. While Risten has told me some, it probably would be best to hear that tale from Risten herself."

Suddenly the stories I had heard began to make sense. "And your brother blamed it all on you."

Zofie nodded. "Everything. Father's death, the massacre, he said I had engineered the plan to steal the throne, and he had only been saved by his swordsman, Wort. The proof was in who had drained my father's myst. Any myst user worth half their salt could see that I had done it."

"So you're trying to get the sword and take back your kingdom."

Zofie sniffed and wiped her eyes. "That's Risten's plan, although I would be happy to just get this curse off me."

I glanced over to where Risten was sleeping and noticed that her blanket was empty. I looked around. Where could she have gone?

Zofie looked down and shook her head sadly. "No, I'll never get my kingdom back. You need someone that the people will follow, and as you can see, they won't follow me." She looked away. "Plus, I really am a murderer. It was I who sucked all the myst from his body. I should have realized what was happening sooner. Perhaps if I had listened to Risten." She turned her sad eyes to me. "So that's the other reason you really don't want to be friends with me. With this open connection between us, I could kill you. Suck every bit of myst out of you without even meaning to. I don't want to be a murderer again."

I suddenly felt a presence beside me, and a voice whispered right in my ear. "You know I could have killed you ten times over."

I leaped up in surprise and whirled to face Risten, squatting behind where I had been sitting, an evil grin on her face. I put a hand over my chest. "Don't do that! You nearly made my heart leap out of my chest."

Risten stood and went to sit next to Zofie. "Serves you right for getting too friendly." The sword-master settled beside her cousin and turned to her. "Did you give him the old memory magic? I hope you didn't show him my last bath or something."

Zofie chuckled. "Definitely not. I was just showing him that time I walked in on you while you were on the chamber pot."

Risten wheeled. "What!"

Zofie ducked. "I'm jesting. You know I wouldn't show him something private."

They both laughed. It was evident the two women were very comfortable with each other. I couldn't help but envy their closeness.

We were silent for a moment, until Risten cleared her throat. I could tell she was working up to something. "Can you do that memory thing with me? I haven't had a chance to show you how Master Ginneley helped us and... you know."

Zofie nodded resignedly. "I know, but I was dreading it all the same." She glanced at me and seemed to come to a decision. "Risten, could Coren see it too? I think it would be good for him to know."

Risten glared at me for a moment, but finally nodded. "I guess so. Just nothing private."

Zofie sighed and took both our hands. She steeled herself for the magic, seeming to dread what was coming. I couldn't help but wonder what could possibly be worse than what I had just seen.

Zofie bowed her head and tightened her grip on my hand. Then, in the next heartbeat, I was there, back in the castle's banquet hall. Only this time, I was looking through Risten's eyes...

I knelt inside my ethereal myst cage, defeated and in complete misery. Both my master's sword and my own lay useless beside me. I hadn't been able to do a damn thing. The king had been assassinated. The guests had been slaughtered. Wynn had cursed Zofie. And my master was dead. I had utterly and totally failed. I should have died instead.

*Why had my master done it? If it hadn't been for me, he would still be alive. There was no honor in the way he had died. Why just that morning, he had been talking about giving up his post with the king and just finding a quiet cottage to settle in. And to my shock, maybe even marry his one love. Creator knows he had enough coin to do it, and certainly the goodwill of the king.*

*It just wasn't right.*

*Movement outside my cage made me look up. Wort passed close by, the evil sword at his side. He paused to talk to Wynn.*

*As I watched him through the red hair in my eyes, I felt my anger ignite and flash within me—a burning flame of rage, hot and ugly. He had killed my master with a magical sword. There was no honor in a weapon like that. And the man deserved to die just as my master had. I beat at the cage's green-tinted bars with my bruised and battered fists. He would pay. That man would pay. I slowly got to my feet and sheathed my own sword safely at my belt. But I clutched my master's in my right hand, feeling its weight and deadly beauty as if for the first time. I would kill him, and I would use this sword to do it. I didn't know how. But I was going to get out of this cage and kill him, as my master would have done had I not gotten in the way—even if it cost my life.*

*I felt something tap me on the shoulder, and I jumped in surprise. I wheeled to find a disembodied hand beckoning me closer. It extended toward me palm up as if it wanted me to do something. I reached out, and it immediately latched onto me, unexpectedly yanking me forward—hard.*

*I fell and sprawled onto the floor of someone's bedroom. A myst-casting! I turned to find a night-dressed butt standing there without a visible torso. It was like her top half had disappeared behind a curtain of invisibility.*

*A moment later, the person's torso re-appeared holding a small unconscious monkey. I was relieved to see it was Mistress Dorhty Ginneley—Zofie's tutor. Probably the only one of the old king's friends that hadn't been at the party.*

*She was an elderly woman, thin and frail—a little on the short side. Even in the summer's warmth, she was wrapped in a shawl. Zofie spoke very highly of her, saying she was a brilliant myst-seer—the best of her generation—but I never cared much for the woman. And from my limited dealings with her, the* feeling was mutual. Ginneley and Master Valervick had some kind of falling out many, many years ago. Unfortunately, I was guilty by association.

Breathing hard, Ginneley shuffled over to her bed and seemed to more collapse on it than sit, with Zofie cradled in her lap. The woman looked exhausted. Zofie had mentioned before the party that the woman was very ill.

I got to my feet, sword still in hand. "Wynn used Zofie to kill the king and..."

"I know," she said, the depth of her misery evident in those two words. She stroked the unconscious Zofie's fur. "When I felt the beginning of a myst battle, I looked to see what was happening. By then, it was too late. That swordsman used Havoc's Sword. A truly terrible weapon." She slowly shook her head. "They're all dead now... even Arnest." She gave a sad smile. "How I loved that bastard."

Arnest was the familiar name of my own Master Valervick. It puzzled me that she referred to him that way since they had barely interacted over the years. But then again, they had known each other since long before I had been born.

I stepped forward. "Send me back! I will avenge Master Valervick." I held up his sword. "I will kill that traitor with this very blade."

Breathing in short gasps Ginneley, stared at me. "I can," she said. "But pulling you both out nearly did me in. I have maybe one more good spell left in me, and then that's going to be it." She grimaced, with her hand making a fist, she laid it over her chest. "I don't have much time left anyway. This old heart is just about done." She gave a short, bitter laugh. "I guess it's been broken one too many times."

The elder looked up at me, the exhaustion in her eyes evident. "So what will it be? You possibly getting your revenge and dying in the process, or you living and protecting someone you swore to defend at all cost? Pick quickly before they figure out it was me and storm my meager defenses."

I opened my mouth—but hesitated. I had been going to say send me to my revenge. But then I looked at Zofie in her new form and remembered my oath, and my love for my cousin.

Ginneley looked down at the transformed Zofie and gently stroked her head.

"She can't do myst-casting now. The curse eats up all her myst. And she can hardly fend for herself in this form. At best, she'll end up in a cage as someone's pet or more likely on someone's dinner plate."

I turned away in anger. The woman's logic was maddening. And irrefutable. I gritted my teeth. "What do I need to do?"

Ginneley stood and laid Zofie on the bed. "Good choice, because I can't save her. Only you can." She shuffled to me, and I turned to face her.

"First thing we need is a disguise," she said. "That part is easy." The small woman looked up at me critically. "Going as a servant would make you more invisible, but your progress would be slow. Plus wielding the kind of coin you'll need will make you a target, and likely reveal your sword-master skills." She tapped her chin with a single finger. "Better I think to try the other way." She turned to the side and reached through empty air, her arm vanishing from sight. A moment later it returned with an elegant dress and shoes. My eyes went wide when I recognized it: a light blue dress with a white ribbon around the sleeves and collar. It was already sized to fit me.

"There is no way I'm going to wear that brat's dress," I spat. "That's the one he gave me for the party."

"All the more reason to use it. It's the only dress in the castle already made to fit. You won't have to wear it long, just until you're well away from here. Now put it on and quickly! Remember you're doing this for Zofie."

I grumbled, but quickly disrobed and put on the dress and shoes. The dress felt strange and confining. It no doubt looked stupid on me.

Ginneley handed me two hair combs. I looked at her, not understanding since mine was too short to hold them.

Ginneley sighed and grimaced again. She swayed for a moment but steadied herself on a nearby table. "Your red hair makes you too easy to spot, and its length means you're not a lady." She poked my middle.

My scalp began to tingle while something began to brush my neck. Glancing behind me, I saw that my short red hair was growing and extending down my back. Its radiant waves not stopping until it reached the top of my butt. However, the length wasn't the only change, I was shocked to see that my new hair was no longer red, but a golden blonde. I would bet that my freckles were gone too. I quickly put the combs in my hair to hold it back from my face.

I caught movement out of the corner of my eye and, when I turned, saw it was my own reflection in a small mirror on the wall. My mouth fell open as I took in the transformation. I looked nothing like my usual self. While it was still the face I was accustomed to seeing, it was not me. Instead, returning my gaze was—a lady. Something I would have never thought possible. I shook my head and turned away. I didn't have time for this now.

I put my old clothes and swords in a large cloth bag which Ginneley provided and a few other things that I might need. "Here," the old woman pushed a sizeable purse of coins at me and a freshly penned note. "Give the paper to the man at the docks and a gold coin. He'll ask for two, but tell him you'll find someone else for that price, and he'll take the one. Tell him you're not getting along with your new husband, and so you're going to Iron Landing to visit your uncle. He won't ask questions. And no one will notice you. Everyone will be looking for the trousered, short-haired, sword-master, not elegant Lady Brightmare." Ginneley paused and took a step back. She sadly shook her head. "You look so much like your mother. She had the same shade of hair."

My eyes went large; the deep hunger to know the woman that had abandoned me. "You knew my mother? And you never told me?"

The old woman frowned. "It was her wish, not mine. Maybe you'll meet one day." Ginneley grimaced and nearly bent over in pain. "Hurry! Get Zofie and stand in the middle of the room."

I did as I was told, cradling Zofie in my arms and the bag in my free hand. "But what's in Iron Landing? It's just a small river port town."

Ginneley took a deep breath and began tracing patterns in the air. With each stroke, a line appeared and glowed. She spoke as she drew, turning the lines into a complex myst-casting. "You need to find a man named Spraggel van Deviante. He is your key to getting the curse off Zofie."

"So he can remove it?"

Ginneley smiled fondly as she drew. "Spraggel couldn't use a myst-spell if you drew him a picture. Although, he was able to use that pocket spell I gave him." She started drawing the center pattern in precise, intricate lines. "No, Spraggel can't remove it. But he knows someone that might. A young lad who I made a special amulet for not long ago."

The old master finished her pattern. "When I open the portal, step through quickly. It will only be open for a few seconds at most."

"And what about you? Aren't you coming with us?"

Ginneley paused and put a hand on my shoulder. "No, child. This is it for me. This will be my last spell and is my last gift." She gently patted my arm. "Please take care of my student. Tell her that I love her and not to feel guilty. I do this of my own free will."

I gasped, suddenly understanding the cost of this last spell. My eyes welled up in sorrow, but I refused to cry. This gift deserved better.

Ginneley raised her hands and the glowing lines brightened, and with a soft pop, vanished, leaving a hole in the air. Through it, I could see the port.

The old master grimaced in pain. Her arms started to falter. "Go!"

I stepped through and found myself on the docks, wet with recent rain. The man I was supposed to see was just ahead. I turned to wave to Ginneley, but the elder didn't respond. She grabbed her chest with both hands and seemed to crumble. She fell face forward, and the portal collapsed.

I fought back the tears. "Thank you," I whispered. And paused for a moment as the weight of our situation settled in. All of our friends and family were gone.

We were totally and absolutely alone.

I turned toward the docks and wondered if perhaps dying while fighting Wort might have been the easier choice.

I blinked in momentary confusion as the campsite came back into focus. *Oh Creator, that was bad too.*

Zofie was squeezing my hand as if to break it off and openly sobbed.

Risten's eyes also glistened in the firelight. She put an arm around Zofie. "Don't weep. She said not to feel guilty."

"But she didn't say I couldn't miss her. She was the first person besides you to treat me as just plain Zofie instead of some princess."

We sat in silence for a while as Zofie quieted her tears. Finally, she pulled her hand from mine and stood up. "It's about time for me to transform back," she said, pulling the hood of the robe up and hiding her chimera face. "I think I'd like to be alone for a bit. I have a lot to think about." She then turned and started to step away, but I reached up and grabbed her arm. She paused but wouldn't look at me.

"Let her go, Coren," warned Risten.

"No," I said, shaking my head and standing. "No, I won't." I'm not exactly sure what got into me, but I just pulled her into my arms and hugged her. "Zofie, don't push me away, I want to help. I know I can't take your pain away, but at least let me share it."

She relaxed into my arms and laid her head on my shoulder.

"You shouldn't Coren. It will only lead you to ruin. I've been branded a murderer. And I could kill you without meaning to. You'd best not get too close."

I pulled her tighter against me. "I think it's too late for that."

# CHAPTER EIGHTEEN

# Cumulative Error

I gave Spraggel a puzzled look. "If we're looking for an island, shouldn't we be heading toward the sea instead of the mountains?"

The sun was barely illuminating the horizon as Spraggel, Risten, and I got our horses ready for the day's journey. Zofie had transformed back to her latest bird form just before first light and flew off to see if we were being followed.

Zofie and I had spent most of the night just chatting about different things, mostly about my life and childhood—she seemed fascinated by the everyday events of a commoner. She eagerly devoured every detail and even laughed at my not-so-funny jokes. I really enjoyed her company. So I had to say I was ever so sorry when she said it was time and transformed back to her bird form.

Which left me one very tired man.

I tried to rub the sleep out of my eyes while I chewed on some dried meat. What I would give for some real breakfast food. Actually, what I would give for a little sleep. Or even better, breakfast in bed.

Risten had finally given my shirt back. I had immediately slipped it on only to find it now smelled like Risten—roses and leather. I had noticed this before. I couldn't figure out where she got her rose scent from, unless she had it in her soap. I guess I should have been happy she didn't smell like something foul, but I wasn't. In fact, it bothered me. I wasn't exactly sure why. Maybe because I hadn't noticed a scent from Zofie, which I could only attribute to her cursed chimera form.

As we saddled the horses, Spraggel and I were discussing our next destination. But I couldn't believe he was serious. It seemed ludicrous to me to have an island in the mountains.

Spraggel made the final adjustment to his saddle and stood. "The instructions were quite clear. It's in the Skyblue Mountains. I was interrupted before I could pin down the exact location. But it's definitely in the mountains."

Over Spraggel's shoulder, I could see Risten finish up saddling her horse. "So, you don't have a clue where it is," she called to us.

Spraggel looked over his shoulder at her. "I know more than just a clue, my dear." He seemed uncharacteristically irritated. "It's in the mountains, due north and somewhere in the Skyblue Mountains." He turned back to me. "I do wish Wort hadn't interrupted us. It would have made things so much easier."

Risten threw up her hands in frustration, turned on her heel, and headed for the oak tree that caught our flight.

*What is she up to?*

Spraggel continued to babble on about the nature of the scroll, and how the author had written the text, the references to names and places during the time of the war with the Dark Avenyts.

Meanwhile, Risten jumped up and caught the lowest branch of the oak tree and pulled herself up into its foliage.

I returned to my discussion with Spraggel. "Could the name Averet Island, be a reference to the Supterian god of water? If it is, then we should try due south off the coast."

Again, watching over Spraggel's shoulder, Risten leaped down, holding the Spear of Flight we had used last night. About that time, Zofie returned and landed next to her. They talked, or rather Risten talked and Zofie nodded, but I was too far away to make out what she was saying. Especially over Spraggel's lecture.

"Nonsense. Averet is indeed a Supterian god, but it's the one for thunder. Which indicates clouds. Maybe it's a figurative island, like when the mountain top sticks up from the clouds surrounding it...."

Risten stepped away from Zofie and wrapped the spear with a scarf. Then she hefted the weapon as if she was going to throw it but gripped it through the cloth. Zofie raised her wings like she was preparing to fly. I couldn't help but look puzzled at what they were doing. Risten shouted loud enough that I could hear her. "Take me to Averet Island!" and threw the spear, pulling her hand away at the last moment. The spear sailed on, and Zofie took flight behind it.

*Zofie? What's going on?*

*Sorry,* she answered. *I can't talk. I have to concentrate.*

All right. I guess I needed to go to the source.

Risten walked back toward us while Spraggel continued his discussion of the allusions in the literature of the time. I stepped to one side of Spraggel. "What did you just do?"

She had a very pleased look on her face. "Rather than argue it to death, I just sent the Spear of Flight to find it for us. Zofie's following it, and she'll come back and tell us which way it's heading."

"But..." I started to protest but drew up short—what she had done sinking in. "Actually, a brilliant idea."

Risten just crossed her arms and gave me a cocky smile.

Spraggel started to wind down. "But all discussion about the island's name probably isn't important." He sighed. "I guess the best thing to do would be to use the Spear of Flight to find it."

"Uh... Master, I think Risten just did that."

He brightened. "Excellent! Then let's get started." He climbed into his saddle.

Risten shook her head. "Men."

We mounted up and headed in the same direction Zofie had gone. I was afraid we might not hear from her for a long while, but a little over three hours later, she came back carrying the spear.

We had just stopped to rest the horses and take a much-needed break. I didn't know about the others, but my landing in the tree had left bruises everywhere, and I was a little stiff.

"What happened?" I called to her.

*It was headed in the direction of Mount Eternal,* explained Zofie. She fluttered to a halt beside us, causing the horses to shy away.

*But the spear seemed to run out of myst after only an hour of flying. It just stopped mid-flight and fell! You two were lucky you didn't fall from the sky yesterday.*

Probably another reason the spear had fallen out of use. Those using it likely had a high mortality rate—and not from battle.

I relayed the information to the others.

Spraggel put a finger to his lips in contemplation. "Mount Eternal lost its peak a long time ago. Perhaps it left a crater when it did, which filled with water and left an island in the middle. Which means we'll have to climb it. No one's been up there since its top was blown away, or at least no one will admit it if they have. The people living along its base say it's haunted. And those that have gone up it to explore have never returned."

I threw my hands up in the air. "Oh, great. A haunted mountain."

Risten smiled. "What's the matter? Are you scared of ghosts?"

I guess I was a little irritable from lack of sleep. "Ghosts, no. Man-eating monsters, yes."

Spraggel interjected, "It must be something fairly serious since the priests of Daili haven't been able to get to the shield."

I turned to Spraggel. "You think there is something to the stories?"

"I do."

I pushed the dirt around with my boot. "I have an idea. Let's just let Wort go ahead of us and get eaten. Then we wouldn't have to worry about it."

Spraggel nodded. "While that would be nice, remember he's got the sword. I doubt much could stand in his way. No, our best course is to get there first and take the shield."

Risten turned to Zofie. "Speaking of the bastard, did you see him anywhere? Is he following?"

She flapped once and nodded. *I did see a group moving in the same general direction as us. But it's much larger than Wort's original party of six. There looked to be about twelve people in all.*

I relayed this to the others.

Spraggel shook his head. "That's not good. Likely Wort and Benzel have teamed up. Apparently, we severely wounded their pride."

I shook my head. "This just gets better and better." I started walking in a small circle. "So we're being chased by not one enemy but two, and we have to climb a mountain that no one returns from, *and* get back down before our enemies catch us. All to get a shield which no one's seen in a thousand years. Doesn't all that sound a little... I don't know... *difficult*."

They all just stared at me.

I sighed heavily. "Well, at least we understand the odds."

We mounted up again and pushed our horses as hard as we dared. The horses had served us well to this point, but even they had their limits.

Speaking of limits, I hit mine at mid-day. I was used to dozing in the saddle now, but I must have been exhausted because I nearly fell off my horse.

I looked around to make sure no one saw. But behind me, Risten was smirking. Yeah, she'd seen.

I needed something to occupy me, so I didn't really embarrass myself. I turned my wrist up and examined my curse-anchor. I sure could use some more information on my curse. On impulse, I reined in my horse, coming to a stop in the road. Risten passed me and gave me a puzzled look.

"You go on ahead," I told her. "I want to try talking to my curse again, and I don't want you to think I'm crazy."

She snorted. "It's too late for that."

When I thought they were out of earshot, I spoke to my wrist. I had to admit that it felt really strange talking to my hand.

"Abhulengulus. Can you speak to me? I have some questions."

The eye on my wrist slowly opened, staring right at me. *I think we've already had this conversation,* came that deep, resonating voice. *I only answer the questions I want to, and right now, I don't want to.*

I frowned, remembering what Zofie had said. Perhaps he was trying to avoid answering me. "I don't believe you," I said firmly. "If you really didn't want to, you would just ignore me. There's more to it."

All I heard was silence. I took that as encouragement.

"I think you're obligated to answer my questions... and you're trying to avoid your obligation."

Silence.

"I require you to answer my questions right now, giving the best possible answer."

More silence. I was beginning to have my doubts.

"Why are you called the Thief of Curses?"

*Just for the record, you're a rotting piece of flesh, and this is just a royal waste of time. But I am called Abhulengulus because I like the name.* He sounded very annoyed.

I smiled. "And?"

*Oh, all right. My creator chose the name because I am a curse that takes, or steals, other curses. I then incorporate them into my being so that I can use them and have more tools at my disposal, so to speak. Thus the name.*

Now we were getting somewhere. Spraggel turned in his saddle and looked back at me with an odd expression. I just waved him on and pointed to my wrist.

"So how many of these tools do you have?"

*Probably higher than you can count. Have you learned to use your fingers AND your toes yet?*

"Answer the question."

I heard an almost human exasperated sigh. *One.*

I started laughing. "You're a thousand-year-old curse, the famous Thief of Curses and you've only stolen one curse?"

*It's not my fault, dammit! I lose all my curses every time my host dies. And you, my unfortunate sack of meat, have only touched one in your ENTIRE LIFE! I've been on your wrist for well near a decade, and you've only touched the one. And I have to say your girlfriend's was the worst curse I have ever seen. Clever, but sloppy. It looks like a child put it together. It took me three tries to get it incorporated. Next time, do me a favor and get one put together by a professional.*

"You said hosts? I guess you mean people like me. I knew my grand-father and father had it, but there must have been others. How many have there been?"

*Including yourself, there have been forty-two men and women.* He sounded almost smug.

This was going better than I expected. I had so many questions. "So how come you can talk... or speak in my mind, or whatever it is you do?"

But there was no answer.

"I command you to answer me."

Silence.

"How come you won't answer me?"

I heard cruel laughter.

*Because I don't have to! You've had your three questions. Now I'm off the hook for a whole day!*

"You mean I only get three questions per day! That's stupid. I command you to answer me."

*Command all you want, you sack of meat. I'm not answering. So until tomorrow.*

And the eye on my wrist closed.

"Abhulengulus, you answer me!" I hit my wrist with my fist, but all that did was hurt *me*. "Abhulengulus!" But the eye stayed closed.

"Dammit!" And we were making such good progress.

I sighed. I decided I *would* get my questions answered. It just might take a while.

That evening after making camp, I explained to Risten and Spraggel what I had learned from the curse. Zofie was out hunting. She claimed she didn't have time during the day.

Spraggel leaned back against a tree. "You had best consider carefully what you want answered. It appears to be a bit of a trickster, but it should have knowledge of how it is used. It might even know of a way to remove itself from you."

I nodded. "While that would be great, I have some other things I want to ask first. Like how to get Zofie's curse off. She's suffered so much. That's what I'm going to focus on."

Risten threw another stick on the fire. "You mean you're not going to ask about the island or how to get rid of your own curse first?" There was a twinge of bitterness to her voice.

"Well, Zofie's suffered so much... actually you both have. If I can shorten that by even a day, I think it would be a good thing."

Risten leaned away from the fire. "Having Zofie uncursed would definitely be my wish."

I nodded. "And after that, perhaps it can tell me what I need to do to use it." I looked up at the stars. "But I've just got this feeling it's not going to be that easy."

Just then, Zofie fluttered down beside us. She looked more tired than usual. Risten noticed it too. "Are you all right?" she asked.

Zofie nodded her large owl head and settled her wings. *I'm fine. Just tired. I have been flying all day, you know.* While I repeated this for Risten, Zofie swiveled her head to look up at the moon. It was just a finger-nail's width. *I think I'm going to go to sleep. I've flown most of the day, and it took a lot out of me.*

I started to stand, but she held out a wing. *You don't need to Coren. I've found a tree sturdy enough for me to perch in just over there, and I'm just too tired right now. Maybe we can talk tomorrow.*

"If you're sure?"

*I am. Tell Risten that I'm just tired.* And she launched herself into a nearby tree.

Risten and I both looked at each other. Zofie didn't look like she was feeling well. And I couldn't shake the feeling that there was more to Zofie's curse than we knew.

It made for a very sleepless night.

The next day, I started in with my questions right after breakfast. But Abe didn't answer. I kept trying at intervals, but it wasn't until mid-day that the eye finally opened. I had once again dropped back so the others couldn't hear me.

"About time," I said as the eye finally opened.

*A curse has got to get their beauty sleep.* I could almost have sworn I heard him yawn. *What does my sack of meat host want from me today?*

"Can you remove Zofie's curse?"

He sounded amused. *I would never have guessed that one was coming,* he said sarcastically. *I already told you I stole it. I control her curse now. My curse can rule them all.*

"Then why didn't she change back?"

*Because she CAN'T! Whoever created that curse didn't reset her to her* original form like it was supposed to. You've probably noticed by now that when she returns to human form, she retains part of the animals she's transformed into. She's having what's called a cumulative error—with every transformation, she gets a little further away from her true self. And it gets worse.

"Worse?" I didn't like the sound of that.

Listen, sack of meat, most curse composers cast them because they want their victim to suffer for as long as possible, and they build in protections to make it last. You know: killing them isn't punishment enough thing. But this curse is gradually leaving things unfixed. Oh, just little things, like ALL HER INTERNAL ORGANS! They're getting moved around and not being put back in exactly the right place. I'm sure you noticed that she only eats or drinks when she's in one of her animal forms, right? Well the reason, meathead, is because she can't eat otherwise now. These transformations are not only making her look ugly, they are killing her! One of these cycles coming up, she'll revert to her supposedly original form and not be able to survive. And from the last time I saw her, she doesn't have much time left. I'd give her only one or two more transformations at most.

My heart sank. Zofie was dying?

"Is there anything I can do to keep her from... you know..." I hated to say it.

And that my lovely host is something I can't answer. I can only answer questions about my function and some basics on curses. That's it. I'm not some oracle with an answer for everything. I can stop her from transforming further, but that will only delay the inevitable. Her body is so warped it won't work properly. It's just a matter of time before it stops.

I pulled my horse up, bringing him to a stop. I took a deep breath and tried to get my emotions under control. "Thank you *Abhulengulus*. That's all the questions I have now."

*What! I was sure you were going to beg me for some more answers. You hitting your own wrist yesterday was a hoot.*

"Not now Abhulengulus. I'll have some more questions tomorrow."

*Fine!* And the eye on my wrist closed and I immediately felt alone again in my thoughts.

I hung my head. It made perfect sense.

Zofie was dying.

She had to know it too. She was smart and was a myst-seer herself. What had she said when we first talked? Something about time being short?

I looked up and realized my vision was blurry. I nudged my horse forward, and he moved to a faster pace to catch up with the others. I had to blink my eyes several times to get my vision to clear.

I didn't mention what I knew to Zofie when she joined us that evening. She said our followers were still far away, so we risked a small fire and fixed a meager pot of beans for our dinner. I noticed Zofie didn't stick around while we ate, saying she had to get her own food.

As we finished, Spraggel was his usual energetic self, keeping up a monologue on the history of Mount Eternal and the theories of how it lost its top. But Risten was quiet too. I caught her looking in my direction more than once. I wondered if she also knew about Zofie.

After dinner, it was my turn to clean the small pan and bowls, so I went to the nearby stream to wash them. I had hung my amulet up in a tree branch so I could see around me. I was distracted, thinking about Zofie and running through what we could possibly do for her, when Risten startled me by squatting down beside me.

"Did you ask your curse how to help Zofie?" she asked softly.

I took a deep breath and let it out slowly before turning in her direction. "I did. There's nothing Abhulengulus can do for her."

Risten looked into the water and nodded. "You're sure?"

"That's what he said. I'm going to ask some more questions, but he was pretty blunt about it."

"So there's nothing we can do for her?"

"Not that I know of."

She nodded slowly. Abruptly, she sprang to her feet and threw me onto my back. Her knife leaped into her hand and came to rest against my throat. She sat down hard on my stomach, and I felt the sharp blade press into my skin just enough to let me know it was definitely there. "You don't know?" she hissed through her teeth. "Or is it you won't admit it! Maybe you do know and are just too coward to say it!" She loomed over top of me. I could feel her tears splatter on my cheek. "What I do know is you wear her curse anchor. So if I kill you, then her curse goes away."

I didn't dare move. "Risten, it doesn't work that way."

"*Then what will?* Killing you is not what I want, but it's all I've got." She swiped her tears with the back of her hand. "I've come to like you, Coren, but I won't hesitate to trade your life for Zofie's. My own damnation from your murder would be a small price. I'd cut out my own heart if it would save her. "

I considered what I should say and realized there was nothing I really *could* say. I tilted my head back and to one side, giving Risten plenty of room to make her cut. "If you really think it will help her, go ahead. You're not the only one that would die for her."

I felt her tense and was pretty sure she was going to do it, but instead she jerked the knife away and slammed it into the ground blade first. I could see its blade reflect the feeble light. She sat up and beat on my chest, but her blows had no real power behind them. "Then why have you been so quiet tonight? I was sure you knew something."

I grabbed Risten's fists and stilled them. I could see her eyes glistening in the dim light.

"Zofie's dying," I said softly.

Risten stared at me for several heartbeats and then stood, stepping toward the stream. She wrapped her arms around herself and stared into the darkness.

I picked myself up and brushed the dirt from my clothes. "Abhulen-gulus told me. Her curse is gradually killing her. That's why she's been so tired and doesn't eat when she's in her human form."

Risten looked to the sky. "That bastard. I bet Wynn did this on purpose. A safeguard to ensure she died even if she escaped."

I put a hand on her shoulder and gently turned her to face me. "We'll figure something out."

She nodded. "But we can't tell Zofie. Not yet."

Absolute heartbreak was on her face. I stepped in her direction and pulled her into a brief hug.

"I'm sure she already knows."

I heard the flutter of wings and then Zofie's voice in my mind. *Well, I know now. I suspected you were only being nice to the ugly girl. But it's clear you've had feelings for Risten all along. I'll just leave you two love birds alone. No pun intended.*

I turned toward the sound of the wings disappearing in the night. "Zofie! It's not what you think!" I turned to Risten. "Zofie heard the last part of our conversation. She thinks... you and me."

Risten's eyes got large. She brushed past me and ran after Zofie. "Come back!" she yelled. "I don't like shit for brains! We were just talking!"

*Tell Risten to leave me alone for a bit.* I could feel the distance between us growing. She must really be flying hard. *I'm actually happy for both of you. I just need a little time to come to terms with it.*

"Zofie, it's not what you think."

*Coren,* her voice was very faint now. *You're really a good fellow. You really deserve someone like Risten. Not a monster like me.* And then her presence in my head was gone.

*Zofie!*

No answer.

I sighed and shook my head.

*What a mess.*

Risten came back a few minutes later breathing hard. "I couldn't catch her. She's really in a state. I don't know what to do now."

I pursed my lips. "Well, I do."

Risten gave me an expectant look.

"We'll just have to save her."

# CHAPTER NINETEEN

# Missing Bird

The next day, I had my questions ready when Abe woke up. We were still on the trail heading toward Mount Eternal, and Zofie was acting like nothing had happened the previous evening, giving reports on the trail ahead and how far back our pursuers were. But I could sense the forced cordiality she projected.

I had to find a way to fix this.

"Abe, wake up. I need to ask you some questions."

*Abe is it now? Do you know that I've had that nickname twenty-two times among the different hosts?*

"But Abhulengulus is so long."

*So's the name Coren. At least, for you it is. I'm surprised your mother was able to teach it to you. Want to know what my other names were?*

"I'm not wasting one of my questions to find out."

*Damn, he's learning.*

"First question. If I were to die, then what happens to the curse's you've stolen?"

*Ah, he's starting to think. Now, that's scary. Well, the best way to explain it is that... nothing happens. The curse freezes in place and vanishes. Whatever state it is in, it just stops.*

I frowned, not completely understanding, but going on to my next planned question. "So for Zofie, when I die, does her transformation cycle stop and leave her a non-transforming bird forever?"

*Oooh. I'm impressed. He's started planning his questions. In most cases yes, it would stop dead, leaving her a bird forever. However, that was not the intent of your girlfriend's curse. Hers was designed to not only torture her, but to waste her myst—basically keeping her from using any of her spells. It continually transforms her into a bird over and over again, and only stops when her myst drops below a certain point. That's why she comes out of it during a new moon. Without her anchor, she would immediately go to her neutral state. She would basically be that hideous monster for the rest of her life. Admittedly, her short life. We talked about that last time.*

"She's not a monster."

*Heh, to each his own.*

I sighed. So killing me wasn't an answer. I couldn't decide if I was happy about that or not.

Now my final question. I could be wasting it.

"Abe, is there any way I can get more questions during the same day, after my original three are exhausted."

I heard deep laughter. *They all ask that eventually. And I do love giving this answer. Yes, there is, but you have to give the secret word to increase the questions.*

"How do I find out this secret word?"

He laughed. *Oops, you're out of questions. I guess that's all for today.* He laughed out loud for a full minute.

I leaned my head back and shook with frustration.

●  ☽  ○  ☾

The next day, Mount Eternal was definitely looking closer, and the land was tilting upwards. Zofie still would only say a few words to me. I noticed Risten sharpening her knife again, which definitely wasn't a good sign.

"Abe! Get your butt up!"

*I would like to point out that I don't have a butt. You, unfortunately, have two: you're sitting on one, and the other I'm looking at.*

"First question. What is the secret word you mentioned yesterday to grant me more questions?"

*That's the second question they always ask. And I love this answer more than the other.* I heard him make a clearing throat sound. *The answer is... I don't know. My maker didn't tell me—it's a secret!* He laughed long and hard. *They fall for that one every time. It never gets old.*

I beat my fists on my forehead in frustration before going to my next question.

"Second question. When we were back in Daili, you transformed the high priest into a woman. What triggered that?"

*That was such wonderful timing with that curse. Did you see the look on his face when he saw he was a woman? It was priceless! Or would that be on HER face? Either way, you triggered the curse. You wished very hard for him to suffer being a woman, and then you spoke it aloud. So my interpretation of that was to transform him into a female using the curse I stole from your girlfriend. As you probably just figured out, if you don't specify exactly what to do with the curse, I make it up as I go. And usually, the person being cursed won't care for the result.*

"But how could you transform him into a woman using that curse? It only transforms Zofie into animals."

*My dear bag of meat, you ARE animals. From my perspective, you are nothing but an ape that walks upright and chatters annoyingly. The statue of their goddess gave me a convenient female image, so I just set the curse to use the image and invoked the curse. Then poof! He transformed into a she.*

I couldn't help but wonder if *all* his parts transformed.

I flinched at Abe's sudden laughter. *Ooh. Naughty, naughty. You're wondering if he's truly female. And I assure you she's now completely woman with all the monthlies, cramps, and having babies included.*

It was a little unnerving that Abe answered my unspoken question. "How did you know what I was thinking? Can you read my mind?" I'm not sure I liked that idea.

*Do you really want to know?*

"Yes."

*I could almost feel him grinning. Then see you tomorrow!*

I pounded my leg with my fist. He was *so* frustrating.

The next day with Mount Eternal closer, but still a way away, we started up into what could be considered its foothills. This made the going just a bit more difficult. This was one big mountain.

I asked Zofie if she could see the top, and she confirmed she could. But she didn't see anything resembling water up there. Just lots of rock.

*Then where the heck was our island?*

At mid-day, I once again attacked Abe with my questions.

"Abe, time to wake up."

*Ah mother, is it that time already?*

"I'm not your mother."

*And I thank the Creator every day.*

I took a deep breath to calm myself. He was really getting under my skin. And he knew it too.

"First question. Can you read my mind?" I had debated long and hard about this question, but it bothered me so badly, I had to know.

*I'm impressed, Coren. Your questions are getting more and more STUPID! Of course not! Why would I want to read your mind anyway when I can easily guess what you're thinking? Remember, I'm only a thousand years old. Do you know how many times I've had this exact conversation?* His voice softened. *The better question is how many times have I suckered them into wasting one of their questions by asking.* He chuckled. *And guess what, that count just went up by one more.*

I gritted my teeth and shook my head in frustration. It took me a couple of minutes to get myself back under control. "Second question." I really didn't want to ask this one, but I had to. I might need it. "How do I activate one of the curses you've stolen?"

I think Abe must have realized he had almost pushed me too far. He softened his tone. *Most of my previous hosts asked that question a lot sooner. But then again, their significant other wasn't about to die. Well, except in that one case, but she wanted her significant other to die.*

"The answer."

*It's simple. Point to the object of the curse—usually a person that has really pissed you off—then say, 'I curse you' person who has really pissed me off. Or if you don't know the person's name, you can give a description such as fat man or woman in a red dress. Then to finish it up, just add the curse I'm supposed to use. Of course, it has to be one that you've stolen. I don't make those things up, you know.*

"That doesn't sound too hard."

*However, and there is always a however, if activation of the curse will endanger your life, I can either refuse it or substitute something that won't kill you. It's a safeguard my maker built into me to save STUPID PEOPLE LIKE YOU! Also, if you don't name the curse, I get to choose. For instance, if you say to me, 'I curse you Mr. blah blah' but don't give a curse, I might choose a lightning curse or a drowning curse, provided you ever steal one.*

"All right, final question. Why do you protect me?"

He gave a long sigh. He sounded uncharacteristically sad. *That's a question I can't answer. I can't speak for why my maker forced that one on me, but I can speculate. I think that one day, I really pissed him off, and that became my curse. I have to protect you from harm to the best of my ability until you die a hopefully natural death. Then I move on to my next host, losing all the curses I've accumulated. The next host being the closest relative with a weak cache of myst.*

"But shouldn't that be a *strong* cache of myst?"

*Wouldn't you like to know? Until next time!*

"Dammit!" I shouted. Everyone looked back at me but knew enough to let me suffer in peace. I closed my eyes and rubbed them. This was getting old.

The next day, I tried again. I started right in after waking Abe up.

"So what exactly are you? Are you a cursed person, who's been cursed into being a curse?" My mind sort of reeled around that one.

*That's such a disgusting thought, but thank my maker, I'm just a made thing. I think I would kill myself if I found out I used to be a human.*

"Who was your maker?"

*That's one of the questions I'm forbidden to answer. It is sealed. That secret word thing again.*

"Why?"

*Ask my maker.*

"What?"

Abe yawned. *That was a record. You went through three questions in about three seconds.*

"I didn't ask three questions."

*Oh yes, you did. 'Why' counts.*

"Dammit."

He just laughed and closed his eye.

"You know you're a real bastard."

*He laughed. Thanks, I've had a thousand years to perfect it.*

The next day, the going became more difficult as the elevation increased. Mount Eternal still loomed over us, barely closer than the day before. I knew the mountain was big, but now I was convinced it was enormous. The ground was growing increasingly rocky, and the trees began to thin, changing from oak to mostly pine. The faint trail we had been following also thinned and became hard to see among the overgrowth. I wasn't sure how much longer we could stay on horseback. Spraggel thought we were still two or three days away from reaching the top.

When we stopped for the evening, Zofie said she could still only see bare rock at the mountain's summit. No island. This put us in a bit of a quandary—were we headed in the right direction? So after a brief discussion, we decided to try the spear again.

At dawn the next morning, Risten took the Spear of Flight, wrapped it with a piece of cloth, and threw it much as she did before, only pointed away from the mountain. The spear took off but quickly curved back toward Eternal. Zofie immediately took off after it.

This time we agreed that Zofie should keep up a running dialog as she flew. I, in turn, would relay the information to the others. We were hoping that it would give some clue the others might recognize.

*It's continuing to climb the mountain,* came Zofie's voice in my head. *I'm having a little trouble staying with it. I have to build up speed and catch updrafts, while it doesn't.*

"Just do your best Zofie," I said to her. "Please don't hurt yourself."

*I'm fine.*

This is the first time she'd said more than a few words to me since she saw Risten and I. I wasn't going to waste the chance.

"Uh, Zofie," I said softly, trying not to let the others hear me. "You know there's nothing between Risten and me. She still thinks I have manure inside my skull."

*Coren, now's not the time to talk about that. I'm a little preoccupied.*

Spraggel was oblivious and was writing in a journal he had materialized out of his myst pocket. Risten gave me a funny look, but I plowed on. "But it's the first time you've talked to me. I need to explain. Risten was just having a bad time that night. She's terribly worried about you, and it just got to her. We just figured out how bad your curse really is."

She went on with her narrative as if I had said nothing. *The spear is still climbing. I'm having to circle while I build up speed and climb, so it's getting ahead of me. I can still see it though.*

"You're ignoring me again," I said.

*Dammit, Coren. You were embracing each other. I'm not stupid. Besides, she's a very lovely woman. Much stronger and definitely much prettier than I'll ever be.*

"But she's not you."

*Coren, I can't...*

I sighed heavily. Risten had moved a little closer pretending not to be listening to my whispers. "All I ask is that you talk to me when you come back. Just talk. I'll explain everything."

There was a pause. *All right. Maybe this evening when we camp. It better be good. Hang on, the spear is rising above the ridge now, but it's overshooting for some reason, heading up a lot higher than it should. Like it's arching over something. But there's nothing there but perfectly flat bare rock. Wait...it's turning back toward the mountain top now, angling down.* There was a pause. *What just happened?*

"Zofie, what is it?" I asked, concerned.

*The spear... it just disappeared in mid-flight.*

I relayed this to the others.

"Did it fall?" I asked.

*No, it was flying one minute and then gone the next. I had just gotten high enough to see over the edge. And it's simply not there.*

Risten gave up pretending to eavesdrop and came to stand beside me.

*I'm following along in its path now. It was right about here...* There was a long pause. *Well, I'll be. There's an illusion barrier around the top of the mountain. Which makes it huge! And there's a lake up here. A huge one that takes up most of the mountain top and I can see an island in the center of the water. It looks like when the mountain blew, it created a crater. Oh, I see the spear, I'm going to try to catch up to it. It's over the water now and heading right for the island and... and... what is...?*

Her thoughts became a jumble. I couldn't make out what she was saying. Something about a party. I grew worried. "Zofie?" I asked in concern. "Are you all right? What's happening?"

*The music...* She sounded almost gleeful. *It's so beautiful...*

"Did you say music?" I asked in panic. "Zofie, what's going on?" But there was no answer. "Zofie! Answer me," I cried out. Risten hovered nearby, and Spraggel joined us.

But I heard nothing more from her.

I strode to my horse and began to pull supplies together to climb the rest of the mountain on foot. "Something's happened to Zofie." I explained to them our conversation and that the island was really there. "I'm going to climb the rest of the way on foot. It's too rocky and steep for the horses. They'll end up breaking a leg."

Risten began to pull together her own supplies. "I'll go too."

Spraggel nodded. "You young people go on ahead. I'll just slow you down. I'll stay here and take care of the horses. I'll find somewhere to hide so Wort won't find me."

I patted him on the shoulder. "Sorry master. I hate to leave you behind, but speed is important. She may be hurt. And no telling what we may have to climb over."

His eyebrows went up in surprise. "Oh, I nearly forgot." He reached into his pocket. "Now let's see. Where did I put it?" He felt around and then dug deeper until he had almost his whole arm down inside. He always amazed me when he did this. "Ah! Found it." He then pulled out a coiled length of rope and handed it to me. "I thought we might need some before we left Iron Landing."

It wasn't very long, only about five times my height and of a rough weave. Not to mention, it had been heavily used. Probably some cow rope. I couldn't see how it would be much use, but I took it anyway and looped it across my shoulder. If it got to be too burdensome, I would just cast it aside.

It only took Risten and I a few minutes to pull together our supplies into crude packs. Risten, like me, was going light for speed. Then I saw her pull out a hatchet and slip it into her belt. Well, I guess going light didn't mean she couldn't be deadly.

As I was finishing up mine, I touched something in the bottom of my saddlebags: it was one of the exploding spheres I had gotten from the Temple of Daili. I hefted it thinking it was too heavy and started to set it aside. But on impulse, I decided to take it. One never knew. I just hope it didn't slow me down too much.

We took off at a brisk clip up the mountain. While both of us wanted to run, we knew that way lay disaster—breaking a leg wouldn't do Zofie any good. So we moved quickly, but deliberately over the rocky terrain. I just hoped that if Zofie was injured, we made it in time.

# CHAPTER TWENTY

# The Barrier

A t mid-afternoon, I asked Risten if we could break for a few minutes so I could ask my questions of Abe. While we were having to carefully blaze our trail, we were making good time. Risten wasn't wild about the idea of stopping, but reluctantly agreed. She knew we couldn't afford to miss this opportunity to get some answers.

I squatted next to a rock and tried to take a little rest. "Abe, wake up. I'm in a hurry."

*Anxious over your friend?*

"As a matter of fact, I am. I understand you had something to do with this mountain blowing its top. Can you tell me anything about what might have happened to her and why the top is protected by an illusion barrier?"

*I have you know that's two questions, but I'm going to let it slide this time because the answer to both is the same. All information on that time period has* been sealed. I am unable to comment. It was like he was reciting it. *But I will let you in on a little secret. I'm dying to find out what it is myself.* He laughed.

He was so annoying. I looked up at the sun in the sky, wishing I didn't have to ask this next question. Risten was pacing, so I had better get on with it. I sighed and braced myself. "Next question. You've told me how to activate curses that you already have, but how do I... you know... steal someone else's curse."

*Took you long enough*, he said rather smugly. *Up until you asked, I was choosing when to steal a curse which is how my creator wanted it for some reason. And it was intended to last until the host was ready to take the reins. But now, da-da-dah! You've asked the question, so I turn control of acquiring curses officially over to you. The question was a signal that you're ready, and I'm not allowed to do it for you anymore. While I will likely recommend the ones we take, I won't do it on my own now.*

I wasn't sure I agreed with him on being ready for this.

Abe continued. *Now, to take a curse, you have to touch the person and say something like, 'Your curse is now my curse,' and I will take it. The other person will go to their neutral state, whatever that might be, and you get a new curse anchor.*

That explained why he was avoiding my questions. He didn't want to give me control. The sneaky bastard. But I wondered when he had stolen Zofie's curse? I thought back to when Zofie and I were in the Sylph village, and she was a wounded squirrel. Zofie had gone to her neutral state while we were in the hut. Abe must have used that to hide the stealing of her curse.

*Now... what's your next question? Please, oh please make it a good one. I haven't had this much fun in a long time.*

I opened my mouth to ask—but on impulse decided against it. For some reason, waiting seemed best. There might be something I needed to ask him. "Go back to sleep. I'm going to save my last question for today. I might need it later."

The curse gave a deep sigh. *That's no fun. You're starting to figure out this question thing. Just remember that if you don't ask by mid-day tomorrow, you lose the question.*

I looked to Risten. "Let's go."

She picked up her pack and slung it over her shoulder. "That didn't take long."

"It never does. He's a real bastard to get information out of."

*I heard that. You had better be careful, or I'll do something to make your life really miserable.*

"No, you won't," I replied. Risten gave me a funny look over her shoulder but kept on walking. "You'd have done it already if you could have." I was following close behind her as we climbed over some rough terrain. I was having to focus on where I placed my feet.

*Oh really. Then how about I curse your traveling partner? Maybe turn her into a giant frog. That might slow you down.* He chuckled. *And to free her, I'd make it so you had to kiss her frog lips. Which I'm certain is something you couldn't do, because frogs don't wear clothes, and you'd be thinking about kissing her while she's not wearing anything. You're just too modest.*

It was my turn to chuckle. "You're mistaken. Having Risten's clothes on or off wouldn't make a difference to me. I wouldn't mind kissing her."

Suddenly, I bumped into Risten's back. She whipped around to glare at me. "You might not mind it, but I do. You get anywhere near me while I'm not wearing clothes, and I'll hack you to tiny pieces."

"What?" And then it hit me what I had just said out loud.

Abe broke out laughing. *Now, what were you saying about me not being able to make your life miserable?*

Risten and I pushed ourselves hard up the mountain, but our path was becoming increasingly difficult as the terrain continued to tilt upwards. While the summit wasn't that much further, our forward progress had slowed considerably. There were some sparse shrubs and grass up ahead, but not much else—mostly rocks and loose soil. Also, the wind had been getting stronger, and despite the season, the temperature was slowly dropping.

But it was the quiet that was unnerving. The only sound was the wind rattling the shrubs. No birds or animal sounds. Not even any insects. It was creepy.

And I couldn't help but feel we were being watched.

I leaned up against a boulder and caught my breath. Risten pulled up beside me and resettled her pack. "It sure is spooky up here." She looked over her shoulder. "I've looked twice for something I noticed out of the corner of my eye—only to find nothing there."

"Me too," I answered. "I'm beginning to understand why they say this mountain is haunted."

I started moving again, my sense of unease growing. I jumped when I knocked a loose rock free, and it tumbled down the steep slope. *That could have been me*, the thought came unbidden. *Rolling and tumbling down until I was dead. Empty eyes staring at the sky.*

I shook my head, trying to get rid of this feeling of impending doom. I reminded myself, we had to find Zofie. It was what we were here for. I looked behind me and saw Risten several paces back, just standing, staring up at the mountain with the first look of fear I'd ever seen on her face. I followed her gaze and likewise froze in place. Despite there being nothing but barren rocks ahead, it seemed so evil. I knew I didn't want to go up there. We should turn around and go back to Spraggel. Zofie would come back on her own. We didn't need to go up there.

I turned to leave and saw that Risten was already heading back down the mountain. I took two steps down the trail with a sense of relief with each step. Zofie would come back...

I stopped dead in my tracks and looked over my shoulder. The fear returned, and I had to fight just to hold my place. I shook my head in denial. This wasn't right.

"Risten!" I yelled. "Come back. We've got to get Zofie. I think there is some kind of fear spell on this mountain."

Risten drew up short and turned to look at me. "I... can't. There's crawly black things up there. I just know it."

"Think Risten! Is this normal? Does your fear usually rule you this way? Would it keep you away from your cousin?"

"Zofie?" she asked. She wore a very puzzled expression. But then determination blossomed on her face. "Zofie. She needs us." Risten climbed back up beside me. I could tell that each step was a challenge for her.

When she reached me, the fear hit me again, even harder. This was not normal for either of us. It had to be some kind of spell. Something to frighten people away.

"There's some kind of fear illusion here. I bet it was connected to the illusion Zofie had mentioned. It's not real!"

Risten took a deep breath. "I'm not normally this afraid."

"Which means someone is keeping us from Zofie. And we've got to find her." I held out my hand. "We'll go up together. Both of us are stronger than this."

She looked at my hand for a moment, considering I supposed, if she could. She finally reached out and took my hand, giving it a reassuring squeeze. I didn't hesitate further, lest the fear overcome me, and turned back up the mountain. Risten followed half a step behind, continuing to tightly hold my hand.

Gradually the feeling of fear subsided. It was nearly gone by the time we reached the final leg of our climb—a nearly vertical rock face that wrapped around the mountain's summit. It had to be twice my height but appeared to be the final obstacle to reaching the top. Fortunately, handholds were plentiful, and we made quick work of it.

Risten and I, tired and out of breath, finally crawled out onto the summit. We both stood at the edge in awe, looking across the flat bare rock that stretched all the way to the other side. It had to be at least a couple leagues across. It was as if someone had just sliced off the top of the mountain. Zofie had said it was an illusion, but it sure looked convincing.

"That illusion wall Zofie mentioned should be about here." I took a step forward and smacked right into something hard.

*What the?*

Risten bumped into me from behind. "Hey, what are you doing?"

I held out my hand and, despite only seeing air, felt a barrier in front of me. "There's something here. Feel it for yourself. I've never encountered anything like it."

Risten moved up beside me. She probed the air until she found the barrier and rested her palm against it.

"It's smooth like finely crafted glass but completely clear." She laid her head against it and sighted across it. "There's no distortion of the light, so it's not glass."

I pulled out my sword and gave it a whack, but it only bounced off. Picking up a loose rock, I pounded it against the surface until the rock crumbled. When I closely examined the invisible wall, I could find no trace of where I had hit it, not dust, nor scratch.

Risten pulled her sword and started swinging at it with the same success. She stepped back breathing hard. "How did Zofie get through this?"

"Maybe she flew over it. I remember her saying that the spear seemed to overshoot the edge—going higher than seemed necessary. That must be why. It was trying to clear this... wall."

I looked around and found a small stone. Then stepping back to the very edge of the summit, I threw the stone toward the top of the wall. It went twice as high as my head and bounced off. Risten got the idea and did the same. She had a better arm than me, and her stone went three times our height. It sailed slightly beyond where the vertical barrier would have been—and disappeared.

"So there *is* an invisible wall. And a tall one at that."

Risten came to stand beside me. "What if I stand on your shoulders?"

I shook my head. "I don't think you could reach it, and even if you did, there's no telling how sharp the edge is. You could jump up and grasp it, only to lose all of your fingers." I pointed to the right. "Let's explore along the wall and see if we can find a gap." There was maybe twenty-five feet from the summit's edge to the wall, so we had plenty of room to walk. I just hoped it maintained that distance further on.

I quickly built a pile of rocks to mark our starting point, and together we began to walk the perimeter. I noticed that a fine line of dirt was piled up against the barrier in some places. I guess it was dust that got blown up against it and then slid down. Once I knew what to look for, it was easy to make out the edge.

When the sun touched the horizon, and the light began to fade, I realized we were going to have to stop. The top of the summit was littered with loose rocks, crags, and large cracks. Even if I used the light of my amulet, it wouldn't be enough. One of us would end up breaking a leg, or worse, falling to our death.

"Risten, I hate to say it, but we're going to need to stop for the night. It's too dangerous up here in the dark."

She was in the lead and turned to give me a dirty look. "We can't stop now. Zofie may be hurt."

I stopped and pointed toward the half of the sun still over the distant horizon. "I know how you feel, but we need to take shelter for the night. It doesn't do us, or Zofie, any good if one of us gets hurt. And to find a place to go through this blasted wall, we're going to need to see clues. I don't think they're going to jump up at us."

"Just a little longer then. We can make camp in the dark." She turned to continue.

"No Risten. It's going to get cold. We need to find something that's out of this wind before it gets dark."

She stopped walking but didn't turn to look at me. She knew I was right, but her guilt must have been eating her alive.

"We can start again at dawn," I said.

"Just a little more... Please!"

I sighed. "All right. Just a bit. I'm going to keep an eye out for a place to camp." I pulled out my amulet. "But let me lead. My light will help a little."

She didn't say anything. She didn't look at me as I passed her, just followed along behind me.

As darkness fell, I became increasingly uncomfortable traveling. The stars came out, but there was no moon yet to help guide us. And what had been a pleasantly cool breeze when we started had continued to decrease in temperature and was now a constant frigid wind. I trailed one hand along the wall, choosing my steps carefully. My feeble light wasn't cutting the blackness. Also, the mountain ledge had narrowed, leaving us only about ten feet to the edge. I thought it was time to turn back. I looked over my shoulder. "Risten, we should..." Suddenly the ground under my left foot gave way, and I fell against the wall. But it provided no friction, and I began to slide into nothingness.

Risten grabbed my jacket and quickly jerked me back from the brink. I landed on my backside breathing hard, with Risten standing behind me. "That was close," she said.

I stared at her wide-eyed, trying to still my heart. I took off my amulet and held it out in front of me to get a clearer view of our broken path. In the dim light, all I could see was some sort of deep crack in the rock blocking our path. As I neared the edge, another piece of the rock dropped away into the darkness. I held my breath, waiting to hear it hit—but it never did.

I carefully backed away from the edge. Risten gave me a sheepish look. "I guess we should stop now."

I slapped the barrier in irritation. "An excellent idea! I wish I had thought of it."

So we backtracked, looking for a place to stop out of the wind, but all we found was a slight depression in the ledge. It didn't really provide any cover, but it did help block the wind a little.

Together we ate a cold meal of dried meat and tough bread, but it put something in our bellies. Neither of us spoke, too occupied with thoughts of Zofie. We pulled out our blankets and wrapped up in them and huddled in our depression. Now that we had stopped moving, the wind seemed to suck the warmth right out. And the ground was cold too. I imagine that snow had covered this area only a few weeks ago. I lay on my side, arms crossed in front of me and hoped the sun would come up quickly.

I was just about to drift off when I heard Risten sit up beside me. "I'm too cold to sleep." I heard her teeth chattering. "I guess I should have brought my other blanket."

I held open my blanket to her. "Come here. We'll share."

She didn't hesitate to shift under my blanket and throw her own over top of us. She settled with her back against mine. "At least you're warm," she commented.

I didn't say anything. I was actually a little uncomfortable having a lady that played with swords snuggled up to me. I tried to get back to sleep, but she seemed uncharacteristically talkative this evening. No doubt afraid of the dreams awaiting her.

Risten cleared her throat. "Have you tried contacting Zofie with your mind trick thing?"

I sighed. "I've tried many times, but I don't get anything. It's like she's asleep."

"Unconscious maybe?"

"Could be. I'm just not sure."

"I pray that nothing has happened to her. I don't know what I would do..." She broke off and didn't finish the thought.

I reached my hand back and patted her knee. "Don't worry. I'm sure she's fine. She'll probably ask what took us so long."

She brightened a little. "Yes, you're right. That's exactly what she would say."

I couldn't help myself. "What was Zofie like when she was a child?"

I could hear the pride in her voice as she answered. "I used to tell her she was like the weather: comforting as a clear spring day, as stormy as a summer squall, as beautiful as the autumn leaves, and when angered, as cold as ice." She laughed. "Don't let her cool and controlled exterior fool you. She's got a bit of a temper. She's learned to control it as she's grown into an adult but, believe me, you never want to cross her."

"And what about you, Risten? You've never talked about yourself. You once mentioned how you started caring for her after her mother died, but you haven't said anything about your parents."

Risten sighed. "There's not a lot to tell. My father, Bernard Xernow, was King Xernow's younger brother and I was his bastard daughter. Actually his only child, at least that we know about. My father never married. From what I heard, he was a bit of a womanizer. Although he did love his brother and helped him with the kingdom when needed. But one day, he ended up on the wrong side of a duel and was killed. I barely remember my father, and my mother not at all. Apparently, when I was five, I showed up on his doorstep with a note from my mother saying she could no longer care for me, and so, was giving me back. When my father died, the king took pity on me and brought me into his house." She pulled the blanket closer. "But I was a bit of a wild one. And woe to anyone that even mentioned my bastard status. The only one that treated me well was Lady Winstella, Zofie's mother, so I sort of helped take care of Zofie, when I wasn't terrorizing the other children."

We were silent for a bit. Sleep began to creep up on me when Risten spoke again. "Do you like Zofie? I mean as more than just a friend."

I was surprised at her question. "I've never had someone I've fancied before, so I'm not exactly sure what it should feel like. But I do know that when I look at Zofie, my heart beats a little faster. When she laughs, the world just seems to sparkle a little brighter. And when she's angry at me, I want to crawl under a rock." I sighed. "But I'm not sure she feels the same. She seems to hold me at a little bit of a distance." I shifted slightly. "I understand it, actually. She's a princess, and I'm just an apprentice scribe. Don't get me wrong. She's been very nice to me, and I feel like she trusts me now. I would do everything in my power to help her. But..." I shook my head. "I'm not a fool. There's no way she would truly consider someone like me. I'm sure there is a prince out there somewhere that would just love to be hers."

It was her turn to pat my arm. "Don't underestimate yourself, Coren. You're the Thief of Curses."

"True. But what exactly does that mean?"

I felt her shrug. "I guess it means... whatever you want it to."

# CHAPTER TWENTY-ONE

# Dark Water

The next morning, I awoke slowly, relishing the warmth of the blankets. I opened my eyes to see the sky just turning a deep blue, and the stars beginning to fade overhead. Thankfully, the wind had died down, but there was still a nip in the air. It took me a moment to realize that the warmth I enjoyed was coming from another person under the blanket. I turned my head to find Risten had rolled to face me during the night. While the light was still dim, there was enough to see her sleep mussed hair and a few loose strands hanging across her face. Even with the smudge of dirt on her cheek, I had to admit she looked very pretty.

Surprisingly, her blue eyes were open, and only a hand's-breadth from my face. Even more strangely, she seemed rather content. "About time you woke up." Her lips drew back in a sly smile. "Of course, you realize that when a man and woman sleep under the same blanket, they have to get married."

I rolled out from under the covers and was standing in only two heartbeats. "Tell me you're joking?"

Still laying on her side, she propped up on her elbow and grinned evilly at me. "Of course, I'm joking, you idiot. Do you think I would let something like that happen? Especially with you!" She threw the blanket back. "But it definitely got you going."

We ate a quick breakfast while gathering our blankets, and with just enough light to travel safely, we retraced our final steps from the night before. It didn't take us too long to get to the place where I had nearly fallen the previous evening. It was easy to see the problem. The path had narrowed with the summit much closer to the barrier—Risten and I could fit side by side with only a hand's-breadth to spare. But in front of us, a small gully had been cut into the mountain: a very deep and wide V-shaped gouge in the rock face—too far to jump. The sides of the gully were loose rock and gravel, which made it especially treacherous.

I squatted down and examined it more closely. Risten was right there with me and noticed the same thing I did. What remained of the rock in the gulley had been dug out at the base of the barrier, forming a depression where the gully met the stone underneath. No doubt the cycle of freezing and thawing over the years had weakened the rock face. A sparkle in the morning light caught my eye. I stared in disbelief. Out of that depression came a tiny trickle of water.

My excitement rose. If water was coming out, then that meant there might be a way in. I lay down on my stomach and scooted over the edge as far as I dared. The rock under the barrier was cracked with several pieces loose and ready to just fall off. I smiled to myself. It might just be possible to make that slight depression in the rocks into something bigger.

I leaned out experimentally and extended my arm, but it was too far back. I pushed forward a bit more but drew up short when a piece of cracked stone under me broke loose and tumbled into the gulley. It bounced against the sides, once more against the bottom of the gulley, and then sailed out over the edge where it quickly disappeared out of sight. It was a long way down.

I looked to the depression and sighed. So close, but how to reach it? And even if I could, how do we dig out the rock? Then I remembered the exploding ball I had taken from the Temple of Daili. If I could place it against the rock, it might blow a hole. It had certainly done that with a wall.

Risten lay down beside me, and I explained my idea. She nodded. "We could use the rope Spraggel gave you, then one of us hold the other while they swing out and plant the ball. We'll just have to make sure to get away from it in time."

I made a face. "Do you think the rope is strong enough?"

She shrugged. "Do we have a choice?"

I shook my head. "I guess not."

I pulled out my rope, and Risten started to tie it around herself, but I stopped her, explaining that while she might be a little lighter, my curse would provide better protection. She reluctantly agreed, and I secured our makeshift safety line around my waist. After retrieving the black ball from my sack, I laid on my stomach and scooted out as far as I could. Risten used the rope to support my body while I leaned way over the edge. But it was still a stretch. I moved just a hair further... and heard Risten grunt at the effort to hold me. "Hey, don't lean out any more. My arms aren't that strong. Any more and I might not be able to hold you."

I took out the ball and carefully placed it on a tiny ledge just beside the trickle of water. It was slightly muddy there, and it helped hold the ball in place. Now the tricky part, from what I saw previously, it took an impact to set it off. And then I had about seven heartbeats to get away. I managed to snag a fist-sized rock and yelled to Risten over my shoulder. "Ready!"

"Just hit the blasted thing. You're killing me."

I struck the black ball with the stone. "Now!" And then waited for Risten to pull me back.

And waited.

"You're too damn heavy! I'm losing my grip!" she yelled.

I panicked as I felt myself side toward the black ball instead of away. I tried to reach behind me, but I was too far out. Finally, Risten started to swing me over to the side...

The black ball exploded, sending debris flying, and water pouring out...

And I was thrown down the gully toward the edge of the summit. Thankfully, Risten held fast, and the rope acted as a tether. I arched through the gully and out into the open air beyond the edge of the mountain. As the rope reached its limit, I momentarily hung motionless, staring down the sheer side of the mountain and marveling at just how small everything was below me. I was sure I had pushed it too far, and I was about to fall to my death.

But the rope held, and Risten was able to hang on. I arched back inside the gully to slam against its nearly vertical wall, hanging completely from the rope. For a moment, I couldn't breathe from the severity of the impact; the world seemed to dim. In my daze, I struggled to find purchase to pull myself up, but the rock offered no easy hand-holds. I heard Risten screaming at me as if from far away. The rope slipped, and I felt myself go further over the edge. Fear gripped me as I realized that I wouldn't be able to help Zofie.

*Zofie!*

I blinked, and the world finally came into focus. "Coren!" Risten yelled. "I can't pull you up. You'll have to do it yourself. And make it quick, you're slowly dragging me toward the edge."

Frantically, I tried to find a purchase but felt none. The wall here was completely vertical—and completely smooth with the edge tantalizingly out of reach. No wonder Risten couldn't pull me up. My entire weight was on the rope.

In desperation, I looked to the hole blasted into the rock. It was still wet from the initial deluge, but the water had quickly slowed to a trickle. And the blast had not only created a hole, but a small muddy ledge under it.

"Hurry Coren. I can't hold you!"

I quickly measured the distance and the length of the rope. It just might work. Using my legs against the rock face, I started swinging back and forth. "Risten!" I called up to her. "I can't find a way up. So I'm going to try something. When I say let go, let go of the rope."

"Are you *crazy!*"

"Trust me. It's the only option we've got."

I worked on swinging back and forth and was trying for just a little higher.

"I'm losing you!" Risten yelled.

I started swinging toward the hole. "NOW!"

The rope released and I sailed the last few feet into the hole. I landed with a loud smack as the mud and water sucked me in. I scrambled for a hold and found one in a stone wedged in the side of the hole. I had no doubt my curse had somehow helped. Thank goodness Abe was looking out for me.

"Coren!" I turned to see Risten had laid down at the edge. Real worry was on her face. It passed to relief when she saw me.

"I'm right here." I looked down at myself. I was covered in mud with dampness soaking my clothes.

*Creator, I hated being wet.*

I helped Risten follow me through the newly made hole beneath the barrier. We emerged into what had been a small overgrown pond— now just mud and reeds since our hole had drained it. We crawled through the muck and up onto a small pebble-covered bank. We paused to stare in awe at what lay before us.

From this side, the barrier around the mountain had a milky white translucent appearance, allowing light in but not letting one see through it. As I tracked its path into the distance, I could make out how it curved around the mountain's summit and appeared to be completely unbroken for as far as I could see. Above it about thirty to forty feet, I could see blue sky and a few wispy clouds, which must have been how Zofie had gotten in.

But what was truly amazing was the lake.

Just ahead of us, down a gentle incline, was a rocky beach, lined with tall grass and a few stunted pine trees just higher than my head. Beyond that was a large lake—at least half a league across. Its waters were dark—almost a midnight black in color—and so smooth there was hardly a ripple. If not for the gentle lapping at the shore, it would look like a giant sheet of obsidian stretching into the distance.

And I was instantly terrified.

Just looking at the dark depths made me shudder, and I stood there frozen in fear. All that dark water, waiting to pull me under....

I was jerked out of my thoughts by Risten stepping forward. She pointed out across the water where a single island sat in the middle of the lake: no doubt the Averet Island mentioned in the Scroll of Nobem.

*What was wrong with me?* The river at night or going over Dragon Falls hadn't bothered me this bad. These waters were placid, nothing like the swollen river that had drowned my father. And yet, the water's blackness called to me; its dark depths promising an embrace from which I would never escape.

I closed my eyes and fought back my panic. Zofie was on that island. I knew it. And I had to get to her. Forcing my eyes open, I swallowed my fear and followed Risten—one hesitant step at a time.

We drew up at the water's edge and stared out into the distance.

"How are we going to get across that?" Risten asked. She squatted down and began to calmly wash the muck from her hands.

I tried not to think about how deep the water was. "I'm not sure," I answered. Then added. "I can't swim." It seemed important to say it.

Risten shook the water from her hands, either ignoring or not noticing the tremor in my voice.

"I can swim some," she said. "Paddle mostly. But I doubt I could make it that far, especially if I have to carry anything." She leaned a little closer to splash some water on her boots and rub some of the muck off. I almost reached out to pull her back. I could feel myself sweating.

She gazed out across the lake. "The water is strangely warm. I would have thought it would be ice cold. If we had time, I would take a bath." Sighing, Risten stood, pushing up on her knees. "So I guess we need something that floats."

"Agreed." I eagerly turned away from the water, but I could feel it still there, waiting for one misstep.

I nodded up the slope toward a clump of the stunted pines—their trunks only the width of my arm and just over head high. "Think we can make a raft out of those? None of the trees are very thick."

Risten pulled the hatchet from her belt. "Only one way to find out.

Divided between us, the raft building went faster than I expected. Risten cut down the few trees around us while I carried them to the shore and lashed them together with Spraggel's rope. Pretty soon we had a serviceable raft. It was a little smaller than I had hoped, but there just weren't that many usable trees. I prayed it would be enough to get us across.

As we were shoving it into the water, something stung me on my thigh. Then another came directly on my buttock. I beat at my pants and tried to shake whatever it was out the leg, but the stinging kept up. I had to get whatever it was out, and there was no way I was going to drop my pants with Risten standing there.

I made a beeline for a thick scrub bush.

"Where are you going?" Risten called after me. She was moving our sacks and swords onto the raft. It seemed to be floating pretty well.

"I'm going to wash the mud out of my pants. I've picked up a bug or something."

"Be quick about it. We need to get to Zofie."

I didn't answer. I just waved and jogged a short distance away, where I stepped behind a scrub bush next to the shore. I quickly dropped my pants to my ankles, and sure enough, there was what looked like ants on my legs. Vicious little things. I looked at the lake in trepidation and took a deep breath. I really didn't want to get in the water to wash them out, but those pesky things weren't going away on their own.

And then I heard it.

My head came up. *What was that sound?* I listened closely. A sound like bells, light tinkly bells, so beautiful and dreamy. I was immediately enraptured, and my head slowly turned toward the source of the music: the island across the water. There was no question about it, I had to go to it. I had to see it, touch it, *worship it.* It seemed such a reasonable desire.

With my pants around my ankles, I hobbled forward and promptly fell on my face. I shoved at the pants but couldn't get them off. I rose and tried to shuffle forward again, but my pants snagged on a rock, and I fell once more. I fought with them, but for some reason, I couldn't figure out how they worked. My mind was filled with a strange fog, and even though I knew it wasn't right, I had to get to the raft and float to the island. The desire was so intense I could taste it. I tried to stand again and managed to shuffle toward the raft.

Up ahead, Risten was wading the raft further into the water. She climbed aboard without looking back at me. She picked up the long pole we had lashed together, and gazing intently in the island's direction, shoved off toward it with all her strength.

I hurried after her and waddled a few steps into the lake. I fell again into the water, and without a thought for my fear, dragged myself deeper. I had to reach the raft. My head went under, and suddenly the sound of the bells was gone.

Instantly, sanity returned. *What am I doing! I'm in the Creator damned lake!* Spitting, I stood up in waist-deep water. Once more, I felt the hypnotic pull of the bell music. Although I fought the urge with all my might, I took a step forward, tripped, and again fell into the water. This time, when my body became my own, I stayed under. It had to be the music that was making me go toward the island. I put my fingers in my ears and stood up.

Although I could barely hear the bells, I still felt the pull. Fortunately, it was not overwhelming and something I could resist. Across the lake, I saw Risten well on her way, and no matter how loud I yelled to her, she paid me no attention. I watched in frustration as she floated away. I shook my head. This was no doubt what had happened to Zofie. And now Risten had been caught, too. Creator only knew what fate it drew them toward. I prayed the spell wouldn't affect her so badly that she would step off the raft before reaching shore.

I tried to think of something to stuff my ears with, but quickly realized that was going to be damn difficult while I had my fingers in them. Looking down, I suddenly realized I was standing in water up to my ribs. *I was actually in the blasted lake!* My breath caught as the dark water lapped against me. I started to back away but caught myself. There was really only one option. Afraid I wouldn't be able to do it if I hesitated, I ducked myself back underneath the water. I pulled my knife and managed to tear a strip of cloth from my shirt, no easy trick while wet. Carefully, I plugged each ear with the damp pieces. Then standing, I finally got to pull up my pants.

At least the ants were gone.

I quickly waded out of the water—relieved to be out of it—and sat down on the shore. I wasn't sure what to do. Unfortunately, building another raft was not an option.

There were still a few trees of suitable size available, but the only tool I had to cut them down was my knife. Everything else was on the raft with Risten, and even if I did, I had no rope to lash them together. We'd had barely enough to finish the first one. I could likely build another using just my knife and weaving some grass twine, but it would take a day to hack my way through a single tree, and I had no idea how to make twine. I gave a heavy sigh. I was stuck.

I sighed again. There really was only one thing left to do, and I wasn't really looking forward to it. Maybe a little flattery would help.

"Abe? I called tentatively. "Thanks for helping me avoid that siren's call."

*Just doing my job, you worthless sack of meat.* He almost sounded pleased with himself.

Now my real question. "I don't suppose I could curse myself into being a bird or something to get across?"

*Sure, you can curse yourself all you want. In fact, if I were as miserable as you, I'd curse myself all the time. Now, if you mean can you* put *a curse on yourself, the answer is a big, fat NO! Simply isn't allowed. The fundamental rules of myst usage only allow for one curse per person, and for you, I happen to occupy that slot. It has something to do with how myst cycles through everything. And as for the 'or something' part of your question, only humans can be cursed. Again something to do with the myst cycles.*

I sighed. "Any idea on how to get across?"

*Oops, look at the time. Since I've answered the remaining question from yesterday, it's time for me to go!*

I shook my head in disbelief. "But it's almost when my next set of questions start. Can't you give them to me early?"

He laughed. *Do you really want me to, considering you just asked a question?*

I clenched my fist. "You know, you're a real bastard."

*And I'm good at it too!* He laughed and faded away.

Damn! I looked forlornly out across the black water at the island. It was just ahead—right *there!* But it might as well have been on the other side of the world. I slapped my knee in frustration. There had to be a way. I refused to give up.

I glanced around at what was left. Not much. The limbs we had hacked off the trees to make the logs were scattered about—quite a lot of them actually. But there was no rope to tie anything together. *Could I swim out there?* Maybe with something to help me float? Then I thought about all that dark water that would be under me, and I shivered. I barely managed to hold my panic at bay.

And it made me angry. Why was I afraid of a little bit of water? As my anger grew, I leaped to my feet. There had to be a way across. In my fury, I picked up one of the branches lying close and shoved it at the water. I leaned my head back and yelled at the sky in frustration. "I refuse to give in! Creator, you had better help me because otherwise, I'm going to come up there and give you a piece of my mind! I bear the Thief of Curses!"

But the Creator chose not to answer me and, with my ears plugged, all I heard was silence. The only response was a cool breeze caressing my cheek. I sat back down, my anger having played out. That actually hadn't accomplished anything, but at least I felt better.

I looked down at the water and noticed the branch I threw was floating, and the breeze was blowing it toward the island. Rather quickly, in fact. My eyes widened. I looked back to the branches lying on the ground, seeing them in a new light. And I moved quickly to begin gathering them together in a pile by the water's edge. I went to the few standing trees that had been too small for the raft and managed to whack off a few other limbs with my knife. When I had a reasonably decent pile, I wove them together into a dense bundle and bound them together with strips from my shirt. I crawled on it experimentally and thought it just might work.

I pushed it into the water and crawled on top, laying down to spread the load and help hold it together. Thankfully, it only sank a little under my weight. And as I expected, the breeze pushed on the pile, and we gradually floated away from shore. I couldn't suppress a smile. My crude raft, if one could even call it that, wasn't exactly the best boat I'd ever seen, but I thought it would get me across. I tried using one of the denser branches as an oar to help the process along, but the rocking tended to make the branches want to separate. I finally decided that going slow was better than going under, so I stuck the branch upright as a sort of sail and just lay still, forcing myself to let the wind do the work. I tried not to look at the water, keeping my eyes fixed on the island. It was hard because my fear ate at me the whole time, the darkness nipping at me from the corner of my eye. But I knew if I looked, I would panic.

So instead I faced forward and tried to make my crude raft go faster by force of thought alone.

Zofie, Risten—I hoped I wasn't too late.

# CHAPTER TWENTY-TWO

# A Dream
# To Die For

The going was slow, but I finally did reach the island by early afternoon. Unfortunately, the shore was very rocky, and my raft pile snagged a little way out. So I had to abandon my craft and wade the rest of the way in, not to mention getting myself covered in mud as I tried to climb the bank.

I quickly found Risten's raft and, along with it, my sword and both our sacks—all abandoned without a thought. I could easily see where she went. Her trail led up a high, steep bank and cut through some tall grass. So after washing the mud off, I donned my spare shirt and set out after her.

I topped the rise and was surprised to see a large willow tree, standing by itself in a clearing, and whose long thin branches almost touched the ground. The leaves and branches hung so densely the trunk was hidden.

Nothing moved around me. Even the grass was eerily still—the breeze that had pushed me to the island was suddenly gone. I couldn't help but feel like an interloper.

Risten's path went right into the branches of the tree. I cautiously stepped closer, pausing at the edge, looking for some sign of her, Zofie, or what was causing the siren song. All had to be close by.

I slowly stretched out my hand to part the branches... when the air suddenly filled with a beautiful tinkling sound. Like thousands of tiny bells ringing in perfect harmony. I thought that very odd since my ears were plugged—but then I lost the ability to care. It seemed the most natural thing in the world to reach up to my ears and pull out the plugs.

Suddenly, the green of the tree became greener, and the blue of the sky became bluer—everything took on the ultra-rich colors an artist used on a canvas.

The branches stirred, and a young lady stepped from within them. My heart skipped a beat at the sight of her. Saying she was beautiful was the same as saying the sun gives light. Her brightness hurt my eyes; her beauty was absolutely blinding. Her hair was a dark red, and she wore it long and pulled back with clips on either side. She had pale skin, a smattering of freckles across her nose, and a lovely dress of blue which drew out the same color of her eyes. I instantly knew it was Zofie. The princess in her true form.

She stepped closer, and I noticed she carried Havoc's Sword loosely in her right hand. She smiled, her whole face lighting up and tiny dimples gracing her cheeks. "Look, Coren. I found the sword. We can go home now!"

Something stirred in the back of my mind, but I pushed it away. "You're not a bird now?" The question sounded stupid even to my ears. I could clearly see she wasn't.

She laughed. It was like music. "Something turned me back to my old self when I touched the sword. Isn't it wonderful!" Zofie leaned forward and hugged me tightly.

When she leaned back, we stood in the castle I had seen in her memories. Only now, Zofie's hair was put up in a tight braid wound atop her head. She wore an elegant blue gown with long flowing skirts, something very suited to her station as a princess. Over it, she wore a jacket which sparkled with jewels and gold.

Zofie smiled at me. "We can't be late to see Father. He's been eager to meet you." She picked a piece of lint off my own splendid coat.

"I thought your father was dead?"

Zofie laughed. "Silly. We all thought he was dead, but that was just a cruel joke my little brother played. Father is fine. And Wynn apologized for giving the sword away." She looped her arm in mine. "Now enough of that. It's time to meet the king."

And she pulled me down the aisle of a large chamber with hundreds of on-lookers on every side. They broke out into applause and cheered as we neared the front. The king sat on his throne at the front of the room, fully robed in the royal colors of his family. He beamed proudly at us. Risten stood on his left along with Spraggel, while Zofie's brother Wynn stood on the right. All were dressed in their finest, smiling with their love and adoration. I nervously stepped forward and bowed, simply glad I didn't trip.

But when I straightened, I couldn't help but notice a tapestry hanging just behind the king. Unlike the rest of the brightly colored room, it had a plain dull brown background and only a single stylized eye drawn in black on it. The eye seemed to be looking at me. And I recognized it from somewhere. But where?

"Coren!" The king announced, jerking my attention back to him. "You demonstrated such bravery in getting Havoc's Sword back, I have decided to offer you my daughter's hand in marriage."

Zofie rushed into my arms and we kissed...

But when she stepped back, the hall had changed. It now was decorated with blue ribbons and pink flowers. I stood at the front, and Zofie was walking down the aisle wearing a brilliant white wedding gown with a train that reached half the length of the hall. Six maids carried it for her. And Zofie was smiling in rapture.

I took her arm, and together we turned to face the priest. I stared at him in surprise. He was a stick-figure, the kind a child might draw to represent a person, with nothing more than lines for arms, legs, and body. But the head was different. It was larger than a normal man's and contained a single stylized eye, forming some kind of symbol. I knew that symbol from somewhere. I could feel it on the tip of my tongue. I turned back to Zofie, and she threw her arms around me and kissed me full on the lips. I felt so happy—the happiest I had ever felt.

When I pulled back, the floor had been cleared, and there were dancers all around, twirling and spinning. Zofie was in my arms, and she was laughing. She looked so beautiful, and to think she was now my bride. I felt a tap on my shoulder, and I turned to see the odd stick-figure man with the stylized eye for a head. "May I cut in?" he asked. His voice was so deep it rattled my insides.

Zofie stepped to one side but, instead of going to her, he took my hand, and we began to dance.

Why was this stylized eye so familiar to me?

The figure cocked its head to one side. "Don't you think it's time to let this little fantasy go?"

I felt recognition dawning on me. I knew who this was. I knew!

I shook my head. "No." I shook my head harder. "No! I don't want to."

Zofie gently pulled me away from the stick-figure man.

Suddenly, Zofie and I were getting into a fine carriage. A joyous crowd surrounded us. They were shouting blessings and pelting us with tiny flowers. Zofie settled into my arms as the carriage started moving. The coachman leaned down. "Where to, sir?" he asked.

I looked up at him and again saw the stick figure man with the eye for a head. "Where to?" he repeated.

And with an aching sadness, I knew the answer. It would be so wonderful to stay. But I was needed. It wasn't done. I glanced beside me to the smiling Zofie, knowing I would likely forever regret what I did next. My mouth went dry, and my lips didn't want to move, but I forced the words out. "Take me back."

Zofie took my face in her hands and tried to kiss me, but I grabbed her wrists and pulled them down.

"Don't you love me? Don't you want to stay with me forever?" I saw a tear roll down her cheek.

"I'm sorry," I whispered. Only I wasn't sure if I was sorry for her... or for myself. "I have to go back. It's because I do love you that I have to."

"Please, no," she cried.

The carriage stopped. I opened the door and stepped out—

My eyes fluttered open and I blinked in the dim light; the last vestiges of the dream falling away—one that I would have been happy to dream until I died.

I lay under the willow tree with its branches forming a ring around the ground I lay on. I looked toward the trunk and saw a skeleton propped against it. I shivered.

*Damn! That was a nasty one.* Abe said into my head. *I almost didn't get you away from that bitch.*

I sat up and my head spun. "I feel like my head is full of fluff."

*Well, it is full of fluff, but we already knew that. The willow tree has a powerful siren curse on it. A really good one too. Very finely crafted. I bet that one was done by the old masters. It's rare to run into those nowadays. You have a wonderful dream and die a few days later from exposure. Then your rotting corpse feeds the tree. Pretty clever, huh?*

"I don't know about it being clever." I shook my head, noticing my earplugs were gone. "I hope the dream doesn't come back."

*Nope, it won't. You broke out of it, so you're immune to it now. And don't worry; you weren't out all that long. It's only been a few hours. Just right before sunset, to be exact.*

I leaned forward and sat up. The ground underneath me crunched and popped. When I put my hand out to steady myself, it almost felt like twigs and branches, but smooth and brittle. I bent and examined the ground more closely and saw the area was littered with bones and skulls from all kinds of small creatures, including bugs, birds, and a few small mammals. I stared in shock. No wonder the area was so quiet. The siren tree had pulled not only humans to it, but every living thing—where they had cheerfully died to provide nourishment for the tree. I shivered.

Standing, and with my feet crunching the bones beneath me, I spotted Risten lying on her side, facing me a short distance away. She was smiling blissfully, her breathing regular as if asleep. And a little beyond her, closer to the trunk, lay Zofie. She sprawled in a most un-birdlike way. I walked over to her and knelt beside her, gently smoothing her feathers. She didn't wake. And she didn't seem to be breathing all that well either.

*By the way, your lady friend was quite the looker when she was human. The tree must have pulled her likeness from either sword-girl's mind or maybe even her own. Very clever indeed, but a dead give-away. The curse outsmarted itself since you didn't know what she looked like.* He paused, his tone softening. *You know I had to join your dream to try to get you out, don't you?* The question was most uncharacteristic, almost like he was apologizing. *My maker felt that dreams were private, and I'm normally not allowed to visit them, but you were in danger, so I had to make an exception. I hope you didn't mind too much... AND IT'S TOO BAD IF YOU DID!*

I shrugged. "I didn't mind. We're pretty much joined at the hip... I mean curse anchor, anyway."

*Ha Ha!*

I considered the willow tree for a moment. "If I cut down this tree, will it wake them?"

*Sorry, but no. The tree bears a curse. If you cut it down now, you will stop the curse dead in its tracks, which will keep anyone else from becoming trapped. But... for those already cursed, theirs will never end, and they will sleep until they die. The only way to wake them is for you to steal it. Once I have control, I can end it, and they'll revert. Just go up to the tree, touch it, and say the words.*

I sighed. I was really uncomfortable with this curse business. It was one thing to be cursed, but quite another to be the one manipulating them. It was almost like I was being forced down a path I didn't want to go. Plus it made me feel... dirty almost. I stroked Zofie's feathers and shook my head. But did I really have a choice?

I stood and faced the tree, then reluctantly reached around the skeleton to touch the bark, finding it cool and rough. I took a deep breath and said the words Abe had told me. "Your curse is now my curse."

I felt a welling of power from my left wrist quickly followed by a sting on my chest. A yellow glow spread out across the tree, and then it began to morph and change. Its branches contracted, pulling into itself, where it gradually took on a human shape. I gasped. *Human?* When the glow lifted, an elderly woman lay where the tree had been.

I heard a groan and a crunch behind me. I glanced over to see Risten sitting up. "What happened?" She scratched her head and yawned. "Where's our children?"

I turned to look at her. "Our children?"

Her eyes went wide, and she had a very uncharacteristic sheepish expression. "It was a dream, wasn't it?" Then she did something I had never seen her do. She blushed. She quickly stood and turned her back to me. "Where are we?" she asked to cover her embarrassment.

Zofie groaned and opened one eye, but she did not rise. She lay limp, a rather large pile of feathers, her one eye swiveling around slowly to take her bearings. Gradually, she gathered her strength and sat up as a bird might sit on a nest, looking quite dazed.

"Zofie, are you all right?" I asked, concerned.

*Coren... I... we were...* She swallowed. *I'm not sure.*

"Both of you just take it easy," I said. "You were under a powerful siren spell. Everything since hearing the music was a dream."

Risten turned back in our direction. "A dream, huh." She glanced at me, blushed again, and quickly turned away. "I had better have a look around."

*That must have been one very good dream,* I mused.

I heard another groan, only this one came from the elderly woman. I rose and knelt beside her. She lay on her back, wearing only a simple white gown. Her eyes were open, staring at the sky. But when I entered her line of sight, she turned her head slightly in my direction. She slowly licked her lips. "How long has it been?" she asked in barely a whisper. "How long since the Dark Avenyts?"

"About a thousand years."

Her eyebrows went up briefly in surprise. "That long? Then my watch is done, I'm long overdue for a respite." She closed her eyes.

"What do you mean, your watch is done? And how did you get turned into a tree?"

She sighed deeply. "I'm tired. Let me rest now."

And she gave one last long breath, and quietly died. I sighed sadly. *Who was this woman? And how did she get turned into a tree? Could she have been here for a thousand years? It didn't seem possible.*

I started to stand but stopped as I noticed the woman's body continued to age, turning gray and growing gaunt. It was like time was catching up with her all at once. Her body gradually caved into itself and collapsed to dust. The whole process had only taken a few minutes.

Curiosity got the best of me. I should be due some questions. "Abe," I asked. "Do you know anything about the woman that had been turned into a tree?"

He didn't answer immediately, as if mulling over his answer. *I do not know her. But her curse is familiar. I've seen it before, just not sure where.*

I pulled up my shirt and saw that next to Zofie's curse anchor, I now had another. This one was a circle with a willow tree in it. My second.

I wondered what happened when I ran out of chest.

I pulled my shirt back down. "Abe? How come that lady was cursed? While Zofie can't, this woman turned back into a human."

His answer was almost subdued; most unlike him. I couldn't help but wonder if he knew more than he was telling me. *I don't know why she was cursed. The motivations for being cursed, I'm not so good at. As for why she turned back, that's exactly what the curse was supposed to do. When the curse ended, it transformed the person back to their original state. Most well-designed curses do.* He paused, and I opened my mouth to ask another question, but he continued, quickly regaining his usual swagger: *And that, my sack of meat, is the last question for today. Although, I have to say it's been the most interesting day I've had in quite a while. You may have shit for brains, but you're a trouble magnet.* He laughed, which gradually faded to silence.

I went over to Zofie, who was now looking more alert. *Do you have any water? I'm parched.*

"I can certainly believe you are. You've been out for a day and a half." I held my water skin to her mouth and dribbled some on her out-stretched tongue. She then tilted her head back to drink it. We repeated this several times until she was satisfied.

When she was done, she flapped her wings once, but quickly folded them back against her body. *I don't think I can fly. I'm feeling too weak.*

I glanced at the horizon and noticed the sun was just about to set. We needed to make camp. I surveyed the area, looking for a likely spot.

With the tree gone, I now had a clear view of our surroundings. The little bit of grass that had been between the tree and the lake ended abruptly just a few steps away, before turning into clear flat rock stretching into the distance. And just beyond the grass were a series of tall stones evenly spaced in what appeared to be an enormous circle. But it was what was beyond them that caught my eye. The setting sun behind me illuminated a few small squat structures toward the island's interior, and in the middle of them rose a single vertical column extending high into the air. And on its top was a man-sized figure, its left hand extended toward the sky. And in his hand, he held what looked to be a shield.

*Ruin's Shield.*

I sighed. Our goal was finally in sight. But instead of feeling joy, I instead felt dread. So far, every step had been a challenge. I couldn't help but fear that the worst was yet to come.

# CHAPTER TWENTY-THREE

# Trap

We walked a short distance to a couple small boulders and made camp beside them. There was no wood for a fire, so I placed my amulet on a rock in the center to provide a little light. We settled around it as best we could. Zofie was the weakest I'd seen her. She took water but refused the dried meat. She said even smelling it made her sick. I'd have to ask Abe in the morning, but I was pretty sure her curse was taking its toll on her.

Risten lounged on her blanket nearby, staring up at the moon, no doubt thinking the same as me. The moon was only a day from being completely full. And Zofie would transform, yet again. That would likely be her last transformation before she died. Which led me to a decision.

"Zofie. There's something I need to ask you. It's related to your curse, and I think it's pretty important."

She turned her big eyes on me and looked at me unblinkingly in the way owls do. She didn't say anything, so I jumped into the speech I'd been preparing in my mind.

"I've been asking Abe questions related to your curse. And I found out that as the Thief of Curses, I can use him to take over your curse. I can stop your transformations."

She stared at me a moment with those huge eyes. *But you can't return me to my human form, right?*

I looked down and answered carefully so Risten could follow Zofie's side of the conversation. "No, I can't return you to your human form, which is why I'm asking." I cleared my throat. "There's one other thing too." I looked to Risten. "I'm sorry Risten, but I think it's time Zofie knows."

Risten glared at me a moment with her jaw set, then nodded and looked away.

But Zofie answered before I could continue. *Know what? That I'm dying? That the transformations are killing me? I've known that since my second transformation when I didn't revert completely back to my original form. I knew it was only a matter of time.*

My head came up in surprise. "You've known all along?"

Risten sat up. "And you didn't tell us?"

*Yes, and probably for the same reason you didn't mention it to me before now... I didn't want to worry you. Worrying over it doesn't help. It's not something that can be changed.*

"Then do you know that you only have one transformation left? Abe says the damage the transformations are doing is pretty bad."

She looked away for a moment, then looked at Risten before returning her gaze to me. *I knew it was soon, but I didn't realize it was that soon.*

I gazed at her levelly. "So do you want me to take your curse? That way you can at least live. Maybe we can find a way out of it."

Zofie shook her head before looking up at the moon. *Thanks for the offer, Coren. But, I'm tired of fighting it. Please just... leave it.*

I stared at her in shock. "You don't want me to? Creator, why?"

Her wings moved in what I interpreted as a shrug. *I don't want to live like that. The next time I transform, I should be some type of big mammal. I almost enjoyed being one of those.* She turned those large eyes on me. *I'll have about another month to live before my final transformation. It won't be so bad.*

I glanced over at Risten and passed on the information. Tears came to her eyes. I stood and went to Zofie and stroked the feathers on the side of her head. "Are you sure? I could save you."

She reached out a wing and gently stroked my face with her feathers. *I'm sure. Living in that chimera form, barely being able to breathe, or little alone walk somewhere unaided. I don't want that.* She turned to me and closed her eyes. Her wings were restless. *But... I'm afraid. Could you... be with me until then? Both of you?*

I put my arms around her, my own cheeks wet. "I would be honored, my lady."

Risten stepped forward and also hugged her.

Zofie enfolded both of us with her feathers, and we sat there for a very long time.

The next morning, we got off to a slow start. Zofie was feeling better but was still weak. Risten and I both were bone tired from sleeping on the hard rock and worrying over our friend.

As we walked toward the center, the ground transitioned to bare granite, with occasional patches of gray dust. A few scraggly bits of grass grew out of some cracks, and they rustled hauntingly in the breeze. The area seemed even deader than where the tree had been. Even the plants were having trouble.

Zofie worked up the strength to take a short flight over to the tower. She said there was nothing living for as far as she could see. I cautioned her against flying too close to the shield, or Creator forbid actually trying to grab it. There was no telling what other traps we might run into.

Reluctantly, she agreed with my logic and landed a little bit away from the statue area, sitting down to wait for us to reach her.

When we caught up, we discovered the base of the column was surrounded by a short wall only about waist high. And at each of the four major compass points around the barrier, there was a life-size statue of white marble—beautifully crafted. Each was posed in the robes of master myst users: two men with long beards and two women with long hair tightly woven into braids. All had their arms upraised and appeared to be looking at the top of the column. And in the center rose the towering statue itself going up at least a couple hundred feet, a solid round column of stone going straight up and so wide that if I wrapped my arms around it, it would only cover a tenth of its perimeter. At its top, I could make out another statue of the same white marble carved in the form of a man wearing a short tunic. His left arm was raised toward the sky, and in his hand, he gripped a golden shield. Ruin's Shield.

As I studied it, I couldn't help but think that atop a tower was really an odd place for so valuable an item. It was not only out in the open and clearly visible, but also completely exposed to the elements. Something just wasn't adding up. I shook my head. Regardless, we had best retrieve the shield as quickly as we could and leave before Wort caught up to us.

I saw something fluttering in the wind and was surprised to see it was a feather tied to our old companion, the Spear of Flight, sticking point first into the ground at the base of the tower. Apparently, it had continued on after our last throw and found its target despite Zofie going under the siren spell. I pointed it out to Risten, and we had a good chuckle.

I turned to Risten and Zofie. "So this is it. We've finally reached it."

Zofie flapped her wings. *We should probably check around the perimeter to make sure there are no traps.*

"Agreed."

Risten and I each made an independent circuit of the area outside the short wall. There was no opening in it—or cracks for that matter—just a completely unbroken circle of stone about a hand's-breadth wide. It was something one might find protecting a garden. The sun was leaning toward afternoon when we finished our inspection with no traps found.

I rubbed my chin. "There has got to be another trap around it. I can't imagine this being so exposed and not have one."

Risten nodded toward the wall. "Maybe it's inside."

I drew my sword and, holding it as far from me as I could, poked it into the area inside the wall. Nothing happened. I brought the tip down and gently tapped the top of the stone wall. Again nothing.

I perched one hip on the wall and looked around the tower. There was nothing I could see, just dirt and a flat stone floor. Zofie flew up and landed on the wall beside me while Risten joined me on the other side. "What could it be? I certainly don't see anything."

*Well, there's only one way to find out.*

And Zofie launched herself into the circle.

"Don't...!" I yelled. But it was too late. Just on the other side of the wall, she screamed and fell to the ground. Immediately, burning pain shot through my chest. Risten quickly moved to get Zofie, but I managed to lunge for her and tackled her to the ground.

She fought with me. "Get off of me. She's in trouble."

"No!" I yelled. "You'll get caught too!" I quickly climbed to my feet and watched as Zofie began to glow and quickly reverted to her chimera form. But she didn't rise. She raised a feeble arm in my direction, but it dropped to the ground. Her breathing was labored, and the pain in my chest didn't ease. For a moment, I couldn't understand why the sensation hadn't stopped when her transformation had completed. Then I realized what it was—she was continuing to pull on my myst.

"Stay back!" she croaked. "It's a Myst Siphon, and it's drained all of mine. I should be dead, but it's now drawing from you. You've got to cut off the curse. Otherwise, I'll drain you dry. And then we'll both die."

Risten came up beside me. "I'll run in and get her..."

"NO!" Zofie yelled. "You won't make it two steps before you die."

She turned her pleading eyes on me. "Hurry and cut off the curse. I'm as good as dead anyway. Please! I don't want to kill you like I did my father."

My heart pounded in my chest. I didn't want to let Zofie die. Not yet. But something was eating at the back of my mind.

"Abe! Can I steal this curse? This Myst Siphon thing?"

He answered instantly. *Yes, you can steal it. There is a curse on the northward statue. Unfortunately, the only way to take it is from inside the Myst Siphon. The curse appears to be a wonderfully complex one. I would dearly love to add it to my collection.*

"That doesn't help me any. How..." *How can I get inside without dying?* Was what I was going to ask, but then a strange thought occurred to me. Abe knew the trap was there, *and* he knew I was tethered to Zofie. Yet Abe didn't stop her from going in. There could only be one explanation.

Abe didn't consider it a threat.

I rose to my feet. "Risten, stay here. I'll be right back."

"Hey?" she protested. "What makes you think you can go in and not me?"

"Because I can steal the curse."

I leaped over the wall and immediately felt my pain double, causing me to stagger. Swallowing my discomfort, I wobbled over to Zofie, lifted her in my arms, and carried her back over the wall. The pain in my chest instantly released. I laid her down on the ground, and Risten knelt beside her and took her hand.

This was the first time I had seen Zofie in the revealing light of day. My heart ached—she didn't even look close to a human. Her gaze met mine, and then she looked away, clearly not wanting me to see her that way. I grabbed one of the packs and pulled out a blanket and drew it around her.

I sighed. But my job wasn't done yet. I leaped back over the wall and ran to the statue Abe indicated. I touched it and spoke the words, "Your curse is my curse." I felt a sting on my chest, and at the same time, the statue began to glow, gradually changing into an old man. Only this one was very old. I tried to catch him as he toppled off the pedestal, but I only managed to break his fall. I laid him down as gently as I could, but he never opened his eyes. He took two breaths and died. And as I watched, his body collapsed to dust just like the woman who had been a tree.

Had these people been forced to take those curses? That would have been exceedingly cruel. But for some reason that just didn't feel right. What had the lady of the tree said: *My watch is done.* Could it be these people had volunteered? I couldn't shake the feeling I was missing something. Something big.

I felt a sudden chill breeze where there hadn't been one before. Looking up, I realized that the barrier surrounding the top of the mountain was gone. Apparently, it and the myst siphon were somehow connected.

I went back to Risten and Zofie. The princess seemed exhausted. From what little I knew of myst depletion, it could cause one to have weakness, sweating, and even loss of consciousness. And to my untrained eye, she had two of those and was just a hair's breadth away from the last one.

A concerned Risten looked up as she held Zofie's hand. The water bag lay close by, and Risten had arranged the blanket to conceal most of her chimera features, leaving only her huge eyes peering out.

Zofie turned her head in my direction. "How did you do that?" she asked weakly. "The siphon was not only sucking out your myst but was also pulling my portion out of you too."

I shrugged and knelt down beside her. I explained my theory on Abe not considering it a threat. But I could offer no idea as to why it didn't affect me. The only explanation was that there was more to my curse than we knew.

She reached up her arm and stroked my face. "I'm just glad you're all right."

I took her hand and kissed it. I probably shouldn't have—her being a princess and all—but it just felt right. "There is only one thing left to do now." I looked toward the top of the column, the sun's reflection glinting off the shield's golden metal. "And the sooner I get it, the faster we can get off this accursed mountain."

"Watch for traps," Zofie cautioned as I stood.

"Of that, you can be assured, my princess." I gave her an exaggerated bow then in my overconfidence, tried to leap the wall, but caught my foot and nearly fell. Embarrassed, I looked back over my shoulder to see Risten shaking her head.

On the far side of the column, I found a series of handholds built into the side. I looked them over carefully but didn't see anything that could be a trap. I was also going to need some way to find out what parts of the shield I could touch—and I didn't want to lose a hand figuring it out.

At a sudden idea, I bent down and picked up a few loose stones to take with me in case I needed to test the shield. I placed them in my pouch. Then thinking it might be windy at the top, I also donned my coat. And with my final preparation done, I started climbing.

Considering the column's age, the handholds were in excellent shape, but I still went slowly and deliberately, testing each handhold before putting my full weight on it. But while the going was slow, it was thankfully uneventful. I only made the mistake of looking down once. And I promised myself, I would not do it again.

Finally, I reached the last rung and carefully snaked over the edge and onto the top of the column. I crawled over to the statue and sat down at its base for a moment to let my arms rest. While I was in no immediate danger of falling, I was still on top of a tower that was on a tall mountain. So I was pretty damn high. From my vantage point, I had a view that went on for many leagues. The sun had moved toward late afternoon, and there wasn't a cloud in the sky. I could see where the willow tree had been and beyond that, the lake surrounding the island, and beyond that the distinct edge of the mountain, and still beyond that, the deep blue of the surrounding countryside. It was definitely beautiful...

But it was scaring me to death.

I didn't dare step to the edge to look down at Zofie and Risten. In fact, I wasn't sure how I was going to work up the courage to go back down. I shivered. Guess I'd figure that out when I got to it.

As I was turning away, the glint of something shiny below caught my eye close to where the willow tree had been. I studied the area it came from but couldn't find it again. It must have been the sunlight reflecting off a pool of water or perhaps a piece of crystal. The sun was low enough to do that.

I sighed. I guess I had put this off long enough. Moving carefully, mindful not to touch the shield, I slid up the statue's legs and waist until I found a spot to stand on his bent leg. The sculpture was roughly twice human size, which put the shield over my head. Shuffling around to get a better angle, I examined the interior of the shield more closely. It was perfectly round and much larger than I expected. The ones I'd seen were only slightly more than the length of a forearm. However, this one was easily the length of my entire *leg* and maybe just a bit more. Whoever carried this in battle, must have been huge.

The shield itself was attached at an upward angle, with a thin metal bar running its diameter and affixed to the concave metal interior. There was some kind of metal mechanism clamping the shield to the statue's raised forearm, and surprisingly there was not a hint of rust on it.

I dug in my pouch and pulled out one of my small stones. Before I went to the trouble of taking it down, I thought it a good idea to test it.

I lobbed a stone over the top of the shield, letting it arch over to hit the front. The stone instantly went poof and turned to dust. I blinked. That was pretty impressive—best not to touch the front. I tossed a stone at the underside, and it bounced off unaffected. I gave a sigh of relief. I had been afraid both sides might have been set up to destroy.

Now to get it off. I looked closely at the mechanism holding it in place and ran my fingers along the bar. There was a lever in the middle attached to some kind of sliding metal clamp. I grasped it. Now if I pulled the lever...

It didn't budge.

I jerked on it and even tried with both hands, but it wouldn't move. I stared at it a moment in consternation. *I was not* going to go back down the tower just to find some sort of tool. Finally, I pulled out one of the remaining rocks and slammed it against the lever. That did it, moving just a fraction. I kept at it until I was able to move it all the way using just my hand. Then I reached up, grabbed the crossbar, and lifted the shield free. Surprisingly, it was as light as my sword, despite its much larger size. I gave a prayer of thanks that it wasn't that windy of a day as I carefully climbed back down from the statue.

Holding it away from me, I carefully slid around the stone figure to where the ladder was. I eyed the spot in frustration. *But now how to get it down?* I briefly considered just dropping it and letting it glide to the rock below, but there was a chance it could fall face down on the ground. And with its spell of defense, it would likely start eating a hole in the earth.

I finally decided to secure it to my back using my coat. Then I carefully, *very* carefully, maneuvered back over the edge.

Going down seemed to take a lot longer than going up. And I was so glad when my foot hit solid ground. I gave a long sigh of relief and immediately pulled the shield off my back, lest I accidentally brush something with it. But looking around, I was surprised that I didn't see either Zofie or Risten. I stepped over the short wall surrounding the statue's column, but they weren't anywhere in sight.

"Zofie!" I called. "Risten!"

Suddenly, there was a shuffling sound to my right, and I heard an unexpected voice which seemingly came from just in front of me. It was a voice I really didn't want to hear.

"Oh, how touching," said Wort. "He can't find his friends."

And as if a covering drape were pulled back, Spraggel suddenly appeared. Wort stood just behind him with one arm locked around my master's throat, and Havoc's Sword pointed at his heart.

Wort grinned evilly. "I think you have something I want."

# CHAPTER TWENTY-FOUR

# Surrounded

Wort wore a smug expression as the unveiling continued on around me. One by one, the others of his party appeared, forming a rough semicircle around me. I ground my teeth in frustration. I should have guessed. *A concealment charm.* That speck of light I had seen from the top of the column was likely from the spell distorting the surrounding air. They had been following us a little more closely than we had believed possible.

I counted twelve men total—six of Wort's and six priests—plus one additional pissed off woman, the high priest Benzel. I easily recognized those in Wort's original party from our past encounters, as they did me. Dai, the helmeted man that tried to kill me back at our keep, nodded in my direction and grinned, while Rid, with the scar across his eye, blew me a kiss. I shivered. The priests all wore the traditional black robes, but each was armed to the teeth with several swords and knives apiece.

At the very last, Risten and Zofie were revealed sitting on the ground within the semicircle of men. Risten's hands were bound behind her, and she had a developing bruise on her face. Zofie, while not appearing to be tied, sat with Risten, leaning heavily against her cousin with the blanket still draped over her. Unfortunately, Zofie looked paler than before; her condition seemed to be getting worse. The myst depletion, along with her curse, had definitely taken a toll on her.

Spraggel, for the most part, looked unharmed, although his hair was mussed, and his robe was stained with dirt in a couple places. His hands were bound behind him, and Wort had a restraining arm around his throat. While my master said nothing, I could see the anger in his eyes.

Wort grinned. "About time you got the damn shield down." He motioned toward me with his head, and two of his men moved forward. "Now what say you let us have that shield, and your friend here won't get hurt, *Thief of Curses*."

I froze. "How do you know about my curse?"

He shrugged. "The young master mentioned I might run across it. Not that it was specifically you, but that this Thief of Curses could be with his sister. The hint was when you used the exact same curse on Benzel that my master used on his sister—a strange coincidence unless you had taken that curse for yourself." A grin returned to his face. "And my master was very clear, that if I ran across this curse, I was to bring it back with me. And under no circumstances should I directly threaten you. Something about your curse providing protection."

"Me?" My voice cracked. The boy-king who killed his own father, cursed his sister, and had dozens of others killed—wanted *me!* That couldn't be good.

Wort nodded. "I'm not sure what he plans for you, but he said you would definitely be useful in conquering the neighboring kingdoms." He held out his hand. "*Now give me the shield..*"

I didn't move. "You realize having the sword and the shield together is dangerous. If one touches the other, you'll have death on a massive scale. All the myst will get sucked up."

Wort made a face. "You actually believe that if the two touch, each one will try to best the other until all the myst within their reach is consumed. And in the process, kill off every living thing in the world?"

I nodded, a little surprised. "Well, yeah. That's a pretty good description."

Wort grinned again. "Do you honestly think the ancients would be so stupid not to account for that? They built a safeguard into them. So how about giving it to me before I separate this old man's head from his body."

Spraggel shook his head. "You're wrong, Wort. There are no such protections. It doesn't work that way."

Zofie raised a feeble hand, but quickly dropped it. "He's right, Wort." She panted. "My brother lied to you."

Wort frowned, raising his sword. "Then why don't we test it right now." He swung toward the shield.

"NO!" I cringed back.

Thankfully Wort stopped mid-strike and grinned. "Well then, why don't you just hand it over? That way, the shield doesn't get hit."

I just stared at him.

His eyes narrowed. "You had better hurry. I'm not a patient man. You're out of options."

Unfortunately, I had to agree. I lowered the shield. "I can't put this down. I'll have to walk it over to you."

I slowly stepped in his direction and extended my arm.

Wort and I locked gazes. I could see his confidence, his sureness that he was going to win. And I knew without a doubt he was going to kill us all.

Wort shoved Spraggel away, reached out, and easily took the shield from me. Dai and Rid pinned my arms behind my back.

Wort laughed. "I have them both! I finally have them! I am the strongest man alive!"

The female Benzel stepped forward. "What about my curse? I want this thing off of me."

Wort shifted his sword to point at me. I noticed he was careful to keep the shield pointed away from it. So maybe Wort wasn't quite so sure of his young master after all.

"Do as the high priest says. You're the Thief of Curses, so take hers away. I'm extremely tired of listening to her nagging—worse than having a wife."

Benzel glared at Wort. "You will refer to me as a *he*. I am not an accursed *woman!* I am a man!"

Wort gave him a dismissing wave.

Dai whistled. "And a right pretty man too!"

Benzel's face turned red, and the priests stiffened at the remark, but she chose to ignore it and faced me. "Now, remove my curse."

I frowned at Benzel, not really wanting to cooperate. I looked at him levelly. "You don't deserve this." I looked to Wort. "I have to touch... er... him to steal the curse."

Wort nodded to his men, and they released me. I stepped forward and looked Benzel in the eye. "You understand your original form has been lost, and you can't go back entirely to what you were. You'll likely be mostly a man, but some part of you may still be a woman."

"I don't care," he snarled. "Get this curse off of me."

"All right. You've been warned." I reached out a single finger and touched Benzel. I recited the words. "Your curse is my curse."

I braced for the sting in my chest and the transformation glow to start...

Only nothing happened.

I poked Benzel's chest again and repeated it. Nothing.

In my head, I heard an explosion of deep laughter: so loud I thought my brain was going to vibrate out. *I can't believe it.* Abe said. *It's hysterical. I can't steal the curse back!*

I put a hand up to conceal my mouth. "Uh, Abe," I muttered. "What's going on?"

If he had been human, I'm sure he would have been bent over and slapping his knee in complete roaring laughter. *The guy just couldn't pass it by. Curiosity is a bitch.*

Benzel's scowl was growing. "Why haven't I turned back? Do it now or your friends die!"

I held up a hand. "Give me a moment. I'm trying." I whispered, "Abe? Can you enlighten me a little?"

*In all my years, I've never seen anything like this, so yes, I'll answer the question. In fact, this one's on the house. It's just too good.*

"So the answer."

*It's one of those strange quirks of myst transformations. Only one curse per person, as they say. Our good old boy Benzel here, the one that hated women so badly, did a little hanky-panky in the darky-parky.*

"I'm not following you."

*Come on... you're not that naive. You know, ride the dragon, a little under the covers work with a favorite pal.*

I shook my head not fully understanding. "So he took a woman to his bed. He's done that before. What's different?"

Abe chuckled. *It wasn't... with... a WOMAN.*

It took a moment for that to sink in. "You mean he's had... ah... with a man? But he's..." Now that was a little surprising considering his taste for female sacrifices. "But what's that got to do with Benzel's curse?"

*I can't steal his curse, BECAUSE HE'S WITH CHILD!*

I thought my brain was going to explode. "With child?" I turned an open mouth to the high priest. "You're kidding me."

*Nope. I couldn't make up something like that. If I were to steal his curse, he would transform back into a man. But the baby inside him would create a paradox. You can't be male AND be pregnant. So the transformation just doesn't work. He's stuck, at least until the baby is born!* Abe laughed again. *I would pay gold coins to be there for the birthing.*

I glanced over at Benzel. She was really angry now.

"So Abe, what do I tell her?"

*That, my friend, is YOUR problem.*

I blew out my cheeks and turned to face her. At least now I knew what sex to consider Benzel. "I can't take your curse," I said.

She drew her knife and held the blade against my throat. "And why not?"

I gritted my teeth and forced a grin. "You're going to be a mother. Congratulations."

Benzel stared at me in shock. Then shook her head violently. "I can't be. It was just the one time. There's no way."

Wort roared with laughter, as did the rest of his men.

Risten yelled over at him. "How many of your female sacrifices have you told that line to!"

Benzel, on the other hand, wasn't pleased. She lunged for me. Thankfully, one of Wort's men caught her and held her back. She struggled and was so angry she spat. "This is all *your* fault. *I will kill you!*"

Wort, with his laughter subsiding, shook his head. "Not yet, high priest. Or should I call you holy mother now?" That drew some snickers from his men, but the priests remained deadly silent. Benzel's face became even redder. She lunged for me again, nearly making it this time. "This one is *mine!* I will peel his skin back bit by bit. I will pluck out his eyes and feed them to the crows. He will know such pain as he has ever known."

"Easy, high priest," said Wort sobering. "Unfortunately, I have to bring this one back alive. My young master was quite clear on that." He surveyed his prisoners. "But you bring up a good point. I can't take all these back with me. Let's see." He nodded toward Spraggel. "I'll need

the old man to keep the boy under control." He turned to consider Risten and Zofie. Risten glared at him, while Zofie continued to lean
heavily on her cousin's shoulder.

Wort nodded in their direction. "The princess's curse makes her as
good as dead. Killing her would be a mercy. However, Risten Brightmare has been a thorn in my side." He grinned, but there was ice in his
voice. "Bring her here. I think I should try out my new shield. And I
have the perfect candidate in mind."

Two of Wort's men jerked Risten up, leaving Zofie, who had been
leaning on her heavily for support, to fall over on her side. She hardly
moved. The effects of the myst depletion were getting worse.

Risten struggled, but they bodily dragged her over to Wort, forcing
her to stand before him. She raised her head high and glared at him.

Wort was wearing a very satisfied grin. "Now, my dear, you have
the privilege of trying out my new shield for me. Before I go into battle
with it, I have to understand what it can do to people. Surely you
understand."

She just stared at him coldly. I remembered what the rock had done
when I had tested it on the tower. I shuddered to think what it would
do to flesh. I couldn't let Wort do that to her.

I still had my sword, which apparently meant he didn't really consider me a threat. Unfortunately, with the guard restraining me, I
wouldn't even be able to get it out of the scabbard. And even if I did, I
was in no way skillful enough to beat these men. No, I needed to get
the sword to Risten.

So I used the only weapon at my disposal.

My big mouth.

"Wort!" I yelled, a little louder than I needed to. "I wouldn't do that
if I were you. The rock I tested on the shield just exploded into bits. But
a human...? Think of all the blood and guts that's going to cause. Quite
the mess!"

Risten turned her glare on me. I grimaced. I guess that did sound a little harsh. But it accomplished my true intent and got through to the men holding her. They glanced nervously at each other and stepped back a little, attempting to stretch her out by her arms, but with her hands tied, they couldn't get very far away. Wort huffed at their discomfort and motioned to one of the guards holding me, who stepped forward and cut her bonds. She struggled briefly, but she was no match for their strength. They each took an arm and stretched her taunt between them.

"Hold her tightly men," Wort commanded. "She's stronger than she looks."

Wort took his position in front of her. He extended the shield toward her and laughed. "This is going to feel so good... for me at least."

I flicked my eyes left and right frantically. There had to be something I could do. The one guard remaining had a firm grip on me, but how could I shake him off? Benzel stood close to me loosely gripping her dagger but watching Risten's pending execution with keen interest.

Hmmm.

Just as the shield was about to touch Risten, I did the only thing I could think of. I jerked toward Benzel, catching my guard unaware, and kicked her. Hard.

And just as I expected, the priest screamed.

Benzel leaped for me, slashing with her knife. I grappled with her for the weapon.

Just over the priest's shoulder, I saw Wort whip in my direction, the shield coming with him and away from Risten.

And then Risten smiled.

She twisted and kicked one of her guards in groin. He crumpled. With one guard remaining, she moved close and slammed her palm into his jaw. His head rocked back, and he collapsed.

I used the distraction to pin Benzel's arms behind her and slammed her into my guard, sending both of them tumbling to the ground. This bought the few precious seconds I needed. I quickly pulled my sword, reversed it, and tossed it toward Risten. I watched as it sailed in her direction, and she snatched it from the air.

One of Wort's men slammed me to the ground, and all the breath went out of my lungs. He jerked my hands painfully behind me. I strained to raise my head (and get my breath back), so I could see what was happening. Wort took a step backward as Risten brandished her sword. She looked in my direction and smiled at me—it was as if in that instant, she had completely forgiven me for any wrong I had done. It was her old master's sword and very fitting she would use it to fight his killer.

Wort faced off with her. He chuckled. "Do you actually think you can beat me with just a single weapon? I have both the sword and the shield."

Risten quickly stepped to the guard she had downed and took his sword. Unlike hers, it was of a simpler design with a rather wide guard and only one sharpened side. Holding a sword in each hand, she leveled the one in her right and raised her other in her left. "Doesn't matter," she said. "I'll still beat you." And she launched herself forward.

Wort raised his shield in defense, but instead, Risten danced to the side. Wort followed swinging with his sword, but away from the shield. It was then I noticed how much trouble Wort was having to maneuver the shield. For one, it was too large to be used effectively with his long sword. Secondly, he only had the metal bar going across its center to control it. Whoever had designed the shield had done a poor job of providing a way to hold it. It was like it wasn't intended to be used in battle.

Wort lunged, and Risten danced out of the way, while slowly backing toward the tower. Risten bided her time, and Wort seemed to be becoming increasingly frustrated as he fought not only with Risten, but with the awkwardness of the shield.

I spat dirt out of my mouth. I was still pinned to the ground with my arms pulled behind me, and it was getting increasingly hard to breathe. The man holding me was brutally strong. "Hey!" I yelled. "How about letting me up!"

Above and behind me, I felt a sudden jerk—the man holding me groaned and slumped to the side. I quickly rolled to my back to find Benzel standing over me, a bloody knife in her hand. "While Wort's occupied, lets you and I play. He says your curse won't let me kill you, but perhaps it will let me remove your manhood and let you see what it's like."

"I wouldn't do that if I were you," I warned. I tried to crab crawl away, but she planted a restraining foot on my chest, pinning me to the ground.

Dai grabbed her arm and pulled her off me. "Lord Wort says..."

He was cut off as one of the priests applied a club to the side of his head, and the man collapsed. Immediately, several small skirmishes broke out between Wort's remaining men and the priests. I, on the other hand, wasn't completely sure my curse would save me from an assault on my privates, so I used the distraction to scramble to my feet and flat out run.

Benzel took off after me. None of the men standing close by interfered with her pursuit since they were occupied with their own fights. "None of you touch him!" she yelled. "He's mine!"

Something must have happened in Benzel's transformation, where the high priest had once been a flabby middle-aged man, she was now an athletic mature woman, who was clearly faster than I was and rapidly closing the distance.

With nowhere else to go, I leaped the short wall around the statue and ran toward Risten's and Wort's fight. There were now several large gaps in the barrier where Wort had cut through them with his sword.

Risten was still managing to taunt and dodge Wort's blows. I gasped and nearly stumbled as Wort swung, and Risten brought up her own to counter. *Is she crazy? It'll be sliced in two!*

At the last moment, she shifted the angle of her sword and deflected it by striking the flat side of his sword. I was amazed. So that's how she was surviving. She had apparently figured out that the cleaving magic was only contained in the cutting edge of the sword—not its body. Striking there gave her some limited defense.

It was also clear Wort was becoming increasingly frustrated with the shield: it had become more a liability than an asset, yet he dared not set it down.

As I drew closer (with Benzel on my heels), I yelled: "Hey Wort! Can you do something about *her!* Your master won't be happy if she succeeds in cutting off my manhood."

Wort eyes shifted momentarily in my direction.

Risten smiled at the distraction. She flipped the sword in her left hand, end over end, and grabbed it by the blade. *What is she doing?*

She then extended the sword toward Wort and hooked its guard over the edge of the shield, pulling downward as hard as she could. This rotated the shield face toward the ground and completely exposed Wort: leaving the sword in her right hand to attack. Wort jerked back hard on the shield while trying to dodge her swing. This ripped the reversed blade from Risten's grasp, and in rebound, sending the shield over his head. Unfortunately, the shield also came free of Wort's grasp and quite unexpectedly—no doubt with help from my curse—caught the wind and flew straight at me.

I immediately jumped to the side, and it passed me at waist height. Benzel, like me, had enough sense to leap aside, but the priest behind her leaned in to catch it. I grimaced, expecting a sudden explosion of flesh and blood. But instead when he touched it, the man simply staggered and toppled over, instantly dead. He flopped to the ground, and the shield fell faceup beside him.

So flesh was treated differently. It may be slightly tidier, but it was still just as deadly.

Realizing this was my chance, I rushed to get the shield, but unfortunately, Benzel was closer and reached it first. She stuck her knife under the shield's edge and lifted it up until she could get under it and grab the bar. But I was right behind her. She gave me an evil look as my hand fell on the bar beside hers. She immediately slashed out with her blade, but with my free hand, I managed to grab her wrist. With both of us holding the shield and the knife, we were deadlocked—unable to attack, nor pull away.

For several moments we struggled. She was strong and quick—I wasn't sure I could take it from her. I pushed against her with what remained of my strength, forcing her to take a step back. Her heels hit the body of the downed priest, and she lost her balance. I quickly jerked the shield away, managing to wrench it from her as she sprawled on the ground most unladylike.

The remaining priests began to close in on me while Benzel slowly stood with knife in hand. I stepped away from them, swinging the shield from left to right to ward them off. This was not going well. A couple of the priests made lunges for me, and I was able to keep them at bay with the shield. That too wouldn't last long. My only hope was to get something solid to my back.

I glanced over toward Risten and Wort. They were still at it, but Risten looked to be tiring, our adventures and hard traveling had taken its toll on her. I was afraid it was only a matter of time before she became too slow to avoid one of his swings.

Wort, on the other hand, didn't even seem winded. Losing the shield had worked to his advantage. And his strategy appeared to be to drive her toward the statue's column. No doubt he was trying to make it difficult for her to dodge him.

Zofie sat on the ground nearby, taking cover against the statue and uncomfortably close to where we fought. Spraggel was kneeling beside her, trying to offer some small bit of aid. He had somehow gotten his hands free and had helped her away from the action, only now the action had followed her.

I carefully retreated toward the statue until I felt its cold stone behind me. Risten continued to be beaten back as she dodged and avoided Wort's attack. Wort's longer reach was definitely a problem for her. She glanced over her shoulder at me and moved in my direction. She stepped to block with her angled sword tactic, when she unexpectedly lost control of the blade, and Wort knocked it from her grasp. She flattened herself against the huge stone column just a few steps from me. She looked defeated, her arms hanging limp as she stared at him in shock.

Wort's lips grew back in a grin. "You put up a wonderful fight, Mistress Brightmare. But, as they all do, you die." He reared back for a powerful nearly horizontal swing—his final death blow.

At the last moment, Risten ducked and rolled toward me. I raised the shield to protect her, forcing Wort to slightly alter his swing—

The blade passed cleanly through the stone column, leaving a neat line across the granite. For a moment nothing happened. Then we heard it: the sound of cracking stone.

From the slice in the column, a spider web of cracks began to spread through the stone. A shocked expression came over Wort's face. The web of cracks quickly grew, snaking up the side with chunks of the rock falling away—small at first, but growing gradually larger. The column started to give out a groaning sound, and the statue slowly began to topple our way.

The whole towering, massive chunk of solid granite began to collapse over our heads.

# CHAPTER TWENTY-FIVE

# Sword
# Versus Shield

ocks began to fall around us. Wort backed away before turning and breaking into a full run away from the collapsing
column; his men, Benzel, and the priests followed suit, all of
them making a break for it. A boulder-sized chunk of rock landed just
in front of us, and I knew we'd never make it. I grabbed Risten, and we
quickly moved to where Zofie and Spraggel were. I raised the shield
over our heads, and we huddled close together. We barely fit beneath
it. We were about to find out just how good the shield actually was.

Large chunks of stone slammed against the shield to instantly turn
to dust. I could see a constant rain of powder as it slid off the edges.
From our side, the shield gave a few loud pings, which quickly turned
into a deafening roar, sounding like a summer's hailstorm on a metal
roof. Dust flowed under our shelter, darkening the air and making it
hard to breathe—we covered our faces as best we could. The noise
grew louder and louder, until finally there was a deafening crash.

Suddenly, it was quiet. Just the occasional ping of debris as everything settled. I waited a few moments to be sure nothing else was going to fall, and then I poked my head out. Around us rock was piled higher than our heads, forming a crater with us at the bottom. Jagged blocks of stone lay in heaps around us, covered by thick dust apparently supplied by the shield. I looked around in awe, shocked we had survived intact.

Fearing an avalanche, we carefully picked our way out of the crater and across the remains of the column. Risten carried Zofie on her back, and I wielded the shield, ready to bring it into play should any more attacks come.

When we reached the edge of the wreckage, we paused to catch our breath and shake off what dust we could. In the distance, I could see the shapes of men moving slowly away from us headed toward the lake. I spotted several priests, Wort's men, and even Benzel herself. But no sign of Wort. *Had he been crushed in the falling rock?*

Risten let Zofie slide to the ground and propped her up against a large stone. She squatted down beside her cousin and tried to wipe away the dust and make her more comfortable.

Spraggel stepped down from the pile and tried to brush some of the powder off his cloak. He was rewarded by a choking cloud and started coughing uncontrollably. Being careful to hold the shield to one side, I stepped closer and patted him on the back.

"Coren?" Risten called behind me. "Did you happened to see our packs?"

I turned toward her and froze. To my horror, Wort was right behind her: his face cut and bleeding, but with eyes bulging in rage. He rose to his full height behind the unaware Risten and raised his sword high, no doubt intending to cleave her from head to toe. I instinctively grabbed Risten and pulled her toward me, while bringing the shield around to protect her.

And then the unthinkable happened. Something we had tried so hard to prevent. Havoc's Sword, the ultimate weapon of destruction, and Ruin's Shield, the impenetrable barrier—

Touched.

I expected some kind of explosion, or flash of lightning, or something dramatic to signal their contact. But there was nothing. At first, I thought maybe Wort was right, and the ancients had put some kind of protection between the two. But when I tried to pull the shield back, it wouldn't move. It just hung there in the air. I peeked around the corner and saw Wort jerking on his sword, but it wouldn't come free. He gave a mighty pull, the muscles on his arms bulging, but it refused to yield.

And then I felt it. A brush of cold coming from the shield. I looked at the inside, and a layer of ice had formed on the surface. I stepped away feeling the cold grow. Wort staggered back. I saw an icicle hanging from the sword hilt.

I felt a tugging on my leg and looked down to see Zofie looking up at me from where she sat. Her eyes were bright. "You've got to get them apart," she said. "They're each drawing in myst to defeat the other. They have no governor on them, so they won't stop. They'll consume all the myst in the world until everything is dead."

Wort turned and fled off the rubble pile. He looked back over his shoulder. "This is all your fault."

I watched warily as he leaped clear of the debris pile and sprinted toward a shaft sticking from the ground. *Creator be damned.* The Spear of Flight had been on the side away from the collapse and clearly visible to those who knew what it was. Wort plucked it from the ground and quickly hefted it.

"Take me to the young master," he shouted as he threw the spear. It jerked him into the air.

"You coward!" I yelled after him.

He waved as he sailed away.

It would be fitting if he didn't survive the landing.

I turned to Risten, who was kneeling beside Zofie.

"Take her and get out of here," I said. "I'll see if I can pull them apart."

Risten looked up at me and shook her head. "It's no use. There's no-where far enough to run." But she relented and gathered up her cousin.

I turned to go, but Zofie grabbed my arm. She gave me a weak smile. "Don't die saving us."

I smiled back. "Best advice I've had all day."

Risten settled Zofie into her arms and took off at a trot. Spraggel went after them trying to keep up.

I took off my shirt and wrapped it around my hand. I then went to the sword and tried to pull it, wiggle it, or just get it to move. But it didn't. Ice was pooling around it, and the burning cold cut through my shirt wrapped hand.

And there was something else. I felt that old burning sensation in my chest, which meant something was drawing myst from me. So it really was only a matter of time.

I sighed. So this was it? I was never going to be that famous knight-scholar-explorer I had dreamed of. And I would never have a chance to be free of this stupid curse... this Thief of Curses.

A sudden thought came to me. Wasn't a spell a sort of curse? Could I take them?

"Abe," I asked aloud. "Question one."

*Oh for Creator's sake, what could you possibly want? You've already let the shield and the sword come together. You do realize that was a bad thing, right?*

"Unfortunately, yes."

*And you're also aware that you're all going to be dead before the sun touches the horizon, right?*

"Sure am."

*And that this mudball of a world is going to turn into an icicle just a little before it blows out the flame in the sun, right?*

"We kind of figured that out."

*All right, just wanted to be sure you knew... Now what did you want?*

"When I stole the curse on the willow tree and the statue, they turned back into humans. Would this shield by chance also be someone cursed?

*That's preposterous! There is no way a shield of that power could have been a human. Besides, I'm not getting a curse feeling from it. For them to be a cursed human, the curse itself would have to be hidden. Only someone talented, no, EXTREMELY talented, could pull something like that off.*

"I think you're wrong. Look closer. There might be some sort of illusion over it."

*There is no way I'm wrong, but I'll check. This might take a minute. I've got to look for some hint of an illusion."*

"Thank you, Abe. Just please hurry."

I watched as Risten, now some distance away, stopped and put Zofie down to rest. She looked back over her shoulder at me.

"Abe? Got anything."

*Well, I hate to admit it, but as for your curse idea, you might be right. There is something odd about the spell on both the shield and the sword. They might be under a concealment charm. And I'm not too good with those.*

"Then let's go find out. We're going to die anyway, might as well go out with a bang."

I quickly went to the pile of rubble and the joined weapons. The ground was frozen, and my breath fogged. The ache in my chest was getting worse.

*You know this is a bad idea, don't you? It's very difficult to steal a curse while operating. It's kind of like lifting a cart being pulled by a galloping horse. It's a lot easier if both are still. And if that wasn't enough, you have to steal both curses AT THE SAME TIME! That is going to take a hell of a lot of myst and is way outside what I was designed to do.*

I shrugged. "So I die either way. At least this way, I die trying."

*Creator, how did I get stuck with you! Don't you know that if there is a myst backlash because of this, not only will the world not make it past your next breath, but it will suck out your soul and eat it. Not only will you be dead, you will be DEAD, DEAD! You will cease to exist. Period. No afterlife for you.*

I shrugged again. "Well, I guess I had better not die then."

Abe laughed. It was a deep, hearty one. *You are so stupid it hurts. But you know, it hurts in a good way. So, let's do this! You're going to need to touch both of them at the same time. And it's going to burn like hell.*

I wrapped my shirt around my hands and carefully selected where to touch them. I took a deep breath and said a quick prayer to the Creator: *please let this work.*

I extended my hands and touched the sword and shield. "Your curse is my curse."

I tried to jerk my hands away as the burning started, but they wouldn't budge. I felt the power growing inside of me, which hurt as much as my hands. The draw of power kept increasing as it tried to take the curses—I could feel it in my very core, like my insides were being hollowed out.

*Dear Creator, I'm not going to make it...*

Suddenly, I was standing in a place of all gray: everything around me, for as far as the eye could see was a dull light gray. I looked around, not understanding what had just happened.

Beside me stood a stick figure, arms and legs nothing more than simple lines, with Abe's curse anchor for a head—the same figure I had seen in my dream of Zofie. And before me were two other stick figures with curse symbols likewise in place of heads. Only these, I had never seen before: one with a sword inside a circle, and the other, a shield. They had to be the curses of the two weapons.

Looking closer, I sensed movement inside their heads: the movement of tiny gears and flecks of light, rapidly whirling and flashing. It was almost hypnotic. The arms of each stick figure were locked in struggle, pushing against the other. And directly under where they stood, was a dark, dark pool of nothingness. As I looked at it, I could feel the draw. It was just waiting to suck me in. I was instantly re-minded of my father's death. The water had been just as black, just as dark, just as menacing—and it had sucked him straight down....

I shivered and shoved the memories aside, returning my focus to the two struggling figures. There was only one explanation: I was now in *their* world. The world of curses.

I shouted. *"Stop! You have to stop!"* My voice echoed strangely in the grayness, like it was eating the sound of my words.

Their heads, consisting of nothing more than their curse symbols, slowly turned in my direction. *We can't*, they said in unison. *We have to do what we were made to do.*

"You will cease to be if you don't stop!" I shouted. "I know you're just doing what you were made to do, but you have to stop for just a mo-ment. Just the barest moment. Before you destroy *what* you were designed to protect!"

They made no pretext of halting their struggle. *We do not want to de-stroy this way*, they answered again in unison. *But we are unable to go against our making.*

I looked over my shoulder at Abe, and he shrugged. I couldn't help but notice that Abe also had tiny gears in his head, but they were not rotating or flashing. This gave me an idea.

Turning back to the two struggling figures, I gritted my teeth. "Then if you won't stop, I will just have to make you."

I grabbed the arm of the figure with the shield head and tried to pull him away from the other, but the arm wouldn't budge. It was like I was pulling on an iron bar—a very flat iron bar the thickness of a piece of parchment. The moving gears in their heads caught my atten-tion and I smiled. Perhaps there was another way. I reached out and inserted the index fingers from both my hands in the gears of each of their designs. Strangely there was no pinching as they snagged on my digits, but to my satisfaction, they began to slow.

*STOP!* they yelled. *You're interfering with our purpose! We must do what we were made to do!*

"Not if I have anything to say about it!" And I held firm, inserting my whole hand and pushing against the gears as they slowly ground to a stop. The stick figures dropped their arms to their sides in defeat. It was then that Abe reached across me and touched them—

I blinked in the sudden light as I found myself back in the real world. The sword and shield fell away from each other like they had just discovered gravity and landed on the ice-covered ground. Immediately, the sword and the shield began to glow and transformed into an elderly woman and man. Like the others, they wore the ancient robes of myst users. Both seemed incredibly old.

As for myself, I felt like every ounce of strength had been sucked out of me. I collapsed to my knees in exhaustion beside them.

The woman opened her eyes and looked at me. "Thank you for stopping us. Our time is long past."

The man slowly reached out a hand to the woman, and she took it gently.

He whispered ever so softly. "I never thought I would see you again, my love."

The woman nodded. "Nor I."

And then they shut their eyes and died turning into dust only a few moments later.

Exhaustion finally caught up with me, and I sank to the ground, leaning back against a large stone. I couldn't help but stare at the piles of dust the cursed pair had left. Who were those people? They were obviously friends, maybe even lovers at one time. What had caused them to be cursed? It was almost as if they had willingly taken them on. I would have to talk to Spraggel about this. Maybe he had a clue as to why.

I sighed. Dreading what I would see, but already suspecting the answer, I looked down at my bare chest. Two more curse anchors were lined up against the others. I had quite the collection going: Zofie's imperfect transformation curse, the siren tree, the myst siphon, and now a sword and a shield transformation.

I rolled my head to the side, too tired to lift it, and noticed evening was falling. And on the horizon, I could see the moon beginning to rise. Ice gripped my heart. Zofie would transform soon. It would be her last time.

After the cycle ran out, and she tried to change back to human, she would die. If there was anything that I could do, it had to be now. There would be no second chance. What was the good of having this power over curses, this Thief of Curses, if you can't even save someone you care for?

I ran a hand through my hair in frustration. How could I save her? For the millionth time, I reviewed the facts of Zofie's curse in my mind. But no matter how I looked at it, I just couldn't see how to fix things. And yet, deep in my gut, I knew there was something I was missing. My thoughts kept going back to that time in the Temple of Daili...

I raised my head and blew out a long sigh. "Abe, I have a question. I think its number two."

*Don't I get a break! You save the world and think I'm supposed to be at your beck and call. You really are worthless. Yes, it's question two!*

"When you transformed Benzel, where did you get her human form?"

Abe chuckled. *The statue of Daili's mother, of course. It was clearly visible behind you. I know you saw it. When the eye on my curse anchor opened, that was the first thing I saw. In fact, it's the only female form I've seen with my own eye since we've been together.*

I perked up—an idea beginning to form. I stood as quickly as my tired legs would let me. "In the dream with the willow tree, were you really inside it with me?"

*Unfortunately yes. Somehow, I got dragged into it. Only in that one, I only had the barest bit of influence inside. And did you see my body! It was absolutely horrendous! Now your girl was definitely a looker. I'm not that much of a judge of human females, but I think she was pretty high up there.*

I smiled, suddenly excited. Could it be that simple? "Abe, can you..."

*Coren,* he interrupted, sounding uncharacteristically subdued—almost apologetic. *I know you want to save the girl and all, but I can't answer any more questions. I have to follow my making of only three. I have no choice.*

I closed my eyes and sighed in irritation. "Abhulengulus," I pleaded. "Can't you make an exception just this once?"

There was silence for a moment. *I'm sorry,* he answered sadly. *I can't go against my making. Not for... anything.*

"Creator be damned," I sighed deeply. I couldn't check out my idea, and I wasn't sure if it would work—failure could cause Zofie to die not a month from now, but this very evening. Did I want that responsibility?

As the sky darkened and the first stars came out, I picked my way over to where the others were gathered. Zofie lay panting on a slab of stone just high and long enough to make her a crude bed.

Risten knelt beside her, looking exhausted... and heartbroken. She refused to meet my eyes. "You did good, Coren," she said. "You saved us all." But I could tell she was really concerned over something much more important to her than the world itself.

Spraggel sat on a stone nearby, clearly exhausted and upset at the scene before him. I had no doubt he had tried to think of a solution too.

As I walked up, Zofie looked at me with pain in her eyes. But she still smiled. "I see you took my advice about not dying."

I couldn't decide whether to cry or to smile. For her sake, I chose the latter and broke into a sad grin. "I always try to listen to the advice of those I care about."

I knelt beside her across from Risten.

Zofie gave me a tired smile. "Does that mean you care about me?"

I leaned toward her. "More than you know."

She reached up and stroked my cheek. "I think I might understand a little." She turned her gaze to the moon just coming over the horizon. "I'm glad this will be the last time I have to go through this. I'm so sick of this transforming."

I took her hand again and held it tightly. "Zofie, I..."

She shook her head. "No, Coren, I don't want to live my remaining days as this monster. Let me have this last transformation. Don't take it away from me. If I can't have my true body, then I don't want to live."

"Zofie, I want to try something. I may have a way..."

"No, Coren, there is no other way...."

"Zofie, *please* let me try this one thing. If it doesn't work, I'll curse you myself. Just this one thing."

She looked at me with pleading eyes. "Coren..."

I don't know where they came from, but the words of The Poet appeared on my lips—a line from one of his sappy plays about a princess and a knight on the eve of the story's great battle. "And though we walk through Death's door," I quoted. "I will never release your hand, nor will I ever let you fall from my sight..."

Her eyes grew wide in surprise. "...For you are my true love, my true hope, and my life..." Her voice caught, but I finished it for her.

"...Not only for this humble knight, but for all future generations to come."

She gazed at me steadily for several heartbeats. She closed her eyes, and a single tear slid down her cheek. "You know that was a dirty trick, don't you? How did you know that was my favorite of his plays?"

I squeezed her hand and smiled. "It was just a good guess."

Zofie hesitated before finally asking, "What would I have to do?"

"Nothing. I will have Abe make a change to your curse. If it works, you'll be able to live. But it has to be done before you start your next transformation."

"And if it doesn't work?"

I sighed. "I could end up killing you today."

Risten jumped up. "You can't be seriously considering this. We might be able to find a way out of her curse in a month's time. Don't bet everything on this."

Zofie looked over at her cousin. "Risten, I love you like a sister, but do shut up and sit down. This is my decision to make. I chose him. Remember? I'm not backing down now." Zofie looked back over to me. "All right, I'll do it. But only because you said the magic words."

I looked into her eyes and brushed a strand of her hair away from her chimera face. "And what words were those?"

She smiled, a twinkle in her eye. "I'll let you figure that one out."

I nodded and stood. "This will likely hurt... a lot."

"Wait," she exclaimed and drew up the blanket over her head. "I don't want you to see me transform. Especially since it might... ah... go badly."

"I understand." I gently took her hand.

Risten glared at me over top of Zofie. "Coren, if you kill her, you'll be next."

I nodded. "And if I do, I'll gladly accept whatever you decide."

I looked up at the rising moon and gave the Creator a silent prayer. *Please let this work.*

Sighing deeply one last time, I said the words: "Your curse is my curse." And I felt the familiar stinging sensation in my chest. I heard Zofie struggling to breathe. I had to act fast. I laid my finger on Zofie's chest. "Princess Zophia Olwenna Xernow of Brethnach, I curse you..." I broke off, licked my lips, and tried again. *What if I was wrong?* I shook my head. *No, this was our only hope.*

Choosing my words very carefully, I continued. "I curse you... to forever transform every cycle into..." I dropped my voice to the barest whisper. *"Your true self."*

Zofie screamed in pain, and her body spasmed as the transformation started. The blue light enfolded her, but as I watched, I sensed nothing was happening.

*Coren!* Abe spoke loudly in my head. *I can't complete the transformation. I don't know what her true form is! It's been lost! My eye has never seen her.*

"Yes, it has," I whispered.

*It has?* he asked in surprise.

"The dream. You were in the dream. And your eye was open. It was your whole head."

Abe paused. *Coren, I...*

Suddenly, the blue light intensified. The pain in my chest became a white-hot poker, and I fell to my knees in agony. Zofie screamed again. The progress of her change was concealed by the blanket, but her form beneath it seemed to shift from human into a lump which writhed as if searching for what it wanted to be. Around the edges of the cover, the glow of her transformation burned bright enough to cast shadows in the dim light. The glow intensified until I couldn't bear to look at it...

Suddenly the light vanished. The evening became eerily quiet. The night was dark to my light deadened eyes. I fumbled for my broken amulet and found it had somehow gotten thrown over my shoulder. I held it up to see Risten looking from both her to me in worry. And on the slab where Zofie had lain was a single human-sized lump under a blanket. Only, it lay perfectly still.

No movement.

I stared at the lump in disbelief.

Risten shook Zofie's shoulder and cried out her name, but there was no response. She turned accusing eyes in my direction. "You killed her!" she shouted. "You killed my Zofie!"

I fell to my knees and bent forward to lay my forehead on the ground. No, please no. Creator, tell me I didn't just kill her.

Risten openly sobbed, and Spraggel came over to pat her shoulder. I got to my feet and fearing the worst, tugged on a corner of the blanket, slowly pulling it back.

The shifting covers revealed the young woman I had seen in my vision. Her red hair was mussed, and with her eyes closed, it looked like she was sleeping. She looked so peaceful.

I bent forward, and with tears in my own eyes, gently kissed her. "I'm sorry Zofie..."

And to my amazement, her eyes fluttered and opened. They focused on me, and an amused smile curled up her lips. "A little forward, isn't it, to steal a kiss from a fainted lady?"

My eyes grew wide in shock. "You're alive!"

Risten shoved me out of the way and hugged her cousin. "I thought I had lost you!"

I couldn't believe it. Zofie was herself again! Well, at least until the next full moon.

Abe laughed inside my head. *Very clever. I can't believe you did that. I might actually have to start calling you by your real name. You knew I had seen her true form and so you just cursed her to cycle through transforming into herself. Not bad. Not bad at all. You might catch on to this cursing thing one day.*

Zofie clutched the blanket to her chest while she examined her arm and then felt her face. She lifted the blanket and peered beneath it. "It's me. The old me. How did you do it? How did you take my curse away?"

I grimaced. "Actually, I didn't. You're still cursed."

"But, I'm me!" she protested, slowly sitting up while clutching the blanket.

"Yes, but that's just the form I chose. I just changed it so that the animal you transform into is human—and every time, it will use your old form for the appearance. Unfortunately though, you still won't be able to use myst and every full moon, you'll still return to your chimera form for a while. But with each transformation, you'll pick up a piece of what you had lost, and eventually, little by little, you'll go back to your original form. And when everything is the way it was, I just take the curse away completely."

She threw her arms around me and gave me a kiss.

I could get used to this hero bit.

# CHAPTER TWENTY-SIX

# The
# Princess Chooses

It was dark, we were hungry, and we were all exhausted from our battles. So we made a cold camp on the back side of the rubble, hopefully concealing ourselves from the others on the mountain.

We had spotted Benzel and the rest of Wort's men off in the distance by the shore of the lake. They had built a couple small fires. We, on the other hand, didn't dare—no sense in attracting unwanted attention. Instead, we huddled together and shared what meager food we had and ate by the concealed light of my amulet. We were fortunate that Spraggel had been able to pick up our traveling packs and stuff them into his ever-mysterious pocket. When we got back, I was going to have to ask my master about getting one of those.

Seeing our exhaustion, Spraggel agreed to take first watch. A deep weariness had settled over me, so I was extremely grateful. He was to wake me later so he could rest too.

Zofie, on the other hand, was delighted with returning to her human form and seemed to be overflowing with energy. She and Risten went behind some fallen rocks and came back with Zofie wearing a broad smile and some of Risten's spare clothes.

"Do you realize I haven't worn clothes for almost a year?" Zofie plucked at her shirt. "This is wonderful. I can dress up again!"

Risten snorted. "You always were the one for new clothes."

Zofie looked in my direction. "What do you think, Coren?"

I settled myself against a large rock and draped a blanket over me. But I couldn't help but smile. "You look great. Of course, you could wear a sack and still look good."

"Oh, you." She was practically beaming.

As the cousins chatted, I noticed Risten was carrying a sword. My sword, in fact. She saw me looking and patted it. "I found it lying in the rubble like it was waiting to be found. And don't worry. I'll give it back."

I waved it off. "It's the only sword we have now, so it makes sense you carry it."

She nodded in satisfaction.

I couldn't suppress a yawn. My exhaustion was rapidly catching up to me. My eyes wouldn't stay open. "I'm sorry, ladies. I'm going to lay down. I'm exhausted."

Zofie nodded. "That's probably from myst depletion. You must have used a lot today, especially for someone that's not a myst user. In fact, most myst users wouldn't have been able to do what you did. You must have one huge supply of myst—very unusual." She gave me an evil grin. "Maybe later, I'll check you over."

"Later." Risten and I both said in unison. We both looked at the other in surprise.

I stretched out on the hard ground and watched sleepily as Risten motioned Zofie over, and the two huddled together whispering. They were talking about going back, but their whispers turned to a gentle noise as my eyes closed of their own accord...

*There was bright light in my eyes—whiter than snow, more brilliant than* the sun—its intensity hurt. As the light faded, I found myself in an unfamiliar room. There was a window nearby, and outside I could hear the clop of horse's hooves and the jingle of a harness. Gentle embers burned in a stone fireplace to my right, and I could feel its warmth on that side of my body. The air smelled of damp and roses and wine.

I looked down at myself and found I was dressed in pants and jacket of fine black leather, while seated at a long oval table made of highly polished oak. Around the table with me were three men and four women. I couldn't help but notice that one chair was unoccupied and for some reason that concerned me. Those gathered around the table were into middle age and dressed in various costumes. I knew from the illustrations I had seen in Spraggel's books that their manner of dress was old—very old. Fashions from roughly a thousand years ago.

What the creator is going on? I asked myself. Where am I?

The man across from me leaned forward, face drawn in worry, obviously agitated. "Time is short," he said in a thick Ellish accent—one I could barely make out. "They are almost upon us."

The woman next to him nodded. She wore a dark robe with a brightly colored tunic underneath. Even by older standards, it was quite elegant. "It is time to act."

"But the cost!" I found myself saying. Only it wasn't my voice, and it used the same thick accent. Why was I talking like this? Or was it even me?

My voice continued. "Each and every one of you I count as a friend, nay, more brother and sister. But this plan will mean you have to give up your freedom forever... even worse, give up your life!" My fist pounded the table. "I do not want to do this. It is too much."

I felt a hand on my shoulder, and I turned to the woman sitting on my right. Her hair was long and woven into a tight braid down her back. Her eyes were gentle and kind yet filled with concern. I somehow knew this woman meant more to me than the others. Much more. More than the world itself.

"And yet," she said. "It is something you must do. It is the only way to defeat the Dark Avenyts."

*"Please Evelend, I beg you. Don't make me do this..."*

I jerked awake.

My eyes opened to a cloudless sky of a vibrant blue promising bright weather for the day. The sun was just rising over the horizon, its bright rays illuminating the surrounding pile of broken stone. I blinked as I oriented myself. I was back on the mountain at our make-shift camp beside the ruins of the giant statue. I sat up and found Risten and Zofie sharing a blanket a couple paces away. Spraggel was sitting by himself on a rock nearby, his head drooping and nodding as he struggled to stay awake. I snorted and shook my head. The old fool must have decided we all needed to sleep and kept watch all night.

Stretching, I thought back to the dream. I didn't know what else to call it. It had been so real. *What the hell had it been?* And I wondered who Evelend was? The name was vaguely familiar. I slowly stood, feeling every stiff and sore muscle in my body. And I had quite a few of them. I wasn't sure how many muscles there were in the human body, but I was pretty sure all of them were complaining this morning, and they made for quite the choir.

I hobbled over behind some rocks and took care of my morning business. When I returned, Risten and Zofie were sitting up. Zofie smiled at me, and the aches in my limbs suddenly didn't feel so bad.

"Good morning," I said, returning the smile.

"And a good morning to you, my good sir."

"Would my lady care to break her fast with me?" I bowed in deeply exaggerated politeness.

She grinned and bowed politely in return. "I would love to, but only if Risten can come along."

I nodded. "Of course, my lady. Your chaperone is more than welcome, although your cousin would surely cut my head off if I didn't invite her too."

Risten rubbed her eyes. "Would you two stop it? I can't stand all this honey sweetness first thing in the morning. It makes me sick."

Zofie and I laughed.

I looked over at Spraggel and saw him watching us bleary-eyed. "Nothing happened, so I thought I would just let you sleep. I did notice that Benzel and the others are gone now. They were up well before dawn and crossed the lake back toward their home. They didn't give us a second look." He shrugged. "I guess we were too much trouble."

I settled down and pulled out our remaining dried meat. We would have to leave soon ourselves. We were running out of supplies. I handed out our shares and sat down on a rock to chew on mine.

I looked into the distance. The vision still fresh in my mind. "I had the strangest dream just now. It was so real." I told them about it quickly. "The strangest thing was the woman's name. *Evelend.* Seems like I've heard it before."

Spraggel blinked. "I seem to remember it too." He thought for a moment and held up a finger as he remembered. He reached into his pocket—deeply into it—and came out with a book. It was the book on curses.

I couldn't help but comment. "You put that valuable, one of a kind book in your pocket? The magical one that puts stuff Creator knows where?"

Spraggel gave me an unconcerned look. "Well, I was in a hurry when those men found me. I needed somewhere to hide it."

He opened the book to the first page and held it out to me. The author's name was simply listed as *Evelend.* No family name was given.

I looked up at him in surprise. "*She* wrote this book on curses?"

Spraggel shrugged. "We don't know that... it could be a coincidence. The name may have just been popular at that time."

He put the book back in his pocket. "This is something we definitely need to research."

I nodded agreement and looked over at our other party members. Like me, they had settled on rocks nearby, with Risten leaning against a tall one and Zofie seated on a stone with her legs dangling off the edge. I noticed the two women were exchanging looks, and from their worried expression, I was pretty sure there was a disagreement between them. I bet I knew what it was.

"So," I said, taking another bite of breakfast. "Since our quest is done, what are you two going to do now?"

Risten looked away, and Zofie guiltily stopped in mid-chew. She was really going to have to work on hiding her facial expressions if she expected to rule one day.

Zofie dropped her hands to her lap. "I have to go back and face my brother. Somehow make him pay for my father's murder."

Risten snorted. "And get yourself killed in the process."

Zofie ignored her cousin's comment.

I forced down another bite and pointed to her with my dried meat. "You realize that you're still cursed. When the next full moon comes around, you'll transform just like you did before. And you can't use your myst either. The curse still consumes it all."

Zofie looked at me steadily. "I know. But it's something I must do. I will have justice."

Risten opened her mouth, but I gave her a dirty look, and she closed it for once.

"What about you?" asked Zofie, her expression hopeful. "What's next for you?"

I inclined my head toward Spraggel. "I have to get this old goose back to Iron Landing safely. And then, I guess I'll research my curse. We have the book now, so surely it says something I can use."

"Oh." The disappointment was thick in her voice. "I was hoping you might... you know... come with us."

"Is your highness ordering me to come with her?" I asked quietly.

She looked at me in shock. "No, I wouldn't order you. I thought..."

"That I might like to," I finished for her. "Maybe even want to be by your side."

Her breath caught, but then she slowly nodded, her eyes large in sudden apprehension.

Risten huffed. "Zofie, you can't. You know you can't. You have to remember who you are... actually, what you are."

I sighed deeply and knelt before Zofie. I took her hand in mine. "Risten's right. You're not a normal girl. I'm just a lowly scribe apprentice. I don't deserve to stand at the side of someone of your station. You're royalty."

She reached out and gently stroked my cheek. "You're not just a scribe apprentice. You saved me from death. You beat back Wort's men, and saved the world. Not to mention, you gave me back my body. I knew it the first time I saw you. You're more powerful than you know."

"But Zofie," I patted her hand. "You'll be the Queen."

Zofie's eyes grew wet. She blinked and turned away. After a moment, she nodded. "You're right. And I guess I need to start acting like one. I need to remember my responsibilities and draw the powerful close to me... negotiate for the betterment of my kingdom." And then she smiled evilly. It was as if I could see the gears turning in her mind. "I need to choose my advisers wisely."

I shrugged. "I think so."

Risten stood. "Don't Zofie!"

Zofie held out a halting hand toward Risten. "Silence!"

Risten jerked in surprise, like me, startled at the voice of authority.

Zofie pointed to the ground beside me. "Now attend me. As your Queen, I so command."

Risten still in shock knelt beside me on my left.

She looked to Spraggel still sitting on his rock and looking highly amused at the whole affair. "And you, Spraggel van Deviante, master of Revenhill Keep, would you also attend me? But please do not kneel, for I respect your advanced age."

He moved to the indicated spot on my other side and bowed. "Thank you for your consideration, your highness."

Zofie sat up, her back straight, and her head high, leaving no doubt of her heritage. "I hereby call my court to order," she announced. "First, I wish to establish the senior advisors of my court." She looked to her cousin. "Risten Brightmare, you have proven yourself in battle, and your sword arm has no equal. For services rendered to the throne, I ask that you accept my appointment to be the Commander of my army. Will you lead them to victory in my name?"

Risten recovered quickly from her surprise. She bowed her head and placed a hand over her heart. "I swear before the Creator to do my best in your name."

"Thank you, Captain Risten Brightmare. Please take your station." Risten moved to stand beside Zofie just in front of her stone throne.

Zofie then turned to look at my master. "Spraggel van Deviante. You also have served me well with your knowledge of history, science, and culture. I ask that you accept as my senior adviser, to keep me informed of the mistakes of the past, record the deeds of the present, and help me guide the kingdom into the future."

Spraggel bowed at the waist. "It would be an honor, my queen." He then moved to stand on Zofie's other side.

Zofie held her hand out toward Risten. "My sword, please. I have need of *Majestic*."

Risten stared at her for just a moment before moving to comply. She pulled my sword from her belt and handed it hilt first to Zofie.

My mouth fell open. It was the same one I had been carrying since our adventure began, the one that had appeared in my bedroll that first night, and the one that I had passed to Risten to beat Wort. I had no idea that all this time, I had been carrying the King's Sword, or more formally known as *Majestic*. The blade was legendary, and only certain people were allowed to carry it.

Zofie laid the sword lengthwise across her lap and fixed her gaze on me. "Coren Hart, I, Princess Zophia Olwenna Xernow, soon to be Queen of Brethnach, have a boon to ask, will you hear my plea?"

From my kneeling position, I bowed my head. I formally answered. "I would gladly, your majesty."

Zofie paused as she chose her words. "Coren Hart, you have saved my life, and throughout our travels, exhibited a quick mind and a brave heart. I have need of a champion to fight for me against my brother. I need a knight of the highest caliber. Would you do this for me? Would you win the kingdom back from my father's murderer? Of course, you wouldn't do it alone." She waved her hand to indicate Risten and Spraggel. "You would have the help of all my court."

I was shocked. A knight? I had dreamed of it since I was little, but was it something I could actually do?

"Your majesty," I protested. "I am not qualified for such a role."

She leaned forward, ice in her voice. "Do you doubt your future queen's judgment?"

"No, your majesty, it's just..."

"Then perhaps you wish a reward to go with the title and lands. Very well, I am a little short of funds at the moment, but perhaps I have another currency."

I looked up at her, clearly puzzled.

She continued. "If you accept, I will declare you one of my suitors—of course, that doesn't guarantee marriage, but it would give you a chance to formally court me."

I looked up at her in disbelief. "Are you sure? That is a rather large reward."

She smiled. "I think it a suitable one."

I couldn't help but smile back. "Then I accept. I will be the best knight you will ever have."

She was working to suppress her grin, but it wasn't working too well. "Then you may rise, Sir Coren Hart." I rose, and she scooted off her throne and stood with me. She presented the sword to me, resting on her palms. "I grant the King's Sword into your keeping. Use it well."

I took the weapon and bowed.

"Thank you," I said. But Zofie didn't turn away. She seemed to be waiting for something else. Then it hit me. "Ah... I believe it's customary for a suitor to seal their relationship with a kiss."

"Indeed it is." And then she whispered. "I was afraid you were going to miss that part."

"Never." And I leaned in and kissed her.

She put her arm around my neck and held me to her lips for several seconds before relaxing her hold. Pulling back, I whispered in her ear. "I think I've been manipulated."

"Of course," she whispered back. "It's a lesson you'll have demonstrated many times."

Risen cleared her throat. "This court is adjourned because I'd like to start back home. I'm sorely tired of being on this accursed mountain."

We all nodded in agreement and began to gather our few belongings.

In only a few minutes, we were ready to leave. We quickly decided to take another path down the mountain, preferably away from the other men. Settling my pack on my back, I turned and gave the area a last look. We certainly had caused quite a bit of destruction. The stately statue was in crumbles, the shield gone, and all its traps disabled. Maybe now the mountain could go back to the way it was before.

Then why, deep in my gut, couldn't I shake the feeling that I was missing something again?

Suddenly I caught movement out of the corner of my eye. Looking up, I saw the strangest thing. Up in the sky, suspended from nothing I could see, was a small square, slanted downward at an angle. And while fairly high, it looked to be lined with stone and had a small door hanging down.

"Hey," I called to the others, pointing. "Look at that."

They turned and Zofie gave a gasp, "What is it? It looks like a trap door."

And indeed it did. A trap door in the sky. You could even see the shimmering shadow of something just within it. As we watched, a thin pole extended through the shimmering area and probed the air around it. After doing this for a while, it quickly withdrew and, a minute later, was replaced by what looked like a large, dark hand that emerged from the shadow of the door. I gasped. It was too far away to be sure, but I thought the hand seemed oddly inhuman being short-fingered and having too many joints. Had we not been almost under it, I would not have seen the detail. The hand extended through the opening and seemed to feel the air—like it was probing for something. Then it grabbed the door and pulled it closed. The square vanished completely.

*What the hell had that been?*

I looked beneath the square and then traced where the statue would have been. The opening would have been directly over where the statue stood. In fact, the shield would have been in that same area.

And a sudden realization hit me, sending a shiver down my spine.

The siren tree, the myst siphon, the towering statue, and finally the shield itself. I shook my head in disbelief. It couldn't be.

Zofie noticed the change in my expression immediately. "What's wrong, Coren?"

I hopped up on a large piece of the fallen statue and looked around the top of the mountain with new eyes. And indeed I could see it.

I shook my head as I measured the distances with my eye. "We got it wrong," I said in disbelief.

"Wrong?" asked Spraggel. "What are you talking about?"

I pointed into the distance. "Everything. Look at how the land is devoid of cover gradually sloping up to the statue, exactly like what would be needed for a battlefield. And the water circling the top—that's not a lake. It's a moat. Which means the other things: the siren tree to pull in those on the mountain, the myst siphon where nothing could live, and finally the shield raised high in the air where the top of the mountain would likely have been."

Zofie shook her head. "What is it, Coren? I don't understand."

"Don't you see?" I hopped down. "We've been looking at this all wrong... The shield was blocking a portal. And those traps weren't meant to keep us out."

Zofie's eyes went wide in horror. She whispered. "They were meant to keep something *in*."

I nodded slowly. "And we just broke them all."

Risten stepped forward. "Then what we just saw up in the air..."

Spraggel gasped. "The worst invasion in history. The world's darkest hour."

The Dark Avenyts were back.

And we had just thrown the door open for them.

The story continues in
Book 2 of the
*Chronicles of Coren Hart* Series

# QUEEN
# OF
# CURSES

# Acknowledgments

*Thief of Curses* would not have happened had it not been for the help of many others. Thanks go out to Jennifer, who was a major help with proofing and copyediting. I also need to thank Rebecca and Kasey for their writing advice and many corrections, as well as Daniel, who was one of my beta readers.

I also need to thank the creative team at Mibl Art for their fantastic cover art. I much appreciated their creativity and patience as we worked through the many drafts and adjustments.

And finally, my wife deserves major kudos for putting up with my cranky, whining as I worked through the plotting and multiple re-writes, as well as, the many nights I left her alone watching old reruns while I tried to type some coherent words. When I got discouraged, she knew the magic words to make me turn around and try again.

# About The Author

*Thief of Curses* is Jessie Eaker's first novel. His short fiction has appeared in Marion Zimmer's Bradley's *Sword and Sorceress* and *Fantasy Worlds* anthologies. A native of North Carolina, he currently lives in central Virginia, and has been there so long, he's lost his southern accent (much to his wife's disappointment). When not writing, he watches anime, reads, and works on his ever-growing list of things to fix around the house.

Check out jessieeaker.com for his latest works and updates.